OUR LAST NIGHT

The Hope Center Book One

Rory London

Five Hearts
PRESS

Dedication

For Fred.

Content Information

O*ur Last Night* is an emotional, slow burn, second-chance love story. The themes and events captured in the book are sometimes on the heavy side, although this is not a dark romance.

Please be advised of the following content warnings (this list includes semi-spoilers for the story): Childhood trauma and neglect, substance abuse, medical emergencies requiring hospitalization, assault, including sexual assault, socioeconomic hardship, death of a parent, police interactions, insensitive and homophobic language, and scary situations.

If any of the above are deal-breakers for you, please take care and we'll catch you for the next happily ever after.

Part One

CHAPTER ONE
Cori

PRESENT DAY

Curious eyes would be on me tonight, but I deserved it. I'd surprised the hell out of everyone.

The email had gone out to all JBC employees at eight o'clock this morning. I knew my choice would be unexpected, but I hadn't anticipated the level of shock that immediately began filling my in-box. *Was I absolutely sure? Was this a joke, Jason and Brad playing one last prank before settling into new roles at a big boy company?* I dodged the questions by working from home most of the day, but this party was unavoidable.

An evening breeze came in from the sound as I hurried across the intersection on First Ave. RIP blowout. My pencil skirt strangled my legs, but I did my best to power walk in heels. Reaching the lobby of our office building, I stopped to smooth myself out, then used my phone camera to touch up my lipstick.

As I stepped off the elevator into the open space of JBC's third-floor suite, one of our senior account managers approached me.

"Hey Cori, you made it," Leon boomed, shaking my hand. "I was hoping to run into you." His features tightened as his arm dropped. "I have to admit, the email this morning caught me off guard."

There was a question in his statement. My neck heated, and I sent up a silent thank-you for the top-of-the-line AC system we'd installed last year. It combated Seattle's early September weather. And Leon's inquisitive stare.

I smiled and looked him in the eye.

"It's the right move for me," I said firmly. "And of course I'd never miss the party. I would have gotten here earlier, but I had a lot of loose ends to tie up, as you can imagine."

"Well, we will certainly miss the 'C' in JBC," Leon said. "You did a great job ironing out the guys' rough edges."

I couldn't help my small chuckle. We both knew "rough edges" was code for *occasionally acting like overgrown frat boys*. I had a reputation for being the grown-up in the room at JBC. Professional and consistent.

I peered over near the bar, catching my former partners' eyes. They tipped their glasses at me. It was strange that we'd started the business together, but I doubted we'd be more than passing acquaintances after today. Still, I was fond of them and said as much to Leon. "I think being part of a larger operation will be good for Jason and Brad."

"But not for you?"

"No."

He directed another probing glance at me, but I didn't elaborate. A server passed by with a tray and I grabbed a Merlot. Taking a sip, I darted my eyes around. Having skipped lunch in favor of Pilates, food was my objective.

"So what's next, Cori, since you're not making the transition to TremMark?"

"Honestly, I don't know. I'm taking my time to decide."

I'd been contemplating leaving JBC for more than a year. Six months ago, we'd agreed to sell to another large biotech firm. TremMark made me a great offer—chief organizational operations director—to stay on once the acquisition was complete. Instead, I'd taken my seven-figure portion of the sale and walked away.

I stepped aside before Leon could ask more questions.

The menu displays promised tacos somewhere. On one side of the room, I found plates with shot glasses in the center, resting on whole basil leaves, filled with what looked like chunky tomato soup and stale breadsticks. Was this supposed to be the bruschetta? Gross. Another table held crackers with dollops of raw hamburger meat on top. Tartare—hard pass. I never understood the mental gymnastics people went through to convince themselves raw ground beef was somehow elegant and not completely revolting.

The food at these events was always so bougie and pretentious. I wouldn't miss that.

The last table had to be the tacos. I kept my chin down so no one would try to engage with me, even as I felt their eyes on my back.

More than one hundred people crammed into the open lobby. Their voices echoed off the exposed brick walls and wood flooring. At least I'd talked Jason and Brad out of hiring a DJ. With limited space and an open bar, I didn't need my last memory of the company to be watching my coworkers get sloppy and grind on one another.

I wondered how those staying on would do. Even though Jason and Brad could occasionally be mistaken for douchey tech bros, with their jeans-and-hoodie uniforms and cringeworthy habit of referring to themselves as "disruptors," they were decent people and brilliant scientists at heart. I joined them five years ago because I honestly thought they could help cure cancer. Hopefully, working at TremMark didn't stop them.

But I couldn't worry about that now. I'd made my decision. I headed toward the third table.

Aubrey from HR stepped into my path.

I attempted to shuffle around her, but she matched my movements and stayed in front of me. "Cori, you got all the docs I sent, right?" Like Leon, she looked at me like she wanted to ask if I'd fallen and hit my head.

Aubrey was exactly my age at twenty-nine, but I doubted anyone would guess that. Most of the TremMark folks in attendance wore suits and dresses, while only a few JBC employees had changed into party attire. She remained in her office clothes of baggy jeans and a Grand Teton National Park T-shirt. I was also in my work attire—long, fitted gray sheath dress under a tailored black blazer. Sensible yet sophisticated Louboutin Sab pumps.

"I received the papers, Aubrey. Thank you."

She twisted her hands together. "You know that once you sign these last ones, everything is...final."

It had actually been final for a while. The papers were merely a formality. But I guessed that she, like Leon, was still struggling to process my departure.

"I know, Aubrey. Thank you." Her lips stayed flat as I angled past her.

It was a new experience having the worried frowns of my coworkers directed at me.

Staying on with TremMark would have been the safe choice, the expected choice, so of course I'd raised eyebrows when I turned it down. That was why I waited until this morning to make my decision widely known. I'd only told Jason, Brad, and the TremMark executives a few months ago, asking them to maintain discretion. We'd all agreed it would be better to avoid giving folks more time to speculate about my leaving.

The last thing I wanted was for my decision to cause concern that something was wrong with this buyout, or that I didn't support it. I honestly believed the acquisition would give the vital work being done at JBC a better chance to flourish. With additional money and access to resources and top talent, the science could progress more quickly.

Forty feet away, I caught the eye of TremMark's chief science and technology officer, Graham Turner. He gave me a chin lift and began walking over.

Graham had been great throughout the entire process even though he seemed sorely disappointed when I told his team I would not be accepting their offer to stay on.

"Everyone keeps sneaking glances at you like you're a celebrity, but they're trying to play it cool." He smirked. "Guess it's to be expected now that you've finally clued people in on your plans."

I sighed. "Pretty sure they're worried I've been body snatched by aliens who forced me to turn down the job with you guys."

"Is that what happened?" he teased. "Because I will fight some little green men if it means you'll reconsider."

I laughed and, not for the first time, noticed how attractive Graham was, with his artfully floppy dirty-blond hair and tall, gym-honed physique. He had a great personality, too. He'd charmed the support staff at JBC with his sharp wit and dry humor, helping to ease the transition for everyone. But even though he was single, I'd never been able to think of him in more than a professional capacity. I wished I could because he was certainly what most women would consider a catch. The chemistry just wasn't there.

"You don't need to punch out any aliens. I assure you, this decision was all me."

He nodded, and an admiring look crossed his features. "I understand where your employees are coming from. You surprised me as well, Cori, and that doesn't happen very often. I'd heard you were the sensible one at JBC, so I figured you'd be the first to jump on board with us, as opposed to that duo over there." He gestured to Jason and Brad, who laughed loudly as they watched something on Brad's phone.

"Those guys are actually pretty cool." I defended my colleagues. "And they're very good at what they do."

"I don't doubt it," Graham spoke genuinely. "I sense the brilliance beneath the *Zelda* hoodies. We're expecting great things. But that doesn't mean we won't miss you."

"Thank you."

"If you ever change your mind, the offer remains on the table. There will always be a place for you at TremMark." Graham ran a palm through his hair, and I imagined a *swoosh* sound as it fell perfectly back into place. "You have my number." He shook my hand, holding it as he added in a low voice, "I'd love to hear from you."

My breathing hitched. Was he flirting? I couldn't tell. This was what happened when you went more than a year without getting laid.

"About the job?" I blurted.

His cheek ticked. "Sure. You can call me anytime...about the job." He squeezed my fingers lightly before stepping away to speak to someone else.

Now *that* definitely felt like flirting. Too bad I still didn't feel a spark.

I resumed my taco mission, finally reaching the third table.

Except... These were... What?

I grabbed one of the little square plates and stared. A whitish circle rested in the center, its texture mooshy and gelatinous. It was the same thickness as a tortilla, but not like any I'd ever seen. A square of something meat-like sat atop it. There was a halved grape tomato in one corner, and a green sauce smeared across another. I looked up at the server in confusion.

"It's a taco," she said with about the same level of conviction I felt. I peered at the plate again as she continued, "It's, uh, like, deconstructed. A pressed cauliflower tortilla with seasoned tempeh, tomato, and avocado crema. Vegan and gluten-free."

I smiled tightly.

My brain conjured a memory of sitting on the steps of the Center eating Rosa's tacos. Little corn tortillas filled with spicy carnitas and topped with radishes and lime. They'd been so juicy I'd had to hunch over, balancing a paper plate on my lap while keeping a wad of napkins handy. I shook my head at the recollection.

This was what I couldn't explain to Aubrey or Leon. Jason or Brad or Graham. Or the dozens of other employees who kept sending anxious glances my way. I'd spent over a decade trying to be the kind of person who could imagine smooshed cauliflower when I saw the word "taco." But I wasn't a foodie. I wasn't many of the things people assumed I was.

Everyone here was celebrating the success of JBC, the company I'd helped found and been the chief financial officer of, the start-up that had become an industry leader in bioinformatics in less than half a decade. But as hard as I'd worked to be in this room, I needed to step away before it was too late.

I had been the last to arrive at the party, but I was the first to leave.

CHAPTER TWO
Cori

My best friend Britta had borrowed my SUV for the weekend to go camping, so I ended up taking two rideshares to get home after the party. The first was to the Chipotle in the U District, where I picked up a burrito—chicken, because their carnitas never tasted quite right—and a large order of chips and guac. The second drove me to my house in Wallingford.

Last year, I'd moved into the new-build, row-house-style four-plex near Meridian Park. There weren't many houses like this in Seattle, where the front door hugged the sidewalk. My home was a testament to the city's chaotic decades-long building boom. Whenever one beautiful old Craftsman went down, four to six whatever-was-popular-at-the-moment-style townhomes or condos went up.

But even if my sideways shoebox of a house looked a little odd, I loved the place. Its three bedrooms and two-and-a-half baths were a step up from the downtown apartment I'd been renting. I preferred the quieter neighborhood too.

I told the driver to drop me off on the corner so he wouldn't need to worry about navigating the one-way street.

As I approached my door, I saw a familiar figure sitting on the front steps.

He was hunched and trembling, elbows on his thighs, forehead resting against his clenched fists. I recognized the dark gray jeans with holes in the knees and tattered sweatshirt as the same outfit he'd been wearing the last time I saw him, over a month ago. Did he even have a spare change of clothes? He must have heard my heels striking the sidewalk, but didn't look up to acknowledge me until I stood directly in front of him.

"Johnny."

"Hey, Sis."

His red-rimmed eyes appeared vacant and bloodshot. He ran a shaky hand across his face. I smelled the acidic rankness of his clothing. Or possibly his body. I had no idea where he was living these days, let alone whether he had access to a proper shower. Band-Aids wrapped around most of his knuckles, and scabs lined his jaw, along with several open sores. It didn't take much deductive power to conclude that my brother had been using.

"What are you doing here?" I asked gently but with an edge in my tone.

"Ouch. Do I need a reason? Maybe I just wanted to visit."

I hmphed. At least he was cognizant. Coming down, I guessed, based on how hard he shivered in the mild air.

"You don't need a reason. You just usually have one." I gave him a half smile as I stepped past to open the door, motioning for him to follow me inside. I glanced around to see if any of the neighbors were watching.

Johnny clocked the move. "Don't worry," he said. "I've only been here a few minutes."

"Sorry."

"You shouldn't be." He waved his arm around as he sat down at my tiny kitchen table. "I'm fucking proud to have a little sister like you, who lives in a neighborhood where I stick out like a dookie in a fruit basket." He sighed as I removed the food from the bag. "Better you be ashamed of me than like me."

"I'm not ashamed of you, J."

He pressed his lips together, letting the untruth pass. I wasn't ashamed, exactly, but I'd certainly done my best since college to distance myself from him. Between his short stints in jail or rehab, Johnny had been like a ghost in my life for most of the past decade, slipping in and out without truly being a part of it. He'd only met Marcus once before my former fiancé and I ended things, and I'd never introduced him to any of my other friends or JBC colleagues.

I broke the rule about unwrapping the foil from the burrito as I put it on a plate and sawed it in half.

"Will you eat something?" I asked.

"Nah," Johnny replied. "Already ate." He leaned back and patted out a quick rhythm on his stomach. I grimaced. At five foot eleven, he weighed maybe one forty soaking wet, the purple veins under his pale skin protruding and ghoulish. In another world, he was healthy and filled out, with a full set of teeth.

But even missing a few molars—mercifully, all his front teeth remained—his smile still charmed as he beamed at me. Johnny was a good person underneath the addiction, and I mourned the loss of the brother I could barely remember.

I sat down with my food across from him. He took the soda I offered. As I ate, he rubbed the fingers of one hand over the knuckles of the other, and I gestured toward the Band-Aids I'd noticed earlier. "Get in a fight?"

"Ah...no. Just some friends messing around with poke and stick tattoos." He darted his eyes from side to side and wrung his palms.

"Look, J, it's nice to see you. I mean that," I said honestly. "And we can sit and shoot the breeze or whatever if that's what you want... Or maybe you should just tell me why you're here." His eyes appeared conflicted, almost guilty, so I added bluntly, "You know I can't give you any money."

He startled at my candor, then exhaled. I'd learned the hard way that any money I gave him went straight into his pipe or his veins, so I hadn't made that mistake in a long time. I still tried to buy him clothes or meals when he'd let me, and I occasionally paid a landlord directly on his behalf during the few periods when he was sober enough to live in steady housing. As far as I knew, he'd been couch-surfing or unhoused for the better part of a year. The thought of him sleeping on the street or in those awful tent encampments horrified me, but I was aware he did that sometimes when he used. I'd never let him stay with me longer than a night or two—mostly because he refused to get clean, but also because I hadn't wanted my worlds to collide. I'd been riding the fine line between loving my brother and keeping him separate from the rest of my life since college.

Johnny didn't say anything, so I assumed I'd guessed correctly. But I spared him the indignity of forcing him to admit he'd come to ask for money. I took a bite of chicken, chewing thoughtfully as some of the tension left the air.

"Can I crash on your couch tonight?" he asked after a minute.

"Yeah. You can stay a few nights if you need to, as long as you don't bring any *stuff* into my house." He nodded, and I nudged the tortilla chip bag his way, raising my eyebrows in challenge.

Johnny let out a lazy chuckle. "Fine." He took a chip, bringing it to his mouth dramatically before chomping down. "Holy shit!" he exclaimed, licking his lips. "This is fucking delicious."

My cheeks lifted. "I know. I can't tell if it's the lime or the salt or what, but the chips are the star of the show."

Johnny snatched the bag from my hand, and I watched with satisfaction as he ate almost the entire thing. He even took a few bites of my burrito. It was the most I'd seen him eat in a while and it occurred to me that, with this new phase in my life, I could potentially spend more time with my brother without having to worry about compromising my carefully curated persona. I wasn't delusional that I could get him to clean up his act, but perhaps I could do more to ensure he ate and had clean clothes.

We sat for a while, and I told him about JBC and the acquisition. I laughed out loud when my brother became the last person that day to ask if I was sure about not going to TremMark.

After attempting to find out what he'd been up to the past few weeks—questions he'd brushed off by turning the conversation back to me—I gave up. I doubted it was anything I'd want to hear about anyway. I focused instead on having him here in my living room, sober-adjacent and happy for the moment.

He refused the guest bedroom, so I made up the couch while he took a shower. We watched a replay of the Mariners game before going to bed, and I realized I hadn't spent time like this with my brother in ages.

In the morning, I discovered the blankets folded neatly on the couch. Johnny was nowhere to be seen. I tried not to be upset. At least we'd had a great night. Hopefully, there would be more soon.

I looked around the living room, attempting to decide what to do with the rest of my Saturday. It would be strange adjusting to not working, even on weekends. Perhaps I'd travel or do some volunteering, maybe catch up on watching all those Marvel movies Jason and Brad loved so much.

I decided to treat myself to coffee and a pastry from the little place a few blocks away.

Slipping on jeans and a light sweater—Prada, but at least it was casual—I gathered my hair into a ponytail. I grabbed the purse I'd used yesterday off the kitchen counter, humming when I observed it clashed with my outfit.

By the time I pulled out my wallet to pay for a soy latte and double chocolate muffin, an indulgence I planned to make more of a habit, I felt almost giddy. But when I reached for my credit card to use in the old-fashioned reader, I encountered only a leather sleeve where a plastic rectangle should have been.

———

*KNOCK, KNOCK...*TWENTY SECONDS...*ding-dong...*

I alternated knocking on the door with stabbing my index finger against the doorbell. I'd been expecting the location to be a little seedier, picturing Johnny's usual friends, but once the rideshare dropped me off in front of this bungalow in a suburb north of the city, there was no turning back. This was the only lead I had to find my brother.

The barista at the coffeehouse had been nice about giving me their biggest muffin. I think she'd sensed my frustration when I'd had to dig out my backup card to pay for breakfast.

Johnny didn't have a phone, so the best clue I had as to his whereabouts was this single-story olive-green house with neatly cut grass and freshly painted cream trim.

About six weeks ago, he'd shown up on my doorstep looking for a place to crash. I'd been handling a lot of meetings and paperwork from home at the time, shepherding the acquisition, and I was worried one of my coworkers might show up. I'd only let Johnny in long enough for him to tell me it was cool, that he could stay with a friend instead. Feeling guilty, I offered to send him there in a car, using my app, and this was the address he'd given me.

*Knock, knock...*twenty seconds...*ding-dong...*

Why wasn't anybody answering? A huge construction truck and a little sedan sat in the driveway. Someone had to be home, right? It was eleven o'clock on a Saturday morning, a time when most humans were awake. Of course, based on my brother's track record with his friends, everyone on the other side of the door might be passed out.

I'd gone online to cancel my card and saw transactions for large purchases made at two local department stores, as well as several online retailers. Apparently, Johnny's plan was to get money through reselling, a scheme that had landed him in jail for a short time in his early twenties. The credit card company offered to open an investigation to dispute those charges, but I didn't want to create a situation where Johnny might be in real trouble if things escalated. I simply told them I believed my card was compromised and asked for a new one.

Leaving it there had been an option. I could have chosen to move on from the fact my brother had stolen from me and gone about my day, lesson learned. After all, I'd spent a lifetime perfecting the art of not getting sucked into his problems. I could lock up my purse the next time he came around, and we could both pretend this never happened.

But, dammit, I thought we'd turned a corner last night.

My mind kept drifting to our easy conversation, the best one we'd had in years. Laughing over dinner. Had it been hard for him to steal from me after that? I pictured the blankets folded on the couch this morning and imagined it had.

But I needed to know for sure. I needed him to say he was sorry. Too bad for Johnny, I'd just abandoned the script I'd used to guide my entire adulthood. And like my colleagues at JBC, my brother was in for a surprise. I wouldn't be letting him walk all over me just to maintain appearances.

Knock, knock.

Ding-dong.

I paced back and forth on the small front porch. An old man in enormous glasses peered at me from behind the curtains next door, and a woman pushing a stroller gave me the side-eye as she passed. For all I knew, Johnny had punched in a random address and didn't even know this house. I wished someone would answer the door so I could find out.

I wanted to have this conversation with my brother and bring things to a head for a change. To engage in the conflict instead of avoiding it.

The minutes ticked by. Still nothing.

Shaking my head, I exhaled in defeat. Clearly, whoever lived here wasn't home.

I turned to leave when I heard feet shuffling toward the door on the other side. *Finally! A sign of life—hurrah!* The deadbolt clicked, and I gathered myself in time to see a man silhouetted behind the screen.

"Sorry," he said, moving to unlock it. "I was in the backyard and didn't hear the bell at first."

As the door opened, I straightened.

"That's okay." I yanked my purse onto my shoulder, positioning a hand over my eyes to shield them from the sun. "Sorry to bother you. I'm looking for—" I stopped cold as he stepped into the doorway. Disbelief clouded my mind. "Oh my god…" My arm lowered in slow motion. "Deck?"

Either the stress of the past few days had caused an intense hallucination, or Arturo Decker stood right in front of me.

My heart hammered. The sensation of tightening lungs gripped me, binding my chest like an iron band. A shockwave traveled down my spine.

"Deck?" I whispered again.

He stared at me, slack-jawed. His dark brown eyes blinked, then blinked again.

Those eyes. Big and round and stormy. With the soulful gaze that had fueled so many of my teenage daydreams.

For twelve years, I'd tried to forget those eyes. Tried to forget the haunted look he'd given me the last night I'd seen him.

The worst night of my life.

CHAPTER THREE
Deck

PRESENT DAY

I stuck the shovel in the ground and leaned against it, the task of digging a massive hole in my backyard nearly complete. My arms ached like I'd just pitched nine innings, but the Japanese maple in a pot on my patio deserved a permanent home. I had almost psyched myself up to keep going when the *Dope Gardening Songs* playlist blasting from my soundbar went quiet between tracks, long enough for me to hear the buzzing of my doorbell.

Leaving my muddy shoes outside and turning off the speaker, I gave my hands a quick rinse in the kitchen before making my way to the front of the house. As I opened the screen door, I hoped Johnny would be on the other side. I hadn't seen him for a few weeks, and he'd looked pretty strung out that last time. It would be nice to see him safe and—

"Oh my god...Deck?"

Alright.

Not Johnny.

Mierda.

Since I started talking to her brother again a year ago, I'd been expecting this moment. Dreading it. Even as I did my best to avoid it.

"Hey, Cori."

I lifted my arm, like maybe I was gonna shake her hand, but it turned into a clumsy little wave at my waist. It didn't seem like she noticed. Her eyes looked unfocused, dazed.

"Deck?" She appeared to be catching her breath. "Deck..." More deep breaths. "I can't believe... Wow."

As much as I'd anticipated running into her eventually, I still felt unprepared. Even more so when I registered her expression.

Why did she seem so surprised to see me? She'd shown up on *my* doorstep. Had Johnny given her the address? Was he okay? Was *she* okay? I wanted to ask, but the words wouldn't come. The only ones that came were, "Yeah...wow."

She glanced up at the sky and shook her head before muttering, "W*ild*," beneath her breath. Leaning back on her heels, she eyed me up and down. Her expression remained unreadable. I stood, not speaking, my hands buried in my pockets.

"I take it this is...your house?" she asked.

"Yeah."

A few more seconds passed.

Finally, her upper lip twitched. "So are you going to invite me in?"

"Oh, shit." I backed up and held the screen open wider. "Sorry. Yes, of course, come in."

Cori stepped over the threshold and into the small entryway of my house. She eyeballed the cardboard container filled with boots, as well as my sock-clad feet. "Should I take my shoes off?"

I looked down at the *small items* U-Haul box I used to hold the steel-toed Wolverines I wore to jobsites.

"No. It's fine."

She nodded, and I motioned her into the living room. Thankfully, nothing too embarrassing was lying around. A few baseball caps and a jacket on the couch, some mugs left out on the *medium items* box I had repurposed as a coffee table, and small piles of junk mail on top of the six other boxes stacked against the wall.

I moved around hurriedly, gathering up the loose items. "Sorry, I wasn't expecting company."

"It's fine," she said. "I wasn't exactly expecting to see you today either." Her tone stayed flat, but she smiled tentatively, as though to test my reaction.

The smile hit me in my gut.

Cori sat down, and I looked anywhere but at her. I'd already noticed enough. The high ponytail exposing the long line of her throat and neck, the expressive sky-blue eyes behind dark, blunt lashes, and the two tiny brown moles on the apple of her left cheek.

Memories flared. I'd been young. Cocky. I'd wanted to kiss those moles.

Pushing the thoughts aside, I decided the stacks of mail needed straightening. Right that minute. The jacket and hats had to be put away neatly in the front closet.

Forcing myself to forget about her had been the right thing to do. It was still the right thing. But it was impossible to ignore her when she and her two tiny moles were in my living room. I evened out the already even boxes against the wall.

I had no idea how she'd ended up at my house since seeing me on the other side of the door had obviously been a shock.

"I...I can't believe you're here," she said, mostly to herself.

"Uh-huh."

Cori peered at the boxes along the wall. "Did you just move in?"

"Um... It's been about two years."

She sucked in a breath. The silence stretched and knotted in the air. "You've been back...two years?"

I nodded, shifting my weight from foot to foot. When I didn't elaborate, her eyes moved around the room, taking in my sparse living space. Eventually, she asked, "Do you...live alone?"

"Yeah... Just me." I raised my arms at my sides.

After another beat of silence, Cori gestured to the bare walls. "Not much on decorating?"

"Not really." I looked down and ran my hands over my shirt—muddy from planting—then stuck them into my back pockets.

"And you were...gardening?"

"Mm-hmm."

Cori scrunched her nose. "I gotta be honest, Deck. I remember you being more of a talker." A nervous little guffaw left her throat.

Carajo.

I needed to get myself together. I might be stunned to see her, not to mention afraid of her ability to draw me in like a magnet, but none of that was her fault. If I'd wondered if anything had changed in twelve years, just having her in my house for ten minutes had proven that it hadn't.

But she deserved better than me acting like a *pendejo*. Of course she was confused. The Artie Decker she'd known before had talked a lot of shit.

"Sorry, Cori. I guess I'm just surprised to see you. I asked Johnny not to tell you I was here. Or that we were back in contact."

She recoiled slightly at my words but seemed relieved I'd finally uttered more than a few in a row. "He didn't tell me. I snooped out this address on my own, thinking he might be here...long story. I didn't know it was your house."

I sat down next to her, maintaining a careful distance. "So you came here looking for your brother? Is he alright?"

She sighed thickly. "That probably should have been my opener, huh? I guess I got distracted...seeing you. But yes. I'm looking for him. And I don't know if he's alright. That's why I need to find him."

Cori explained how she'd ended up here—Johnny staying over last night, the stolen credit card, the address in the app, and hanging out on my front porch for twenty minutes, ringing the doorbell. Part of me wanted to tell her she'd been foolish to leave her purse on the counter, that of course an addict was going to take that opportunity, but I understood what she meant when she said, "I think I'm always trying to prove my brother still cares, in his way. Subconsciously, giving him easy access to my purse was like a test of our relationship." She stood, agitated. "He failed."

I watched her pace across the builder-grade beige carpet in my living room, ponytail whipping around. Good thing we had an urgent task to focus on. I needed something to think about other than how beautiful she looked. She'd been can't-argue-it attractive as a teenager, but this grown-up version...*peligrosa*. Fucking dangerous.

"Don't worry, Cori, I'll help you find him." What else could I say? She looked so lost. And I had an idea where Johnny was.

She stopped moving. "Thanks. And, so we're clear, I realize it was kind of insane showing up at a random house. I know you could have been an axe murderer. But it's also been a hell of a morning on top of a really weird few days." She reached into the purse that was still slung over one shoulder and pulled out a slim black cylinder. "In my defense, I brought pepper spray."

"Hey, I get it," I reassured her, almost smiling. "You don't grow up where we did without becoming at least a little insane and a lot fearless. I'd have given teenage Cori at least fifty-fifty odds against an axe murderer, so I wouldn't expect thirty-year-old Cori to be scared of a quiet house in Mountlake Terrace in broad daylight."

"Watch it. I have six more months of my twenties." She laughed before sobering. "It's just that Johnny's never stolen from me before. And I'm mad at him, but I'm mostly worried."

I decided not to upset her further by admitting I'd also been extremely concerned about her brother lately.

My stomach dropped as her expression turned grave. Grave and eerily familiar. Unbidden, an image of her face on the last night I'd seen her surfaced in my mind. But I couldn't allow myself to think about *that* right now. Not if I wanted to function while she was near me.

"Try not to get too freaked out yet, Cori. I have a thought about where he might be."

"Well, thank goodness for that, because I'm officially out of leads. Honestly, I can't believe Johnny didn't tell me he was talking to you again. He never mentioned a thing."

"Like I said, I asked him not to."

"I know you said that. But...why?" She frowned, letting out a deep, slow exhale before asking, "Why have you been back two years, and I didn't know?"

I eyed her levelly, speaking in a low tone. "I think you can guess."

An exasperated huff left her. "I'm not sure I could, Deck." Her shoulders sagged. "But we can leave it for now." Blowing out another massive breath, she sank back onto the couch. "This is all so surreal, seeing you and—"

A poofy gray hurricane jumped up on the cushion. Cori looked at him, disbelieving, as he rubbed against her and purred noisily.

"Is that…" She glanced at the feline again before whispering reverently, "Bastardo?"

"Yep," I replied, glancing down at the furry little intruder. "Mamá was more than happy to part with him when I got this place. In fact, the day I closed escrow, Pop showed up and dropped Bastardo in my living room. I believe his exact words were, '*Es tu problema ahora, tonto.*'" I did my best impression of my dad's *gringo* accent.

Cori gave Bastardo scratches under his chin, and I recalled her doing the same thing in our kitchen fourteen years ago. She looked up at me with a grin, and I couldn't help but return it. Maybe I could convince myself it was merely a fond smile between old friends. That our reunion was simple. After all, I'd gotten good at pretending. I'd spent the past two years pretending she didn't exist.

———

IT WAS A TESTAMENT TO THE HISTORY between us that Cori seemed fine getting into the truck with me. She didn't have her own car because she'd apparently lent it to a friend for the weekend. Her face got a little lopsided when I told her we were heading to the old neighborhood, but she didn't change her mind.

My truck was extremely reliable and necessary in my line of work, but I wondered what she thought of the beat-up old Ford. At least it was neat. I always got on Juan about how his truck smelled like french fries. My time away had taught me that I felt more in control when I kept things tidy. Call it a tic, but it worked for me.

Also, the truck wasn't flashy, an advantage for where we were headed.

Cori seemed unfazed by the rusty wheel wells as she climbed into the cab. She sat up straight with her purse in her lap, hands folded neatly over it. Although she appeared calm, I registered the tightness of her jaw. I remembered that tough facade. Seeing it in my truck now felt surreal.

Surreal. She'd used that word in my living room. It triggered another memory. She used to come over to my house to watch Marisol—my parents never made me do that unless they were desperate—and I helped her practice SAT words. Cori had these shitty homemade flash cards, rectangles cut up out of old cereal boxes, and I would quiz her at my kitchen table after my sister went to bed.

I'd memorized those words along with her. No way would I have learned them otherwise.

Cori's shoulders tensed as we merged onto I-5, heading north. My eyes gauged her expression. *Mercurial. Inscrutable. Enigmatic.*

"Do you want music?" I asked. "Or maybe I should turn on the AC?"

"I'm good. You can put on the Mariners game if you want."

"Sure."

She liked baseball. I'd forgotten. At one point, I had known, but...I'd managed to forget. Forced myself. That was what would happen if it took too long to find Johnny. I'd start remembering more and more. Things I'd worked so hard to shut away. We need-ed to find her brother, *inmediatamente.*

But even though my brain knew that, my eyes were drawn to her as they'd always been, trying to solve a puzzle.

Her clothes fit like a glove. Just jeans and a sweater, but still, she looked expensive. Buttoned-up, hair tight, unlike before. As a teenager, she'd never been very social, but had always tried to fit in enough to fade into the background. It was safer that way in our neighborhood, especially for a white girl with red hair. My pops was as Irish as the guy on the Lucky Charms box, but all my looks came from Mamá, so I'd never had to deal with it. Cori and Johnny, on the other hand, had to work hard not to stick out.

She was definitely gonna get noticed once we got to Everett. We needed to do something about that.

Cori blew a loud raspberry when the Mariners went down one-two-three in the bottom of the fourth.

The mid-inning commercials came on, and she lowered the volume, angling her head toward me. "I know you said we're going someplace near the old neighborhood, but why do you think Johnny will be there?"

"I've picked him up there before. When I let him crash with me."

She curled her fingers into her palms. "I haven't been back to Everett since my mom died."

"Not at all?" Cori and Johnny's mom had passed away over a decade ago. I knew from talking to Johnny and my family that Cori didn't make it to Everett much, but I hadn't realized she'd never been back.

She shook her head and pulled one of her feet up to the bench seat, looping her arms around her knee to rest her chin on top.

"After she died, it felt like there was nothing left for me there," Cori said. "Nothing but bad memories." I flinched but kept my eyes on the road, not daring to look at her. She leaned back in her seat and continued, "Then I ran into Rosa six months ago, randomly at the mall. I hadn't seen her since I took off. That was around the same time we got this incredible offer at my company, and it felt like the universe was trying to tell me something. Rosa and I talked for almost three hours. She let me buy her one of those jalapeño pretzels she loves, and she treated me the way she always had, like no time had passed. It reminded me that there were some good things...good times. Maybe I didn't have to leave *everything* in the rearview."

I hummed, considering. "I saw Rosa a few weeks ago when I visited my parents. She and Mamá made dinner. I'd never leave that lady in the rearview because then...no tacos."

Cori huffed. "Don't say tacos."

"Huh?"

"Never mind."

"Actually, Rosa seemed pretty upset about something. She was having a heavy conversation with Mamá when I came in. But she wouldn't tell me about it. She just grabbed my chin and hit me with the 'don't worry, *mijo*.' Maybe if you see her again, she'll tell you."

"I seriously doubt that, Deck, since our little conference over mall pretzels was literally the first time I've seen her in years. I've emailed and texted a few times since, but we mostly just talk about stupid stuff. The Center. Her birds. My job. Not sure we're at the *spill-your-secrets* phase quite yet."

I shrugged. "I don't think that matters. You were really special to her back in the day."

Cori turned her head to look out the window. "I'll see what I can do. We're overdue for another meetup, anyway." She exhaled heavily, fogging the glass. "I have time to figure it out, though, right? Since I'm guessing we won't run into Rosa wherever we're headed. Unless you're thinking Johnny is sitting in her kitchen right now, drinking Jarritos?"

My jaw flexed. "Sorry."

She angled her head to watch as we passed an industrial area on the side of the freeway. After a minute, the game came back on, but she didn't turn it up. Instead, she asked, "Why did you tell Johnny not to let me know you guys were hanging out?"

"*Caray*, Cori...this again?"

"C'mon, Deck. It's crazy that I'm just now finding out you've been back *for two years*."

"Did you need to know?" I snapped, not wanting to open this subject. "Why does it matter, since it sounds like you've been pretty done with the old neighborhood? And all the people from your past."

She squeezed her eyes shut and put her foot back on the floor of the cab before fisting her hands in her lap again. "That's...fair," she gritted out. "Like I said, I've been...reevaluating...those decisions lately. And that's on me. But you're not just some random person I used to know."

"No?" My voice pitched as she entered dangerous territory.

Her gaze shifted in my direction. "Please don't play dumb," she murmured, her voice laced with hurt. "Don't do that to me."

I wished she'd stop pushing. We didn't have to talk about this. We could leave it in the past, in the dirt where it belonged.

"You know why," I rasped. My pulse sped up as my body rebelled against the thoughts, the creeping guilt like a hand choking my neck.

She stared at me, narrowing her eyes. I looked away.

"It wasn't your fault, Deck."

I shuddered.

The things that happened. I would never forget her terrified face. And at the end, when her face changed. Accusing.

That had been the last time she'd seen me. A dozen years ago, but still a vivid image in my brain.

I'd been terrified too. Out of my mind. Almost naked. And covered in blood.

It didn't matter if she blamed me or not. I blamed myself.

I turned the radio up.

CHAPTER FOUR
Cori – Age 14

FIFTEEN YEARS AGO

After sprinting to the Decker house, I paused in their driveway to catch my breath. It was 4:58, and I'd promised to be there by five.

I'd lost track of time unloading a Costco order with Rosa. She'd let me help more at the Center lately, putting things away, cleaning up, and answering the phone. We'd been chatting about the book I'd just read for English, *Brave New World*, while we stacked cans of diced peaches and boxes of Ritz crackers in the pantry.

The last-minute babysitting request came in late yesterday after one of their older daughters had to back out because her car had broken down. Of the seven siblings, only Deck, Marisol, and their brother Raymond still lived at home. Fernando had graduated from college and moved to California. Justina and her twin sister, Angelina, lived in the dorms at Seattle University, and Emilio had an apartment near the community college where he attended part-time.

Raymond played the violin in the high school orchestra and had even won awards for it. He wanted to attend a prestigious music college. Michael and María needed a sitter so they could watch him at an important audition. Since everyone respected Deck's refusal to watch Marisol alone, I was the next best option.

As I ventured up the walkway of the Deckers' mint-colored Craftsman, I saw Bastardo on the front step grooming himself. I leaned down to pet him.

Marisol's parents had gotten her the kitten last year. She spent so much time in bed, they'd figured he could keep her company. Unfortunately, the only household member the charcoal-colored tabby seemed to tolerate was Deck—and me, when I visited their house. The touchy feline they'd initially named Baxter had gone on to become a staple of the neighborhood, earning the obvious nickname "Bastard" as he roamed around digging up flowers, sleeping on freshly washed car hoods, and hissing at children. "¡*Ay, Bastardo!*" was a common refrain heard on the Deckers' street.

I was about to knock on the door when it opened, and Emilio came out.

"Hey Cori, you're watching Marisol?" he asked with his usual friendliness.

"Yeah. I didn't know you'd be here. Your mom said you and your sisters couldn't do it."

"That's true. I'm on my way out. Just came by to do laundry." He held up the black duffel by his side. "I would have stayed with Mari except I have a ride-along scheduled with the EPD tonight for this criminology course I'm taking."

"That sounds interesting. Maybe you'll get to be in a high-speed chase or something."

Emilio let out a small laugh. "That would be fun. But I'm expecting it to be *muy tranquilo*."

"Well, I hope they at least let you switch on the lights and sirens."

He smiled, lifting his hand to show crossed fingers. "Bye, Cori. Thanks for helping. It means a lot to my parents, to all of us."

"It's no trouble," I assured him as Bastardo scurried into the house between our feet. "Your house is way bigger than mine. Plus, your parents let me watch TV, and there are always good leftovers in the fridge."

"*Seguro. Mamá's* cooking *es la mejor*."

He shrugged on his coat and winked at me as he walked out to the fifteen-year-old Sentra in the driveway. His pride and joy.

Emilio Decker radiated charm. Not to mention, he was smart and gorgeous. If I didn't already love Arturo Decker with my whole heart, I might have considered crushing on his older brother instead.

I walked into the light-filled kitchen, which was decorated like the rest of the interior in varying shades of red, orange, and yellow. Marisol sat at the table, squeezing Hershey's syrup into a glass of milk. It had been a while since she'd had any surgeries, and she appeared more energetic than usual. But even during these in-between times, her parents worried about her being outside too much and exposing herself to germs.

After washing my hands, I sat down with her while she swirled a spoon around her glass.

"Hi there, little miss. What should we do tonight?"

She grinned toothily. "Will you read to me?"

"Sounds like a plan."

Leaving her milk on the table, she went to her room to choose some books. Marisol always loved being read to. Now that she was seven, she was also reading simple books on her own. I felt guilty about sometimes getting impatient while she sounded out her words. I had no idea how Rosa managed to help kids who struggled with their homework every day at the Center.

María and Michael rushed into the kitchen. He scooped up his keys and wallet, while she put on her earrings.

"Thank you, Cori, you're a lifesaver," María said. "We should be back before nine. Artie's here now, but he's leaving soon. There are enchiladas warming in the oven. Marisol should eat around six, and I'll be disappointed if you don't help yourself as well."

I would have watched Marisol regardless, but Mamá Decker's cooking was a nice perk. The most my mom ever did was boil noodles to eat with jarred spaghetti sauce.

The Deckers hurried through the back door. Michael called out, "Marisol, be good for Cori. Bye, Arturo. Be home by eleven."

After they left, and with Marisol still hunting for books upstairs, I peeked into the living/dining room. I saw Deck hunched over the dining table, mumbling to himself. One of his pointer fingers moved back and forth across the page of an open textbook. His other arm hung by his side, gripping a pen.

Even agitated and annoyed, he was still the most beautiful boy I'd ever seen. I'd known him for almost four years, but now just looking at Deck made my heart beat faster. The change had happened so slowly I hadn't even noticed it at first. It was like one day I looked up and realized the boy I'd known forever was exactly the same person he'd always been, yet somehow, completely different.

From my place in the kitchen archway, I admired him. He had on beige chinos and a white tank top. The gold chain he always wore rested between his chest muscles. Evidently, the hours that he, Johnny, Cruz, and Eliazar spent lifting weights in his garage were paying off. He'd slicked his hair back into a low ponytail, a style that highlighted his broad brown shoulders.

At school yesterday, I'd overheard one of the girls in my eighth-grade class talking about him.

"You remember Artie Decker? I saw him skating at the park this weekend. Damn, that boy has gotten fine as fuck since starting high school. Imma shoot my shot next year when we're back in the same building."

While her friends laughed, I'd frowned at the reminder Deck would never look at me like I looked at him. The hot girls wanted him. He was beautiful and mysterious and sexy, and I was...his best friend's little sister.

Still, he was always nice to me, and I spent a lot of time with him, even if it was mostly because of Johnny. Deck might not *notice* me the way I wanted him to, but he'd never made me feel invisible.

I was busy checking out the definition in his biceps when he groaned in frustration. "Fuck!" he shouted, slamming the textbook shut. "Fucking shit assignment."

I backed away before he could see me.

Retreating into the kitchen, I intercepted Marisol carrying a stack of books from her room.

"Should we sit on the couch?" she asked.

"Actually, I think here is good. We don't want to disturb your brother while he's doing homework."

But then Deck came tearing through the kitchen, heading toward the back door. He stopped short when he saw me.

"Oh, hey, Cori. Mamá told me you were coming." He brushed his hands across his thighs before running both hands over his slick hair. "How'd the essay turn out?"

Deck also knew I was studying *Brave New World*. We'd talked about it at the Center when he came to meet up with Eliazar the other day.

"Okay, I think. It was nice of you to listen to me about it."

"No worries. I had to read that book in eighth, too, but I didn't really get it. You should have been my teacher." He waggled his eyebrows.

My cheeks heated. "Thanks."

"Nah. I should be thanking *you* for watching my baby sister while your brother and I get up to no good," he teased.

At least, I hoped he was teasing. Johnny had come home smelling like weed last weekend.

"It's no problem. Marisol and I only got halfway through the book on Jesse Owens last time, and I need to find out how it ends." I turned to his sister and gave her a small salute when she produced the book in question.

"Cool. I tried to read to her a few days ago, but—"

"He's not good at it," Marisol interjected innocently. "He goes too slow, and then he just makes the words up."

I winced at Deck's immediate expression of embarrassment.

"Marisol, I know you didn't say something mean on purpose, but how do you think those words make your brother feel? Especially since he was trying to do something nice for you."

I didn't know if my admonishing his sister made the moment better or worse for Deck, but at least it would make her think twice before saying something similarly careless in the future.

Marisol's face fell. "I didn't mean... I wasn't trying to say anything bad about Artie." She looked helplessly at Deck.

"It's okay, little squirt," Deck said quickly, reaching out to ruffle her hair. "I shouldn't have tried to fool you anyway with the words. You've got all those books memorized, right?"

"Right." Her grin returned.

"Reading's just not my thing, *hermana*. But maybe I can teach you to ride my old bike someday."

Marisol wrinkled her nose and giggled. "Don't be funny, Artie. You know I'm not allowed to play outside."

She returned to her books, unaware she'd just sent an arrow through her brother's heart. Even though Deck preferred not to be left alone with Marisol, he still loved her fiercely. I could only imagine what the reminders of her limitations did to him.

"Maybe someday, squirt," he whispered, giving me a searching glance before bolting toward the door.

I watched from the kitchen window as Deck headed into the street. Johnny walked over from the direction of our trailer park with Eliazar close behind him. A moment later, Cruz drove up in his silver Escort, and the four of them took off to who-knew-where.

"Can we finish Jesse Owens?" Marisol asked my back. I turned and nodded.

"Yeah, but let's go in the living room. You're right. It's more comfortable there."

We sat on the couch and finished the Jesse Owens biography for kids, before moving on to Babe Ruth and Mary Lou Retton. Marisol loved reading about famous athletes. I imagined it was her way of being into sports since she couldn't play.

But perhaps she would one day. She wouldn't always be so fragile. Deck hadn't been completely off base in suggesting she might ride his old bike one day.

Maybe then he could forgive himself.

CHAPTER FIVE
Deck – Age 16

FOURTEEN-AND-A-HALF YEARS AGO

"Mamá, I'm leaving soon."

Cruz would roll in any second. It was midafternoon, but I had just woken up a few hours ago. I'd managed to shower, shave, and eat a bowl of cereal. Plus watch HGTV. I'd never tell my boys, but I was addicted to those shows where workers turned condemned houses full of old cat poop and graffiti and shit into fancy mansions.

After pulling on a white undershirt over my black Carhartts, I used the gigantic bottle of Costco-brand gel my family shared to slick my hair back, twisting a rubber band around it.

Searching for my wallet, I faltered when I found it sitting open on the kitchen counter. Had one of my siblings messed with it? Seen what I'd paid fifty dollars for yesterday? Or had I just tossed it there like *un idiota* when I snuck in last night? Anything was possible. I'd been pretty wasted.

After confirming that the driver's license for *Jose Alvarez, age twenty-six, resident of Lake Stevens*, remained safely tucked away, I released a relieved breath.

Mamá called out from the back bedroom as I shoved the wallet into my pocket.

"No, *mijo*. Don't walk out just yet. First, go to my car and bring in that little tote with the stuff from the pharmacy. I'm changing your sister's bandages, and her new ointment is in there."

I knew better than to argue. It was just the three of us in the house. Pop still wasn't home from his shift at the airport, and none of my other brothers and sisters were around.

Only Marisol. She almost never left the house.

I found the bag my mom needed and brought it to the bedroom, placing it on top of the dresser near the doorway before attempting a quick getaway.

Mamá sighed from her chair near the bed. "I raised you better than that, Arturo. Bring it over to me so I don't have to get up." She met my eyes. "I could use a little help, too."

"Cruz is gonna be here any minute."

"Entonces probablemente deberías ayudarme rápido, ¿verdad?"

Stepping slowly toward the bed, I glanced down at my sister. Her *Kim Possible* bedspread was bunched at her feet, and the sheets were a sweaty heap resting on her midsection. Her breathing was shallow, a result of pain and pain meds, and I wasn't sure if she knew we were there.

"¿Qué necesitas, Mamá?"

"That's more like it, *cariño*. I'm just going to pull these off and use the cool water before putting more ointment on. Then fresh bandages. Not too complicated. If you can hand me everything as I go, it'll be quicker."

I steadied myself. The process itself wasn't complicated. But seeing the tight silvery skin pulling across my baby sister's neck and jaw, the fresh red across her chest and shoulders, puffed up and angry after her most recent skin graft? That part was torture.

Five years and dozens of procedures later, it was still hard to look at. I did what my mother asked. Handed her the sponge. The little scissors. Gauze. All while keeping my eyes on anything but the bed.

We weren't quite finished when I heard Cruz pull up outside. Mamá took pity on me. "You can go, *mijo*. I have it from here."

I gave her a kiss on the cheek. As I passed through the kitchen to the side door, I ran into my pops coming in.

"Cruz is outside."

"Yeah, we're gonna pick up Johnny and go to Eliazar's to play video games, or maybe head over to a friend's house."

He grabbed my shoulder as I tried to pass him.

"Artie, we have enough to deal with after your sister's surgery. We don't need any more nonsense—"

"I know, Pop." I interrupted, annoyed.

"Don't think we didn't hear how late you came home last night. Stumbling around." His grip tightened as he looked past me out the window, to a clear view of Cruz sitting stoically in the driver's seat of his car. "I mean it. Don't get up to anything."

"Sure, Pop." I twisted out of his hold. "I'll be good."

<hr>

CRUZ AND I PULLED UP TO JOHNNY'S double-wide earlier than planned. I assumed Cori heard the engine because she opened the door before I could knock.

"Johnny's in the shower," she said, not quite meeting my eyes. "You can wait here for him to finish up if you want."

A blush spread across her cheeks, and her mouth turned up in a shy smile. I clocked the cute little moles on the side of her face. On school days, she wore makeup like all the girls did, but now I saw every freckle on her nose. Johnny would probably punch me in the face if he knew how much I'd been thinking about those freckles lately.

I turned around and yelled to Cruz that Johnny wasn't ready yet.

"Imma go get Eliazar then," he shouted back from the driver's seat. "You stay here and make sure Johnny keeps his ass moving."

I smiled and waved Cruz off as I stepped into the trailer, shutting the door behind me. It was a running joke in our crew that Johnny moved at the speed of a stoned turtle. He took going with the flow to the next level, always running into the store to get one thing and coming out with another, losing his keys, or forgetting his backpack somewhere. One time, he left his jacket at my house. The rest of us hung in the car while he went inside to grab it. After ten minutes, Johnny still hadn't come back out, so I went in. That fucker was sitting at the table with Pop talking football, chilling, like we weren't sitting out in the driveway waiting for him.

But it was impossible to stay mad. Johnny never meant anything by it. He just loved people—loved making them laugh and loved when everyone was happy.

I'd known Cruz and Eliazar since kindergarten. Johnny had shown up in fifth grade, feeling like a long-lost relative. Johnny and Eliazar were on the younger side for our grade, while Cruz and I were older. But the four of us fit together perfectly. Especially Johnny and me. I'd never had much in common with my musical genius brother Raymond, and Emilio and Fernando were a lot older than me. Johnny was my brother from another mother.

And, of course, with Johnny came Cori.

Pop called Cori and Johnny "Irish twins" because they only had thirteen months between them. On the other hand, Cori and I were almost two years apart. When we were kids, those years felt like a wide, gaping *chasm*, to use one of her flash card words. Johnny pretended to get annoyed when she followed us to the minimarket or begged Eliazar for rides on his handlebars, but really, he didn't mind. And because Johnny and I were so close, she felt like my little sister too. But somewhere along the way, things had changed. I was determined to ignore it and had been mostly successful in pushing the newfound awareness down.

Until last Monday.

The evening began the way many had over the past year. I came home to find Cori at my house, babysitting my little sister.

While Cori was upstairs putting Marisol to bed, I sat at the kitchen table, getting pissed at my history textbook. It felt like every time I finished a page, I immediately forgot all the words. I kept having to go back and re-read, and even then, most of the information didn't stick.

I was trying to decide between throwing the book out the window or setting it on fire when I felt a tentative hand on my shoulder.

Everyone thought I was a cocky, indifferent student. I let them believe it because the alternative—people knowing I was just plain stupid—was way worse. Cori never bought into either scenario. She always spoke to me like I had smart things to say and didn't judge me for having difficulties with schoolwork. A few times, I'd been in danger of failing my classes. She'd talked through assignments and textbook passages with me, and never mentioned it to anyone.

But that night, I was too far gone. As much as I loved her big brain, I wasn't in the mood to be tutored or given a pep talk.

I glanced down at the open textbook, where the words still swirled together in a confusing maze of letters.

Cori's grip on my shoulder tightened. "I'm sorry it's frustrating, Deck. That sucks. Especially since you work so hard at it."

I waited for her to say more, but the silence stretched. That was it. No solutions or advice. Just acknowledgment of my misery.

Exhaling, I reached my hand up to cover hers. "*Gracias.* I'm glad somebody sees."

She swallowed. After pausing a few beats, she said softly, "I see things... You know I do."

I sucked in a breath at the murmured words. The sweet sound of her voice. She was right. I knew. How could I not? She was the only person on earth I never put on a show for.

I see things.

Cori saw.

Deck. Decker. Artie. Arturo. All of me.

The world stopped in that long moment. I shivered, and it felt like all the blood in my body began traveling directly to my dick. Tension lingered in the air between us, and I knew for sure what I had been trying to ignore for months. Something with Cori and me had shifted.

I couldn't say anything, of course. Johnny would kill me. Plus, she deserved better than my sorry ass. But at least I could be honest with myself.

To her, I merely said, "Thank you."

She nodded and gave my shoulder one more squeeze before grabbing her backpack and slipping wordlessly out the door.

It had been five days since then, but I could still remember the feeling of her hand on me. Could still remember jerking off to the image of her in my mind. I'd be feeling guilty about that one for a while.

But I was determined to get back to normal, to shake off this weirdness with Cori that had gotten hold of me.

The microwave beeped, pulling me from my thoughts. Cori waited a few seconds before pulling out a bag of popcorn. "Ouch!" She dropped the pouch on the counter and sucked her pointer finger into her mouth, mumbling, "I always forget you're supposed to wait a minute to touch the bag."

I wouldn't have known that. Mamá always made popcorn using kernels in the big pot on the stove, adding melted butter and a pinch of chili pepper. But even if I had known, I would have forgotten, because the sight of Cori sucking her finger between her pink lips had my full attention. *Dammit!* I needed to stop noticing that shit.

"You can share this," she said, pulling the bag at the corners to open it. "I'm sorry I don't have more to offer. I haven't been to the store yet this weekend."

Cori and Johnny's mom never bought groceries. Just left them money when she remembered. Meanwhile, Mamá barely let the rest of us cook in her kitchen.

I pffted. "All good. You know you don't have to, like, *host* me." I stood on the opposite side of the counter, using it to keep some distance between us as I grabbed a handful of popcorn. "Were you at the Center?"

"Uh-huh. Chuck organized some Saturday baseball for the kids whose parents couldn't enroll them in Little League. I told Rosa I'd help him out."

"Why couldn't they do Little League?"

"Lots of reasons. But mostly because it costs money, and Chuck said getting a scholarship is kind of a grind."

With seven kids, I'd heard my parents gripe many times about having to fill out scholarship forms for this or that. But they'd always done it. "How'd it go?"

She shrugged. "I mean...I'm pretty good at carrying water bottles, and I can operate that scoreboard like a boss, but Chuck is gonna have to be the one to teach them to do fancy stuff like hold a bat or catch a ball."

I chuckled. "Whatever. They're lucky to have you." Opening my mouth, I made a motion for her to throw a piece of popcorn in the air. She did, and I caught it, snapping my jaw shut before grinning in victory.

Dios, the microwave stuff tasted like shit.

It was no shock to realize I'd spent my morning sleeping off a massive hangover while Cori had been volunteering. I admired that she seemed to have different priorities than everyone else but still knew how to get along in the neighborhood. Her red hair made her stand out—no help for that—but she did her best not to attract attention. She knew how to avoid a beatdown from other girls in our school by staying off their radars. Yet, somehow, in keeping herself safe, she hadn't grown hard.

I worried about that. It was dangerous for her to have such a big heart.

But not so big it stopped her from throwing a piece of popcorn at my eye.

"Ouch!" I put my hand to my chest and would have fallen over dramatically, except there was no room to do so.

With only two bedrooms in the double-wide, Johnny slept on the couch. His things were everywhere. I flicked a pair of boxers off a chair so Cori and I could sit down at the tiny round table that passed for a dining area.

"Sorry it's messy," Cori said, closing some schoolbooks and stuffing them in her backpack.

"It's fine. I know Johnny is basically a tornado." I winked, and her cheeks turned red again.

An ear-splitting sound wafted through the hallway. At first, I thought *Bastardo* had gone into heat and prowled too far from our house. But it wasn't my demented cat.

Cori groaned as her brother's voice rose over the noise of the shower. "Is he...singing Beyoncé?" She put her face in her hands as Johnny botched a high note. "Why is he such a weirdo?"

I laughed. "And tone deaf."

"And loud."

We listened, silently consoling one another when Johnny launched into Justin Bieber's "Baby." As we finished off the popcorn, my eyes drifted to the closed bedroom door at the back of the trailer.

"Your mom been around?"

Cori flicked the zipper on her backpack and shook her head slowly. "Nope. She might have come by while we were in school, but I haven't seen her in a few days. She has a *friend* she's been staying with lately."

"Oh."

"Yeah."

It was an open secret that the Raneys' mom, Jill, was an addict who tricked when she needed to. Johnny never tried to hide it. He usually played it off like it was hilarious, but I knew he and his sister worried about her. Jill had gotten clean and taken decent care of her kids plenty of times over the years. She just couldn't seem to make it stick. At least Cori was close to Rosa, not to mention my parents, so she had other people if she needed someone.

And Johnny had me, Cruz, and Eliazar. We were boys. Brothers for life.

"What are you reading these days?" I attempted to change the subject.

Cori rolled her eyes. "Do you really want to hear? Or are you just asking because you know I don't want to talk about my mom?"

Now that she asked, I realized I wanted to hear. "I like it when you talk to me about what you're reading. It's hard for me...the words...you know. But I like it when you tell me."

She still didn't seem too sure. "Do you want to know what I'm reading in school or for fun?"

Fuck. This girl. She read *for fun*. "Both?"

Cori nodded. "Well, for school, my honors class is reading *Great Expectations*. I wish I liked it a bit more, but we just started, so maybe it'll pick up." She glanced downward. "For fun...don't laugh at me, okay?" I made the *cross my heart* gesture with my finger. "I guess you'd call it a...small-town romance. With cowboys and stuff..." She took a breath before adding quickly, "It's not like porn or anything. Not even close. I got it in the teen section at the library. But, yeah, it's, um, it's...good."

I didn't laugh as she stammered through her description—I'd crossed my heart after all—but I did smile and bite my lip.

We lived in a neighborhood where couples regularly shouted at each other in the streets, and you had to kick over a couple of meth heads to lock your bike at 7-Eleven, so of course Cori was reading about small-town cowboys.

It made me feel even more guilty for noticing her in a new way, considering my plans for the evening.

I thought about how excited my friends and I were to have our brand-new fake IDs. No more begging adults to buy for us outside the corner store. We'd be purchasing our own Rolling Rocks tonight, *muchas gracias*.

I would have been embarrassed if Cori knew most of what we'd been getting up to lately. She probably had her suspicions, but the fact that I didn't want her to know only proved that I would never deserve her. She didn't need me dirtying up her life.

Johnny turned off the water, mercifully ending his off-key rendition of "Umbrella." He exited the bathroom with a towel wrapped around his waist. Before I could stop him, he came over and shook his soaking wet hair like a dog, spraying our clothes and faces as we held up our hands.

Cori giggled. "Knock it off!"

"Showers for everyone!" Johnny declared.

"Fucker." I wiped the water drops from my jaw. "Go put some clothes on."

Johnny cackled and turned around before releasing the towel, shaking his bare ass at us as he grabbed some wadded-up jeans off the floor and headed back into the bathroom.

"That's my crazy brother. He's on offer if you want him," Cori said, still laughing.

"At least he didn't give us full frontal."

"True." Cori reached over and ran a thumb across my forehead before snatching her hand back. "Sorry," she said. "The water…"

I captured her wrist before she could pull it away completely. Brushing my thumb across the sensitive skin, I fixed my gaze on her. "It's okay."

Our eyes locked. A gulp worked its way down her throat as I touched her.

I knew I needed to let go, but I didn't want to.

Fuck, I didn't want to.

"C'mon, bro." Johnny reappeared wearing the jeans and a gray zip-up. "Cruz just pulled up outside."

I released Cori and stood. At that moment, I wanted nothing more than to stay there and talk about small-town cowboys. To eat shitty popcorn. To lean forward and beg her to touch my forehead again. To do whatever I needed to do to be good enough for her.

But Johnny was already pushing me out the door.

Chapter Six
Deck

PRESENT DAY

Cori and I pulled into a neighborhood near the one we'd grown up in, walking distance to the ancient skating rink and not too far from the freeway. Houses here looked slightly nicer than the ones on my parents' street, with fewer sketchy apartments, but it wasn't exactly Beverly Hills. Weeds still sprouted thickly in the overgrown lawns, pushing on the low chain-link fences surrounding them.

Parking the truck a block away from our destination, I pointed out the drab yellow house to Cori. She took a deep breath and moved to climb down from her seat when I stopped her with a hand to the shoulder.

"You sure about this? I can go in on my own if you want," I offered.

"No. I'll go nuts if I sit here and wait. I'm going."

"I figured. But we ought to do some things so you don't draw attention. I'm not sure exactly what we'll find. It's two in the afternoon, so anything is possible. The party could be finishing up or just getting started, but there definitely won't be any women who look like you in there."

She didn't pretend to misunderstand. "What should I do?"

"First, let's not take your bag in with us. That's just asking for trouble."

I pulled the lid up on the silver lock box in the back of the cab. After taking out the pepper spray and shoving it in her pocket, she put her purse in, along with her phone. "Anything else?"

"Can you, um, maybe take your hair down, muss it up a bit? It'll help if you look a bit...used."

Cori flinched but didn't argue.

With her hair down, she looked somewhat better, but those fancy clothes and clean sneakers weren't gonna work. I couldn't do anything about the shoes, but I could fix the rest. I grabbed one of my work hoodies from the back seat and handed it to her.

She slipped it over her head, no questions asked, drowning in the dingy gray size L with the J&D Construction logo on it. It did the trick, covering up her curves and masking the quality of her jeans.

"That's good," I said. "Stay by my side and try not to look at anyone too close, okay?"

"Yeah, Deck. I know." I sensed the fear in her voice, but also the careful attention. She understood the rules here.

There were no sidewalks. Cars hugged every inch of the curb, so we walked side by side in the street. All the windows had their curtains drawn tight. The only evidence these houses were occupied were the cars, the bikes tossed haphazardly near the porches, and a few yards with faded Little Tikes slides out front. Cori and I spoke quietly in the unnerving stillness.

"How did you know about this place?" she asked.

"My brother Emilio. You remember that do-gooder mothereffer is a cop? About a year ago, he mentioned he'd seen Johnny here, on the job. That's how your brother and I reconnected."

It had been dangerous engaging with Johnny because I hadn't wanted to run into Cori. I'd known since I was a teenager that the best thing I could do for her was stay away. But her brother was a different story. I'd put Johnny in this situation. I owed it to him to try to fix it.

As we walked by a gray house with a makeshift wheelchair ramp out front, two enormous Dobermans came rushing at us, jumping up on the fence and barking viciously. Cori launched herself against my side. My arm came around her shoulders instinctively. After we passed the dogs, I attempted to remove it, but she grabbed on, locking me next to her.

"It might make more sense if we look like we're, you know, together," she said.

I didn't want to have my arm around her. A dozen years on, I still remembered how good she felt there. But she had a point. I nodded and lifted the hinge on the gate. We walked up the path to the door.

My stomach churned as I tapped on the solid wood—memories of Chi-chi's parties threatened to make their way to the surface—but I didn't have a choice. Johnny could be in there.

I raised my fist to the door again, noticing it wasn't fully shut. Eventually, I knocked hard enough that it opened.

Into a nightmare.

The door creaked wide, and we found ourselves on the edge of a putrid-smelling living room. Navy blue sheets were duct-taped to the walls, covering the windows and back door slider. Cori and I squinted, adjusting to the abrupt darkness, and I barely pulled her back from stepping in a puddle of something—vomit, probably, hopefully not piss—as we ventured in farther.

At least five couches were shoved into the room, all with people in various states of awareness on them. A dilapidated coffee table covered in drug paraphernalia held a place of honor in the center. I saw Cori's eyes widen at the sight of burned foil and spoons, lighters and pipes. Needles. One needle stuck up from the carpet, perfectly embedded.

"Watch where you step," I whispered. Her reply was a slight nod.

A couple looked up at us with curiosity, but no one seemed to mind that two random people had walked into the house. It was strangely quiet, just the sounds of breathing, snoring, and a squeak of pleather as someone moved around on a sofa. I imagined this room looked a lot different a few hours ago. Still a nightmare, but one with music and talking. Again, I pushed down the memories that nagged me.

Shuffling on the carpet echoed from our left. A woman came out from the hallway, the straps of her tank top falling off her shoulders and two stringy braids unraveling down her back. She gave us an upnod as she walked by and went through the open doorway of the kitchen, passing close enough that I could make out her blown pupils and the track marks near her elbow. Cori noticed too, gasping a teeny bit before catching herself. At least it was a sign of life. Everyone else looked half dead.

I pulled Cori against the wall, hugging her to me—not that anyone was paying attention—and used that vantage point to check out the people on the couches. None of them looked like Johnny. The guy slumped in the corner was too big. The man on the far cushion was Black. Another couple was on one end of a '70s-era paisley couch, and I realized with disgust that they were more awake than the others, the woman lazily rubbing her hand against the man's crotch while he humped up against it.

Leaning down to Cori's ear, I said, "I don't see him here. I'm pretty sure that *mujer* who just passed us is the only one in the kitchen. We need to check the bedrooms."

She trembled slightly as I rested my hand on her lower back, keeping close as we made our way down the hall. The first bedroom door was wide open. Four people were on the bed—three women who might have been teenagers, and one man who looked like he was in his thirties, all naked. I assumed they were passed out until the man glared up at me and shouted, "Shut the fuckin' door, bitch!"

I shut the fucking door.

His loud roar reverberated like an earthquake after the quiet we'd walked into. Cori and I held up for a tense moment, worried his yelling might have alerted someone who would object to our presence.

Nothing happened.

"Shit, that was close," I breathed out.

Next up was a bathroom, the door cracked open. I checked quickly and saw just one man, lying in the bathtub, needle still in his forearm. The oppressively sour smell radiating from the pool of vomit in the sink of the unvented space almost made me throw up, but I choked it down in time. "Nothing in here," I said to Cori, shutting the door quickly.

It was a small house, two bedrooms, so there was only one door left to try. Had I brought Cori into this hellhole to come up empty on finding her brother?

Pushing open the last door, I registered that this room was darker than the other. A double coverage of sheets blocked the light from its one window. A beat-up dresser missing two drawers took up almost half the real estate in the tiny space. Atop it was a bunch of pipes, needles, spoons and foil, a rubber band—the same stuff that had been on the table in the living room. I could barely make anything out with only the dim light of the hallway as my guide.

On a twin bed pushed against the wall, a lone occupant lay still and unmoving. My breath stuttered.

"Johnny!" Cori whisper-shouted, pushing past me to kneel beside her brother. "Johnny." She ran her fingers through his hair. Tears began streaking down her face as she rasped, "Johnny, can you hear me?" She frantically slapped his cheek, lightly at first, and then a few times with more force. "Johnny, wake up...please."

Her brother lay on his side, legs curled up. He had on his hoodie and boxers but no pants. As Cori continued to plead with him, I discreetly pulled the needle she hadn't noticed out of his toes.

I saw her stick two fingers on his neck and press her other hand against his chest. I held my breath as her face went pale, but then an expression of pure relief washed over her. "He's alive, Deck. He's not waking up, but he's breathing."

Thank fuck. "We need to get him out of here."

I found Johnny's pants shoved behind the bed and slid them on him quickly. I still had the sense we were on borrowed time. It would have been helpful if Johnny could have woken up a bit, but he was basically in a coma. Cori and I needed to make do.

We hoisted him up between us, and I bore the brunt of it as we draped his arms over our shoulders. Johnny probably weighed fifty pounds less than me, but *maldita sea, dios*, he felt heavy. Pure dead weight. His bare feet dragged on the carpet as we carried him down the hallway, but there was no help for it. As we passed the other bedroom, I was grateful the man inside had forced us to shut the door.

No one on the couches looked up as we went back through the living room, but the woman in the kitchen—now drinking a Gatorade—cocked her head at us.

"J okay?" she drawled.

"Yeah, *está bien*. We got him."

She nodded, and I exhaled shakily as we hobbled outside. It had only been twenty minutes, but the sun already felt foreign.

Cori must have sensed it too. "It's like coming out from another dimension," she said.

"Hundred percent."

Her face twisted. "A horrible dimension with needles and naked girls and nobody giving a crap about anything. Just the drugs." She spat out the raw words.

"Cori—"

"The world where my brother lives." She shook her head, even as she did her part to keep Johnny steady between us. "I didn't know, Deck." Lifting her shoulder to wipe a tear from the bottom of her jaw, she continued softly, "I mean, I knew, but...not really. Not like this."

We got to the truck, and I hoisted Johnny into the back seat. He seemed fine there, uncaring when I buckled him into the middle with just enough slack to lay him down. He let out a small grunt when his head brushed up against the door, the first sign he was coming down.

"What do you want to do, Cori?"

She remained stonelike for a moment, hunched in the passenger seat with her hands clasped in her lap. Eventually, she asked, "Can you take us to the hospital?"

Johnny would hate it, but it was the right call. "Yeah."

"And Deck?"

"Hmm?"

"If the doctors have questions, I'm not sure how much help I can be. Will you stay with me there for a while? Just until I have an idea of what's next. Maybe you can tell me more about him, what you know about his situation."

At that moment, it dawned on me. I wouldn't be able to keep pushing her away. Not entirely. For Johnny to survive, he needed as many people as possible in his corner. And it wouldn't happen overnight. I thought I'd been helping him this past year. I got the feeling Cori thought she'd been doing the same thing. But we'd just been passing time.

This didn't mean we had to be back in each other's lives. I didn't want that for Cori, didn't want to risk hurting her again. But we needed to work together to save Johnny. I owed her that much. Then I could stay away for good.

CHAPTER SEVEN
Cori

PRESENT DAY

Deck stayed with me at the hospital through the day and into the night.

When we first arrived, he gave me the rundown on the time he'd spent with my brother over the past year. It sounded like his experience had been similar to mine. Lots of hopeful conversations and episodes of Johnny camping on his couch for a few days, only to be followed by the disappointment of Johnny leaving to score, and then radio silence.

After filling me in on those details, Deck didn't talk much. For hours, I sat in the same sagging slate-blue chair, watching as he moved from one seat to another, paced behind me, investigated the vending machines, flipped through magazines, and just generally fidgeted like a toddler drinking Mountain Dew.

We had been relegated to the main waiting area for the emergency room. We hadn't received an update since our arrival, other than one doctor coming out early to inform us that Johnny was stable and that they were running tests and administering fluids. The ER stayed busy with Saturday afternoon triage. From my home base in the chair, I watched as a cavalcade of people—some clutching limbs, some sniffly and red-eyed, and at least a dozen doubled over in pain—came and went.

As the seats emptied throughout the evening and into the overnight hours, a nurse informed us we could see Johnny once they moved him to a room, something that likely wouldn't happen until the next day. I'd expected them to revive Johnny and send him home quickly, which had happened before, but the doctors saw something in his initial results that prompted them to run more tests and keep him longer.

"I think the coffee cart in the main lobby is open twenty-four hours," Deck said at around three in the morning. It was the first time he'd spoken in over an hour. "Do you want a latte or something? I remember you used to like the vanilla ones."

"No, I'm good. Thanks."

He nodded and walked through the glass doors into the maze of the main hospital corridors.

It was probably past time for me to tell him it was okay if he wanted to leave, but for the first time in a long while, I found myself reluctant to be alone. Even subdued, I liked knowing Deck was there.

I just needed to get used to this wary adult version of the boy in my heart.

He no longer had the slicked-back ponytail. His black curls were shorter, framing his tanned face and brushing his collar haphazardly. But even with less hair and little wrinkles beginning to form around his eyes, he still felt familiar, and his presence was a comfort.

If Britta and Marcus weren't camping, I felt certain they would have been willing to sit with me at the hospital. There were acquaintances from JBC, particularly Jason and Brad, who would have come if I'd called. But nobody from my adult life knew much about my eating-SpaghettiOs-from-a-can childhood. They didn't know about the extent of Johnny's issues, and this didn't feel like the time to introduce them to all-things-considered Cori. Hiding that piece of myself had been my habit for so long, I couldn't even imagine it.

No. Even if it was incredibly awkward between us, and I had no idea what Deck was thinking right now, having someone with me who understood my past was a blessing.

My eyelids drooped, and I felt the adrenaline I'd lived on the day before leaving my system. I should have taken Deck up on his offer of a latte.

As if by magic, he returned carrying two cups.

"I got you one, anyway." He shrugged. "You might want it later, or you can just throw it out if you don't."

"Thanks." I grabbed the cup from his hand and took a grateful sip.

He surprised me by dropping into the chair next to mine for the first time since we'd arrived.

Gripping his coffee tightly, he said, "Look, Cori, I just want to say that I'm sorry this happened... That I didn't help him more."

I let my breath out slowly as I shook my head. "It's not on you, Deck. I mean, I was eating burritos with him two nights ago, thinking he seemed fine. I didn't stop this either. At the end of the day, this is on Johnny."

I talked a good game. But deep down, I understood Deck's sentiment. Logically, I knew it wasn't my fault Johnny was an addict, but I questioned if I should have done something more for him.

I'd offered rehab in the past, but I'd never been able to convince him to accept my help.

"I'm not just talking about yesterday." Deck slumped in his chair. "I should have seen it when we were kids, kept him away from certain things. When it started getting bad, I could have paid attention instead of always fucking around. I should have kept a better eye on him...and Eliazar."

I felt tears spring to my eyes at his unexpected mention of Eliazar. He had been part of Deck and Johnny's crew growing up and therefore a fixture of my childhood. The kid who always shared his candy and gave me rides on the handlebars of his bike. Small, with joyful brown eyes, forever drowning in his cousins' hand-me-downs, Eliazar was everyone's little brother, the follower. But he'd also been the first person who showed up when you needed someone.

"Deck, I don't want to make this day any worse, but I was just wondering if you heard about—"

"Eliazar. Yeah." He cut me off. "My pops told me. Wrote to me when it happened."

I closed my eyes at the catch in Deck's voice and the expression of pure regret on his face. He took a long pull from his cup.

"I don't want Johnny to die," I whispered.

Deck put his hand on the armrest of his chair, inching it sideways so our pinkies barely brushed. He left it there three seconds before pulling back.

Long enough.

AROUND SEVEN O'CLOCK IN THE MORNING, Deck looked dead on his feet, and we still hadn't heard anything definitive from the doctors. I thanked him for keeping me company, saying I could text him later with an update.

But when I handed him my phone so he could put his number in, he hesitated.

I sighed. "What's the matter, Deck? Worried I'm going to try to sell you a timeshare or something?" It hurt that his instinct was still to keep his distance. "Are you kidding me right now?" I huffed. "Okay, fine. Apparently, you don't want to know me anymore or whatever, but how else am I supposed to let you know how Johnny's doing if I don't have your number? Or do you not care?"

"C'mon, Cor, you know I care. And of course I'll..." He exhaled slowly and started punching the numbers on the screen.

"Well, you don't need to be weird about it."

He ran a hand over his cheeks, pulling the skin taut across his face. "I'm not trying to be weird. I'm just trying to be clear about...boundaries."

"Right." My insides tightened in frustration. I'd done nothing to Deck, not on purpose. It wasn't my fault that seeing me reminded him of something he wanted to forget. He wasn't the only one whose life changed that night.

But I supposed Deck had processed those events differently than I had.

I'd gone to therapy.

He'd gone to prison.

With that in mind, I tried a different tactic. Doing my best to understand where he was coming from.

"Look, Deck, I'm not going to pretend I don't know what's bugging you, that for whatever reason, you think everything that happened to me was your fault. To be honest, until I saw your face yesterday, I'd sort of thought that maybe you were mad at me, that you blamed me for going away—"

"Cori, you know I would never—"

I put up my hand. "We don't need to hash it out. Not after everything we've been through with Johnny. Maybe not ever. But since I can't force you to see it my way, how about I agree not to send you a text unless it's important information. You don't need to worry about me just trying to be friendly. I think I understand your *boundaries*."

My head spun. After everything, was our relationship truly going to come down to a limp *I'll only text you if it's important*? This was what Deck wanted when we were finally in the same room again? To be nothing to one another?

At his house yesterday, he'd been taciturn and closed off, words I never would have applied to teenaged Deck. That kid had been a bundle of energy and ideas, a natural leader people gravitated toward. Back then, he'd done everything to make me smile. Now, grown-up Arturo Decker remained stone-faced, careful and controlled as he held my phone.

After we exchanged numbers, he left. I decided to go home to shower and take a nap. It didn't seem like anything was happening with Johnny. I went to the reception desk and let them know I'd be back in a few hours, making sure they had my number.

At home, I realized I still had on Deck's hoodie. I placed it carefully on my dresser to wash later. After a quick shower, I stretched out on top of my bedspread and pulled a throw blanket over me. I set my alarm to chime at noon and fell into a fitful slumber, but I didn't get to rest even that long. My ringing phone woke me up just after eleven.

I reached over and answered quickly, terrified it might be the hospital calling about Johnny. "Hello. This is Cori Raney."

"*¿Mija?*" a familiar voice questioned over the line.

"Rosa?" I let out a relieved sigh.

She didn't miss the tension in my voice. "Cori? *¿Qué pasó, nena?*"

"Nothing. Sorry." I woke up further as I realized this was the first time Rosa had called since we'd met up at the mall months ago. We'd texted and emailed, but the fact she was calling had me sitting up in bed. "Are *you* okay?"

"Oh, my girl…" Her voice pitched higher before catching in her throat. She sniffed as she continued, "I'm going to be okay, but I need to be honest with you." I heard muffled talking, like Rosa had a hand over the phone while someone spoke to her in the background. "*Dios*, I wanted to ease into this slowly. I've been thinking about it ever since we ran into each other outside Macy's, something I was hoping to avoid, but I've run out of time."

Instantly on alert, I put the phone on speaker as I began tugging my socks up. As long as I was awake, I might as well get back to the hospital. "Run out of time for what?"

"I'm calling because I need some help." Her thick accent grew even more pronounced with the admission.

If it had been anyone else calling me out of the blue after barely speaking for six months, on top of not communicating for the dozen years before that, I might have been suspicious about their motives. But this was Rosa, the woman who'd helped raise me. A woman who had been a mother to all the kids in the neighborhood. I knew her pride. If she was asking for help, it was serious, and it was also a last resort.

"What's the matter?"

I heard more indiscriminate arguing on her side, followed by Rosa speaking to someone else. "*Está bien dejar que ella nos ayude. No eres una carga.*" To me, she simply said, "Lupe is sick."

The words hit me like a spear. Lupe had lived with Rosa for as long as I could recall. I didn't know the specifics of their relationship since Rosa hadn't gone around sharing her personal life with teenagers, but I'd always assumed they were partners or wives. "Sick?"

"Cancer. First in her breast ten years ago. We caught it then. She had a surgery. But about a year ago, it came back, and now it's…aggressive. Spread to her brain and her lymph nodes." Rosa's voice quivered. "She has six months. Possibly a year."

My movements stilled as I sat down heavily on the bed. "Oh. God. Rosa, I'm so sorry. So, so sorry."

My mother had paid for her hard living with too many physical and mental scars to count, her body ravaged by addiction. But in the end, it was cancer that claimed her life. Pancreatic, mercifully quick. Three weeks from diagnosis to death. I could only imagine how devastating it was for Rosa to watch Lupe slowly fade away.

But I wasn't a doctor. Why was she calling me? "How can I help?"

"*Mija*, I've been taking care of her. You know I had to."

"Of course."

"I kind of let things go…at the Center. I know you've been successful with your company. And you mentioned when we ate the pretzels that you might be between jobs soon. Right now, I have a finance person who does all the accounting and a part-timer who handles grants and events. But I've always done most of the fundraising myself, and I haven't been able to do as much this past year. Because of Lupe."

"You want me to help with fundraising?"

"No, *nena*." She exhaled heavily. "It's hard for me to admit this, but I think it's possible things are so bad we can't be saved. I have a few calls I can make to donors who can provide us with enough funding to sustain us for a few months, possibly through the new year. But if you're willing to do it *gratis*, I'd love to have you look at the books. I want your opinion on whether you think there's something I'm missing, if you think it's possible to stay open."

I sank further into the mattress. The REACH—The Ronald Ernest Althurst Center for Hope, named after some long-forgotten founding donor and usually referred to simply as "the Center"—had been a staple of the neighborhood for over sixty years. It had been my second home. The idea that it could close was unthinkable.

"Of course I'll help."

"When I ran into you, it seemed like a sign. If there's a way to save it, you'll tell me. If not, I know you'll be honest about that too."

Her faith in me was a gift, especially on this hard day. "I'm grateful you trust me with this. I do love the Center."

"Of course you do, *mija*." I heard the tinge of optimism in her voice. "Can you come by later this week?"

"Yes. Definitely. I'll text you. I have some things to take care of, but I'll make the time."

"Okay, *nena*. Enjoy the rest of your Sunday."

"You too. And Rosa..."

"*¿Sí?*"

"Take care of yourself. And give Lupe all my love. I'm so glad you called me."

Two things crossed my mind as I finished pulling myself together to go back to the ER. One, a person who had probably saved my life many times over was finally giving me the chance to do something for her, and two, the opportunity was a godsend because it would give me something to focus on besides Johnny. I needed a task to ground me, to make me feel useful and competent while I sorted out the rest of my life.

When I returned to the hospital, the person at the intake desk informed me that Johnny had woken up and that someone would be out soon to take me to see him.

I texted Deck.

ME: Hey Deck. Just letting you know Johnny is awake.
ARTURO DECKER: Thx. Want me to come?

Did I want him to come? It pained me to admit it, but I was afraid to face my brother alone right now. Even though Deck had been clear that he wanted space between us, he'd been equally clear that he wanted to help my brother.

ME: Yeah. I'd appreciate that.
ARTURO DECKER: NP. On my way.

I went to the desk and informed the person there that Arturo Decker would be coming in to see Johnny, requesting that he be directed to my brother's room upon arrival. She was the same woman who had been on duty when we'd arrived yesterday. I had irritated her when I kept asking for updates, until she informed me coldly that the doctors would be with me when they could and to please stop interrupting her. She seemed no more sympathetic today.

"Is he a family member? Visitation in the ICU is for family only."

A decade working at a tech start-up had taught me nothing if not how to remain calm when presented with a potential setback. "He's family."

"It says on these forms your parents are deceased and that you are Mr. Raney's only sibling."

I blanched. *Seriously, lady, what's with the forensic deep dive? Did they mess up your order at the coffee cart or something?* If I said Deck was a cousin, would that get him in? I wasn't willing to risk it.

"He's my husband. He was here with me yesterday. Just went home to get cleaned up a bit."

Her eyes narrowed, but I saw in her expression that she recollected a man had accompanied me the day before. She nodded curtly.

The nurse who took me past the emergency room beds and into the ICU seemed to be having a better day than grumpy desk lady because she said cheerfully, "I'll bring your husband back when he gets here."

Darn it. Apparently, we would need to make this story stick. I texted Deck.

ME: By the way, you're my husband
ME: Only family can visit

A minute went by, and I could visualize Deck frowning.

ARTURO DECKER: Got it. I'm your husband

Rolling my eyes at the name he'd punched into my phone, I changed it quickly to "DECK" before slipping the device into my pocket. The idea of Deck playacting as my husband would have made fourteen-year-old Cori spin out with excitement. But twenty-nine-year-old Cori smarted from him doing so only under duress.

CHAPTER EIGHT
Deck – Age 17

FOURTEEN YEARS AGO

"I'm trying! I swear!"

"Don't give me that bullshit!" Pop yelled as we faced off in the kitchen.

"But I am!"

He had pulled up my grades online after getting an email from my teacher.

"You're never going to graduate with marks like this. And I'm not sure what you think you mean by 'trying.' I don't see you putting in much effort. All I see is you going off in Cruz's car to do god knows what!"

My blood boiled. Pop never believed that I tried. That I studied and read, and even told my friends I was busy playing video games when, in reality, I was in my room trying to make sense of *Fahrenheit 451*. He didn't understand that pretty much everything about school was hard for me. Harder than it seemed to be for everyone else.

I slammed my hands down on the counter. "Well, I'm sorry, Pop. I'm sorry I can't be college material like Nando or the twins. A wannabe cop like Emilio. Or a musical genius like Raymond! You had seven kids. At least one of us had to be a fuckup! Guess I drew the lucky number."

"Stop telling me you're a fuckup! You're not! You just need to put your head down."

He didn't get it. I had put my damn head down. My classmates would clown on me if they found out how much I'd studied for that history exam. But when I sat down to do the multiple-choice part of the test, I couldn't understand how to answer. Like those fucking questions were designed to trick you. And the essay part—¡*mierda*!—I knew what I wanted to say about the invasion of Normandy. I just didn't have enough time to write it.

"Look, Pop. I said I'm sorry, and I am. I think I can still pass the class with some of the other assignments and stuff." Luckily, this teacher gave high percentage points for attendance, and going to class was something I actually did.

"So that's it?" Pop shook his head. "Your plan is to scrape by?"

"What the fuck more do you want from me? I said I'm trying!"

He sighed, slumping down into a chair at the table. "We're talking in circles now, son."

I hated his disappointed face. And I knew if Mamá were here, she'd be making the same one. I leaned my elbows back against the counter and watched as Pop rested his forehead in his hands.

Dios. I needed to get out of there.

The sound of shoes shuffling across the ancient linoleum sliced through the air. Marisol walked into the kitchen, wide-eyed.

"I heard shouting," she said softly, scratching at her neck. She was always itching her bandages. "Is Artie okay?" She directed her question to Pop, but looked at me.

"I'm okay, little squirt." Exhaling, I walked over and kissed the top of her head. "I was just leaving."

"Deck—" Pop lifted his head to meet my eyes.

"I need some air. I'll be back later." Pushing against the screen door, I didn't look back.

Without a destination, I let my feet and frustration guide me, ending up at a tiny park ten blocks from our house. It wasn't safe there after dark, so no kids were around, just a few older folks from the dilapidated senior housing place by the highway trudging out to let their dogs take shits, along with the addicts and homeless people who seemed to occupy every park bench and staircase in the city after the sun went down.

I sat down on the lonely swing set, digging my toes into the dusty bark below as I twisted the rusted chains in circles.

A few minutes later, Chi-chi Mendoza arrived. He gave me an upnod from thirty feet away before walking in my direction.

Chi-chi was older than me. He'd been in the same class as my brother Fernando, and Nando was twenty-four now. I remembered Chi-chi being a little punk, dealing dime bags by the bleachers and mouthing off a lot. He once tried to date my sister Justina until Mamá threatened to take away her phone. Turned out, she liked the idea of dating the school bad boy less than she liked having access to her texts. Chi-chi lived in his *abuela*'s old house, not far from ours, but I hadn't seen him up close in a few years. In the unlit park, he looked the same as before. Short and stocky with dark tan skin that shone in the moonlight thanks to his clean-shaven jaw.

"You need something?" he asked, pointing at the black backpack he carried.

"Nah."

Folks in the neighborhood acted like Chi-chi was some sort of big-time gangster. Mamá and Pop had warned me to stay away from him more than once. But how important could he be if he was hanging around the park?

An old maroon sedan pulled up to the curb. Two guys in black hoodies got out, walking on the path beside us. Chi-chi went over, moving them into the shadows before he pulled something from his backpack. Whatever he gave them looked bigger than a dime bag, and I realized it was the reason he was here. Not to deal to random teenagers on the swings. I was curious but kept my head down. Not my fucking business.

I figured Chi-chi would leave after that. But he didn't. He came back over to me.

"You're Nando and Emilio's little brother, right?"

I huffed. "I'm also Justina, Angelina, and Raymond's little brother."

Chi-chi grinned with crooked white teeth. "*Lo siento.*" He sat down on the swing next to me. "You sure you don't need something, *bróder*?"

"Nah. I smoke sometimes, but not feeling it tonight. I don't mess with anything else."

He pumped his legs a little, and the swing moved backward. "Just wanna stay pissed, huh?"

My boot dug into the bark. "Fight with my pops." I almost added that it was about my grades but stopped myself. It seemed like such a kid thing to get upset about.

Chi-chi grunted. "Yeah. I guess it's tough keeping Daddy Decker happy."

"Something like that."

He hoisted his backpack on his shoulder. "Well, if you want to kick it at my house sometime, just stop by."

"Really?" I asked, coughing away my high pitch.

I knew about Chi-chi's house. Everyone did. On weekends, the street outside his little broken-down bungalow was so full of cars people couldn't pull into their own driveways, and music blasted out until early morning. Neighbors had given up on calling the cops a long time ago. Even with my attitude and tendency to find trouble, I hadn't thought about getting an invite. But I didn't want to seem too eager.

"Sure," Chi-chi replied. "My boys are always around. I'll tell them you're chill." His gaze hardened. "You are chill, right?"

I stopped moving, meeting his eyes. "I'm good."

"Yeah…" He nodded slowly. "Yeah. I thought you might be." Chi-chi's shoulders eased. He pulled cigarettes from the inside pocket of his coat. Tapping the pack, he held it out to me. I shook my head.

He shrugged. "I've seen you around with your boys. On the court and at the little market on Twelfth." Putting the cigarette to his lips, he cupped the lighter in his hand and clicked the flame on. "Your friend drives, right?"

"Cruz, uh-huh."

"Hmm." He puffed on the cigarette, blowing the smoke into the air. "Well, you can bring them to my place on Saturday if you're down. After ten. There'll be people from the neighborhood. And other friends of mine."

Chi-chi took it for granted that I knew where he lived. Why wouldn't he? My heartbeat sped up. This was probably a terrible idea. Cruz, Eliazar, Johnny, and I had gotten into our share of mischief, but that wasn't the same as hanging out with the neighborhood dealer. Still, the idea of going someplace where I wasn't constantly being nagged at or reminded of all the ways I didn't measure up had its appeal.

"Yeah, maybe."

Chi-chi chuckled. "Ten o'clock, *compadre.*"

CHAPTER NINE
Cori – Age 15

FOURTEEN YEARS AGO

Principal Hardcastle caught me in the hallway before class on a Friday. As one of the school's top students, I knew him fairly well, having been on the receiving end of multiple honor roll handshakes and Student of the Month certificates. But his determined expression set off my internal alarms.

"Cori, can you please come to my office for a minute? There's someone who would like to speak with you."

Oh shit. From his tone, I gathered that the *someone* was not a person I wanted to meet.

My mind flashed back to last week, when one of the newer teachers—I didn't even know her name—caught me giving myself a washcloth bath in the sink. I had tried to avoid running into anyone that morning, arriving over forty-five minutes before the first bell. But Ms. Overeager-and-Way-Too-Peppy must have used that same logic to assume it would be a safe time for her to enter a student restroom. She walked in to find me in shorts and a sports bra, running a small towel over my arms because the shower in our trailer had refused to turn on that morning. Her eyes darted to the change of clothes I'd draped over a stall door.

When she asked what I was doing, I told the truth. Because it didn't seem like a big deal.

Except she responded with a funny look. I should have known then what would happen.

There were two kinds of teachers who called CPS. The ones who took their roles as mandated reporters so seriously they wanted to log every little thing, mostly to cover their own butts in case something happened. And then there were the ones who were so naive they believed in the system, that the state somehow had the magical ability to move children from not-so-ideal situations into homes filled with love and care.

I guessed the teacher who caught me in the bathroom was the second kind. Idealistic idiot.

Johnny and I were teenagers. Why would anyone honestly think a group home would be better for us? Sure, our mom wasn't around much, but she was good to us when she was there, plus we had food and stuff. We also had consistent lives at school and with our friends. I knew this was the reason Rosa didn't call CPS for every small thing when it came to teens at the Center. Little kids might get a good foster, but going into the system was usually a disaster for older ones. Unless she suspected true neglect or physical abuse, Rosa tried to help in other ways by providing meals, a supportive environment, and fun things to do. Like our teachers, she was a mandated reporter, and I knew it hurt her when she had to make those calls.

I bet the teacher who found me in the bathroom hadn't even considered what would happen after she did her "duty." Luckily,

I doubted CPS would be overly concerned with a *suspected neglect* call. I could handle this. I'd done it before.

ME: Are you at school yet?

JOHNNY: Cruz just parked. Why?

ME: Pretty sure CPS is in the office

JOHNNY: Fuck

ME: You need to go home before Hardcastle calls for you

JOHNNY: Got it

JOHNNY: Cruz said he'll cut and take me

ME: Good. I'll keep the worker busy. There's probably only one of them so I doubt anyone will show up at the house until I'm done

JOHNNY: I know what to do

ME: I heard Mom come home last night so that's good. Make sure she's awake. Also, I think she barfed out front on her way in. Maybe throw some dirt on it or whatever.

JOHNNY: I KNOW WHAT TO DO!!!!

ME: Stop shouting, fucker. I'm nervous enough

JOHNNY: Sorry

ME: Get Cruz to stop by the Center on your way. Rosa is packing the weekend bags for the kids. She can give you some food.

JOHNNY: On it. Deck says to remind you he's there in school. He wants you to check in with him at lunch

ME: Okay

JOHNNY: Good luck on stalling the nosy assholes. Luv u

ME: Love u 2

I mentally cataloged what needed to happen. Despite Johnny being a royal dummy sometimes, I trusted him to handle this. He needed to go home and get our mom to wake up and look alive.

She'd come home last night, but I had no idea if she was hungover, coming down, or what. At least her being there made things easier. Thank god the park manager fixed the shower yesterday. Johnny also had to get the house picked up and rearrange things so it looked like he slept in the first bedroom and our mom used the pull-out in the living room. Rosa would give him extra food, something CPS always checked on during a home visit.

Johnny needed to take care of cleaning the trailer and getting our mom up and ready for questions. My goal was to convince CPS they didn't even need to bother with a home visit.

The mid-forties woman who met me in the principal's office, dressed in an ill-fitting suit jacket and sensible sneakers, appeared bored and tired. I could work with that. An overzealous do-gooder might dig too deep.

"I'm Michelle," the woman said, shaking my hand as Principal Hardcastle stepped out. "Cori, I won't drag this out any more than I need to. Since you're fifteen, I'll be honest and say that I'm here from Child Protective Services to make sure you're okay. Someone called our office to let us know they suspected you might be having some difficulties at home?"

I stopped myself from rolling my eyes. Social workers were always deliberately vague. It was one of the voodoo mind tricks they used to get people they interviewed to fill in details. To tell them things they hadn't meant to. Luckily, I'd played this game before.

Shrugging slightly, I scrunched my face in confusion. "I don't know why someone would think that. Everything is fine."

I kept my hands in my lap. Used a respectful tone. My jeans and sweater were clean. My shoes were newer. I assumed Principal Hardcastle had already told her both Johnny and I attended school regularly, and that I was an honor student. I hoped those things painted a solid enough picture of functionality to keep her off our backs.

"Everything in your house is in good working order? No issues there?"

"Nope." I popped the p and attempted to smile.

Michelle looked down at the manila folder in her hand. "It says here that you've spoken with CPS before."

"That's true," I answered slowly, straightening my posture. At least four times that I could remember, although it had been a minute since the last one. The caseworker stared at me as though I might say more, but I stayed quiet.

Principal Hardcastle knocked on the door before popping his head in. "Cori, it looks like your brother didn't make it to first period?"

"Yeah. He wasn't feeling well this morning when I saw him at the house. He probably stayed home sick." My voice contained zero hesitation, although my heart hammered as the lie slid off my tongue. "I'm sure our mom just forgot to call and get it excused."

"That's too bad," Michelle interjected, eyeing me carefully. "I'd like to speak with him too." She looked at the principal. "He usually comes on time?"

"Yes, like I told you earlier. Johnny's been here this whole week. Both Raney kids have good attendance records."

I mentally patted myself on the back for all the times I'd insisted Johnny go to school for this exact reason. Even if he barely passed his classes, it was okay. Actual truancy would have had the state up our asses faster than anything.

"Hmm." Michelle looked back down at her folder as Principal Hardcastle left again. "Alright, well, like I said, I know you've spoken with CPS before, so some of this might feel familiar, okay?"

"Okay."

"Cori, do you feel safe at home?"

"Yes."

"Are you left alone often?"

"No."

"Really?"

"I mean, I'm fifteen, so it's not like I'm not on my own some-times. But it's a pretty small trailer. I'd actually love to have some more alone time." I hoped my gamble with levity softened her.

She smiled. *Whew.* "I understand. How about food? Do you have enough to eat?"

"Yes. Definitely."

"Would you describe your home life as stable?"

"Well, I guess it isn't perfect, but I think it's as good as anyone else's around here."

Michelle flattened her folder on her lap and fixed her gaze on me. "Out of curiosity, Cori, even though CPS has never found anything significant, why do you think multiple adults have called us to check on you and your brother over the years?"

The unanticipated question took me aback for a moment. "Honestly?"

"Of course."

"I think some folks just don't like poor people."

The last time I spoke with a CPS worker, I was twelve. I went to the Center afterward, upset and frustrated. Ironically, the inves-tigation came during one of my mom's most lucid and involved times. No neglect had been occurring then. Not even close.

That day, Rosa sat me down and delivered a hard truth. Many adults, even well-meaning ones, confused poverty with neglect.

Michelle leaned back in her chair. She didn't have an answer. I imagined working for CPS made her see things the same way as Rosa.

"Thank you for telling me that."

"Are we done?" I asked.

"I know you want us to be." Her eyes held genuine sympathy. "But I'd really like to talk to your brother."

"He'll probably be feeling better tomorrow."

Based on her answering nod, I couldn't tell if talking to him at school on Monday would satisfy her, or if there would still be a home visit.

I wanted to cut class and head home to check on things, but I worried it would cause too much suspicion. I doubted that Principal Hardcastle enjoyed having CPS come to the school any more than I did, so it seemed like the best course of action was to continue as if it were a normal day.

Lunch was a bright spot. I usually ate with my friend group, other honor students I only hung around with at school, or sometimes with kids from the Center. But Deck insisted I eat with him and Eliazar that day. He kept making dumb jokes and buying me cookies, trying to get my mind off the CPS visit. Being around him made me feel better. Deck always did.

I raced home that afternoon to find Johnny and my mom sitting at the little table working on a jigsaw puzzle. Puzzles were the only normal hobby my mom had. She had raised my brother and me on them. Some of my favorite childhood memories were taking thumbs-up photos in front of ones we finished together.

More importantly, Mom looked sober, and the trailer looked spotless. They'd even hosed down the exterior.

I laughed as I walked through the door. "All we need to do is put some cookies in the oven, and it's basically a sitcom."

My mom stood and gave me a long-drawn-out hug. "I'm so sorry you had to go through that this morning, baby girl. You know how sorry I am—"

"Mom!" Johnny and I yelled at the same time.

"We agreed no more apologies after last time, remember?" I reminded her gently. "Johnny and I don't need them, and it only hurts you and us more when you make promises we all know it's hard for you to keep."

"Fuck, I'm so—... I mean, I just wish..."

I held her close, wincing at her bony frame. "It's okay, Mom. We know you're trying."

My breath left me with an *oomph* when Johnny slung his long arms around both our shoulders, smooshing us into a tight huddle. "What Cori said," he agreed.

"How did it go today?" my mom asked me once we sat back down.

"Good. She asked the usual questions, so I'm guessing she was just going through the motions. Checking a box. But I couldn't get a read on if she'll come here, or if she'll wait and talk to Johnny in school next week."

"Well, we're ready if she comes," Mom said. "And cookies sound good. I think I'll go get some of that rolled chocolate chip dough from the corner market."

"Get two rolls," Johnny said, grinning.

We made cookies and finished the puzzle. Michelle never came by. Not that night, and not over the weekend. Mom stayed home even though she kept fretting about needing to "work," something Johnny and I didn't dare ask too many questions about.

On Monday, no one came to talk to Johnny in school, and again, no one came to the house.

No one came the rest of the week, either.

The CPS visit began to feel very much in the past.

My mom was gone the next weekend. Johnny went out with his crew. I went to the Center and stayed on top of my schoolwork. Mostly, I had the trailer to myself.

By the following Friday, I felt comfortable that Michelle and the state of Washington had closed the case. Or forgotten about it. Maybe I had convinced her I wasn't neglected. Just poor.

Chapter Ten
Deck – Age 17

FOURTEEN YEARS AGO

My friends and I started spending most of our weekends at Chi-chi's. Some weeknights too. At his place, we could just chill. Smoke a joint or drink. Play video games and listen to music. No expectations. We seemed to be the youngest of all the folks who hung out there regularly, but no one asked us about school. Or our families. No one cared.

But as nice as it was to escape for a while, I realized pretty quickly that these weren't my people. I was raised to respect my parents, the law, and even corny shit like hard work. At Chi-chi's, I found myself around shady dumbasses who bragged about check-cashing schemes, back-alley gambling, small-time dealing, and petty theft.

Still, for the first few months, I ignored the jab of my conscience and lost myself in the loud, pounding music and the excitement of meeting new people. I played *Mario Kart* and passed the bong with guys from the neighborhood I used to avoid making eye contact with. The girls who hung around Chi-chi flirted and made me feel like a king. Cruz lost his virginity in one of Chi-chi's back bedrooms to a girl he only ever saw that night. I got a few offers, even kissed a few *chicas guapas*, but that was all.

My friends assumed I had already lost my virginity, but other than a few handies and an unsuccessful blow job from a girl I went out with freshman year, I'd only ever kissed anyone. Sure, I was a horny seventeen-year-old, and I wanted to get my dick wet as much as anyone, but every time I got close to doing the deed with one of Chi-chi's hangarounds, the hollowness in my gut stopped me.

There was a simple explanation for that, a reason I admitted only to myself.

No one else was Cori.

Johnny's sister was still not for me. That was truer now than it had been a year ago when I'd first noticed her that way. But knowing that didn't mean I could just turn it off. Instead, I tortured myself. I found excuses to be near her, to give her small touches, to enjoy whatever pieces I could get.

I sat next to her on the couch while she watched cartoons with Marisol, letting the coconut smell of her shampoo drive me crazy. She had this way of smiling when something was funny, but not funny enough to actually laugh. Thinking about that smile made me happy.

She made me happy.

Wanting Cori and not being able to have her still felt better and more honest than being with any other girl.

But even though I wasn't good enough for Cori, I was pretty sure I was too good for Chi-chi. After that day in the park, I'd gone to the parties and encouraged my boys to come with me because it felt special, like Chi-chi had chosen me. Now, I realized the huge difference between being chosen and actually belonging.

I didn't belong at Chi-chi's house. Neither did my friends.

Because a lot more went on than video games and passing the bong. There were skinny guys who went down to the basement to smoke things besides weed. A glassy-eyed girl who barged in on me in the bathroom and offered to suck my dick for ten bucks. People who came in and immediately disappeared into one of the back bedrooms with Chi-chi and his backpack.

And then there were the constant offers of *opportunities*. Small jobs to earn a little cash. As much as my grades told a different story, I wasn't stupid. I knew the reason Chi-chi had invited me to his house was because he wanted to recruit me and my friends into his operation. I still wasn't sure exactly what he was involved in, or how deep his connections ran—I didn't want to know—but he'd been dropping lots of hints lately about how easy the money was. About the excitement of the game.

We'd said no so far, but each weekend there was a little extra pressure, and Cruz seemed more and more interested in the money. It scared me.

But what scared me more was when Johnny and Eliazar tried smoking meth. I would have stopped them if I'd noticed them going down to the basement. They appeared okay after, but still, crank was fucking savage. We'd all seen the neighborhood addicts, thin as rails and begging for change. Cruz and I ripped them new assholes over messing with it. They promised it was a one-and-done, just curiosity, but being around it was probably a bad idea. Those motherfuckers were such go-alongs.

My friends and I were in over our heads. We weren't criminals. Or addicts. Cruz had been to juvie once for beating someone up, but that was it.

The novelty had been fun for a while, but it was past time to stop going to Chi-chi's.

I said as much when they picked me up one night, four months after the first party we went to. Sitting next to Johnny in the back seat, I suggested we skip Chi-chi's, saying it would be better for just the four of us to hang out. Like old times.

"Maybe next weekend we can do that," Cruz replied slowly. "But I have business with Chi-chi tonight."

"*¿Qué?*" I asked, narrowing my eyes at him. "What do you mean 'business'?"

"He just needs me to drive him somewhere. No big deal." Cruz clenched his lips.

"When did you and Chi-chi make this plan?" I pressed.

"Last weekend. He told me to come around tonight to finalize."

"Shit. How did I not know this?"

"You knocked back more than a few last time, *guey*. You don't remember falling asleep on the couch?"

Johnny laughed. "You were totally snoring, bro."

I punched him in the shoulder and kept my hard gaze on Cruz. "Alright. Fine. So you talked to Chi-chi. Do you think it's a good idea to get involved in his business, though?"

Cruz's face remained almost impossible to read, but I saw a flicker of a reaction cross his features, something that looked a lot like...guilt.

"Motherfucker!" I yelled. "You already did a job!" Johnny and Eliazar exchanged a look, seeming unsurprised. I turned to Johnny. "You knew?" I accused.

"Look, it was my choice," Cruz said firmly. "All I did was drop one little backpack off in Seattle. Johnny came along because Chi-chi said it might be easier for a white guy to make the delivery in that neighborhood."

"*¡Madre de Dios!*" I ran a hand through my hair. "*¿Están jodidamente locos?*"

"It's fine, Deck. No one got caught," Eliazar said.

"You knew too?" My eyes flashed at him.

He looked down at his lap.

"Don't get mad at them," Cruz insisted. "Like I said, I was the one who took the job. And I'm the one talking to Chi-chi tonight."

"But why?" My voice lost some of its anger.

Cruz shook his head. "We don't all have Michael and María for parents. I'm not saying I'm going to start working for Chi-chi on the regular, but it's nice to have a little money in my pocket for once."

Johnny and Eliazar nodded in agreement.

"I want to go to the party, too," Eliazar chimed in. "It's been extra shitty with my parents lately, and I need to get out of my head."

The way he said it concerned me, considering he'd been smoking meth in Chi-chi's basement a week ago. But I also knew he'd had a rougher time with his mom and pops over the past few months. Turned out, they were homophobic assholes who couldn't accept their own son.

We'd suspected Eliazar was gay for a while. He never wanted to talk about girls, but would mention celebrity dudes or point out hot guys on the street. Two summers ago—after a trip to the pool where he was very fucking obvious about checking out the men—we asked him directly. He said, "Yes," we all said, "'Kay," and that was it. I gave zero fucks, and once our classmates began to suspect, Cruz let it be known that he would seriously fuck up anyone who messed with our friend. Johnny took a little longer with it, but he eventually came around.

Of course, the neighborhood wasn't exactly forward-thinking. Far from it. There were plenty of Mexican grandmas who still said a Rosary every morning. They gave Eliazar backward glances and expressed sympathy for his parents. A few folks let Eliazar know exactly what they thought, hissing "*puto*" in school or shouting at him on the street as they drove past.

But by the time we started junior year, it was old news. There were a few other *out* kids at our school, although all of them lived in the better part of the district, not on our streets.

Eliazar's parents took a *we're going to pretend this isn't happening* approach to their son being gay. He didn't talk about it, and they never asked. But a few months ago, his pops caught Eliazar watching porn, and since then, it had been fucking on between the two of them.

Johnny put his arm around my shoulders and cocked his head to tap mine. "Looks like we're going to Chi-chi's tonight," he said. "Don't worry. If you fall asleep on the couch, I'll wake you up."

"And we can be just the four of us next weekend, for sure," Eliazar added, always trying to keep the peace.

Cruz stuck the key in the ignition and pulled out onto the street in the direction of Chi-chi's house.

I looked at the back of his head, then at Eliazar, and then at Johnny next to me. Outvoted, I leaned back in my seat. Making this U-turn was going to be a lot harder than I thought.

CHAPTER ELEVEN
Cori - Age 15

THIRTEEN-AND-A-HALF YEARS AGO

Deck turned a card over in his hand. The fabric bracelet Marisol made him earlier that evening slid around on his wrist, drawing my eyes to the muscles in his forearm.

He tapped the card against his head, as though attempting to read it through osmosis. It was one of the first ones I'd made, back when a teacher in middle school explained the SATs to me. Hard to believe I'd finally be taking the PSATs this year. For so long, college had seemed like an abstract concept. Now the concept felt more like a plan. A plan that began with high test scores and good grades. I'd need both to secure the type of scholarship that would cover my tuition and provide me with a dorm room. Allow me to live somewhere other than a stupid trailer where I got woken up every night by Johnny taking a piss or my mom stumbling in with some loser to *entertain*.

I didn't want to go too far—the University of Washington in Seattle was my dream—but I needed to put some distance between Everett and me.

Deck held up a card with *exacerbate* written on it.

"To make worse or increase the severity of."

"Right-o." He held up another. *Provocative.*

"Intending to provoke, inspire, or arouse."

Deck gave a short nod and shifted in his seat.

We sat on the same side of the Deckers' dining table. An open bag of Doritos rested on a chair between us. An hour ago, I'd put Marisol to bed, and Deck asked if I could look over one of his English assignments. He had done a decent job creating his PowerPoint presentation on *Macbeth*, so we finished the small edits quickly. Afterward, he offered to review my flash cards for the gazillionth time. Deck always seemed down to practice with me. Maybe because he didn't have to read anything, just hold them up. He would never admit it, but I also thought he enjoyed learning the words.

Whatever the reason, I never passed up the opportunity to spend time with him. With the beautiful boy who had teased and protected me since I was ten. For years, I had been attracted to him in a little girl's way. And loved him like family. But now, as I saw glimpses of the man Deck was becoming—both good and bad—as he revealed to me the person no one else was allowed to see, my love for him had evolved into something more genuine.

Something with *gradiations*, frayed at the edges.

Something torn and stretched in certain places, stitched tighter in others.

It consumed me and burdened me in turn.

Because I got to see a side of Deck he reserved only for me. Even with his enormous family and how close he was to my brother, I seemed to be the only one who understood that Deck's *I don't care about school or anything* attitude was a front for being terrified of disappointing people. In return, he saw me in a way no one else in my life did. He knew how I played my part to get by in the neighborhood.

We kept each other's secrets.

My longing for him used to stem from the way I felt whenever he was near—the stomach butterflies and wishing he would give me my first kiss. Those things were still there, but now it also sprang from the belief that I was his shelter from the storm, the only person he let his guard down for. He didn't have to pretend to be hard for my sake.

That's why I was pretty sure he loved me back.

Because he let me see the real him.

I loved him despite the fact he and Johnny had been hanging out with Chi-chi, making shitty decisions and acting like fools. I suspected Deck had tried to bring Cruz, Eliazar, and my brother out of the situation. Tried and failed.

Deck felt like the black sheep of his family. His parents didn't know what to do with him. He lashed out at them. María and Michael yelled back. Part of the reason they asked me to babysit Marisol all the time was because they knew that when Deck opened the door for me, his shoulders eased.

I wanted to put my arms around him and offer him that comfort, to reassure him he wasn't alone. I saw what he saw. Johnny experimenting with meth. Eliazar's parents close to kicking him out. Cruz's family MIA for months.

But infuriatingly, he never allowed himself to acknowledge what had changed between us. Some misplaced sense of honor held him back. I knew he didn't think he was good enough for me. But he couldn't bring himself to stay away either.

We gravitated toward one another, but whenever we got too close, Deck got scared. He would hurt me. Pull away.

Like last summer, when we played around in the backyard sprinklers at Angelina and Justina's birthday party. He chased me to the side yard before lifting me and spinning me in circles over the water. I screamed as he made me dizzy. When he came to a stop, both of us laughing, my wet body slid down his until we were eye to eye. Everything around us fell away. All the noise faded to a low buzzing. Deck held our bodies together, my bikini top plastered to his naked chest. He swallowed, and his eyes landed on my mouth. I was sure he was going to kiss me, but he didn't. Instead, he quietly set me down and stepped away. No one seemed to notice other than Marisol, and I wasn't sure how much an eight-year-old would read into the moment.

After that, Deck dated Daria Drysdale for a few weeks. He made a point of inviting her over to make out on his couch when he knew I would be there watching his sister.

Another time, we were watching a movie on the Deckers' couch with Johnny and Cruz. Deck sat next to me, and during the movie, our hands slowly moved closer. By the end, his fingers curled over mine. But when Cruz flipped the lights back on, Deck pulled his hand away and stared down like he couldn't believe it had happened.

Then he went out with skanky Mandy Ramos until Halloween.

He'd been single since then, almost four months. Although who knew what he got up to with girls at Chi-chi's? I'd heard the stories.

All I knew for sure was that Deck seemed determined to stretch the invisible rubber band binding us together to its limits. As a result, whenever he snapped back into my life, it stung. Even as I welcomed the pain.

Like now.

Deck held up another card. *Inscrutable.*

"Incapable of being investigated, analyzed, or scrutinized. Impenetrable."

He kept finding reasons to talk to me. Coming to the Center to walk me home. Meeting up between classes at school. Hanging out whenever I was at his house with Marisol.

Deck couldn't stay away from me any more than I could stay mad at him.

Tonight was an example. He'd been adamant that I work on flash cards with him, but he'd strategically positioned the Doritos between us so we wouldn't be close enough for something crazy to happen, like our knees touching.

Another card. *Ignominious.*

"Publicly shameful or humiliating."

Deck chuckled. "I don't know about that one. It sounds more like the name of a dinosaur."

He reached into the bag to grab a chip just as I did. Our fingers brushed, and he flinched.

"Great," I said. "Now I'm going to forget the real definition and be wondering the whole time... Do you think the ignominious was a plant eater or a meat eater? Scales or horns? Thanks a lot, Deck, you just cost me a perfect score."

I joked, but also harbored a secret fear that despite literal years of studying, I would somehow choke on the test when the time came.

Some of my thoughts must have shown on my face because Deck put the bag of chips on the table, his expression serious. "*Chica,* you know no matter what happens on the test or in school, you're still the smartest girl in any room." He bent forward. Hesitating only a second, he put a hand on my knee. "No matter what the test score says…you're perfect, okay? There's no chance of an *ig-nominious* outcome."

"Thanks," I mumbled.

"You're welcome."

The smile stayed on his lips. I wished more people could see Deck like this. Softer.

He stood, hooking his fingers together and stretching them above his head. "I think that's enough for now." He glanced toward the stairs. "I don't think Mari's going to wake up. If you need to get home, I'm good to stay with her."

I grimaced. I did not want to go home. Did not want to face the lonely, messy double-wide I'd had to set rat traps around yesterday. My mom hadn't appeared in days, and Johnny had gone off earlier with Eliazar. Those two rarely came home before dawn when they went out together, even on school nights.

But I had no intention of invading Deck's space if he didn't want me there. I began gathering my things.

Deck lifted an arm.

"Cori," he said, "I'm not kicking you out. I *want* you to stay. You know being alone with you is—" He sighed. "I just don't want you to ever feel like you…*have to* be with me."

Meeting his eyes directly, I sat back down. "I'd like to stay. You know the trailer is shit when it's cold. Plus, no Wi-Fi."

"Right. Okay, then. Good… And Cori?"

"Yeah?"

"If that changes, and you decide you have somewhere better to be, I get it."

It amazed me that anyone ever thought Deck was unintelligent. Not everyone was smart enough to have a conversation beneath the conversation.

I wanted to shake him, but all I said was, "I understand."

He nodded. "TV?"

I breathed away some of the heaviness in the air and dipped my chin. "*The Wire*?" The Deckers paid for HBO. They were the only ones I knew who did. Deck and I had been working our way through some of the older series lately.

"Uh-huh."

We sat on opposite ends of the couch. He put the chips between us.

"I think Eliazar should watch this show," I said, halfway through an episode.

"Because of Omar?"

"Yeah. Not many shows I can think of with gay guys from the hood."

Deck chuckled and ran a hand over his face, blushing.

"What?" I asked.

He stifled his laughter. "Nothing. You just reminded me. I had an *incident* with Eliazar the other day. And—*chingado*—I support him and all, but I'm still not okay."

By his red cheeks and the way he laughed, I guessed this story was more embarrassing than truly upsetting. "What happened?"

Deck leaned his forehead into his hands as he shook his head.

"Okay, now you have to tell me."

Finally, he looked up. "So we were coming out of Fink's room after sixth period, you know, because Eliazar and I have the same math class." He cleared his throat. "Anyway, I needed some paper and didn't have any. I grabbed Eliazar's backpack to look for some, but I found something...*else*."

I knew Eliazar had been experimenting with more than weed lately, same as Johnny, but finding drugs in his friend's backpack would not make Deck red in the face. Not like this.

My brows furrowed. "What?"

He angled his head against the couch, stretching his neck as he spoke to the ceiling. "I didn't know what it was at first when I saw the box, so I had to ask Eliazar to explain… But I guess it was a…um, you know…like a…"

Deck stopped, looking like he wanted the floor to swallow him.

"Ohmygod what?" I prodded.

"A douche kit," he muttered.

"A…douche kit?" It took me a minute to put the pieces together. Why would Eliazar need—? "Oh…" My cheeks heated. "Oh."

"Yeah, he got pretty awkward telling me. I tried to make him feel better by saying it was okay and all that. That I was just surprised."

"I'll bet," I chuffed. "Poor Eliazar."

"I meant what I've always said. I'll throw down with anyone who messes with Eliazar. He eats enough shit about it at home without having to worry about it coming from his boys. But that doesn't mean I want to think about all the details, you know?"

"Yeah, yeah. I get it." I smiled lightly. "This will be a funny story someday, even if it's weird now."

Deck seemed to relax into the cushion. "I guess he had a plan to meet up with some *hombre* after school."

A brick settled in my stomach. "Is he meeting up with men from those apps again? Is that safe?"

Eliazar was like a brother to me. He'd been a Hope Center kid too, and still stopped by occasionally to see Rosa. If Deck was the leader of their crew, Cruz the enforcer, and Johnny the joker, then Eliazar was the sweet one. The most trusting, most breakable.

"He can handle himself," Deck replied. "He grew up here too. Although I wonder how many of those assholes know he's seventeen."

"Well, you don't have to worry about any app guys tonight," I said. "Eliazar went out with my brother."

Deck hmphed. "Not sure that's much safer these days. The two of them together... They've been getting up to some shit."

I felt the defeat in his voice to the core of my soul. At moments like these, when I knew he needed me, I loved Deck too much to let him keep me at arm's length. I moved the bag of chips onto the coffee table and sat closer to him on the couch, our legs touching. "I get that you're worried. Believe me, I understand."

"I know you do," he whispered gruffly.

His intense stare sent shivers down my spine.

I watched his chest rise and fall as I remained motionless, allowing him to look his fill and letting him find his anchor.

I also waited for him to stand. Push me away. Put distance between us.

He didn't.

Deck scooted his hips away from mine...but only far enough that he could bend over and lay his head in my lap.

"I'm scared, Cori." He whispered the words into my thighs as his arm stretched out to wrap around my waist.

My breath lodged in my throat. But as his fingers dug into my skin, a calmness washed over me.

Dislodging his ponytail, I carded my fingers through his long black hair. The strands crackled with the gel he used to tame them. I pushed through the sticky locks, pulling them apart until they cascaded over my lap. Running my hands down to his neck, I grazed my fingertips lightly across the bottom of his hairline. I pressed in harder, massaging his scalp as I smoothed my palms over his crown. Petting him.

"I'm sorry you're overwhelmed, Deck. I'm here."

He didn't reply, just squeezed me tighter.

I reveled in the moment, even as its rawness disturbed me.

Deck surprised me again by falling asleep. I stayed on the couch with his head on my thighs until I heard his parents pull into the driveway.

I knew he would regret the moment in the morning. He would decide that he had been weak. I wondered how he would retaliate, how he would hurt me to prove he did not need me. Or deserve me. How much would he punish us both?

CHAPTER TWELVE
Deck

PRESENT DAY

I got back to my house intending to go right to sleep. Still in my clothes, I lay down, but my mind wouldn't rest. Around ten a.m., I admitted defeat and dragged myself into the kitchen. Coffee and leftover adrenaline could get me through until that evening.

In my living room, I stared at the space on the couch where Cori had sat. My new reality settled in.

After all my efforts to keep my distance, with one ring of a doorbell, she was back in my life.

Dios, she'd been amazing going after her brother. Even wide-eyed in that shitty house, terrified and stepping around needles, she hadn't allowed the fear to take hold.

Her keeping steady wasn't surprising. She wasn't loud or rowdy when we were kids, but she'd always been tough, not to mention strategic about planning her future. She'd gotten a decent education in our armpit of a public school, utilized every opportunity at the Center, and stayed out of trouble without making herself a target.

At least not until Chi-chi found her.

Unwanted, a picture came to my mind. That night, she'd been fighting back. I shook the image away. I had to stay focused on the present.

On the here and now, where I needed to keep Cori at arm's length.

I had held myself together while we searched for Johnny. But once the rush of getting him out of that house wore off, and she'd asked me to stay with her at the hospital, I hadn't known how to behave. I'd barely talked. Paced a hole into the floor. Memorized the contents of the vending machines. Been a *pendejo* about exchanging numbers. Anything to avoid the way she drew me in like a magnet.

After tying my boots, I went outside to finish planting the maple, a bizarre task considering the previous twenty-four hours. I took another shower afterward, coming out to find two texts from Cori letting me know I'd need to pretend to be her husband at the hospital to visit Johnny.

ME: Got it. I'm your husband.

Mierda.

I knew interacting with her brother would eventually bring Cori back into my life. But even with that, I wouldn't have done anything differently. I'd been helpless with Eliazar. I couldn't stand by and do nothing while Johnny went down the same road.

Still, I needed to handle myself better than I had in that waiting room.

My daily emotional cocktail of anger, shame, and regret assaulted my senses, making my blood run hot. Thanks to a year's worth of mostly-crap court-ordered therapy, I knew I needed to talk this whole situation out with someone or risk putting my fist through a wall.

Usually, discussing things with my parents or my brother Emilio worked fine. They'd never wavered in their support, even while I was inside. But on this topic, my family was not an option.

Mamá and Pop knew I'd been back in touch with Johnny. They were almost as worried about him as I was and had been hounding me for months to reach out to Cori. So had Emilio. They warned me she had thrown up a wall between herself and the neighborhood after her mom died, but I hadn't realized the contact had been completely nonexistent until yesterday.

"Cori doesn't blame you or Johnny for what happened to her," Mamá said to me only a month ago. "Why would she? That's why she wrote the statement for the court."

"It doesn't matter what she wrote. It was my fault. Whether or not she sees that makes no difference."

"That makes no sense, *mijo*. You helped her."

"I'm the reason she was in that situation in the first place!"

Mamá scoffed. We'd had this conversation so many times. I knew she was tired of arguing with me. But her refusal to acknowledge the truth wouldn't change my mind.

Cori's bruised body and the bloody, torn panties on her bed—these images were my constant companions, even so many years later.

"Look, Artie," Mamá said, "You not reaching out to Cori isn't you protecting her. It's punishing her. Once she finds out you've been back and talking to Johnny this whole time, without even bothering to let her know, she's going to be hurt. We all remember you two were getting closer before that night. I'm sure you being gone is one reason she cut ties with the neighborhood and everyone here. But Rosa said she saw her at the mall a few months ago, that she's looking for her way back. Besides, if you're going to do anything for Johnny, you and Cori are going to need to work together."

Mamá had been right. And not just about Johnny needing us both.

I hadn't intentionally tried to hurt Cori by keeping my distance. My memories of that night were bad enough, so I could only imagine what haunted her. Seeing me and dredging it all up would not be good for anyone. And despite what Mamá thought, or even what Cori believed, it *was* my fault. Because I was the reckless one who brought so much pain into the lives of everyone I loved.

I exhaled heavily as I contemplated my phone. There was no way my family could be objective about Cori and me reconnecting.

But my fists were still itching, and since I wasn't in the mood to repair drywall, I reached out to the one person I could always talk to.

ME: Meet for a beer tonight?
JUAN: Something up? Or just thirsty?
ME: Need to talk
ME: Johnny almost died
JUAN: WTF?
ME: He's okay. I think. Going to hospital now
ME: Also you were right about the borrowed time

The three dots appeared and disappeared a few times before Juan's next text came through. But of course, he knew me better than anyone.

JUAN: Cori?
ME: Yeah
JUAN: It was bound to happen
ME: I know
JUAN: 7 tonight? Tubby's?
ME: See you there

A WAY-TOO-CHEERFUL NURSE took me back to a private room, where I found Cori sitting on a rolling stool next to Johnny. She held his hand loosely to avoid disturbing the IV in his arm. He seemed half awake, head lolled over to the side. A sheet covered his shirtless torso to just above the waist. I did a double take at the sight of his body since it was usually hidden beneath an oversized hoodie. Everything about him looked sunken—his closed eyes, the hollows of his neck, the cavity of his chest. Cuts and bruises in various shades of yellow, purple, and blue marked his splotchy gray skin. He was so thin, practically a skeleton. The muscles of his arms stuck out, looking like knotty ropes.

While carrying him out of that house the day before, I'd simply been grateful he was alive. Seeing him like this, I realized what an absolute miracle it was that he hadn't died.

I glanced at Cori. The same horror I felt was written all over her face.

But of course, her emotions weren't stopping her from getting shit done.

"Hey, babe," she said, reaching out a hand and raising her eyebrows at me. "Thanks for checking on the cat. How was your nap?"

I looked at her with a puzzled expression. She hitched her neck at the wall, which was actually just a thin curtain.

"Uh, good," I stammered. "Bastardo says hello."

She patted a stool next to her. I sat.

Cori leaned in and whispered, "Look, Deck, I know this is a lot, but I wasn't sure what to do. I thought I could just have you play my husband today to get you back here, but apparently, one of the nurses needed to make a thing. So I had to put your name on some forms, and you're now officially listed as Johnny's brother-in-law. I also added you as an emergency contact, after me. I hope that's okay."

"Yeah...um, yeah, I'm happy to do that. I want to help."

"I know you do. Whatever's going on in your head right now, I know you love Johnny," she stated plainly. "I don't want to be the only one listed for him, just in case something goes wrong and I'm not available, or someone needs to decide... You get it."

I nodded.

"It shouldn't be a big deal. Just remember we're married and you live in Seattle with me. I doubt they'll notice much beyond that. Although with how that one nurse was giving me the stink-eye, she may ask us to produce a marriage license." At my look of panic, she groaned. "I'm kidding, Deck, jeez. If it comes to anything like that, I'll come clean. For now, we're good, right?"

"Sure," I mumbled, feeling the heat of her knee inching close to mine.

"Cori?" Johnny's eyes fluttered open as his voice croaked. "Deck?"

"We're here, Johnny—" Cori started at the same time I said, "Hey, Bro."

His eyes bounced back and forth between the two of us. "'Bout time you two were in the same room," he ground out slowly, his words a hoarse whisper. "I told Deck it was a dick move to—"

Johnny stopped speaking abruptly as his face turned green and his chest began rising and falling rapidly. I realized what he needed just in time to grab a small plastic tub nearby, coming around to the other side of his bed so I could help him lean over and retch into it, taking care not to tug on the IV or other wires taped to his chest. What came up was nasty, and Johnny's shoulders shook with his efforts. It took a minute for him to finish and roll back against his upright mattress. He ended the episode by spitting a few times into the tub. Cori produced a tiny cup of water, which he used to rinse out his mouth before also spitting that into the container. The room immediately reeked with the acrid smell of vomit. Cori placed the tub on the floor and pushed it as far toward the door as it could go without actually being in the hallway.

She and I moved our stools to opposite sides of Johnny's bed. His eyes closed again, but I didn't think he'd gone back to sleep. Cori balanced her head in her hands, resting her elbows on her knees.

"The nurses said that might happen," she said, pointing one finger toward the tub. "They also mentioned he'd be in and out of it when he first woke up."

I nodded, watching silently as she slipped one of her delicate, perfectly manicured hands into Johnny's grimy one, pulling it to her mouth to lay a kiss on his dirty fingers.

Mamá was right. If we were actually going to help Johnny, we'd need to work together. As a team. Or pretend husband and wife.

A few minutes later, an older man came into the room and introduced himself as Dr. Alvarez.

"Well, Mr. Raney, how are you feeling?"

I immediately liked him. He addressed Johnny with respect. As an ex-con, I was sensitive to the way some people talked down to those they felt were beneath them.

Johnny cracked one eye open. "Honestly, Doc, I've been better."

Dr. Alvarez gave him the courtesy of a smile, and Cori looked relieved to see a trace of the charmer her brother could be.

"Well, it's true you could be better. You need to understand that you're a lucky man. If your sister and brother-in-law hadn't brought you in yesterday, you would likely have died."

Johnny rolled his head toward me at the "brother-in-law," and I made wide eyes, willing him to play along. He was no dummy, smirking as he said to the doctor, "Yeah, my *brother-in-law* is the best. I'm always going on and on about what a great *brother-in-law* I have. I even got him a mug last Christmas that said *World's Best Brother-in-Law* on it."

Luckily, we could dismiss anything Johnny said as the rantings of someone who was still high.

Dr. Alvarez cleared his throat, sitting down on a third rolling stool next to Cori. "Mr. Raney, may I call you Johnny?"

"I definitely prefer it to Mr. Raney."

The doctor chuckled. "Fair enough. Okay, Johnny, we should discuss your test results, and what needs to happen moving forward. Are you okay with your family members staying in the room?"

"Yeah, that's fine."

Johnny seemed more alert now. Dr. Alvarez looked at Cori and me. At his demeanor, alarm bells started going off in my head.

The doctor directed his attention back to Johnny. "The truth of the matter is, this is more than just an incident of accidental overdose. Yesterday, your system was struggling to digest a cocktail of meth, MDMA, and heroin, not to mention alcohol. If I ask you questions about your drug use, will you answer honestly?"

Johnny shrugged. "Yes."

His immediate reply was sincere. I supposed one thing we had working in our favor was that Johnny didn't deny being an addict. He had always been brutally honest with me about what he got up to.

"Johnny, what is your general drug of choice, and how often do you use?"

My chest tightened at the blunt question.

"Usually crank...um, meth." Johnny coughed, and I gestured to the tub, silently asking if he needed it. He gave a slight shake of his head before continuing. "You say I had heroin in my system, but I don't remember that. I'm not sure how—" He paused abruptly. Running a hand across his face, he frowned at the pull of the IV. "Anyway, I guess it doesn't matter. It's mainly meth, and I get high most days."

Cori paled but remained quiet.

"Okay. I see you're thirty. When did you start using?"

"I first tried when I was sixteen, I think," Johnny answered. I winced, remembering the day. "But didn't do crank much in the beginning..." His raspy voice struggled, and words came slowly, but I took his ability to answer as a positive sign. "Used to smoke lots of weed. Some pills... Molly... X... Less hard stuff. I had a good friend who died, maybe eight years ago. Tried to quit after that. It stuck for a bit. But the meth has been bad for a while." He shrugged again.

Dr. Alvarez glanced at the clipboard in his hand, appearing to digest this information.

"I appreciate you being so forthright, Johnny. Many patients in your situation aren't, which makes my job more challenging.

So let me extend the same courtesy to you by being direct. Based on your test results, I would have guessed most of your history. The deterioration of your body, particularly your heart, suggests long-term substance use disorder. I need you to understand that if you don't stop now, it's not a question of whether you will die. It's a question of when. And if you keep on like this, the answer to that question is that you will be dead soon."

Cori squeaked as she caught a cry in her throat. She still held Johnny's hand. I saw him squeeze her fingers, but there was no comfort to be had.

The bad news kept coming.

"Johnny, you have sustained severe heart damage. Quite frankly, you have the heart of an elderly person. You're close to being in heart failure. You'll never be able to heal your heart completely, but if you take control of your health now, you may hope to undo the worst of the damage and live a normal life. But for the time being, you need to refrain from drug use and any intensive activity."

The good doctor certainly didn't pull any punches. He paused, allowing the diagnosis to sink in for a moment.

I was sure Johnny, Cori, and I were all thinking the same thing—staying clean was nearly impossible for someone in Johnny's situation, even under threat of death. This information essentially translated to the idea that Johnny needed to go to rehab. Or die.

"I know this is hard to hear," Dr. Alvarez stated. "But unfortunately, there is more." He leaned back in his chair. "Johnny, blood tests indicate that you are HIV positive. Were you aware of this?"

Cori's jaw dropped. Johnny looked like he'd been hit by a truck as he shook his head. "HIV positive? Like AIDS?"

"HIV positive doesn't have to mean developing AIDS, Johnny. Medicine has come a long way regarding HIV in the past few decades, and we have started you on several treatments. As with your heart disease, it's possible you can still live a relatively normal life with HIV, possible even that the virus becomes undetectable. But you have to take care of yourself."

It felt like we were at the bottom of a mountain. Heart disease? HIV? Get clean or die? I knew Johnny was headed in that direction, but hearing it out loud was still a gut punch.

Dr. Alvarez stayed in the room with us a few minutes longer, letting us know he'd be printing some materials and checking on Johnny later. He gave us the chance to ask questions. Cori had a few about the treatments that had been started and what would happen in the next few days. She mentioned paying for the hospital stay out of pocket, telling the doctor Johnny should have whatever tests and treatments were needed. Damn. Her brother had not been exaggerating when he said she was doing well.

But after the doctor stepped out, her facade broke.

Tears streamed down her face as Cori begged her brother, "Please, Johnny, let me send you to rehab. You can't keep turning me down. We'll find the very best place. I promise. You've got to let me do this for you." She leaned forward to rest her head in his lap. Her muffled voice pleaded softly, "Please, Johnny. Please. I don't want my big brother to die."

He looked at me, and all I could say was, "She's right."

Johnny brushed his dirty fingers through Cori's hair. "Okay, Sis. Okay." He turned his face to the window, asking, "Do you guys mind if I have a few minutes alone?"

Cori nodded. We all needed a break after Dr. Alvarez's bomb-dropping. She gave Johnny one last kiss on his hands as she rose, and I squeezed his shoulder.

As we exited the room, Johnny piped up, "I must have really been out of it if I missed your wedding."

I glanced back and couldn't stop my smile. "Only your dumb ass would have jokes at a time like this. You know it's because of hospital rules."

"I figured. Well, even if it took me almost dying, at least the two of you are talking again."

"That's not funny, Johnny." Cori frowned. "Don't downplay this."

"Sorry, sorry." He held up his hands. "Hey, Cor?"

"Mm-hmm?"

"I'm sorry I took your credit card."

Cori blew out a loud breath. "I know, J. You can make it up to me by not dying."

———

"THE CRAZY PART IS, IF HE HADN'T stolen her card, and she hadn't gotten so mad about it, he'd probably be dead right now." I raised the pint glass to my lips and took a sip. I wasn't much of a drinker, but this seemed like a night for an exception.

It had taken me the better part of an hour to bring Juan up to speed on the past few days. He needed to know, not just as my friend but also as my business partner at J&D. Everything going on was fucking with my head.

Juan waited patiently until I finished.

"Alright, so it sounds like Johnny is stable even though some bad shit went down. And the HIV... That is fucking rough," he said. "But I don't think that's why you're drinking a Modelo and not a ginger ale. How was it seeing Cori? You've been avoiding that too long, man."

I took a swig from the bottle. "Have you been talking to my mom or something?"

"Nah. But if Mamá Decker thinks it's good for you to dig in with Cori, that should tell you something."

"I just don't understand why everyone's on me all of a sudden."

"Come on, *bróder*, it's not all of a sudden. You've got that night all backward in your head. I've told you that. Your parents keep telling you that. But it ain't getting through. Maybe you need to hear it from the girl."

"I already did," I mumbled under my breath.

"*¿Qué?*"

"She already told me." I looked Juan in the eye. "Yesterday, Cori asked why I'd sworn Johnny to secrecy about me. Then she guessed the reason. Went right for the jugular, mentioning that night. Said it wasn't my fault."

It was the same thing she'd written in the letters she'd sent to me in prison. Offering absolution in careful, perfect printing.

"See? She's moved on. So should you."

I shook my head. "You can't spin this, man. Even Cori can't. I spent years locked up thinking about what happened. Even if I protected her that night, I'm still the one who brought the shit into our lives."

"People make their own choices, *amigo*. What Chi-chi did—that's on him. And you...Johnny...Cruz...Eliazar...were all just kids. You weren't responsible for them, and you need to stop blaming yourself. It's okay to talk to Cori. You haven't said it straight out, but I know you had a thing for her back then."

A thing?

Out of control at eighteen, the sanest part of my life had been the secret I'd guarded in my soul—the way I felt about Cori.

Those feelings had stirred yesterday when she sat in my living room. When she walked fearlessly into that house. When she peered up at me from inside my hoodie. And today, when she called me her husband.

Stupid thoughts. The hope of being good enough for her died years ago, before I'd gone away.

That dream was as dead as Eliazar.

"No good can come from me being in her life, Juan. You should see how she looks, all shiny and polished. I don't want to touch that. Even if I've spent the past twelve years reliving that night, if she's moved on, then good for her. She doesn't need me in her face, reminding her." I slammed the bottle on the table.

"You need to stop punishing yourself. You did your time. And you didn't do anything that motherfucker Chi-chi didn't deserve."

That was true. I may have hated prison, but I didn't regret what I'd done. I had other regrets.

"It's not just her," I said.

"What do you mean?"

"You know. There's Cori. But also Marisol. Cruz is sitting in jail. Eliazar's fucking dead, and Johnny's about there! Cori doesn't need my brand of poison back in her life."

I'd pretended to rag on Cori earlier for turning her back on the neighborhood. In truth, I understood her motivation. She'd dealt with the past by walking away from it.

But yesterday, she said she'd been wrong to cut ties. She wanted to reconnect with Rosa. And she would never abandon Johnny, her biggest connection to our old lives. She clearly sought some middle ground.

I just couldn't see a middle ground for her and me. I couldn't take the risk. Better to stay away.

"Look, Deck," Juan began. "As long as I've known you, you've blamed yourself for everything. Marisol's accident, what happened to Cori and your friends. Eliazar especially. People tell you things aren't your fault, and you don't accept it. People tell you they forgive you, and you don't accept it. You've accomplished so much over the past few years to get your life back on track. You can't be afraid to take that ultimate step forward, to forgive yourself."

"I don't know...if I can." Exhaling, I scraped my hand over my jaw. "I wouldn't even know where to start."

"Maybe start by letting Cori decide if she needs to be protected from you."

CHAPTER THIRTEEN
Deck – Age 18

TWELVE-AND-A-HALF YEARS AGO

There weren't any cars parked in front of our house when we pulled in. Good. If I had to suffer this humiliation, I preferred to do it when none of my siblings were visiting. Even Marisol was away. My parents had asked Cori to pick her up at school so they could attend the appointment with me.

Still, it almost surprised me not to see Emilio's piece-of-shit car by the curb. My second-oldest brother had been on my case ever since one of his cop friends ran into me at Chi-chi's. He hadn't said anything to Mamá and Pop, but he'd let me know exactly what he thought of my *friend*.

Well, Emilio could be pissed all he wanted. No one had noticed when maybe it could have made a difference. Now it was too late. My friends and I were in so deep with Chi-chi that I had no idea how to save us. That motherfucker had us by the balls.

I bolted out of the back seat the minute Pop killed the engine. The screen door leading into the kitchen snapped on its hinges when I jerked it back, the metallic clatter igniting the air between me and my parents.

Mamá and Pop hurried in after me, sensing my intention to hightail it to my room.

"Stop!" Pop called out. "We need to talk about this." He pulled out a chair at the table, hitching his neck in a *sit-down* gesture.

I sat. I supposed one thing I could be grateful for in all my dumbfuckery over the past few years was that I hadn't totally jacked my relationship with my family. To be sure, I'd been a terrible son. I'd pretended, stonewalled, evaded, avoided, hedged, and lied. I'd ignored their worried faces when Cruz picked me up and their frowns when I stumbled home wasted. Despite that, I attended family dinners, kept my room straight, watched a game with Pop once in a while, and did enough for them to convince themselves everything was fine. Or at least not entirely out of control.

Now, a crack.

None of what happened at the meeting today was their fault, although I knew they blamed themselves. But it wasn't on them. This shit was all me, and I'd gotten good at ignoring the regret that sometimes threatened to rise from my stomach and consume me whole. I could usually push it down with alcohol, weed, or a new score. I didn't know what else to do.

My mom sat down next to me. "*Mijo*, I know you're disappointed, but it's not the end of the world. You heard what Mr. Carson said. It's only one more year, and you can do it mostly online. You'd only have to go into the school building a few times a month."

"Mamá, you need to let it go. I'm done with high school."

The guidance counselor had been clear. I'd failed too many courses to graduate with my class. Even making accommodations for the diagnosis I'd received at the end of junior year, it was too late.

My mother put her head in her hands. "*Es mi culpa*." Her shoulders shook. She looked up at my father with tears in her eyes. "*No presté atención*."

"It's not your fault, Mamá," I insisted.

Pop put a hand on her shoulder. "None of us were paying enough attention, María. Especially not that fucking school." My pops' Irish cheeks got red easily. He'd worked himself up in the counselor's office earlier, having some choice words for an education system that hadn't figured out I was dyslexic until I was seventeen.

"It doesn't matter." I pushed back my chair. "I can take the GED next year. It's done."

"Is that what you want, son?"

I laughed roughly. "Unless you have a time machine where I can go back and start over, it's really the only option."

I knew my parents thought I was talking about getting the late diagnosis for the learning disability, but they had no idea. The fact that I still attended school at all was a miracle. Maintaining that appearance had been for them, not me. But I felt so fucking far from high school—classes, school plays, pep rallies, prom, football games—all that shit... *Dios*.

Not getting my diploma? That was nothing. That was a problem I could solve.

If they knew about Eliazar...or Cruz...or Johnny...especially Johnny, who they loved like a son. *Fuck!*

The day before, I'd pulled Johnny out of a dumpster. A warning shot from Chi-chi. I'd been lucky to find him at all, except somebody saw two guys toss him in there, and then told someone else, who told someone else, who told Cori. She came to me, crying. She asked for my help and wanted to come with me, but I wouldn't let her. I told her I'd only fish him out if she met us back at her place.

She knew what her brother was. She didn't need to see it up close.

When I'd brought Johnny to her, he smelled like a locker room towel bucket and had pissed himself.

Cori's mouth had trembled as she led him into the trailer's tiny shower. She'd thanked me and told me to let myself out while she got her brother cleaned up. *Remember when I helped you with your SAT words?* I'd thought. The last time had been more than a year ago. Another life.

Mamá sat up in her chair, the motion bringing me back to the present. "We did this," she said to Pop. "We took our eye off the ball."

"Yes," Pop agreed sadly.

"No." I shook my head. "You guys had other priorities. As you should have."

Marisol's name hung unsaid in the air between us, the way it always did. I'd gotten away with a lot of shit because my parents had had to focus on my baby sister. They rarely made me talk about it, but Pop wasn't letting me off the hook this time. His hand moved from my mother's shoulder to mine.

"What happened to Mari wasn't your fault, Artie. We've told you over and over. It was an accident. And Mamá is right. No matter how busy we were, you're our son, and we should have known this was happening."

Again, I felt my regret fighting its way to the surface. They were still talking about school. The learning disability. The grades. They didn't know how shallow that problem was. How manageable compared to everything else.

At least a GED provided an answer. It wasn't a cap and gown, but it was something.

The rest of it, though. We'd been crazy to think Chi-chi was doing anything other than playing with us.

Grabbing at the collar of my T-shirt, I yanked, pulling until the neckline stretched out, freeing my throat.

The regret trailed up through my lungs, settling like a boulder on my chest. The weight of disappointing people.

Shrugging aggressively, I dislodged Pop's hand. "School isn't for everyone," I said, standing. "It's not your fault that I'm...how I am. I've told you before. Some people are just fuckups. I'm sorry."

"*Mijo—*"

"No." I put up my hand. "I don't want to fight. It's done."

My phone buzzed in my pocket. Ignoring my father's down-turned mouth, I stared at the device as messages came through fast and furious.

CRUZ: chi-chi said time's up
CRUZ: said dumpster thing was just a warning
CRUZ: taking a down payment out of J
CRUZ: said E can be the late payment
CRUZ: sent bash to pick E up
CRUZ: I need to do the job. It's the only way
CRUZ: but it has to be tonight
CRUZ: can you make sure J hides
CRUZ: find E soon, k?

"Fuck!" I ran a hand through my hair.

"Language, Artie." My pops took a step toward me but, registering my expression, thought better of it. "What's the matter?"

I looked at the phone. My pulse thudded as I typed.

ME: On my way

"Artie!" Mamá's voice was both firm and terrified. "*¿Qué está pasando?*"

I forced myself to level my voice. "Uh, nothing. Sorry I cursed. It's just... Cruz was supposed to pick me up, and his car won't start."

"You're going out tonight?"

My hand quaked as I stuck my phone back in my pocket. I needed to leave. "There's nothing more to discuss, right? It's decided. About the GED."

Pop put his arm around Mamá again, and they shared a loaded glance. "We thought we could get a pizza. Watch a movie. You, us, and your sister. Cori too, if she wants to stay."

I hated the looks on their faces. Maybe in some other universe, I could have stayed. Stayed and argued over pizza toppings and movie choices and let them cheer up their kid who'd gotten some bad news. Stayed and spent time with Cori.

But I had to fucking leave.

"We were gonna go to a party at another friend's house, but if Cruz's ride is busted, I guess we'll just play video games at Eliazar's. It's okay if I take the car there?"

The lie slipped easily off my tongue. They always did. My parents would be so glad that I wasn't going to some random party. They wouldn't question me playing video games with a friend they knew and liked.

They didn't know Eliazar had been kicked out of his house months ago. That Cruz had just sent me on a mission to rescue him.

Mamá sighed and nodded. "Just don't be home too late."

"Sure, Mamá." I gave her and Pop forehead kisses. "I'll be good."

As I ran outside, I planned. I needed to tell Johnny to hide in case Chi-chi came looking for him. It would have been nice if I could have texted him, but his phone was somewhere in that dumpster.

But I also had to find Eliazar. Because it sounded like Bash was going to take what he wanted.

I couldn't even think about what Cruz was doing right now.

Cori walked up with Marisol as I came out into the driveway.

"Hey!" she called out, waving hesitantly. Leaning down, she said something in my sister's ear. Marisol giggled and disappeared into the house.

I thought about not stopping. I doubted Eliazar had time to spare. Then I realized Cori might be able to solve one of my problems.

"Cori." I walked over until we stood face-to-face in the grass.

She wore a polo shirt from the Center and baggy shorts. There was a heaviness in the set of her shoulders, but her expression remained *indiscernible*.

"Deck—" She paused. "I'm glad I ran into you. So I can thank you...for yesterday." She folded her arms over her chest. "Johnny was pretty out of it. He talked a lot while I cleaned him up." I wanted to interrupt, tell her I needed to hurry, but there was obvious alarm in her tone.

"What did he say?"

"Nothing that made much sense, honestly. But from what I could tell, it sounds like you guys are in real trouble."

Cori fixed her gaze on me. I'd worked so hard to keep our shit from touching her. She knew her brother used, but with the rest of it, we'd drawn a line. Cori had too much going for her. Even with her mom and everything else. She needed to be protected from all the stuff we'd gotten mixed up in.

After the night I'd fallen asleep in her lap, I'd tried to get rid of her hold on me. That conversation had cut too close. I avoided being alone with her and stopped asking her for help with my classes. I even gave in and lost my virginity to one of Chi-chi's hangarounds. It had felt good for ten seconds, but it hadn't done the trick of getting my mind off Johnny's sister. I slept with two more girls before finally admitting that I wouldn't be able to fuck Cori out of my system. My desire for her was soul-deep. Being around her sometimes, even if it meant not having her, was better than nothing. Avoiding her had been nearly impossible anyway. Our worlds were too intertwined. During the past few months, we'd established a rhythm where I didn't actively seek her out, but I allowed myself to soak up every minute I was near her. Every chance encounter at school, with Johnny, or when she came to my house to watch Marisol.

I knew it was wrong to hold on to those feelings. She wasn't mine to dream about. I should have worked harder to stay away. Because now, inevitably, I'd brought the shit directly to her doorstep.

"Cori—"

"Johnny said you owe Chi-chi. What does that mean? What the hell are you and my brother mixed up in, Deck?"

I stared into her stormy eyes.

I'd caused that. The regret bubbled up again. But I didn't have time for it.

"Listen." I clapped my hands in front of my chest in a praying gesture. "Johnny was out of his mind yesterday... But he's not wrong. We had a misunderstanding with Chi-chi. Cruz is trying to fix it now, but in the meantime, is your brother at home?"

"Probably, but why? What do you mean 'a misunderstanding'?"

"I promise I'll explain it all soon, but right now, I really need to go find Eliazar."

"Eliazar? Is he okay?"

"I hope so. That's what I'm trying to make sure of. Because Chi-chi's not fucking around."

Cori's face changed. Even with a bright future ahead of her, she'd still grown up here. She knew how quickly the situation could spin out when you dealt with guys like Chi-chi. "What can I do?"

I put my hands on her shoulders, which she'd squared into steel. "You said Johnny's at your house?"

"He should be, yeah."

"You need to find him and tell him he needs to leave. It's the first place Chi-chi will look. He needs to hide. The dumpster was Chi-chi putting him on notice. Understand?"

Her eyes widened. I could tell she wanted to ask questions, but she didn't. "Let me run in and say goodbye to Marisol and your parents—they'll get suspicious if I don't—then I'll go home and make my dumbass brother go to Rosa's. He'll fight me on it, but I'll get it done."

Dios, she was spectacular.

"Thank you. If you can do that for Johnny, I can concentrate on helping Eliazar."

"I'll handle it."

She bit her lower lip and shifted her weight, knitting her brows as her expression fought with itself. Without warning, she threw her arms around me, pressing her face hotly into my neck. I shivered as her lips skimmed over my pulse. Looping my arms around her waist, I pulled her tight against me, leaning into her embrace.

Cori was in my arms. At last. Where I'd wanted her to be for years. And even with all the shit around us, it felt right. Her breath on my neck. Like truth and home and safety. For precious seconds, she squeezed, and I held on, burning the memory into my brain.

Finally, she stepped away. "Be careful, Deck."

As Cori ran into my house, I thought about my next move. Meaning I thought about Sebastian Roccio.

And the three things I knew about him.

First, Bash had been rolling with Chi-chi for as long as anyone could remember. I'd never quite been able to make out if he was Chi-chi's muscle or just one of his boys, but he was always around. Second, Bash hardly ever talked. I'd heard him order food, pass a joint, and tell someone to look at his phone, but he mostly communicated with grunts and hard stares.

And the third thing I knew about Bash was that he wanted to fuck Eliazar.

At the beginning of the school year, Eliazar got into a relationship with some guy who lived in Seattle. I was pretty sure they'd met on an app, but Eliazar never talked about the men he was with, especially not after the douche kit incident.

When he started dating Seattle Guy, he kept it separate from us, just as he'd always done. I never met the dude, but I once saw Eliazar get into his car—a shiny black Acura that attracted a lot of attention when he parked it across the street from the high school. Pretty soon, it was all over that Eliazar had a boyfriend, and the talk was too much for his parents to bear. They had gone to church nearly every day and prayed for their boy's soul, but somehow, he was still gay. After that Acura had cruised through the neighborhood a few times, they kicked Eliazar out of the house.

He stayed with his boyfriend at first, but then they broke up. Apparently, Seattle Guy liked showing off his hood Latino boyfriend to his yuppie-ass friends, but not enough to share space on the daily.

The *cabrón* also accelerated Eliazar's meth habit. Eliazar had been dabbling since we first started going to Chi-chi's parties, but the boyfriend was a fiend, and he helped turn my friend into a full-blown addict.

We tried to help. Eliazar mostly stayed with Cruz, since his pops was never around, or Johnny, since his mom barely noticed anything. He couldn't stay with my family because they'd ask too many questions. Wherever he slept, we made sure he ate and got to school most days.

But we couldn't stop him with the meth. He'd disappear and come back strung out and quiet. Tell me he missed Seattle Guy. That he didn't see the point of graduating. Didn't see the point of anything. Then he'd get high again and be happy for a minute.

Cori mostly stayed out of our shit, but she wasn't totally ignorant. Once Eliazar started crashing at her house, she asked Rosa for help. Rosa had a soft spot for Eliazar since he'd gone to the Center until middle school. Rosa spoke with Eliazar's parents, but they refused to budge since Eliazar was eighteen. They even threw Rosa's "roommate" Lupe in her face. *Assholes.*

Cori also had to bear the burden of her brother. Johnny wasn't as bad as Eliazar yet, but he was on that path.

Both our friends had been spiraling for months. Cruz and I didn't know what to do, other than keep rescuing them.

Keep dragging Johnny out of dumpsters.

And keep Bash off Eliazar.

The four of us had been pulling small jobs for Chi-chi over the past year. Small because Chi-chi wasn't a big-time gangster, just a neighborhood king with grand ambitions. I dealt MDMA at clubs with Johnny and Eliazar. Cruz used his car to run hot merchandise to Seattle and Portland. The jobs didn't happen often, and I didn't mind the extra cash in my pocket. But we still had some sense. We refused whenever Chi-chi asked us to move real product, knowing it wasn't worth the risk. Except deep down, I'd known Chi-chi wouldn't take no for an answer forever.

A few weeks ago, Chi-chi summoned the four of us to his house to talk business. Leaving Johnny and Eliazar on the couch, Chi-chi took Cruz and me into the kitchen. He had a job in mind. A big one. He'd been "babying" us for years, he said, and it was time to man up. He told us how much Johnny and Eliazar owed him, saying if Cruz and I didn't do what he wanted, he'd be forced to make our friends pay.

Despite the sinister gleam in his eyes, Chi-chi immediately acted like he hadn't threatened us, insisting we stay and hang out. "We'll get to an understanding, bruh." He slung his beefy arm around my shoulders, squeezing too tight. "*Te relajas, vato. No hablamos de chamba.*"

Cruz and I knew we needed to get the hell out of that house, but we had to play it smart. We sat down on the couches where five of Chi-chi's boys were already chilling with Johnny and Eliazar, passing a bong.

Half an hour went by. Chi-chi's friends turned on *Mario Kart*. The game noise competed with the wet slosh of the bong water as the dark green cylinder got handed around. I took a hit but was still as tense as I'd ever been. I'd never wanted to leave a room more.

But we needed to stay cool. Making an enemy of Chi-chi was a bad idea.

Then one of Chi-chi's friends made a shitty comment to Eliazar, asking like a perv whether an asshole felt as good as a pussy. Eliazar's face went red, and Chi-chi's boys laughed like it was the funniest thing they'd ever heard. I restrained Cruz with a firm hand on his thigh. "We can't win," I muttered under my breath. His eyes darkened, but he remained seated.

Suddenly, Bash piped up from the corner, "I want to try."

Slivers of light creeping in through the tightly drawn curtains highlighted the smoke swirling above us.

"What'd you say, cuz?" Chi-chi drawled. "You want a hit?"

"No." Bash licked his lips and took a step forward to where I sat pinned together with my friends on the couch. "I want to try Eliazar."

Cruz's hands balled up at Bash's flat tone. His nostrils flared.

A few of the guys laughed again, but there was a hint of confusion in it.

"What do you mean?" Chi-chi asked Bash, chuckling menacingly. "You *maricón* now?"

Bash shrugged. He kept his gaze on Eliazar but spoke to Chi-chi. "I'm whatever. And he's...pretty."

I wondered briefly if Chi-chi had invited us over with the intention to let Bash have a go at Eliazar to force our hand. But Chi-chi seemed as surprised by Bash's words as we were.

Pure fury radiated from Cruz. Again, I put my hand on his knee. Chi-chi had Bash plus five other guys here. Johnny was so high he'd practically passed out.

Eliazar shrank into Cruz's other side.

I'd heard rumors that Eliazar traded blow jobs for meth sometimes even though he'd denied it when I asked him directly. But even if my friend was tricking, he would never extend that offer to Bash. Or any of Chi-chi's guys.

Bash must have heard the rumors, too, because the next second, he directed his eyes to Eliazar and said loudly, "I'll pay."

An eerie quiet fell over the room. All of us were some degree of fucked up, and I didn't know how much the others were processing. But Chi-chi had told me and Cruz an hour ago that he'd been floating product to Eliazar and Johnny for months. He'd demanded Cruz make a special delivery for him. If Cruz didn't agree, then Chi-chi would get payment from Johnny and Eliazar. One way or another.

Chi-chi gave Cruz and me a dead-eyed grin. He pointed at the hallway. "First bedroom's free."

Eliazar pressed his compact frame against Cruz. "Um...no...no thank you." His voice was small. Scared. His jaw quivered, and I could hear his teeth clanking together.

Cruz stood, holding Eliazar against himself. "He's not interested." Cruz glanced side to side as though daring someone to disagree. "We're leaving." I jumped up too, shaking a strung-out Johnny to awareness.

Bash made a move like he might try to stop us, but a subtle headshake from Chi-chi held him back.

In the entryway, Cruz said, "You'll get your money. We'll figure it out. Then we're even."

Cruz spoke with bravado, but everyone in that room knew the four of us were only getting out of there because Chi-chi allowed it.

Chi-chi rushed ahead of us and opened the door in an exaggerated motion. He leered at Eliazar. "If you ever want to take Bash up on his offer, you let me know, eh, *guapo*." He brushed the hair off Eliazar's forehead, chuckling when Eliazar flinched. "Shit. Maybe

I should try you myself. A mouth's a mouth, right?" He grabbed his crotch.

Vomit threatened in my throat. Next to me, Cruz vibrated.

"Like we said, you'll get your money," I reiterated.

Chi-chi laughed and stepped back. "Maybe so, *muchacho*. Maybe so." We walked out the door into the light, which felt punishingly bright. "But just so you know—" His tone turned to ice. "I don't care what you do. I'm the one who decides when we're even."

That was less than three weeks ago.

Since then, Cruz and I had talked in circles about how to get the money. Four grand, Chi-chi said. There was no way Johnny and Eliazar had smoked, snorted, or shot that much product, but it wasn't like we could argue.

We didn't have the money. Even if Cruz sold his car, we couldn't get that much. But letting Chi-chi fuck Johnny up or having Bash take the payment out of Eliazar's ass was out of the question. We were brothers. No matter that our brothers were messed-up little meth heads right now, we couldn't let them down.

A few days ago, I'd considered coming clean with my parents, seeing if there was a way for them to help. But then we'd gotten the call that I wasn't going to graduate, and I knew I couldn't do that to them.

Dios. How did things ever get this fucked up?

Cruz and I had assumed Chi-chi wanted the money more than he wanted to make a power play. But based on Cruz's texts to me just now, as well as Johnny's adventure in dumpster diving, we'd miscalculated. Forcing Cruz to make that run was apparently worth more to Chi-chi than four grand. There had never been a choice. Chi-chi would still fuck up Johnny and give Eliazar to Bash, just to remind us who was in charge.

I trusted Cori to get Johnny somewhere safe. And it sounded like Cruz had already made up his mind to do the job. My focus now was on saving Eliazar.

Thank fuck I could track his phone.

I checked the app.

Eliazar was at Chi-chi's house.

CHAPTER FOURTEEN
Cori – Age 16

TWELVE-AND-A-HALF YEARS AGO

I rushed into the trailer like a demon was chasing me. It had been about fifteen minutes since my conversation with Deck, so fourteen minutes since controlled panic mode had set in.

"Johnny!"

I liked to believe that *Good in a Crisis* would be written on my gravestone when I died. I wouldn't allow myself to give in to the fear coursing through my veins until I knew my brother was safe.

My single-minded determination to find him was probably the reason I didn't notice the glass scattered all over the floor until I felt a sharp edge cutting through the sole of my worn-out shoes.

"Motherfucker!" I yelled, jumping up and down as I grabbed my foot.

A large piece of brown glass stuck out. I must have stepped straight down on top of it because it had punctured the bottom of my shoe and lodged in the ball of my foot. I winced in agony as I pulled out the glass, throwing it out the still-open door of the trailer as blood began seeping onto the floor.

Not knowing what else to do, I gently pulled the shoe off while balancing on my other leg, unsurprised to find my sock soaked in red.

The pain was intense, and it wouldn't stop bleeding. *FML.* I needed to save my brother from the neighborhood thug, and apparently, I had to do it while performing an impression of John McClane in *Die Hard.*

We didn't have bandages or really any medical supplies on hand, so I grabbed a nasty dishrag from the sink and pressed it to my foot.

I gripped my ankle, trying to decide my next move, when I finally noticed the rest of the room.

The couch cushions had been relocated to the floor, and everything was knocked off the counter. At first, I thought maybe the place had been tossed. But it didn't look quite messed up enough for that. None of the drawers were pulled open, and our shitty TV still sat on its stand under the window.

The glass I'd stepped on had been part of a broken beer bottle. The neck of the bottle hung off the dining table, like someone had smashed it against a hard edge to prepare for a bar fight.

Was I too late?

"Johnny!" I screamed again, hopping up and down as I worked my way around the shattered glass—with difficulty since small shards were everywhere. I'd almost made it to my bedroom when I tripped over one of my coats, which had been thrown on the floor.

I fell hard on the linoleum, bracing myself with my hands. Another sliver of glass cut across my right palm, while my left hand came down on a sea of tiny glass bits. I saw the evidence of the shallow cuts in my skin as a spiderweb of blood appeared.

Even though my hands were bleeding, they weren't as bad as my foot, so I was able to push myself up.

Stumbling to my room, I grabbed a clean pair of socks from my drawer and put them over my hands as makeshift bandages. The cuts bled through the fabric, but they didn't look nearly as bad as the dishrag on my foot, which was drenched in crimson. I desperately needed to wash these wounds, but I had to take care of my brother first.

Hobbling, I pushed open the door to the main bedroom and found Johnny there, passed out next to our mom. *Thank god!*

I hopped over to him and shoved his shoulder. "Johnny! Johnny! Wake up!"

He rolled over onto his back and flung an arm over his eyes dramatically, like the dim light was brighter than the sun. Mom didn't stir at all.

"Jesus Christ, Cori." He dragged out his words, following them with a lazy stomach scratch. "Why are you shouting?"

"Get up!" I poked him again. "You need to get out of here. And what the hell happened to the living room?"

He turned back onto his stomach, his eyelids drifting shut.

"Nuh-uh." This time, I bent my elbow and used it to crunch down into his shoulder blades. "Don't go back to sleep. You need to get your butt up."

"Ow!"

"Get up!"

"Alright!" He waved his arm in the air to stop me from digging into his back again. "I'm up."

But he wasn't up. He barely moved. It was like he wanted to go back into the dumpster.

"Johnny. Get. The. Fuck. Up. NOW!"

He managed a glare. "I am up. I just said."

"No. Get up! As in, out of bed. We need to move you."

"Wait. Huh?" He sat up a little against the headboard. *Finally, some progress!*

That was when I realized. In all the shouting and jostling, my mom hadn't made a peep. As concerned as I was for Johnny, that wasn't normal.

"What's going on with Mom?"

She hadn't been around for a few days. But the last time I saw her, she seemed to be doing pretty well. I'd been working on schoolwork when she came home, and we sat at the table for an hour eating Chicken in a Biscuit crackers while I told her funny stories about kids at the Center. She had mentioned a plan to spend time with a *special friend* for the next few days, but that was nothing out of the ordinary. Now, as she lay on the bed with her skirt hitched up to the middle of her thighs, I registered the bruises behind her knees and on her arms. One of her ankles looked swollen too.

"Oh. She's just strung out, I think," Johnny said.

"You think?" Shuffling over to her side of the bed, I raised one of Mom's arms. When I released it, it dropped to the mattress like a stone.

"Yeah. You missed it. There was kind of a bad scene, I guess. When Mom came home." I was about to demand he elaborate when Johnny suddenly sat up straighter. He brought a hand to his throat and frowned. "Cor, can you grab me a glass of water?"

When he grimaced again, I looked around and saw a small cardboard box in the corner. Handing it to him, I said, "If you need to throw up, do it in here unless you think you can make it to the bathroom. I'll grab your water."

He scrunched his face at the bloody sock mittens on my hands but didn't ask about them.

I hopped eight feet to the little bathroom at the back of the trailer. I didn't want to risk the gauntlet of broken glass in the main room again, so I picked up a cup from the sink counter—Johnny would just have to deal with the toothpaste residue around the rim—and filled it with water.

When I brought it back into the bedroom, he asked, "Why are you limping around?"

"Glass through my shoe. You need to be careful out by the kitchen till I get it cleaned up. Now tell me about the 'bad scene' you were talking about earlier with Mom."

I sat down on the edge of the mattress, applying pressure to the wound on my foot, trying to slow the bleeding while he talked.

Johnny cleared his throat. "After you helped me shower yesterday, I went right to bed." He stopped to take a sip of water. "It's hard to explain, but my body felt different than it ever has before... I can't remember much about them putting me in the dumpster, but I think Chi-chi's guys might have stabbed me with something."

"Okay." I exhaled. He'd been so out of it yesterday. I'd been terrified. Thank god he seemed okay now, other than looking like he might hurl up his insides.

"Anyway, I slept all the way through the afternoon and night."

"I know. You were still out when I went to school this morning. That's why I put you in Mom's bed instead of the couch, so you could hopefully sleep off whatever was in your system better."

"Right. Well, I was starting to wake up, probably around noon, but what really did it was Mom coming in with some dickbag. I don't know what went down, but there was a loud crash, like maybe a window broke, and then shouting. The next thing I know, this guy is standing in the doorway of the bedroom. My eyes weren't totally open, but enough that I saw he basically flung her down on the bed, and then he—"

Johnny's face contorted with anger.

"What?" I asked.

His eyes narrowed. "This part I remember exactly. He called her a 'stupid, useless whore bitch' and then walked out. I don't even know if he noticed me in the bed."

Stunned, I gulped hard. I loved my mom, and stuff like this never got easier.

There was no way to fill in the blanks until she woke up. I guessed the window-breaking noise Johnny heard was the bottle shattering, and the shouting would explain why things had been flung around the living room. I didn't know who this guy was, or where her bruises had come from. Had he beaten her up? Or was he her rescuer? Was he some sort of pimp? As far as I knew, this was the first time my mom's *work* had ever made its way into our home. It was the reason I never faulted her for being away so much. What seemed like neglect from the outside felt like her watching out for us from the inside. Because it meant shit like this didn't get brought into our house.

But now it was here. And my mom wasn't waking up. And my foot would not stop fucking bleeding.

And Johnny was still in danger.

Sighing, I mentally rearranged the plan I'd had in mind half an hour ago.

"Johnny, you need to get out of here. Go to Rosa's house. Lupe will let you in if she's not home yet."

"Why?"

"We don't have time for questions. I ran into Deck. Chi-chi's after you. Deck said you need to hide while he and Cruz take care of things."

Johnny put the cup down on the nightstand. "Fuck that! This is my shit, too. I'm not going to hide like a little bitch while Deck and Cruz take care of things." He tried to stand but immediately wobbled on his feet.

I pulled him back down by his wrist until he sat on the edge of the bed with his legs swung over. "Johnny! Knock it off. You know full well you're not in any position to do anything. Just fucking lie low like Deck said! Then he doesn't have to worry about you too!"

"Am I a fucking baby, Cori? You think I can't take care of myself?"

I wanted to slap him.

"I think Deck pulled you out of a dumpster yesterday. And then I had to help you shower and take a piss. And right now, you can barely stand. Whether you can take care of yourself is a much longer conversation these days, Big Brother. But at this moment, you need to take your sorry ass to Rosa's and hide until this blows over. She's only three blocks away. I think you're sober enough to walk. I'll text her and let her know you're coming."

"Cori—"

"Johnny, stop arguing! We don't have the time. I've done so much for you, taken care of you so many times. I'm asking you to do this for me. Not make it harder by wasting time and asking a bunch of questions. Maybe you can help Deck later. But for now, you need to get out of here since this is the first place Chi-chi will look for you."

He put his head in his hands before reaching for the water again. After taking a sip, he lifted his defeated eyes to mine. "Okay. I'll go to fucking Rosa's... Because you're right, I do owe you."

"Thank you."

"But you know I don't love it."

"I know." I reached out my sock-covered hand to brush his hair from his forehead before pressing a kiss there. "Now go put some pants on. No one else needs to see your stupid pink skull boxers."

I went back to the bathroom and grabbed the small dustpan beneath the sink. I was able to limp around enough to sweep most of the glass from the floor, set the couch to rights, and pick up the things that had come off the counter. Sadly, the fish-shaped clay blob I made in elementary school that we used as a sponge holder had paid the ultimate price. I sighed, throwing the pieces in the garbage. RIP Nemo.

All the while, my foot kept bleeding. The dishrag still captured most of the blood, but I knew I needed to figure out something else soon.

Johnny reappeared in cleanish clothes with his hair and teeth brushed.

"Tell Rosa or Lupe to let me know when you get there," I said.

"I still can't believe my phone is in that dumpster." He shook his head. "But Cori, if Chi-chi's really coming, it's not safe for you here either."

I'd already thought of that. My original idea had been to go with him to Rosa's, but my mom's presence blew up that plan. Even if Chi-chi came, I hoped it would be okay since I wasn't the one he was after. I'd heard a lot of terrible things about Chi-chi, but I'd never heard of him harming women or children.

"I can't leave Mom when she's like this. She could have a seizure or choke on her own vomit or whatever. Who knows if she has weird injuries we can't see? Honestly, if she's not awake and talking by the morning, I need to take her to the hospital."

"She'll hate that. CPS would come for sure."

"I know. But I don't know what else to do."

Johnny nodded. "You're the boss."

Actually, I'm your sixteen-year-old little sister, but whatever.

After Johnny left, I texted Rosa to let her know he was on his way. Because of her position as a youth leader, I had to use a special relay system to text her. I got frustrated waiting for her reply, but when it came, she said of course Johnny could stay with her, but I'd have some explaining to do later. I expected nothing less. Thankfully, Johnny wasn't a Center kid. Center kids couldn't go to Rosa's personal home. But this situation, while still a big ask, was more the equivalent of her having a family member visit.

I checked on my mom to find her response level unchanged, but I tried to make her more comfortable anyway by pulling down her dress and taking off her jewelry. Her ankle still looked puffy, but I didn't know how to help that. It wasn't like we had a compression brace lying around. I settled for putting a bag of frozen tater tots on top of it while she slept.

In the bathroom, I held my foot over the sink and let the water run over the cut until it ran pink and finally clear. Getting my first proper look at the wound, I registered how deep the cut was. The glass had sunk straight into my flesh. Thank goodness I'd been wearing shoes. I knew it needed stitches, but no way would that be happening. Tossing the disgusting dishrag in the shower stall, I found an old hand towel we could afford to throw away and wrapped it around my foot. After taking off my other shoe and sock so I didn't feel so lopsided, I washed the cuts on my hands with soap and water before putting the socks back on. I could get Band-Aids for myself and an ankle brace for Mom at the Center tomorrow.

But first, we had to get through the night.

While I cleaned my foot, the text came through confirming Johnny had reached Rosa's safely. One less thing to worry about. I checked on my mom—still out cold—and turned off all the lights in the trailer. We didn't have a car. Hopefully, if the place looked dead enough, Chi-chi would assume Johnny had hidden somewhere else.

In the meantime, I lay on my bed, clutching my phone. I texted Deck, letting him know Johnny was alright, but that I needed to stay in the trailer because of my mom. I hoped I'd hear from him soon that he'd found Eliazar safe and sound.

Chapter Fifteen
Deck – Age 18

TWELVE-AND-A-HALF YEARS AGO

I parked my parents' car a few blocks away from Chi-chi's. We always rolled with Cruz, so I didn't think anyone would recognize the old beaten-down Subaru, but it didn't hurt to be careful. The late afternoon light shone too brightly to provide any cover, so I figured my best course was to walk into Chi-chi's like usual. Folks were used to seeing me there, and I doubted Chi-chi had spoken about our disagreement with too many people.

As I reached the porch, two girls I vaguely recognized stumbled out of the house.

"*Hola*, Deck," one of them said, holding the door open for me.

"Thanks," I mumbled, squeezing past her into the entryway.

Four guys sat on the couches in the living room with controllers in their hands. Some cartoonish-looking game was up on the flat screen, but none of them were playing. One had his head lolled back on top of the couch, and the other three were staring into space, eyes glazed over. They were there, but not really. I'd gotten used to the look of a heroin high since I'd started hanging out here, but people this messed up were usually in the basement. It was rare for Chi-chi's living room to be full of people yet so…lifeless. The bong on the table wasn't uncommon, but this time, I also saw white powder, needles, spoons, and a lighter.

"Hey. Anyone seen Chi-chi? Or Bash?" I asked.

One guy turned his head my way but didn't say anything. *Dios,* they were really gone. This was why I almost never went in the basement, why I was so pissed with Johnny and Eliazar for messing with this shit. These *vatos* were fucking zombies.

Unfortunately, they were zombies I needed to get information from. Eliazar's phone said he was in this house, but where? I realized now my plan to rescue my friend had some flaws. I'd been so eager to find him that I hadn't really thought about what would happen once I did. It wasn't like I could fight everyone in this house, although I thought maybe I could handle the vegetables on the couch. I had a vague idea to negotiate with Chi-chi. Now that Cruz had agreed to pull the big job, Chi-chi couldn't complain. If he wanted us to keep working for him, I needed to convince him not to fuck with our friends. Not that I wanted to keep working for Chi-chi, but I needed to buy time.

"Hey!" I tried again, a little louder. "Chi-chi or Bash around?"

I'd search the place if I had to, but a heads-up would be handy.

"Stop shouting, *guapo.*" One of Chi-chi's girls, a woman named Nadia, approached me from the hallway. "Chi-chi's not here. Left yesterday and said he'd be gone a few days. That's why these *idiotas*"—she jerked her neck toward the couches—"thought they could bring their downstairs business upstairs."

I tried to keep my voice level as I asked, "What about Bash? Seen him?"

Nadia's forehead lifted. "Sure. He came in with your friend. The little guy. They went downstairs a while ago."

Rage pumped through my veins. "They're in the basement?"

Nadia gave me a puzzled look. "That's right."

Again, I kept my tone even. "I need to talk to him."

Lighting a joint, Nadia took a deep inhale before holding it out. I was anxious to find Eliazar but didn't want to give it away. Or go in totally blind. I took a quick hit, not enough to affect me.

"I know Bash is pretty quiet," Nadia said, "but don't mistake it. He's just as dangerous as Chi-chi. I wouldn't want him as an enemy."

I blinked at her blunt words.

She kept her gaze on me as I asked, "Why are you telling me this?"

"Because I like you, *muchacho*. It made me a little sad when Chi-chi brought you guys in. Not that anyone turns him down for anything." She took another hit. "And those guys on the couch over there know Chi-chi wouldn't like them shooting up in his living room. But they were a lot less afraid of pissing him off than they were of Bash when he ordered everyone out of the basement half an hour ago."

"He what?"

"I just said. He went down there with your *amigo*. Told them to fuck off. He didn't want to be disturbed."

I glanced at the door to the basement before staring back at her. "Eliazar's one of my best friends."

She nodded. "Your funeral."

I took a deep breath and began walking through the kitchen.

Nadia called after me. "Deck—"

"Hmm?"

"When you get to the bottom of the stairs, there's a metal baseball bat propped up in the corner."

I dipped my chin. "Good to know."

"You didn't hear it from me."

"No. I never even saw you today."

I crept down the stairs one by one, gritting my teeth at every creak and groan of the old wood.

The bat was exactly where Nadia said it would be. I reached for it carefully.

The basement comprised one large main room and two walled-off corners that passed for small bedrooms. An old almond-colored washer and dryer were shoved up against the back wall. By some miracle, the dryer was running, which helped disguise the sound of my footsteps.

Mismatched couches and recliners were crammed into the main room, along with a scratched-up dining table Chi-chi used for "business." I'd always assumed that meant cutting product, but since I didn't spend much time down here, I didn't know for sure. The room was empty, and I could imagine Bash ordering people out exactly as Nadia described. The zombies may have moved their most important *stuff* upstairs, but cans and bottles covered the coffee table. Smoke swirled up from a giant ashtray in the center, where cigarettes had burned down into long, slender fingers of ash.

My heart thumped in time with the tumble of the dryer. I gripped the bat tighter.

Both bedroom doors were closed, but there was noise coming from behind one. As I neared it, I heard the crying sound clearly. Specifically, Eliazar crying.

"No... Fuck... Please."

Everything in me wanted to barrel in there and put a stop to whatever was happening. But I had to be smart. I'd only have the element of surprise once. Bash had done me a favor by dismissing the potential audience from our encounter, so I needed to use that to my advantage.

Assuming I wasn't too scared to use the bat.

I'd been in a few fights, but I didn't think of myself as a fighter. I punched when I had to, but didn't love it or seek it out the way some guys did. My friends and I were more talkers. Well, maybe not Cruz. He loved to fight.

But Cruz wasn't there, and I was. And I would fuck Bash up for hurting Eliazar.

"Bash...pleeeeeeeeeeeeeeeeeeeease."

The anguished whine strengthened my resolve, along with the loud slap that followed it.

Lifting the bat with my right hand, I threw open the door with my left, standing back.

Bash and Eliazar turned their heads toward me and froze.

Eliazar lay stomach down on the bed. Bash was on top of him, shoving Eliazar's face into a dingy pillow while he fumbled to pull down Eliazar's pants. Bash's jeans and boxers were already down to his knees. The sight of Bash's hairy ass in the air while he pushed Eliazar into the mattress had me seeing red.

"Deck, help," Eliazar cried softly.

Everything happened in an instant. Before Bash could make a move, I raised the bat and brought it down forcefully over his back. For a split second, I thought about going for his head, but I had enough awareness to remember it would be a bad idea to murder the guy.

Even if he deserved it.

The hit across his spine was enough to have him screaming and crunching over onto the floor. I could have done without the flash I got of his tiny limp dick as he keeled over, though.

As soon as Bash fell off him, Eliazar hurried away from the bed like it was on fire.

"I'm sorry, Deck," he rasped, reaching up to touch his throat. "He jumped me on the sidewalk."

"Yeah. Chi-chi told Cruz that he gave him the okay." I pulled Eliazar against my side. "And you've got nothing to be sorry for."

From the floor, Bash groaned. "Chi-chi's not gonna like this," he snarled roughly. "There's no place you'll be able to hide."

I lifted the bat and brought it down hard across one of Bash's ankles. There was a satisfying crack of bone. "*¡Pedazo de mierda, violador!*"

Bash opened his mouth as though to scream, but no sound came out. His face went sheet-white, and a moment later, he doubled over and went still. I assumed he'd passed out from the pain but wasn't interested in making sure.

"Are you okay?" I asked Eliazar.

His answer was a silent tear falling from one eye. "I'm just glad you came," he murmured.

"Me too." I glanced at the floor by the bed and saw a bottle of lube. "Did I make it...in time?"

"Mm-hmm. It would have been better if I didn't have to feel his prick against my jeans, but the *pendejo* wasn't able to get it up to do anything. No telling what sort of whack shit he has in his system. He was getting pretty pissed right before you showed up."

It was then I noticed red and purple marks on Eliazar's face and arms. "You fought him?"

Eliazar shrugged. "As much as I could. Bash has like a hundred pounds on me... Oh, he also had a gun earlier. I don't know where it is now."

That surprised me. With as much as I'd been around Chi-chi, I knew he didn't keep too many guns in the house. Probably safer with all the randos and addicts coming and going. I'd seen dozens of them tweak out and lose their fucking minds. His guys took guns out on jobs. He'd loaned them to Cruz before, but I'd never known Bash to carry regularly.

"Where's your phone?" I asked.

Eliazar pointed at a denim jacket flung over a bedpost. "Bash's pocket. He took it away from me first thing."

I reached into the coat and grabbed the phone near where Bash remained curled over.

"Are you okay to walk out of here? We need to leave before Bash can get up or make noise. I don't know if the guys upstairs would help him, but I don't want to chance it."

"I'll be fine."

Eliazar seemed different. I realized it was the first time I'd seen him sober in a while.

We walked up the stairs. Even though it was a bit of a risk to keep it, I didn't dare put the bat back down.

Nothing seemed amiss. The same four guys were still on the couches, the same video game still blared on the TV.

On our way through the kitchen, I caught Nadia's eyes as she sat on the counter, sipping from a coffee mug. She looked down at the bat in my hand. Then she hopped off and walked into a back bedroom, shutting the door behind herself.

After we got to my car, I drove Eliazar to Burger King. I knew he'd been running on adrenaline back at Chi-chi's and wasn't sure if he'd collapse as the night wore on. He seemed out of it, but in a different way than when he was high. He kept tugging on his shirt. Finally, he grunted in annoyance and pulled the tee off over his head, chucking it onto the floorboard of the car.

"Smelled like Bash," he said.

I nodded. It was quiet between us until he popped the last bite of Whopper into his mouth and said, "Just so you know, Deck, I would have been okay if Bash had...done it. I've been through worse shit and come out okay."

My stomach clenched. He said it without inflection, like him being able to power through getting raped was a casual topic of conversation. I didn't want to imagine what *worse shit* he'd been through, although I could guess. He was so deep into the drugs now, same as Johnny. I'd been trying to convince myself that *someday, I'll fix them*, but everything kept getting worse.

I could blame the drugs, blame the app assholes, blame his parents, but really... For the billionth time, I wished I'd never met Chi-chi in that park.

Pulling out my phone to check in with Cruz, I saw a text from Cori letting me know Johnny had made it out alright. But then her next text said she was staying at the trailer. Something about her mom.

What the fuck?

ME: The trailer's not safe. You can't stay there.

She didn't reply. I texted again.

ME: Hey I need to know you're alright.

When Cori still didn't message back, it set my senses on edge. She wouldn't leave me on read. Not with everything going on.

"Eliazar, we need to go to Johnny's."

Eliazar released a hollow laugh. "You remember I'm homeless, right? I don't care where we go."

I gave him a meaningful look across the console. "You're not homeless, *hermano*. Unless we all are, you'll never be."

He turned his face to the car window. "Thanks, Deck." A beat later, he asked, "So I guess this means Cruz is pulling the job for Chi-chi?"

"Tonight." I could barely spare a thought for that. At least, of all my friends, I trusted Cruz to handle himself the most.

"Think he'll be okay?"

"I guess he'll have to be. Chi-chi is a real fucking live wire lately. He never used to be so reckless."

"Just like he and Bash never used to carry," Eliazar said. "Now they do. Chi-chi wants to be big time. Or at least act like it."

"You think that's all it is?"

"I know so. He's not complicated. You don't spend much time in the basement, but I—"

"Eliazar, I can't talk about how much time you spend in that basement tonight."

He hung his head. "I know. I'm only saying that sometimes Bash and Chi-chi talk down there, because they figure everyone is so far gone. A few months ago, I heard Chi-chi explain to Bash how he wanted to pull bigger scores. Make real money."

Eliazar shivered as he spoke. Meanwhile, I felt hot enough to erupt. I pulled my shirt off and handed it to Eliazar. He didn't hesitate, slipping it over his head and burrowing into the fabric.

"Well, apparently his ambition has fried Chi-chi's brain," I said. "Because now he's throwing people in dumpsters and letting his henchmen rape them to prove a point. He's fucking *loco*, acting like we're the enemy."

Eliazar sighed his agreement. I was sure that, like me, he wondered how the hell we were ever going to get out from under Chi-chi's thumb, especially after what I'd just done to Bash.

But that was tomorrow's problem. For now, I needed to find out why Cori wasn't texting me back.

Chapter Sixteen
Cori – Age 16

TWELVE-AND-A-HALF YEARS AGO

The cut on my foot would not stop bleeding. After less than an hour, I'd soaked through the hand towel. I needed to find something else to use, but I'd already wrecked this towel and the kitchen rag. Using a big bath towel was a last resort. It wasn't like we had extras.

In my bedroom, I went into the stacked plastic bins I used as a dresser and dug around, pulling out my *period underwear* from the back. They were clean, and since they already had little bloodstains on them, it wasn't too much of a sacrifice.

My hands were in better shape, so I peeled the socks off them. Even in the dwindling light from outside, I could see that the big cut had scabbed over and the smaller cuts were no longer visible. I didn't dare turn any lamps on to check more carefully. If Chi-chi or any of his guys stopped by, I wanted them to think no one was home.

I wrapped my foot in two pairs of my stained underwear. Looping the elastic around my big toe, I stretched the material over my heel, which put some pressure on the wound. The bleeding had slowed down, but I winced when I accidentally dragged my foot across the bedsheet, smearing blood on it. Awesome.

Something else to deal with in the morning.

After covering my foot, I checked on my mom again, relieved to find that her breathing appeared stronger and more regular.

I pulled the blanket over her. "What happened to you?" I whispered, running my thumb lightly over the purple bruise on her shoulder.

She looked almost peaceful, lying there, and I wondered what kind of life she'd dreamed about when she was my age. I'd asked her once, and all she did was cup my cheek and tell me that Johnny and I were the best things to ever happen to her, that we were all the dreams she needed.

I hoped that was true—that she took joy in being a mother—because, at least to my eyes, it seemed like her life pretty much sucked. Quickly, I banished the thought. She wouldn't want my pity. Or more to the point, I wouldn't want it if I was in her shoes.

The flash of headlights invaded through the blinds. Someone pulled their car up in front and killed the engine.

Quietly, I limped to my room. I thought about hiding in my mom's closet or the bathroom, but if Chi-chi or one of his goons busted into our house, I wanted to have space to run. Or fight. Like I told Johnny, if I was forced to deal with Chi-chi, I'd figure out a way to handle him.

I lay down on my bed, clutching my phone to my chest. It buzzed with an incoming text. I didn't dare turn it over. The light from the screen would reflect in the window like a beacon.

Three loud knocks sounded at the door. "Johnny!"

I held perfectly still. I didn't know if the voice belonged to Chi-chi, but whoever it was, he was angry as fuck.

"Johnny!" This time, the shout came from directly outside my window, like he stood underneath it. His speech sounded slurred. "Johnny! Are you hiding in your house like a little bitch!?"

"Yo, Chi-chi. I don't think anyone's home." A different voice this time, although just as close.

My phone shook again, muffled by my hand. I prayed they couldn't hear it.

"Well, if he's not here, we need to find him. I want to hang onto him until I'm sure Cruz finishes the job. I don't trust that motherfucker."

"He's gonna be pissed when he finds out you gave the little guy to Bash."

The one who was apparently Chi-chi chuckled evilly. "Let him. I already warned him what would happen. Told him to tell that *pendejo*, Deck, too. Three weeks they made me wait!"

The "little guy" must have been Eliazar. But who was Bash?

"I thought you liked Deck. All those guys," the second man said. "Felt kinda fucked up tossing Johnny in the garbage. I've chilled with him before. Always thought he was alright."

"I do like them. But not when they act like pussies. I want loyal soldiers, not little bitches."

"You really think fucking up their friends is the way, *jefe*?"

"Trust."

There was shuffling before one of them pounded on the door again, violently enough to shake the wall.

"Johnny!" Chi-chi shouted.

"I don't think he's here," Chi-chi's far-more-sensible sidekick said a few seconds later.

I squeezed my eyes closed and willed them to go away.

But the banging and Chi-chi's yelling were loud enough to wake the dead. Or, rather, to wake the half dead.

"Johnny?" My mom's low moan echoed through the hallway. "Johnny? Baby?"

Fuck.

"I knew it!" Chi-chi screeched. "Someone's in there."

The knocking began on the door and didn't let up. Two sets of hands this time. "Open up!"

I rolled over the options in my mind. Calling the cops was out of the question. They never came anyway, and I didn't want them to see my mom. Maybe if they kept banging, neighbors would come out and help. But that was a long shot. Besides, most folks knew Chi-chi by sight, and if they saw it was him at our door, they'd mind their own business real fast. I could text Rosa, but I worried Johnny might see and try to play hero. Same with Deck. I thought about just opening the door and reasoning with Chi-chi. If I let him search the place, maybe that would end it. Since Johnny wasn't here. Then again, the dude seemed real fucking crazy.

The decision was taken out of my hands a minute later when the door to the trailer was kicked in. The overhead light in the main room flicked on.

I scrambled up against the headboard, deciding it would be better to meet Chi-chi head-on rather than hide in my bedroom. Lurching to a standing position, intending to face him in the living room, I ignored the stabbing pain that shot up my leg when I put weight on my foot.

But I'd only made it to my bedroom door when Chi-chi appeared in front of me. He dragged his gaze up and down my body, making me feel sick.

He noticed and grinned. "*Hola, chica.*"

From a foot away, I smelled the liquor on his breath and could see the wide dilation of his pupils.

"Johnny's not home," I said with as much force as I could muster. "It's just me and my mom." I gestured to the bedroom across from mine, and Chi-chi peered in.

"Hello, Johnny's mom." He leered at her. "How about you stay in your bedroom while your daughter and I discuss some things?"

"What?" My mom sat up on her bed, wobbly and disoriented. "Cori? What's going on? Why was there shouting?"

I wasn't sure if she'd registered Chi-chi's presence or not, or how aware she was. "It's okay, Mom," I reassured her. "I'll talk to you in a minute."

"Yeah. She'll talk to you in a minute, Mommy." Chi-chi reached back to grab his friend by the arm and shoved him into my mom's room. "My boy Aaron will keep you company while your daughter and I have a little chat."

Blond and blue-eyed, Aaron did not look like any of the other guys I'd seen following Chi-chi around in the neighborhood. He hesitated, evidently having no clue what the script was here. "Are you sure?"

Chi-chi replied with a punishing glare. Aaron held up his hands in surrender before sitting next to my mom on her bed.

"Cori?"

"It's okay, Mom." I kept my eyes pinned on Chi-chi as I spoke. "Hang out with Aaron for a bit."

"But—"

"I think you and I had better talk uninterrupted," Chi-chi said, pushing me back into my room until my knees hit the side of the bed.

He shut the door. I waited for him to turn on the light, like he'd done in the main room, but he didn't. No matter. It was bright enough for me to see the pattern in the plaid flannel he wore over his chinos, and to make out the old-school Sonics logo on his hat.

Chi-chi stepped toward me. I stood my ground, putting all my weight on my good foot.

"Will my mom be alright with him?"

"I imagine so."

Vague, but I'd have to live with it.

"Sit," Chi-chi ordered.

When I didn't comply immediately, he pushed me down. I decided not to fight him. Yet.

"I already told you Johnny's not here," I said. "So you can go."

His right cheek lifted. He sat down next to me, squishing his thigh against mine. "Where is he?"

I wanted to cross my arms over my chest, but I kept my hands in my lap as I answered, "I don't know."

"Am I supposed to believe you?"

I huffed. "You're crazy if you think I'm in charge of my brother, or if I know where he is most of the time." That part was the truth.

"Well, you're crazy if you lie to me." He reached out and ran a hand across my polo shirt, stopping when his palm fell over the Center logo on top of my collarbone. His touch made my skin crawl, and I could tell by the look in his eye that he knew it. Got off on it.

"I'm not lying."

Chi-chi smiled. "I've seen you before, you know," he said, smoothing a circle over my neck before pulling his hand away. "I know all about Johnny's little sister, who gets straight A's and volunteers at the Center."

The reprieve from his touch didn't last. I held perfectly still as he ran his right palm over my knee to the bottom of my baggy basketball shorts. His left hand came up to circle my throat, which he pressured gently.

"Stop."

I moved my eyes around the room, searching for anything I could use as a weapon. My phone was sitting on the bed, but I figured my best bet was a tried-and-true knee to the balls. I just had to wait for the right moment.

"You want me to stop?" The hand on my leg began sliding up under my shorts, inching toward my inner thigh. "Then tell me where Johnny is."

"I don't know." I gulped beneath his hand on my throat. "You're hurting me," I gritted out.

Chi-chi pulled his hands away and stood abruptly. "Fuck." Looking down at me, he spat, "I believe you."

Check me out, being an effective liar! Now I had to get him away from my house.

My phone buzzed again.

Chi-chi snatched it off my bedspread before I had a chance to. His eyes went wide at the preview. When he looked back at me, there was pure malevolence in his gaze.

Shit! Had Johnny been dumb enough to text from someone else's phone?

Chi-chi turned the phone screen to me.

DECK: You need to text me back! Please baby. I'm so worried.
DECK: *heart emoji*

Baby? A fucking heart emoji? After all this time and Chi-chi sees it first? Jesus Christ.

Chi-chi tossed the phone across the room. "Are you...Deck's girl?"

"No." I shook my head vehemently. "Just friends. He's like a brother to me."

The air grew heavy. The clanking of metal filled the room like a cannon shot as Chi-chi loosened his belt buckle. "This time, I don't believe you, *chica*."

I scurried up to sit against the headboard. "Well, you should."

Chi-chi tsked. "Of all your friends, Deck is the one I'm the most disappointed in. I picked him out myself, personal-like, but he never really appreciated it. Maybe if I fuck his woman, he'll get the message of who he owes."

Only in Chi-chi's fucked-up mind did that possibly make any sense. I registered his eyes again. He was definitely on something.

"I'm only sixteen." I was grasping at straws here, and I knew it.

He laughed. "I don't care."

Chi-chi popped the button on his pants and pulled the zipper down. He put one knee on the bed and used his hands to grab my ankles, pulling me toward him. The underwear came off my foot, staining the bedspread bright red.

"This is rape," I tried. A rush of adrenaline kicked in. I thought of my mom, battered and shaky in the other room. Chi-chi might win, but I wasn't going to make it easy.

He laughed even louder this time. "Still don't care."

He swung his leg over to straddle my thighs. Unbuttoning and shrugging off his flannel, he tossed it aside to reveal a flabby chest covered in cheap gold chains and shitty tattoos. Crucially, the move allowed me to assess that, unless he had the world's tiniest gun in his back pocket, he wasn't carrying.

I let him manhandle me, pushing his hands away half-heartedly to convince him that this was all the fight I had in me. My plan was to wait for him to get his dick as exposed as possible and then kick him in the nuts. If I could grab his balls instead, that would be even better. I'd read somewhere that yanking down on the ball sac and twisting hard would incapacitate any man for a minute or two at least. That would give me the time I needed to run. I didn't want to leave my mom with Aaron, but there was no choice. We needed real help.

I hadn't anticipated how repulsive Chi-chi's hands on my body would feel. I wanted to wait until his dick was unclothed, but as he ran his palms up and down my hips and placed spit-soaked kisses on my neck, I decided it would be fine to hurt him through the thin material of his boxers.

Chi-chi didn't bother trying to remove my polo, seeming determined to get inside me as soon as possible. Revolting. He grasped the bottom of my shorts, and I allowed him to remove them since I knew I'd put on enormous granny panties that morning.

I still didn't have a clear shot at his groin when I felt his hands tugging at my underwear. Instinctively, I pushed him away.

He slapped me across the face. Hard. The metallic taste of blood flooded my mouth as my vision blurred. I was pretty sure he'd cut my lip on one of his stupid rings.

Chi-chi yanked his jeans and boxers to his knees, still lying on top of me.

I stretched out my arm from my side, seeing if I could reach his exposed privates.

He clocked the movement and caught my wrist, gripping it so hard I cried out in pain.

"Uh, uh, uh." He shook his head as he ground his dick against my hips. "You can't stop this, so maybe just lie back and relax. You can tell your boyfriend Deck how good I was to you."

Sure, asshole.

With the hand that wasn't holding my wrist, he reached below himself to again pull down on my underwear.

A surge of power, fueled by a mix of determination and desperation, coursed through my body as I surprised him by flipping us over. I slammed my elbow down hard on his groin. His face crumpled in pain, but before he could react further, I followed up the elbow jab with a hard twist of his nuts. It was absolutely disgusting to have to touch those nasty, hairy things, but the look of pure agony that crossed his face was satisfying.

I took a second to pick my phone up off the floor, but didn't bother with my shorts. I swung open the bedroom door with a mind to escape before Aaron realized what had happened.

Deck stood on the other side. Shirtless.

His eyes took in the scene. As I straightened in front of him, panting, I saw him take in my polo shirt and underwear combo, the bruises I could already feel forming on my neck, arms, and legs, and my split lip. Chi-chi lay shirtless on the bed, gripping his dick and breathing hard.

I wanted to fling myself into Deck's arms, wanted him to hold me and wipe away the feel of Chi-chi's hands on my body. He was here. It would be okay.

Baby.

Heart emoji.

But he didn't take me in his arms. His nostrils flared, and I heard the breaths coming out of them. That was when I noticed the direction of his eyes. He was looking at the bloody panties that had come off my foot, now visible on the side of the bed, along with the smears of blood across my bedspread and the floor.

I put my hand on his chin and tried to tilt his face to mine. "Deck, baby, it's okay. It's okay. He didn't hurt me. The blood is from a cut I got hours ago."

He didn't meet my eyes. Didn't seem to notice that I still had my massive underwear on.

That was when I saw the bat in his hand.

"How many rapists do I have to beat down tonight?" he asked nobody.

Chi-chi looked up at him, still breathing raggedly but able to ground out, "Ah...what's the matter, baby Decker? Mad I fucked your girl?"

Deck's face went red as he inched toward the bed. I reached out a hand. "No, Deck. He's lying. It never got that far."

Chi-chi turned to me. "Why do you say that, *chica*? Didn't I just give it to you so good?"

"Shut up, you fucking liar!"

Deck took another step forward.

"You better not be thinking about doing anything with that bat, *bróder*. If shit happens to me, your boy Cruz is going down."

Deck held himself like a statue. Even if I could convince him that Chi-chi hadn't technically raped me, there was no doubt he'd tried to, and that he'd gotten in a good hit before I'd beaten him up.

"Get up!" Deck shouted.

Although clearly still in pain, Chi-chi managed to swing his legs over the edge of the mattress.

"What you gonna do?" he asked, lifting his ass just high enough to pull his pants over his hips, buttoning them with swagger.

Deck's answer was to grab Chi-chi's arm, forcing him past me and out of the room. Chi-chi struggled to move, but Deck held him up, perp-walking him through the main room with one hand as he held the bat with his other. At the door to the trailer, he threw Chi-chi down the three entry steps onto the ground. I attempted to follow, but my foot screamed at me. Deck caught me limping, and his eyes narrowed.

My mom's bedroom door flew open, and she came out, somehow clothed in jeans and a long-sleeved tee. Aaron followed.

Deck leaped over the steps and onto the ground, spitting on the brown grass next to Chi-chi. "Get up! Get up and fight me like a man!"

I grabbed some flip-flops and hobbled to the doorway. Mom and Aaron stood next to me. Eliazar emerged from the passenger seat of Deck's car, yelling, "What the fuck is going on?"

Chi-chi maneuvered into a hands-and-knees position on the ground. "Oh hey, little guy," he said to Eliazar. "Did you have fun with Bash?"

Eliazar froze.

"Shut your fuckin' mouth!" Deck hissed.

"Chi-chi?" Aaron called out, looking stunned.

Chi-chi raised his eyebrows at Aaron, followed by a subtle tilt of his head. I caught the gesture, instantly on alert. Aaron hesitated before reaching behind himself, enough time for me to stick my hand in the back of his pants and grab the gun hidden there. I leaned back onto my good foot and pointed it at him.

I'd never held a gun, but I'd seen enough of them on TV and around the neighborhood to make my stance look convincing.

Aaron raised his hands as Chi-chi shook his head and mumbled, "*Useless gringo.*"

Deck spared me an approving glance before turning to Eliazar. "Check his car."

Eliazar went to Chi-chi's car and found a gun lying on the passenger seat. Chi-chi really didn't think much of my brother to have left it in his car.

"Give me the gun, Cori," Deck said.

I stumbled down the stairs and gave it to him. He handed it to Eliazar, who still held the one from Chi-chi's car.

"Take these and toss them somewhere, okay?" Deck said sternly to Eliazar. He looked back down at Chi-chi. "We're going to do this without guns."

"I'll handle it," Eliazar said solemnly. He shoved both guns into the back of his pants and walked away, heading toward the main road.

Aaron made a motion like he was going to come out of the trailer. Deck extended the bat to him. "This isn't your battle. Stay up there or you're going to feel this across your back." He turned his murderous eyes to Chi-chi. "Just like Bash did."

Chi-chi's cocky facade faltered. He dragged himself to his feet.

"Alright, baby Decker, I'll play. You wanna fight me? 'Cuz you're mad I fucked your girl? Showed her what a real man feels like?"

"Deck, he didn't—"

"It's okay, Cori. I saw the blood. I'm going to make this right."

Stupid, frustrating man. I loved him for wanting to avenge me, or whatever, but I needed him to listen.

Except I knew him. He'd already been manic and single-minded when I ran into him earlier today, when he'd asked me to find Johnny. Something had clearly happened with Eliazar and that Bash person. Now this.

"Get up and fight me!" Deck screamed at Chi-chi. He tossed the bat to the dirt.

"What do you think's gonna happen, *pendejo*? You think you're gonna beat me up and that's the end of it? You're dead, you hear me? Dead."

Deck peered over at me before turning back to lock his eyes on Chi-chi. "You think I care what happens to me now?"

Jesus Christ. Deck might not care, but I sure as hell did. "Deck, stop!"

"Stay back, Cori!" Deck yelled. "This is between me and Chi-chi."

Chi-chi seemed to have mostly recovered. He and Deck circled each other.

"Deck!" I tried one last time, but he ignored me, baring his teeth at Chi-chi. He wasn't in his right mind.

I threw up my hands. Fucking men and their egos. This stupid neighborhood where the only true currency was violence.

Deck struck first, landing a right hook to Chi-chi's jaw that had the other man spitting blood.

Chi-chi responded with a swift kick to Deck's shins. I caught my breath as Deck fell. When he shot back up again, his arm was bleeding. Looking at the ground, I saw that he'd landed on the same piece of brown glass I'd pulled out of my foot and tossed out the door a few hours ago.

Chi-chi yanked on Deck's shorts. Deck fell again, his feet taken out from under him as Chi-chi pulled the shorts off his legs, tossing them aside.

"Look at you, *muchacho*," Chi-Chi taunted him. "Lying there in your underwear." Chi-chi kicked Deck hard in the ribs. Deck groaned as he curled up, clutching his abdomen.

My mom stood behind me, watching, but had yet to say anything. A white-hot rage burned in my stomach.

The tension left Aaron's shoulders as Chi-chi repeatedly kicked Deck in the stomach.

Chi-chi laughed. "I thought we were supposed to be fighting? Why'd you order me out here just to lie down?" He leaned down to punch Deck square in the jaw.

That was when Deck's eyes met mine.

Oh, Chi-chi. You should be better at this game by now. Considering I played it with you twenty minutes ago.

Aaron had the audacity to check the time on his phone. Idiot.

Chi-chi landed one more blow on Deck's rib cage before leaning down next to his ear. "I like your girl, Deck. She's a real fucking wildcat. You may be a little bitch, but you have good taste in pussy."

Quick as a flash, Deck grabbed Chi-chi's ankle.

"What the fu—"

Chi-chi only had a moment to protest before Deck leaned over and sank his teeth into the bony flesh above Chi-chi's heel. Deck held on, chomping down like a rabid dog before Chi-chi fell backward, screaming. Finally, Deck released him, spitting—*oh fuck, was that skin? Did he actually just spit out a chunk of Chi-chi's ankle?*—onto the ground, his mouth covered in blood.

Chi-chi pulled his leg to his chest. From the doorway, I could see the gaping wound. It was gruesome, and I barely stopped myself from vomiting on the spot.

"Holy shit," Aaron whispered.

This time, it was Deck's turn to kick Chi-chi in the ribs. Deck wasn't in great shape—bruises marred most of his thighs and torso, not to mention the cut on his arm—but he still had the strength to kick Chi-chi hard enough to make the other man grunt.

"It's over, Chi-chi," Deck whooshed out, punctuating each word with another kick. "This is all that's left." He held his arms out at his sides, squeezing his eyes closed and staring at the sky before dropping to his knees. "This is the only thing I can do." Reaching his arm back, he brought a powerful fist down on Chi-chi's face. Then did it again. And again.

I heard the sickening crunch of bone and the sound of flesh being pummeled. Blood poured out of Chi-chi's nose.

Chi-chi fell back onto the ground.

Deck pulled his arm back.

"No! Stop!" I screamed, and he paused.

Aaron pushed past me. "That's enough, man. Chi-chi's out."

Deck's irises were pink with rage. He picked up the bat and brought it down hard across Aaron's outstretched wrist. The blond man collapsed to the ground, clutching his obviously broken limb. "I told you what would happen if you came down here!" Deck shouted at him.

"Jesus Christ, Deck! Stop!" I needed to find a way to get through to him. Whatever demons he had running the show in his head right now were blinding him.

But Deck didn't stop. He turned back to Chi-chi and punched him again. Blood splattered up across Deck's chest. A small splash dripped from his chin. It had only taken the first punch for Chi-chi's face to look completely mangled. A few more punches and it looked like ground beef.

That was when two cop cars pulled up, lights flashing and sirens blaring. *Had someone actually called them?*

Four officers raced onto the scene. I saw with horror that one of them was Deck's brother Emilio, who had just graduated from the Police Academy. He ran to his brother and pulled him back into his lap on the ground.

"*¿Qué has hecho hermano?*" Emilio asked him as Deck went limp, sinking into his brother's embrace.

Behind me, my mother pulled the same move, clutching my back against her chest. I felt her shove something into my hand.

My shorts.

I slipped them on quickly before the police noticed us. They were too busy tending to the three men on the ground. I could only imagine how it appeared. Deck was practically naked, and he and Chi-chi were muddy and covered in blood.

That was when Emilio looked up and saw me. Even though I'd put the shorts on, I couldn't hide my lip or the bruises on my face. "*Oh my god,*" he mouthed silently.

An ambulance arrived. One EMT went over to Chi-chi while the other looked at Aaron's wrist.

My eyes glazed over as I watched the professionals triage the scene. Emilio still held his brother. I was fairly certain that wasn't police protocol, but the other officers seemed fine with turning their heads away.

"Don't fucking say anything," Emilio whisper-shouted to Deck. "Do what they tell you and don't make it worse. I don't know how deep you're into this, little brother, but...they got Cruz." A flicker of emotion crossed Deck's face at that, but just barely. "They got him, and now...I don't know what's going to happen...with all of this."

Emilio sounded distraught, which was my first confirmation that the situation was truly dire. This wasn't just gonna be some fight where everyone got off with a warning.

Chi-chi had certainly been punished for attacking me tonight. He still wasn't moving. But at what cost? Would it have been so terrible to call the police? Prosecute him for assault? I would have done it, would have taken my chances.

But that wasn't how things worked here. Things weren't settled at the courthouse. Not if you could help it.

What would happen to Deck? My brother? Their friends? When did this ever stop?

I loved Deck, but now we had this to add to our misery, to deal with in addition to everything else.

Baby.

Heart emoji.

I wanted peace. And a future. I wanted to live in a world where I could get stitches in my foot when I needed them.

I loved Deck, but I also hated him.

Hated him for taking everything away from us.

I watched dully as the cops cuffed Deck and put him in the back of a cop car. Before the door shut, he and I exchanged a long look.

There was a hint of a smile on my face, the ghost of the girl who had always loved him. I needed him to know that—as mad as I was—I still believed we could handle anything.

I hoped Deck saw the love there. That he knew I would do whatever it took to help him get through this.

But he wasn't himself. And I worried he only saw the hate.

PART TWO

Chapter Seventeen
Cori

It took a few days to get Johnny into a rehab facility. Luckily, I found a good one within driving distance. The staff there told me he wouldn't be allowed to contact anyone for thirty days, but after that, we could discuss visitation or possibly release, depending on how things went.

The lack of a definitive plan forward scared me, and so did the fact that the program was voluntary. I worried that Johnny would leave the facility and be out of my reach before I could stop him. I'd been having nightmares about his heart stopping. My whole life, I'd believed money could solve most problems. Yet even having a large bank account at my disposal didn't guarantee Johnny's recovery. Or his survival.

There were so many ideas out there about how to treat addiction, and the more research I did, the more discouraged I became. No matter which type of program or therapy you did, it seemed like the chance of relapse was much higher than the chance of sobriety. And this was all in addition to Johnny having to adjust to new activity restrictions and a regimen of medications for his HIV.

Helping Rosa was a welcome distraction. I felt like the Center had saved my life more than once as a teenager, providing me with the direction and support I needed. In a way, it was saving me again, offering a purpose and a path for me to return to the neighborhood. In the days since Deck and I found Johnny, I'd thought a lot about what I ran away from when I left Everett.

Everything with Chi-chi had gone down at the end of my junior year. My senior year had been miserable with Deck and Cruz gone. Johnny and Eliazar were like ghosts, deep into their addictions. I tried to stay connected to Marisol and the rest of the Deckers, but it was as though the light had left all their eyes. No one knew what normal was anymore. I missed Deck, and I was desperate to talk to him. But he wouldn't see me. Wouldn't respond to my letters.

After he got locked up, I felt keenly how he'd been so much more than a boy I pined for. We were friends. Confidants. He'd *known* me, all the parts of me, maybe better than anyone. I missed our secret language, where he got to drop his guard and I got to share my burdens. I hadn't realized Deck had been my anchor until that night with Chi-chi flung me back into the sea.

The hug in his driveway haunted my dreams. Then I'd wake up alone. After enough mornings like that, I realized I couldn't stay. When my mom got diagnosed with pancreatic cancer just before graduation, my leaving became inevitable. Two months later, I buried her with Rosa's hand on my shoulder and left for college in Seattle. Occasional visits from my brother became the only tether to my childhood. And I tried my best to be a different person.

But after running into Rosa six months ago, I began to think I was ready to return. The decision I'd made at age eighteen didn't need to be absolute.

The ordeal with Chi-chi had been horrendous and shocking, but I'd been wrong to let it define my entire childhood. There'd been plenty of good days. Days when I helped Rosa make meals for kids at the Center, listening as she told me stories and taught me the right way to roll taquitos. There had been fun times at home between the bad—belly laughs I'd shared with my mom and Johnny, not to mention the stacks of puzzles we'd put together. Even the moments when my brother and I had been co-conspirators in making sure our fucked-up little family stayed whole were mostly fond memories. Johnny's friends had also been happy staples in my life. Besides Deck, there'd been stoic Cruz, who taught me how to jump a car battery and change a tire, and sweet Eliazar, who bought me slushies from the corner market, always choosing the grossest flavor like Coca-Cola. There were memorable times with the Deckers. The day Emilio finally saved up enough to buy his shitty car and the neighborhood threw an impromptu barbecue to celebrate. The day Raymond got his scholarship offer to study music in New York. The day Deck taught Marisol to ride his old bike. So many good times before that last awful night.

I'd walked away because of what had happened with Chi-chi and because I'd missed Deck like a severed limb. I'd been young and in pain. Now I was back, and it felt right. Awkward and weird and uncertain, but right.

I showed up at the Center the Thursday after Johnny's hospitalization. As I exited I-5, the route came back easily. And even though it had been almost a dozen years, a sense of homecoming surfaced as I pulled into the dusty parking lot.

The Center was converted from an old warehouse, and new wings had been added over the decades, along with a gym. It looked a little haphazard, both inside and out, because it had been built with function in mind rather than style. There were two play structures, baseball and soccer fields, and a track. The building was secure, with only one main entrance. Since the last time I'd been here, a glass enclosure had been added to the front door, reminding me of a holding pen, where all building visitors had to wait before being buzzed in.

The cavernous main lobby, called "the atrium," contained game tables on one side and couches and TVs on the other. The rest of the indoor spaces were found down four other hallways, extending from the atrium like bicycle spokes, with classrooms, an art studio, a teen-only area, and a kitchen all occupying a section.

Rosa met me at the glass doors. When we walked into the lobby, the staff person sitting behind the front desk immediately jumped up and came running around the counter. Before I could blink, she flew at me and wrapped her arms tightly around my chest.

"Surprise!" She stepped back and grabbed my hands. "I told Rosa not to tell you I worked here."

I took in her dark brown curls and long lashes underneath winged eyeliner, along with her funky vintage housedress. Then my eyes fell upon the tight, silvery-scarred skin running up her neck to her left cheek.

"Marisol?"

"*Sí, mamacita.* 'Tis I." She placed one hand dramatically against her chest and crooked the other on her hip, batting her eyelids like they were hummingbird wings.

Rosa smiled fondly at Marisol and swatted her on the shoulder. "Enough with the silliness, *nena*." Rosa turned to me. "Marisol has been our program director for about a year. When I told her you were coming, she swore me to secrecy."

Marisol smiled widely. "I've really missed you, Cori, a.k.a. best. Babysitter. Ever. I was so glad when Rosa mentioned you were helping out."

I hadn't seen Deck's little sister since she was eleven. She'd been a confident kid, precocious and smart, especially once her more stringent restrictions were eased, and she'd been allowed to go to school and participate in activities. Apparently, her natural exuberance had followed her into adulthood.

"It's just Mari and me here now, since it's early," Rosa explained, pulling a few chairs up to the lobby desk and inviting me to sit. "My fundraiser, Ana, works three days per week and is off today. Quincy, our finance person, is mostly remote. The rest of the staff won't get here until the kids are out of school."

"Ana and Quincy know about the financial problems, of course, but we haven't told the others yet," Marisol said. "Once they notice you're here, we'll fill them in as it becomes necessary."

"Of course." I turned to Rosa. "And I do want to get started, but first please tell me how Lupe is?"

"*Aye, nena. Eres tan amable.* She was sleeping this morning when I left, but she's comfortable, I think." Rosa looked teary-eyed as she turned away. "I'm going to go grab some files from the office, and Marisol can get you started on the computer."

Marisol pulled up another rolling chair. "I'm happy you're here, Cori. I mean that. I know you haven't been back since you went to college, and it's just so great to see you."

There wasn't a hint of passive-aggressiveness in her voice—on brand for the sweet little girl I remembered.

"I'm sorry I stayed away so long. I feel bad now, knowing I could have been here to do more for Rosa."

Marisol clicked the mouse a few times, and an Excel spreadsheet popped up on the screen. "Cori, she understood. We all did. I know it was rough for you after Deck went away. With Johnny, and then when your mom got sick. I'm sorry about not getting a chance to offer my condolences. I only met Jill a few times, but she was always nice to me."

"Thanks. But since you were eleven, you get a pass." I smiled. "Besides, I wasn't exactly in a *receiving condolences* kind of mood. That's why I left so quickly after the service."

"Like I said, I get it." She took her hand off the keyboard and angled her chair toward mine. "You know why I don't think Rosa was bothered that you went so long without returning to the neighborhood?"

"Why?"

"Because she always knew you'd be back."

I hummed. "I certainly left with the idea that I never would, but obviously, I was young."

"Understandable. I had a moment when I considered attending college out of state. Nando is still in California, and Raymond plays in an orchestra in New York. Then I ended up in Eastern Washington and still got homesick."

"Honestly, if I'd had Michael and María as parents, I would have gotten homesick too."

She nodded. "You know they'd love to see you, right? Mamá and Pop."

"Yeah. I'll make sure to catch up with them soon. It's surreal being back. There's so much I've missed."

She folded her arms across her chest and blew out a long breath. "After Deck got out, the first thing he asked my family was not to tell you. When we told him it wouldn't be a problem because no one had heard from you since you left for college, he was surprised. I hadn't thought much about it myself. People leave, right? I'd looked for you on Facebook and Instagram, but—"

"I don't have social media."

"That's what I told Deck. He seemed upset, so I did a quick search and got the basics through your company website. Found out you were still in the area. When I suggested he try to contact you, he bit my head off. It's like he wanted to know you were okay, but he didn't want to see you."

That stung, but I understood more after seeing him last week. I thought about the unanswered letters I'd sent Deck before giving up.

"I don't know what to say, Mari." The nickname still felt familiar on my tongue. "When Deck got taken away... That night was just so awful—"

I didn't know how to finish, and Marisol didn't force me to.

"It was a crazy time when Deck first started getting settled. Once he bought that house and was talking to Johnny again, I figured you and he might cross paths, but it never happened. I hope you're not mad at me for not telling you? Deck was just so adamant. I didn't want to overstep or piss him off by reaching out myself. Since I hadn't seen you since middle school, I wasn't sure if you'd want that."

"Definitely not mad. And I'm sorry you felt like you couldn't reach out. I feel like such an asshole for staying away."

Marisol gave me a wry look, unfolding her arms and leaning in closer. "Cori, I realize I was just a kid back then, but I know there was *something* between you and my brother. What happened that night was terrible. No one can fault you for doing whatever you needed to. We all have our shit. And deep down, we all worry that the worst parts of our past aren't done with us."

I stared at her for a long moment before my lips turned up. "How long have you been waiting to say that to me?"

"Since Rosa said you were coming. Pretty good, huh?"

"Yeah. Pretty good." I shook my head. "Also, when did you stop calling your brother Artie?"

Sadness tinged her expression. "Since I got old and realized all his friends call him Deck," she said quietly. "We're still working on it, but I'd like to be that. His friend."

I pushed down the lump in my throat as something else occurred to me.

"Wait. You said you've been thinking of reaching out since Deck started talking to my brother. You've seen Johnny too?"

"Once. He was sleeping on the couch at Deck's when I went over to drop off some food. I didn't wake him up, though, so I'm not sure if it counts. I haven't actually spoken to him since we were kids."

"Deck told you what happened to him last weekend?"

"Yeah. I hope that's okay. Just the basics to me, my parents, and Emilio."

I had updated Deck on Johnny's entrance into rehab via the short, to-the-point texts we'd agreed on. It was reassuring to know his family cared too. Johnny needed all the people he could get.

I said as much to Marisol before adding, "A part of me thought turning my back on the neighborhood would allow me to reinvent myself. I didn't realize until recently how much I missed certain things—Rosa, the Center, being comfortable in my own skin. It's hard to believe you're not a little girl anymore."

"Well, you're here now. That's what matters."

I hmphed. "I wish Deck felt that way."

She winced. "It kills me to say it, but he's not the same person you remember. Besides the obvious trauma from being locked up, since he got out, it's like he's been determined to convince everyone what a bad guy he is."

"I got that message. He still blames himself for his friends and for what happened to me."

"*Mamacita*, he still blames himself for what happened to *me*." Marisol ran an impressive set of neon-hued acrylic nails over the shiny pink skin covering her face and neck. She'd had a ton of surgeries, but the left side of her mouth still tilted permanently downward a teensy bit, her most obvious scar.

"The fire was an accident," I said instinctively, something we'd all been telling Deck for as long as I could remember.

"*Exactamente*. And what happened with you was on Chi-chi, not our boys. Not to mention Johnny, Cruz, and Eliazar being responsible for their own decisions. But Deck is stubborn."

The picture became clearer. Therapy had helped me move on with my life but hadn't fully healed me. Only time could do that. Walking away from the neighborhood, from Everett, had created a protective layer. I'd insulated myself from everyone who knew, anyone who could remind me. Deck literally went to prison over Chi-chi. He hadn't been able to walk away or relegate it to some deep corner of his mind.

"I think it's good you're finally talking to Deck," Marisol said. "Even though it's because something terrible happened to Johnny. And I have a plan to get you two togeth—"

She never finished her thought because Rosa came back with an armful of files. We ended our conversation, but Marisol gave me the knowing look of someone who reserved the right to revisit the subject later.

———

I SPENT THE MORNING AND MOST of the afternoon going through the numbers. Rosa hadn't been exaggerating. The books were kept meticulously, but that didn't mean the news was great. Once I dug in, I realized there was an overreliance on government funding that was drying up, as well as gifts from foundations that had become significantly less generous over the years.

The Center had historically held a huge spring fundraising drive, but it didn't seem to have happened this year. They'd also missed a few newsletter mailings, which brought in small donations and kept the individual donor list fresh. They were in the final year of a major three-year grant, so that money would need to be replaced with something in the next fiscal year. And there weren't any major gifts on the horizon because Rosa hadn't been doing her handshaking and meeting new donors routine. A gala took place every year before Christmas. I'd need to check with Rosa's fundraiser, Ana, to make sure that the event was still on track.

The Center had enough money to make it through to the end of the year, but beyond that, the outlook was bleak.

I considered making a substantial donation myself. I could probably provide enough funding to get the Center through the next year or two, but that wouldn't be a long-term solution. Since getting bought out of JBC, I would be considered wealthy by many standards, but not to the extent that I could fund the Center indefinitely or establish a meaningful endowment.

Rubbing my temples, I thought about what to tell Rosa. The situation was critical, but I had to believe it wasn't so dire that things couldn't be salvaged. We just needed to find a new income source that would be stable in the long term. Plus, no more skipping newsletters and fundraising drives. Those went a long way toward keeping the Center sustainable.

I found her in the kitchen preparing for snack time. When I'd attended, many of the kids who came didn't eat very well at home, so Rosa always provided a "snack" that was more like a full meal. She pulled four sheets of baked ziti out of the ovens.

"Rosa?"

She wiped her hands on her apron after putting the trays on hot pads.

"*¿Qué te pareció, mija?*"

"Honestly, I think there's a lot of work to be done, but it's not a lost cause." Rosa brightened, coming over to give me a hug as I continued. "But I think you're gonna need more help. I know you want to be with Lupe, and of course you should be, but if this ship is going to get back on course, we can't keep letting the hole get bigger."

The corners of her eyes glistened. "I can't afford more help, *nena*."

I put my arm around her. "It's okay, Rosa. That's why you're going to let me come work here for a while as a volunteer. I'll be the extra pair of hands you need to support fundraising or programs or whatever, and you can do what you need to do for Lupe."

Rosa's internal struggle played out across her features. I knew her pride, but in the end, she'd do what was best for the Center.

"Please don't think of it as charity," I said. "I owe you a ton, and this is something I can do. The timing is right, and I know I can help." She still looked unconvinced, so I declared unapologetically, "You can't afford to turn me down, Rosa. Not if you want to save the Hope Center."

That did it. She nodded as a few of the tears she'd been holding back finally fell. "*Gracias, mija.*"

Chapter Eighteen
Cori

After a lengthy conversation, Rosa and I concluded that she would pay me a nominal consulting fee. It would likely come out to pennies per hour worked, but if it made her feel better to give me something, I could live with that.

Around two o'clock, the staff arrived to set up for the day. I gave Chuck a big hug when I saw he was still around. The rest of the team was mainly comprised of college students, although a few said they'd been there for years. There were also half a dozen volunteers. Marisol told me most of those folks came once or twice a week to lead specialty programs.

The local middle and high schools dismissed their students first, so teens started pouring into the building just before three o'clock.

I experienced déjà vu as the groups came in, laughing and messing around. The clothes and hair were different, but it was essentially the same as when I was a teenager. After spending all day at school worrying about whether I'd accidentally piss off the wrong person or get messed with because I had straight A's, I would come to the Center and finally be able to breathe. I saw that same relief on many of these kids' faces, especially the ones who immediately sat down at the table area and started doing their homework.

Half the teens went into the gym, and I heard the staff calling fouls and reminding them to watch their language. I laughed. Some things never changed.

Several dozen kids followed volunteers into learning labs for classes in knitting, guitar playing, and working on a digital drawing program in the computer lab. A few others flopped down on the couch in front of the TV, which remained off. Video games wouldn't be allowed for another hour. As they kept rolling in, depositing backpacks and coats in the cubbies along the wall, I stood by the desk. Being unfamiliar, I got a few suspicious glances, but no one spoke to me. I remembered that wariness.

Across the room, Rosa slipped into a chair next to a youth who appeared to be simply staring into space. The teen's nondescript jeans, T-shirt, and short, greasy brown hair were unremarkable, but the misery written across their facial features was stark.

"That's Reign." Marisol came up behind me. "They/them pronouns, extremely unsupportive family. I won't say more, but that part's no secret. I'm sure you'll get to know them since they're here every day. Sometimes we can get Reign into an activity, usually art, but mostly they just sort of sit."

"That's so sad," I whispered. Then put my hand over my mouth. I doubted Reign would welcome my pity.

"It's okay," Marisol said. "At least they're here, which is much safer than out there. And besides, there's always a chance things will improve. Maybe they can make a friend or find something they enjoy doing."

I hmphed. "Yeah, I remember. Rosa always used to say, 'Have a growth mindset. *Las cosas siempre pueden mejorar.*' If nothing else, Reign is getting Rosa clucking over them like a mother hen."

"Rosa is busy, but she makes time to talk to Reign every day. So do I." Marisol swung her hair over her shoulder. "Maybe after a while, you will too. They could use more people."

"I'd like that."

Back in the day, I'd been a decent volunteer. But as much as I wanted to connect with these kids, I'd cut myself off from the world they inhabited. I didn't want to claim credibility I no longer had.

"Don't worry about it right now." Marisol bopped me on the back with the ancient iPad she used to check the kids in. "You'll figure out your groove."

I nodded. She was right. Even if I couldn't connect with the kids on the same level as the rest of the staff here, I could still help the Center in my own way. I just had to find a few million dollars.

The elementary kids arrived a short time later, and the building was divided into two sections, with the younger kids occupying one side and the older kids the other. Since there was only one gym, they rotated through it. Everyone received a healthy serving of baked ziti with apple slices for a snack. I spent the afternoon wandering from room to room, getting a feel for the spaces and the activities.

Watching the staff interact with the kids, especially the mindful way they handled behavior issues, made me optimistic that the Center could be saved. Potential funders only needed to see this magic. They'd want to support it.

I knew many of the program participants dealt with serious challenges in life—socioeconomic hardship, criminal or gang-affiliated family members, relatives who were imprisoned, housing instability, or drug-addicted parents like my mom had been. Still, an overwhelming sense of optimism permeated the air. One wall was filled with plaques of Center kids and their colleges. I found my name on the list of students who'd attended the University of Washington. Other spaces were lined with pictures of former participants in their various adult jobs, from stockbroker to teacher to auto mechanic, as well as one '90s-era city councilperson from Everett. No matter the circumstances of their lives, good things happened for kids inside these walls.

I had to help Rosa save it.

Doing my second turn up and down the halls, I stopped to watch a group of elementary kids with the guitar teacher struggle through the world's most adorable rendition of Bob Marley's "Three Little Birds."

That was when an older teen came tearing down the hall. He smashed his fists against the bulletin boards and ripped down posters as he went.

At the front door, he shouted into the atrium, "Fuck you and fuck this place!" Before shoving his way out, he turned around and raised both hands in a double middle finger salute. "See you later, assholes!"

I froze, mildly stunned. Marisol came up on my right side. "Oh, hey, Cori. I didn't realize you were still here." She noticed my eyes trained on the teen now running out onto the sidewalk. "Don't worry about Jayden," she said. "He has meltdowns like that once a week at least. He'll be okay."

I couldn't believe how casual she sounded.

"What happened?" I asked.

"Chuck called him for a couple of fouls in the 3-on-3 tournament. He disagreed."

She and everyone else in the building seemed unconcerned by Jayden's outburst, so I took my cues from them. It had been a while since I'd existed in a world where teenagers hurling obscenities wasn't a genuine cause for alarm.

I had once gotten frustrated in a meeting early in my career at JBC and accidentally tossed the pen I'd been tapping across the conference table. One of our analysts looked at me in horror, as though I'd flung a vial of pig's blood and not a ten-cent Bic. Later, she informed me she had Midol in her purse if I needed it. I'd smiled and thanked her, and it was the last time I displayed any strong emotions at work.

I bet that analyst had gone to a high school with working drinking fountains.

"It's getting quiet," I observed, realizing it was past six. Most of the kids had left or gotten picked up by their families.

"Yeah, we're almost closed. Come to think of it, it's a good thing you're still here." Marisol looked side to side before grabbing my arm and pulling me toward a corner. "Rosa is in the office on the phone with Lupe. Since we have a minute, I want to talk to you about something I'd rather she didn't hear."

Her tone had my spine tensing. "Alright. What's up?"

"Look, I didn't want to burden her with this, but Chuck told me a few days ago that we need to deal with some building things."

"What do you mean 'building things'?"

"I mean, we've been putting off some maintenance projects, but Chuck and I don't think we can any longer."

I glanced around. The facility was certainly old and showing some wear and tear, but it was a youth center, not a five-star hotel. Some dinginess was to be expected. "What kind of projects?"

"As far as I know, nothing huge, but a lot of little things that could turn into bigger problems if we let them."

"Such as?"

"Like a few of the toilets in the gym bathrooms don't work, so we're down to one stall. Obviously, it's disgusting by the end of the day." Marisol made a fake puking gesture.

My cheek ticked up. "What did the plumber say?"

"Haven't called one. Rosa usually handles those types of issues, but she's gone so much lately. Also, we don't have the money to hire anyone, even if she were to delegate the task. We put *Out of Order* signs on the stalls and called it good for now."

I could understand that. The staff was stretched thin, and I'd seen enough of the books to know they'd exhausted their meager yearly maintenance budget.

"Anything else?" I asked.

"Yeah. The freezer isn't maintaining the correct temperature and needs to be looked at. The foam padding on the bottom of the play structure needs to be replaced. The sprinklers on the field don't work. The rubber nonslip stuff on the stairs is peeling off. There are a few holes in the drywall from when things got a little *interesting* between some of the high schoolers. The mirror in the computer lab bathroom is cracked. One van won't start, and they all need an oil change. Baseboards are coming up all over the place. The north court basketball hoop looks like its bolts are coming out of the wall. The atrium roof leaks a little bit when it rains hard. A shelf in the art supply closet collapsed. Some of the outlets don't work. The fluorescents in the main hallway flicker, giving off major haunted house vibes. We tried changing the bulbs, but it didn't work, so I'm guessing the issue is with the ballasts. And the faucet on the maintenance sink shoots water everywhere." She snapped her fingers. "Oh, I almost forgot. The dryer doesn't dry the clothes. It just sort of tumbles them around."

"Jeez, is that all?"

"I might have seen a roach in the kitchen." Marisol snickered.

"And Rosa doesn't know any of this?"

"On some level she knows, and of course we always have stuff like this going on. But I don't think she realizes how bad it's gotten lately. Putting off minor projects is nothing new, except that we're reaching a critical point here. It's just that she's so overwhelmed with Lupe already..."

I met Marisol's eyes in understanding. Nobody wanted to force Rosa to think about building maintenance when she had more important things to focus on.

"Okay," I said. "I agree about not worrying Rosa. It would be different if the building were about to collapse, but it sounds like we just need to call a handyman or something before it gets totally out of control."

"Yeah, but that's not exactly in the budget."

The straightforward solution was for me to simply hire someone and pay for it. But I had a feeling that would cause Rosa and her stubborn pride even more stress. I knew she hadn't invited me to look at the Center's books just so I'd throw money at the deficit. She wanted a partner, not a patron. I didn't want to create a weird vibe between us where she felt she "owed" me. That would make it a lot more difficult for me to help implement a plan for long-term sustainability.

Maybe I could pay someone to come in, but keep it a secret from Rosa? That was tricky, but it could work.

Or maybe I could find someone to do the work for free? There had to be someone who loved the Center who also happened to be a licensed plumber or electrician.

I was about to ask Marisol about it when she suggested, "You should ask Deck."

"Huh?"

"Deck. Now that he's not being an idiot and trying to hide his existence from you and all that. I almost called him myself after Chuck talked to me, but then Rosa told me you agreed to help out, and I realized it would be the perfect opportunity to force you two to speak to one another."

I gave her a dry look as a memory of her making *kissy* noises at Deck and me on the couch when she was eight came back to me.

"Deck works in construction?"

"He didn't tell you?"

"No." Recalling Deck's truck and the J&D Construction hoodie, I realized I should have put it together. Then again, I'd been distracted by Johnny.

"He's a contractor. He owns a business with his friend Juan. They've done really well. Mostly big projects, commercial stuff, so being a handyman for the Center wouldn't exactly be in his wheelhouse, but he loves Rosa, so I bet he'd work *gratis*."

Gratis was what we needed. It seemed like a perfect solution, but I hesitated. Deck had been so insistent on boundaries. Then again, this was important. And we *were* fake married.

"You think he would do it?"

"*Sí*. You know how he is. That part hasn't changed."

I nodded. She was talking about her brother's enormous heart. The one he hid from the world, but which had always been crystal clear to Marisol and me. When we were younger, lots of people had seen Deck's slicked-back ponytail and white tank tops, heard his street accent, or watched him strut down his block, and assumed he was up to no good.

But Arturo Decker had been the first person to put on a tiara whenever Marisol wanted to play princesses. Anytime he saw me walking home from school, he came up next to me and slipped my backpack onto his shoulder. He helped my mom stir pasta when her hands shook too badly to do it, and he stuck up for Eliazar whenever someone uttered homophobic nonsense.

Sure, Deck had made mistakes, but if I wasn't defined by that terrible night with Chi-chi, then neither was he.

Despite his tough exterior, at his core Deck was a big-hearted teddy bear with an instinct to protect people and an innate inclination toward kindness. No doubt prison had hardened him, but I'd gotten enough of a vibe over the past week to know that it hadn't stomped out that part of his nature.

Which was good. Because I needed to convince that big heart of his to fix some toilets.

Chapter Nineteen
Deck

I pulled my truck into the parking lot in front of the Center and killed the engine. My fingers gripped the steering wheel as I stared at the toolbox resting on the passenger seat. I'd drag my ass into the building soon enough, but first, I needed a minute.

My older sisters and my brother Raymond had gone to the Center regularly as kids. So had Marisol once she was medically allowed. I'd always been too cool for it. I still knew Rosa from the neighborhood, and she and Mamá had grown closer since I got locked up, but the building itself was mostly a mystery.

There were snippets of connection, though. The front steps where I'd sat with Cori while she talked to me about school. The bike rack where Eliazar used to lock up his old BMX. The massive parking lot where Pop taught me to drive a stick shift.

The Center was part of the collective memory of all the kids who grew up around here. Whether you attended there your whole life or only went to play baseball or go to summer camp, you knew about it. At the very least, you knew other kids who went. This stayed true even as the outskirts of the neighborhood gentrified.

Unlike the McDonald's that turned into a fancy hot pot restaurant, and the old apartments they tore down to build boxy condo buildings, the Center had stood for generations.

That was why I'd agreed when Cori texted last week and asked me to help fix it up.

Her messages had been short and to the point. She'd spoken to Marisol and hoped I could do some free building repairs while she helped Rosa sort out the place's finances. After talking with my sister, I got more details about what was going on. I'd known about Lupe's illness from Mamá, but Rosa had done a great job concealing the Center's money troubles.

Initially, I thought maybe Juan could do the work. But when I asked him, he reminded me of the conversation we had at Tubby's, telling me again I needed to stop avoiding Cori.

"You need to clear the air with her, *hermano*," Juan had said. "It's not just about repairing the drywall." Pointing to his head, he added, "You need to fix up here."

"I know. It's just... Sometimes it's hard to know how we even got to this place." I stuffed my hands in my pockets.

"*Amigo*, you know I have so much love for you, so I'm telling you this as your friend because I'm tired of having the same conversation. You need to move on. Figure this out. You're so stuck blaming yourself for the past that you've barely been living since you got out."

I glanced sideways at him. "That's not true. I have our business. My house."

"A business you let me make all the big decisions on. We're supposed to be partners, and you act like I'm gonna walk if you don't agree with me on everything. And you still haven't unpacked those boxes in your house. You get up, work, go home. You're still living like you're in a cage—"

"*Bien. Bastante.*" I dug my fingernails into my palms. "I know."

Juan put his hand on my shoulder. "You're allowed to have a life, Deck. Go to the Center. Spend some time with Cori. See that she's alright. Maybe get to know her again as grown-ups. Your baby sister, too. And do something good for the neighborhood while you're at it."

He was right. I'd been keeping myself from having to face her recovery. Her resilience. To admit it might be okay for both of us to move on.

I exhaled and got out of the truck. At the glass-walled entrance, I hit the button, and Marisol let me in.

"So good to see you, big brother." She came around and gave me a hug, always holding on a little longer than anyone else did.

"Thanks, squirt." I held up my toolbox as I glanced around the brightly decorated atrium. "Where should I start? I want to make a list of everything you need, but I'm hoping to knock some easy things out today."

She laughed. "Glad to see you're all business. Chuck should be here in about ten minutes, and he can take you on a walk-through. For now, why don't you head into the office—last door at the end of the second hallway—and check in with Cori." A vibrating sensation bubbled under my skin. Despite my decision to stop actively staying away from her, I hadn't expected to face Cori five minutes after getting out of my truck. My hesitation must have shown on my face because Marisol added, "Deck, you need to rip the Band-Aid off. It won't help anyone if you two are awkward around each other. Go say hi. That's all you need to do. Geesh."

My annoying baby sister had a point. No time like the present. Heading to the hallway, I tried to act cool. Inside, my gut churned.

At the open office door, I saw Cori hunched over a laptop on the desk, humming confidently as she looked down at the screen and made notes on a yellow legal pad.

I knocked on the doorframe.

Her eyes lifted, and I swallowed down my instant reaction to her sky-blue gaze.

She was so beautiful.

Memories flooded my mind. So many times in the past we'd locked eyes like this. Sitting next to her on the couch laughing at a movie, or across Mamá's table as she helped me with schoolwork. Moments when I'd felt everything and said nothing.

I wasn't sure what to say now. I'd behaved badly since she'd shown up on my doorstep, and I needed to reverse course.

The last time I'd seen her, at the hospital with Johnny, our parting had been strained, with me declaring again that we should limit any non-essential contact. I didn't know how to dive into being *friendlier*. My only actual plan was to not be a dick.

Then I remembered the hospital had given us a bit of a roadmap, even if it was for show.

"Hey, wife," I deadpanned.

She startled, head snapping back slightly. When I didn't say anything else, a hint of a smile appeared on her face.

"Yikes. Did Artie Decker just make a joke?"

I shrugged, attempting to return the smile. "Marisol told me to let you know I was here and ready to work. Chuck can take me around when he gets in. That will give me an idea of what equipment I need to bring next time and how long everything will take. And the weather's good today, so if there's stuff outside that needs doing, I might start there..."

Shifting my weight from one foot to the other, I glanced away briefly before meeting those azure eyes again.

Her brows furrowed. "The weather..."

"Uh-huh. Checked my app in the car. Should stay clear all morning."

"Well, then...I guess that's...a smart plan."

I tugged my collar. "So I'll circle back around with you to go over everything and come up with a repair list once Chuck and I talk?"

Cori stared at me. "It'll be good to know exactly what's needed," she finally replied, voice stilted.

"Really, really good," I agreed, trying for enthusiasm, but my high-pitched voice and wide eyes might have tipped into crazy territory. ¡*Mierda*! Why was it so hard to talk to her like a normal person?

Her expression narrowed. "Alright, Deck, what's going on?"

"What?"

"You know what. You only talked to me under duress last time I saw you, making a big deal about *boundaries*, and now it's like you've been body snatched." She leaned back in her chair and folded her arms across her chest.

I inhaled, taking a few strides closer to the desk.

"Look, Cori," I spoke hesitantly. "I thought a lot about it since we last talked, and... I'm sorry. For a lot of things, but especially for not telling you I was back in town." Her eyes shot lasers at me, but I forced myself not to retreat. "I'm working through some shit... but we have a lot of history, not to mention people in common, and I realized that my avoiding you can't be our new normal. Neither can barely speaking. So I'm trying here."

"Just like that?"

"Not just like that. I told you I've been thinking about it. A lot." I tilted my head from side to side before rolling my shoulders. "I want us to be able to be in the same room together."

She sat up straight. "Obviously, I want that too, Deck. It's just a total one-eighty from how you were a week ago." She shook her head, putting her hands against the edge of the desk before rolling her chair back a few feet. "You know what? Never mind. I'm too busy to overthink this. I'll take this *realization* of yours no matter how it happened." She steepled her fingers together. "I accept your apology. And I think it would be great for you to talk to Chuck and then let me know the plan for repairs."

I nodded as a low cracking sound split the air.

That was all the warning Cori got before the two back casters of her chair disconnected from the bottom, causing it to tilt backward. Her arms flailed as she tried—and failed—to grab the desk. Racing to her side, I caught her elbow before she could fall, pulling her up against me as the chair toppled over with a crash.

In the stunned silence that followed, she let out a whoosh of air, and I felt the heat where her palm rested against my chest.

"Well, that was exciting." She chuffed nervously. "Can you please add *fix office chair* to your list?"

I pushed back a strand of red-gold hair that had fallen across her face. "You okay?" I asked softly.

"Mm-hmm." She pressed her fingers lightly against my T-shirt before stepping back as I released her.

Cori pulled out a folding chair from next to a filing cabinet and set it up behind the desk, pushing the broken one to the side. I kneeled to glance at it, quickly diagnosing that the casters were bent beyond repair. On the bright side, the almost-fall seemed to have distracted her from asking more questions about my change of heart.

I stepped toward the hallway. "I'll see about new casters for your chair."

"Thank you." She looked back down at the papers on the desk, mumbling under her breath, "You may turn out to be an okay husband after all."

I hurried out the door. Not thinking too hard about the way her words made my breath catch.

CHUCK'S PROJECT LIST KEPT ME BUSY into the afternoon. Most things would need to wait until I had a chance to visit the hardware store, but I spent a productive morning outside, tightening up loose elements on the play structures and replacing missing steps on the bleachers. After lunch, I got the heat in the dryer working and patched a few holes in the drywall. Some larger repairs would require multiple days of work. Of those, I decided to start with the broken toilets, which had been leaking so long I needed to replace a section of the subfloor underneath before installing new ones. During our walk-through, I also discovered multiple issues Chuck hadn't noticed until I pointed them out.

Marisol found me spackling drywall cracks in the music room.

"Thanks so much, *hermano*. The kids will be here soon. I didn't know if you'd want to stay or come back another day."

My cheeks grew hot. "Am I...allowed to stay? You know, with the kids here?"

It took Marisol a moment to understand. "Oh, Deck." Her face softened. "We have your background check because you're in the building. But since you're not a direct service volunteer and won't be alone with youth, your record doesn't matter. You would need a Class A felony to get booted entirely."

I didn't want to feel ashamed. I'd done my time and gotten out early, taking every opportunity to get an education while I was in to ensure I wouldn't be back. I also had no regrets about putting Chi-chi in the hospital for a month. That motherfucker deserved everything he got. Although I was a little sorry for breaking Aaron's wrist.

"I'll stay if you're sure it won't be a problem. I kind of want to get an idea of how the kids use the space. It might help me identify other potential issues."

"Yeah, Chuck mentioned you found a few things he hadn't caught."

"My eyes went straight to the baseboards. I need to replace all that old wood with rubber. I remember getting mad and kicking the baseboards at school when I was a kid. Apparently, nothing has changed."

Marisol grinned. "They do love to destroy shit—excuse me, *stuff*. I need to put my *after two o'clock* language hat on. We go through a lot of Ping-Pong balls. Occasionally even a snapped pool stick. Good thing we love them anyway."

I watched my sister in her element, trailing her around the atrium as she unlocked doors and put out equipment. My parents had mentioned how much Marisol enjoyed her job. She'd worked for Rosa since graduating from college a year ago.

As the teens poured in through the front doors, Marisol checked them in and asked about their days. They answered easily and asked their own questions about the upcoming teen late night. Some of the older kids came in hot, apologizing when she reminded them to watch their language.

"She's so good with them." My skin prickled with awareness at Cori's voice. I hadn't seen her since this morning when I'd held her against me.

"Yeah." I kept my gaze glued to Marisol.

One strutting loudmouth, who looked about fourteen, reminded me of myself at that age. Tussling with his friends, he accidentally knocked the tablet out of Marisol's hands. I lurched forward instinctively until I felt Cori's grip on my wrist. "Watch," she whispered.

Marisol didn't even have to speak. She simply raised an eyebrow at the kid. He leaned down to pick up the device and handed it to her with a contrite, "Sorry, Miss Mari," before bouncing off.

"I forget she's grown up sometimes," I admitted softly. "Even though she's pretty fucking awesome at being an adult."

"At least you've had a chance to get used to it. When I first saw her, I almost didn't recognize her." Cori laughed. Leaning into my ear, she whispered, "Also, don't say fucking."

Dios, Cori, how about you don't lean into my ear and say fucking.

I turned, giving her a sheepish look before realizing our faces were inches apart. "Sorry."

"It's okay. Must be a Decker trait because I've noticed Marisol drop a few choice words herself this week." Breaking our eye contact, Cori made her way to sit behind the front counter.

Not knowing what else to do, I followed. "Where is Rosa?" I asked.

"Home with Lupe. I told her I could fill in during program time however much she wanted me to. I've been here every day for over a week now, so I feel pretty comfortable with the kids and the routine. It's like muscle memory, too, from when I volunteered back in the day."

"Marisol said it's okay that I'm around when the kids are here."

"Of course," she replied quickly, confused. Then she caught on to why I'd mentioned it. "Deck, be real. If we said that people who'd spent time on the inside couldn't come into the building, half these kids' parents wouldn't be able to pick them up. No one's gonna look sideways at you here."

She appeared thoughtful for a moment before her mouth turned down.

"What?" I asked.

"Nothing," she said, booting up the ancient desktop computer in front of her. "Actually, something about my old job. What you said made me realize not a lot of grace was given when people made mistakes... I'm having an epiphany that that was chaotic in its own way."

Epiphany. Good thing we'd done her flash cards.

I recalled her saying that she'd recently left the company she'd helped found. Or maybe I'd heard that from Johnny. Either way, I didn't know too much about Cori's career, only that it was in tech, and she'd made a lot of money.

"A cutthroat corporate thing, huh?" I questioned.

"I guess." She peered up, looking like she wanted to say more, but didn't. After a moment, she switched topics. "Chuck mentioned that you have quite the honey-do list."

A brief laugh escaped my throat. "Haven't heard that phrase in a while. I forgot you can be such a grandma sometimes."

She took no offense. "Well, since you are my *husband*...the honey-do phrase fits."

"It's a long list, but I'll manage. I might need to bring in an electrician at some point, but I'll see what Juan says."

"Juan. He's your business partner?"

"Business partner, friend, life coach, mentor, occasional therapist, reliable ride to the airport. Dealer's choice." Cori smiled as I stepped away from the counter. "I'm going to wander around a bit. See if I can sus out anything else that needs doing."

I watched a group of boys play pickup in the gym while Chuck did his best to keep them in line. One of the older teens dominated the game, running circles around everyone else. He kept a mean mug on his face, practically daring someone to mess with him.

Reminded me of Cruz.

Moving back into the atrium, I plopped down on one of the couches, putting my head in my hands. I didn't want to think about Cruz right now, rotting away in prison.

I rubbed my eye sockets a few times before glancing up.

And seeing...*Eliazar*?

But of course, it couldn't be him. He'd been gone for eight years. The kid standing in front of me looked a lot like Eliazar, though—short and slight, with clothes that didn't fit quite right. Except this teen didn't have my old friend's shy smile. This face was a storm cloud.

"Hello?" I said to not-Eliazar.

"You're on my cushion."

I glanced down at the couch. "I'm sorry?"

"Can you get up, *please?*" The last word came through gritted teeth. "That's my part of the couch. I always sit there. Every day."

I stood. "Sorry. I'm, uh, new around here."

Not-Eliazar sank down on the seat I'd vacated. Something compelled me to sit in a nearby chair.

"I'm Deck," I offered.

Not-Eliazar stared at me, obviously wondering why I hadn't left.

"I'm Marisol's brother," I tried again.

The kid let out a deep sigh, as though to emphasize the amount of suffering caused by my presence. "I'm Reign. R-E-I-G-N. I'm nonbinary. My pronouns are they/them, and if you have a problem with that, you can fuck right off."

They crossed their arms.

I nodded, blowing out a long breath. "Alright, Reign. That was... very informative. And I'm cool with whatever gender you are. Makes no difference to me."

The pronoun thing seemed to have happened while I was locked up. I'd gotten a thorough education on it when Juan and I did a major roof repair at a local college.

Reign hmphed, still eyeing me with suspicion. "I didn't know Miss Mari had another brother. One came in here a while ago. A cop."

I settled into the lumpy chair. "That's our brother Emilio. We have three older brothers, including him, and two older sisters."

"Are you a cop too?"

I choked out a laugh. "Um, no." My jaw flexed. "I'm not the cop brother. Or the musician brother—that's Raymond—or the pharmacist brother—that's Nando. I'm her other brother, the construction worker." *The ex-con fuckup.*

"Bet," Reign said, whatever that meant. They tilted their head. "Can you fix the toilets in the bathroom over there? It sucks that only one works."

"Yeah. It's first on my list, actually. I also have a bunch of other projects, so if you notice anything, please tell me. I'll be around. You Center kids probably know a lot more than I do about this place."

"That's for sure." Reign's shoulders eased slightly. "Maybe I can watch you do some stuff?"

"Sure, if it's not too dangerous. And if Marisol's okay with it. You interested in construction?"

"Maybe."

I glanced at the front desk and caught Cori and my sister staring at me, open-mouthed. *Shit. Was I doing something wrong?*

"I think I need to go talk to my sister, Reign. It was nice meeting you."

The pained look returned to the teen's face, and they turned away at my departure.

"*Lo siento,*" I said to Marisol, walking over to her. "I know you said I couldn't be alone with the kids, but I didn't realize I wasn't supposed to talk to them. I promise it won't hap—"

"What the hell was that!?" my sister whisper-shouted.

"Huh?"

"You were talking to Reign," Cori supplied.

"Yeah. Like I said, I'm sorry about that, I—"

"No, *idiota*," Mari intoned. "You were *talking to Reign*. Reign doesn't speak to anybody except Rosa. They don't have any friends. Nothing. And you were just, like, talking with them?"

"I didn't know," I mumbled, conscious of not drawing Reign's attention to our conversation. "I just looked up and they were there, and they reminded me of—"

"Eliazar," Cori hushed out. "I thought it was just me."

Marisol's hand flew to her mouth. "Oh my gosh. I never caught it, but of course the resemblance is there. *Dios.* No wonder Rosa has been so protective."

A twinge traveled down my spine. "Does Reign get along with their parents?" I asked.

Marisol shifted uncomfortably. "No. Their parents don't accept that they're nonbinary."

I glanced at Reign, but my mind saw Eliazar. Eliazar being used by men. Eliazar being rejected by his parents. Eliazar never feeling like he fit in, even with us, his brothers.

Eliazar, who I'd never see again.

My heart thudded as I watched Reign sit by themselves on the couch. Dozens of kids walked by, ignoring them. Reign remained stone-faced and silent, taking it.

I hadn't noticed Cori step behind me until I felt her hands on my shoulders. She leaned close to my ear, like she'd done earlier. Her steady voice grounded me as she said, "They're not Eliazar, Deck."

"Not yet." I closed my eyes.

"Not ever," Cori said. "That's why we're all here."

Letting myself lean into her touch was dangerous. But I did it anyway.

Our closeness was as comforting as I remembered.

It felt like I hadn't taken a truly deep breath in a dozen years, the kind where you exhaled something other than air. Where you pushed out some of the shit buried so deep, you thought it would always be a part of you.

I closed my eyes, turning my face to Cori's and resting my chin on her hand.

"Just so I'm clear—I *am* allowed to talk to Reign, right?" I asked quietly. "As long as we're in an area with other people?"

"That's right," Marisol replied, clearing her throat, reminding me that Cori and I weren't alone. My sister eyed us but didn't comment on how close we stood.

"*Bien*. Then, if they're willing, I'll talk to them more, okay? You know, since I'm here," I said.

"Sounds like an excellent idea." Cori squeezed my shoulders one last time before pulling away.

I breathed out a little more.

Chapter Twenty
Cori

I t felt like I'd barely seen my best friends Britta and Marcus since I'd gone looking for Johnny three weeks ago. Resuming our Sunday brunch ritual finally gave us the chance to catch up, something I didn't know how much I needed until I felt a sense of fondness, bordering on relief, watching Britta putter around my kitchen.

"You're enjoying spending time in Everett again?" she asked, unboxing cranberry orange scones onto a ceramic platter. Marcus had stepped outside to take a work call.

I traced the seam of a potholder with my fingers. I'd been so busy that I hadn't stopped to consider how much my life had transformed in less than a month, let alone whether I was enjoying it. With some surprise, I realized I felt...okay. Good, even. I was still worried about my brother, and Deck confused the hell out of me, but on balance, it felt like I'd made the right decision going back.

"I'm not sure 'enjoying' is the word I'd use." Reaching into the oven, I pulled out a quiche. "It's like, I went years without even dipping a toe in and now, all of a sudden, the old neighborhood is a huge part of my life again—first looking for Johnny, then working at the Center." I deposited the pie tin on a hot pad. "But I guess it's reassuring to know I can still fit in after all this time."

Britta smiled encouragingly before handing me a mimosa that was at least two-thirds champagne.

Ten minutes and two scones later, we were discussing the never-ending saga of the 1910s bungalow she and Marcus had been living in and rehabbing for years. As she recounted the headaches of having solar panels installed, I nodded sympathetically, so glad we'd made the time to catch up.

The topic turned to work, as it always did. Britta lamented the office politics of Marcus's and her engineering firm. The familiar stories sparked memories of JBC, but as we weaved between talking about my former company, her job, and my current role at the Center, having a conversation touch on both my adult life and childhood didn't faze me. I even offered an anecdote about flooding the kitchen at the Center as a fifteen-year-old when I'd unknowingly used countertop dish soap in the dishwasher. In my defense, I'd never had a dishwasher at home.

If Britta noticed my unusual openness about my teen years, she didn't comment, listening attentively while occasionally glancing at her husband, who continued to pace my deck.

Through the glass slider door, we watched Marcus gesturing wildly with one hand as he held his phone with the other, grinning at his penchant for animated hand-talking.

Marcus had been my college boyfriend. We'd even been engaged briefly following graduation. A year after realizing we were better off as friends, he fell in love with Britta. They were the only people in my grown-up life who knew the details about my childhood. Not the super gritty stuff, like Chi-chi, but the basics.

They knew about the trailer park, my mom, Johnny, and growing up poor. And they knew I didn't like to discuss it.

But neither of them knew about Deck.

Neither of them knew that having him back in my life again was probably the most *different* thing about this past month.

I'd filled Britta and Marcus in on Johnny's overdose and HIV diagnosis, but I was vague about the man who helped me find him, saying only that he was someone my brother and I knew as kids.

Britta placed her hand on mine as we sat across the counter. "Cori, it's good seeing you like this. Lighter somehow. I know you struggled with your decision to leave JBC, but it seems as though everything's turned out okay."

The slider glass rattled as Marcus came inside, slipping his phone into his back pocket.

"Everything okay at the office?" Britta asked, handing him a drink.

"Fine. Just some interpersonal shit between our new interns, and honestly, nothing that couldn't have waited until Monday." He sounded incredibly irritated, and I recalled how this hard, corporate version of Marcus used to scare me sometimes.

Britta had no such reaction. "Well, you're the dum-dum who took the call, so you don't get to complain about being the employee crisis line."

Marcus's features softened at his wife's playful tone. "You're right, as usual. So let's forget I picked up and get back to whatever you two were talking about."

Before I could answer, Britta said, "We were discussing how Cori is starting to loosen up a little."

Marcus chuckled gently at me. "I'm still having trouble computing that you turned down TremMark. That you're willingly unemployed. Never would have called that."

"And that's a good thing," Britta said decisively. "Letting yourself get lost can be empowering. Helps you discover new pathways and all that."

"You're right that I'm trying to be more open to possibilities," I conceded, choosing my words carefully. "But to be fair, there's not too much uncertainty, at least in the short term. I'm focused on being there for Johnny and Rosa."

My mind went to Deck. All the *possibilities* there.

Marcus eyed me pensively. "Do you remember what I said when I broke our engagement?"

Huh? The random question jarred me from my thoughts. I glanced at Britta. Her chill when it came to the history between me and her husband always impressed me. She appeared more amused than anything.

"You said lots of things," I answered Marcus dryly. "Can you be more specific?"

He ignored my snark. "On the day we split, I wanted to find something, anything, to get a rise out of you. You were so calm. It infuriated me."

"You wanted me to scream at you?"

"We were together for years, and I never saw you be anything other than cool and methodical. Hell, the only time I ever heard you raise your voice was to yell at the TV during a Mariners game."

"I remember. You called me a robot. You said that you didn't think we should get married because I wasn't looking for a husband to love. I was looking for a husband because I thought it was time to get married."

Marcus nodded. "Right. I didn't want to be some box you checked off on a list. And the robot comment—that's what I was getting at just now."

Annoyance threatened, but we'd rehashed this many times. "What do you mean?"

"I'm reminding you that you were willing to undermine your own happiness to stick to some convoluted plan. You would have married me even though we didn't love each other the right way. And I knew it was because of how you'd grown up even though you never talked about it. You just wanted stability. To be settled." Marcus patted the back of my hand. "Maybe this new willingness to be more uncertain, or even just talk about Everett without shutting down, signals a change. When I ended our engagement, I had to force you away from your plan. Now it's like you're finally trying to figure out what you really want. As your friend, I want you to find a life that makes you scream sometimes. Or at least clicks you out of robot mode." He squeezed my fingers.

My thoughts returned to Deck. He certainly made me want to scream. And our relationship was definitely unsettling. Then and now. Being around him made me feel anything but *robotic*.

Britta stared at me keenly. "Where did your mind just go, Cori?"

I shook my head, taking a long swig of my mimosa. "Nowhere." I turned to Marcus. "When did you become such a sage?"

"I have my moments."

"You certainly do," Britta agreed, patting Marcus's ass.

I rolled my eyes as my phone buzzed.

GRAHAM EVANS: Hi Cori. I hope it's okay I'm texting you.

The visual of Graham's name on my phone made my brain tilt sideways. We hadn't spoken since the party on my last day at JBC. Recovering, I replied.

ME: Hi Graham. Totally fine to text. Is everything okay? I hope the JBC folks are settling in at TremMark.

GRAHAM EVANS: All things considered, I'd say it's going smoothly.

I gave my screen a puzzled look, walking away from Marcus and Britta.

ME: That's good to hear. Did you need something else, then?

ME: I hope it isn't to offer me a job again. Because I'm even more sure of my decision to leave.

GRAHAM EVANS: I really admire you sticking to your guns. Like I said, there will always be a job here for you if you want it, but that wasn't why I texted.

ME: ?

GRAHAM EVANS: Yikes. I'm sorry I'm making such a muck of this.

GRAHAM EVANS: The truth is, I've been trying to think of a good reason to reach out, but since it's been three weeks and I can't come up with one, I decided to just shoot my shot. Cards on the table, I was hoping you'd have dinner with me.

My eyes widened.

ME: You're asking me out?

Not the smoothest reply, but my fingers typed before my mind could catch up.

GRAHAM EVANS: Yes. That's why I texted on a Sunday. Because this is personal, not business.

ME: On a date?

GRAHAM EVANS: Yes. If you'd like to.

I pinched the bridge of my nose, picturing the attractive man I'd liked from the start of TremMark's buyout of JBC. With everything going on, Graham reaching out to ask me to dinner had not been on my radar. I'd barely dated since Marcus, loath to try again after having my carefully curated life upset by his refusal to enter into a passionless marriage. After we'd split, I'd turned the entirety of my drive into building a successful career.

Perhaps it wouldn't be such a bad idea to put myself out there.

But Graham? While it was true I hadn't felt a spark with him, maybe that was because I'd been denying that side of myself for so long.

I must have waited too long to respond because my phone shook again.

GRAHAM EVANS: I'm sorry if I was too forward in asking. You can feel free to delete this conversation, and if we ever see each other again, we can pretend it never happened.

ME: Sorry. I just have a lot going on right now. It's been hectic since I left JBC.

GRAHAM EVANS: I understand. No problem.

ME: No. I'm not blowing you off.

ME: It really has been hectic.

ME: I wouldn't mind getting together and telling you about it. Maybe over coffee?

GRAHAM EVANS: Just name the time and place.

ME: Coffee. Not dinner. And just so we're clear, let's not call it a date. I'm not ready for that right now.

GRAHAM EVANS: We'll call it coffee. And no pressure.

ME: I'll text next week once I figure it out.
GRAHAM EVANS: Looking forward to it.

I walked back into the kitchen.

"Well, you're certainly looking...perplexed," Britta said. "Who was that?"

"A colleague. He wanted to, um, ask me out."

Britta's eyes widened. "What? Who? Are you gonna go?"

"One of the TremMark execs. Nice guy named Graham. I'm going to meet him for coffee. Not a date."

"That's wonderful." Britta clapped her hands.

Marcus peered at me skeptically. "You don't seem too enthusiastic."

"Honestly, I never really thought of Graham that way before. But after you guys talked about how great it is not to plan everything out, I figure maybe I should say *yes* to something unexpected for a change."

"That's true," Marcus drawled. "But don't forget the part about how you were willing to settle for something *less than* with me. It's fine getting out there, but..." He twined his fingers with Britta's. "I found the person who makes me feel fireworks all the time. Not box-checking. That's the goal."

Britta kissed him on the cheek. "You are so getting laid tonight." She turned to me. "Marcus is right, love. You deserve fireworks."

"Alright, I get it." I put the scones on the table. "But how about we eat and talk about something other than me and my love life or how I'm unclenching or whatever? I want to hear more about solar panels..."

We spent the next hour discussing their house woes and Marcus's refereeing of his interns. Inwardly, I thought about how Britta and Marcus didn't know I'd already found the person who made me feel *fireworks*.

They didn't know about the invigorating whiplash I'd gotten interacting with him these past few weeks. How he'd infuriated me at the hospital. How I'd shuddered touching his chest when he rescued me from a broken chair. The way it felt watching him be kind to Reign.

I could easily fall for Deck again. Even when we were off-kilter and tense, he made me feel alive in a way no one else ever had.

But we'd just gotten back in the groove of communicating. Upsetting that balance seemed imprudent. Especially with Johnny in rehab. And even if the timing had been perfect, if by some miracle Deck admitted what had always been between us and wanted to explore it, I didn't know if I could go down that road.

Losing Deck the first time almost broke me, and I'd never truly had him.

Twenty minutes after Britta and Marcus left, there was a knock on my door. I blew out a distracted breath as I went to open it.

"What happened? Did you leave your phone aga—"

Johnny stood on my porch.

CHAPTER TWENTY-ONE
Deck

Cori's neighborhood wasn't too different from mine. The houses looked mostly the same, other than these were closer together and cost half a million dollars more. And I lived in the suburbs, so there were chain restaurants and parking lots and strip malls. The block along the main arterial before I turned onto Cori's street had an Irish bar and two restaurants, so you could choose between a twenty-dollar burger or a twenty-dollar burrito.

Still, I'd done plenty of jobs in the city and knew Wallingford was a lot less stuffy than some neighborhoods closer to downtown. There were dive bars, a great donut place, and a weird tchotchke shop that sold bacon-flavored bubble gum and rubber chickens.

Cori opened the door dressed in leggings and a beat-up Mariners sweatshirt, an outfit I'd seen her wear many times as a teen. I couldn't help but notice how perfectly at home she looked standing in the entryway of her cozy row-house, just as she had in her mom's trailer. And on my porch. And behind the front counter at the Center. The expensive jeans had fooled me for a minute, but now I saw clearly.

Back in the day, I'd admired Cori's chameleon-like ability to adapt to whatever circumstances demanded. That talent seemed to have only grown. She'd looked good riding in my beat-up truck and wearing my old hoodie, but I could easily imagine her commanding boardrooms in a power suit.

Then I peeked behind her and saw something—or rather, someone—who did look out of place in this townhouse.

Johnny sat sullenly on Cori's couch, clutching a pillow to his stomach.

Cori opened the door wider, grim-faced as she invited me in. "Thanks for coming, Deck."

"Of course."

Johnny glared at us.

"You texted Deck? Like he's my fucking keeper? I get that you're *married* and all, but what the fuck, Cori?"

This was my least favorite version of Johnny. Defensive. Mean. Acting out like a trapped animal. I'd never met this side of him until we were seventeen, and he started using regularly. Usually, the aggression meant he was coming down, getting twitchy with the need for another fix. But his eyes appeared clear and bright.

"Don't look at me like that!" Johnny shouted, jumping up and tossing the pillow harshly into a chair. "I'm not fucking high, okay?"

I put my hands in front of me, pumping my palms down on the air. "Calm down, J. No one said you were." I tried to smile. "You are being a bit of an asshole, though."

Johnny scoffed, marginally calmer as he slumped onto the couch.

"Of course I texted Deck." Cori sat down next to her brother. "He loves you too. We're both just trying to figure out what's going on."

With the weight of Cori's words to anchor me, I seated myself on the coffee table in front of Johnny, our knees touching. "You're only on, like, day fifteen," I said. "You're supposed to be in rehab."

Johnny stared up at the ceiling before covering his eyes with a crooked elbow. "Day seventeen. And I couldn't do it, Deck. I couldn't stay in that place anymore. The first few days, after the worst of the withdrawal passed, they started talking about therapy. There were group circles and shit. Fucking meditation. Some people there were nice, but..."

He stopped, and I held my breath.

"But what, Johnny?" Cori asked. Her voice was gentle, but I sensed the upset behind it.

"It wasn't for me, Sis."

"What does that mean, it wasn't for you?"

"I don't want to be a dick about it, because I know everyone has their shit. But it was like, one girl I talked to was a student who started using cocaine to get through study sessions. This other guy was some big shot at a tech company who made six figures while mainlining smack every day. There were a few guys my age, but I just couldn't lose that scratchy feeling under my skin. And I don't mean from the lack of a fix. Bottom line, Conscious Horizons wasn't a good fit. So I left."

Cori's face screwed up. "That's it then, *bottom line*?" She stood abruptly. "You didn't even try! It was always going to be hard. Less than twenty days isn't long enough to know!"

Johnny glared at her. "It wasn't the right place."

"It has the best reputation in the Puget Sound!"

"Just because it's the best, doesn't mean it's the best place for me!"

"Jesus!" Cori paced in front of us, arms flailing. "That's a lame excuse if I ever heard one! So, what, you came here to try to get clean on your own? Like, after all this time, you've figured out how to enact that particular miracle!? Or did you just show up so I could watch you die!?"

"Fuck, Cori!" It was Johnny's turn to stand. He took a few strides toward the front door. "If you're going to yell and give me shit, I can fucking leave!"

I jumped up, grabbing him by the wrist.

"Alright, alright, you two. Head to your corners." I turned to Johnny. "You need to look at this from your sister's perspective. Checking yourself out of rehab is obviously a problem. Fuck, man, I'm worried too. Just telling us it wasn't good does nothing about the fact that you have the heart of a Golden Girl and you're dealing with HIV now."

I released Johnny's arm, and he took a few deep breaths.

"Look, I brought my meds with me," he said. "I think I've got that part down." He glanced at Cori. "I really appreciate you paying out of pocket for them. I don't know how I'll ever pay you back—"

"You don't have to—"

"I know. I knew you'd say that. And just so we're clear, I am very aware of what happens if I don't take the meds. Which is why I'm sucking up my fucking pride and accepting the help. Despite what you apparently believe, I don't actually *want* to die. The fact that I'm here and not back out on the street should prove that to you. I just couldn't stay in that place anymore."

Cori's phone rattled. She exhaled resignedly and checked the screen. "It's the rehab. I'm going to talk to them."

"But I already told you—" Johnny started.

"I get it! This is not me babying you, Johnny. I just need to ask about paperwork and payments and stuff like that. They won't tell me about your treatment. It's confidential."

"You can ask them if you want. I'll give my permission. But I already told you. It wasn't the place for me."

"You don't have to keep saying that," I muttered.

Cori pursed her lips and went into a room behind the kitchen to take the call.

I sat down with Johnny at the dining table, glancing at his duffel bag.

"Your meds are in there?"

"Yeah. Right on top, clearly labeled and everything."

"Stop being a dick. We're trying to help you."

"Oh, it's *we* now?" Johnny emitted a low noise that might have been a laugh before smirking at me. "For a year, I've been telling you to work your shit out with my sister. Now suddenly you're fake married and both of you are up my ass like it's a team sport. I'm not sure this was what I had in mind."

I crossed my arms and tilted the chair back, eyeing him. "You couldn't have lasted another few weeks? Not even to make your sister feel better?"

"I couldn't do it, man. Couldn't stay there." Johnny picked at the reddened skin around his fingernails. It drew my eyes to his new tattoos. On his right hand, each bottom knuckle had a number, starting with his thumb: 9-8-2-0-1. Everett's zip code.

"Alright, then." I leaned forward. "You left the bougie rehab. What's the new plan?"

Cori came back into the main room carrying her laptop. She handed it to Johnny.

"They're sending your medical records to your email address."

"Johnny has an email address?" For some reason, I found this funny. Whenever he'd stayed at my house, he hadn't even had a hairbrush.

"Cori set it up for me when she went away to college."

They looked at one another, and I could guess the rest. There had been times while I was in prison when Johnny had been more functional, short periods when he'd held jobs and apartments, and a longer stretch of sobriety after Eliazar died. He'd told me that himself.

"It's come in handy a few times," Cori said vaguely. "Especially because Johnny doesn't always have a phone." She pointed at the laptop. "Log in to your account. Conscious Horizons is sending over all the records from your time there, along with instructions on how to continue accessing your medications. I got that sorted with the online pharmacy they connected me with, so your meds will be sent here. Can you forward everything to me, so I have a copy?"

"*Yes, Mom*. I told you I'm not trying to make this worse. I already knew you'd be pissed enough." He clicked into his email, and ten seconds later, Cori's phone pinged with a notification.

"Well, I guess that's something. I'm relieved you came here, even knowing I'd be mad."

"Your brother was just telling me what his new plan is," I interjected, not wanting to lose the thread of that conversation.

Johnny scraped a hand over his face. "No plan yet." He rolled his shoulders before stretching his hands above his head. "Do you mind if I crash for the night? I'm totally beat. We can figure it all out in the morning, okay?"

Cori nodded, and I knew she was thinking about the last time Johnny slept at her place.

"Will you take the guest room this time?" she asked.

"Sure, Sis." He grabbed his duffel, stopping to give her a kiss on the head as he made his way to the stairs. "I'll see you in the morning. Promise."

Cori sat down on the couch, resting her head in her hands. "Thanks for coming, Deck," she said through her fingers. "Maybe it was overkill that I called you. But I'm glad you came."

"Of course I came." I sat next to her. "That's what husbands do."

"Really pushing that to the outer limit, huh?" She chortled, looking up with tired eyes. "I'll take it."

"Glad I can amuse you."

"I feel guilty saying this, but it's so exhausting. Being scared for my brother all the time." She sniffed, sinking back into the cushions.

The defeat in her voice killed me. "I'm so fucking sorry, Cor. I wish I could snap my fingers and fix him for you." She had no idea how much I wished for it. How deep my regret ran.

She bent one leg and turned in my direction, resting her head on her elbow over the back of the couch. "It's so hard to explain to someone who doesn't understand. The worrying. I've been on my own with it for so long."

"I know. And you've been amazing for Johnny. But now that I'm here, I'll help as much as you want me to. As much as you'll let me. Whatever you need."

I had kept her at arm's length for over a decade, but having a taste of Cori these past few weeks had confirmed that she was still in my blood. I'd spent enough nights in a lonely cell recalling those sky-blue eyes to know she'd never left my system. It didn't surprise me that we'd gone from not speaking to co-conspirators so quickly. I'd missed my rock.

It was the best thing I'd ever been—Cori's friend.

Before I could register the move, she curled her legs up against my side and rested her head on my shoulder. "Don't push me away again, Deck, alright?" she implored softly. "Don't try to be a stranger."

Instinctively, I wrapped my arm around her shoulders. Her hand rose to hold mine, keeping me in place. She nestled deeper into my side, and I felt the wetness of her tears.

Gulping roughly, I grazed my fingers down her arm. "Never again, Cori," I vowed.

She tilted her head back to peer at me. And no one had ever looked so beautiful with tear streaks staining their cheeks.

"I've missed you, Deck," she whispered.

There was so much I could have said. But it had never been our way to say things out loud. Because that would make them true. And there had always been too much going on around us to tell the truth.

She burrowed against me. "Johnny might decide to leave again in the morning."

"I know."

"I slipped an AirTag into his backpack." Cori sighed.

A rough laugh escaped my throat. "Me too."

She smiled, and I felt like I'd won the lottery. We separated somewhat, maintaining the sliver of distance we'd always kept as teenagers. She produced a remote control and, without discussion, put on *The 40-Year-Old Virgin*, which I recalled we both held as a top-ten favorite.

"Do you remember the last time we watched this?" she asked.

"No. You do?"

"Uh-huh. Your senior year, my junior. I'd been babysitting Mari the day before Thanksgiving. Your mom found out Johnny and I had no plans because our mom never did anything on that day. The only turkey I'd ever had said Oscar Mayer on it. María made us come over—invited Mom too, but of course she decided to *work* instead—so Johnny and I spent that day with you all. Your whole family was there, all your brothers and sisters. I remember thinking that Johnny and I were lucky to be a part of it, to have the chance to celebrate a real Thanksgiving. And it never felt like we were intruding. You Deckers just absorbed us. That night, after everyone had gone to bed, you and I watched this movie downstairs. Johnny was asleep next to us. And the reason I remember is because it was a perfect day. Even though you were all far in it with Chi-chi at that point, and Johnny was getting high a lot, it was still one perfect day in the middle of all that. Capped off by this ridiculous movie. And it stuck in my memory because those perfect days were scarce back then. I think I made myself hold on to them because I needed the reminder that they were possible."

"That's deep, Cori."

At the twinge of sarcasm in my voice, she hit me with a pillow. "Extremely deep, fuckyouverymuch."

I deflected rather than admit I knew exactly what she meant. In the middle of the shit, good days were reality without context.

We watched the movie in silence for an hour until Cori spoke again.

"So total subject change—"

"Hmm?"

"Some of the older kids at the Center asked if the teen late night on Friday could be a dance. I told them yes, and I'd like to make it special. Hire a DJ. Grab a few dozen pizzas. I was hoping you'd help me string up lights and hang a disco ball and decorations or something." She spoke enthusiastically, but then she deflated. "I don't know. Some of these kids are so jaded. They might think it's dumb."

I reassured her, "It's a great idea, Cori. And you know better than to let the hard kids get to you. The ones who act tough and talk down about stuff like dance decorations probably appreciate them deep down. I'm speaking from experience here since I was one of those little assholes. And of course I'll help. I think I have some string lights left over from a job, and I bet Mamá would let us dig through her Christmas decorations."

"My plan is to use my own money for the DJ and pizza, call it a donation, since the Center doesn't have the budget. I'm trying not to do that too much because I know Rosa doesn't like it, but I don't think she'd mind this."

Cori crossed her arms over the throw pillow in her lap. She seemed relaxed for the first time that night. Hopefully, putting on a dance for the teens would be a nice distraction from everything else going on. For both of us.

Before the end of the movie, she fell asleep. I gently removed her from where she'd pressed up against my side, pulling a throw blanket over her before standing.

She stirred without waking, and I impulsively ran my thumb over her cheek. I wanted to taste her, wanted to place my lips on that soft skin. Instead, I leaned down and whispered into her ear, "Goodnight, Cori."

Driving home, I thought about that perfect day she'd described. The last Thanksgiving before I got locked up.

Growing up in the neighborhood felt like one of those machines that goes nuts during an earthquake, needles moving wildly up and down. For sure, we enjoyed the highs. The perfect days. But there was always this underlying stress. Just like with the machine, the line never went perfectly straight.

That was why you could never let yourself get too comfortable. You knew better than to expect any sort of sustained happiness. Because the lows always came. Always.

CHAPTER TWENTY-TWO
Cori

Johnny grinned at me from where he sat at the table, eating a bowl of cereal. I didn't think he was sleeping very well because he'd woken up early every morning since he showed up on my doorstep five days ago. But at least he hadn't run off. On the contrary, it seemed like he was determined to stay hidden in my house.

"Why do you have almond milk and oat milk, but not milk milk?"

"Milk milk?"

"Whatever, cow milk."

"I think you mean dairy milk, and I guess because I don't like it as much. I like ice cream and cheese and all that, but regular milk isn't as good as oat milk for cereal and in my coffee."

"What's the almond milk for?"

"Cooking." I sat down and poured myself a bowl. "Any other beverage-related questions?"

"Now that you mention it—" He laughed. "Would you mind picking up some regular Coke at the store next time? Or even the diet stuff. That fancy brand you have in the fridge tastes like booty."

"It's more natural," I retorted. "Like a healthier kind of sweetener. I promise you get used to it."

He shook his head. "Nah. I know my taste buds are probably shit-tastic since the drugs, but even I know the difference between something that tastes good and something that tastes like salad dressing and dirty dishwater had a baby."

I snorted.

"Okay, champ. I'll buy regular soda. No problem."

Johnny dug back into his cereal, and I stole a sideways glance at him. He appeared healthier than I'd seen him in years. His cheeks glowed with color, and his face had filled out a bit. There were no flakes of skin around his hairline, lips, or underneath his nose. No mysterious bruises. Deck had brought over some of his clothes—easier for my brother to accept than letting me buy him a new wardrobe—and Johnny looked like a typical bro in a black sweatshirt and olive-green joggers.

I'd been staying home since Johnny checked himself out of rehab. He hadn't decided on his next move, and it eased my mind to have my eyes on him. Funny how his almost dying had changed my perspective on keeping him close. I knew I'd eventually have to go back to the tough-love approach I'd taken before, but there was no rush on that. For now, I let myself enjoy spending time with the brother who'd been absent from my life for a long time, including when he'd been right next to me.

But even if Johnny wasn't ready to step outside yet, I knew I had to. It scared me to leave him on his own, but I needed to keep my promise to Rosa.

"I'll be back home by six," I told him. "You have the phone I gave you. Don't be afraid to use it if you need to. I plugged in my number, Deck's, and even Marisol's, just in case, since she works at the Center too."

Johnny shook his head. "I can't believe Deck's little sister is, like, a grown-up woman."

"She's pretty awesome. I told Michael and María I'd have dinner with them soon. You should come. They'd love to see you."

Johnny moved the spoon around in his bowl. "We'll see."

I circled the table to give him a hug. "No one's judging. Especially not the Deckers."

He shrugged. "I'll think about it."

For now, I knew it was the only answer he would give me. Johnny's recovery was so new, so tentative. Having dinner with friends probably seemed like the sort of thing other people did. Not him.

I decided to ask Deck about it when I saw him at the Center. Things had been different between us since the weekend. He'd come over—ostensibly to visit Johnny—a few times since then. We hadn't shared another close moment like the one on my couch, but we'd progressed from awkward cordiality into something resembling familiarity.

DECK WAS IN THE BATHROOM OFF THE GYM when I arrived, working on his hands and knees. I stopped short in the doorway, distracted by the perfection of his jeans-clad ass. Catching myself before he clocked me staring, I averted my gaze and cleared my throat.

After exchanging good mornings and catching me up on some of the progress he'd made, I mentioned that Johnny was hesitant to have dinner with the Deckers.

"I get why Johnny might not be ready to hang out with my family," Deck said, pulling up tile from around a hole in the floor where a new toilet would go. "I felt the same way when I got out of prison. It isn't easy to pick up and resume a normal life after you've royally fucked up. It took me months to stop feeling like I had 'ex-con' tattooed across my forehead. He probably feels like 'addict' is on his."

"Yeah, that tracks," I said forlornly. "I wish it didn't, but it does."

Deck pointed at a folding table set up against the wall. "Can you hand me that scraper?"

I held up something that looked like a giant razor blade. "This?"

"Uh-huh. Thanks."

I handed him the tool and leaned back against the door. "But even if it makes logical sense why he wouldn't want to hang out and feel exposed, I can't stop wishing I could help him get there faster. He needs to see that there are lots of people who have his back."

Deck stopped what he was doing and sat back on his haunches, peering up at me. "He will, Cori. If he can stay clean this time, eventually he'll start trusting it more. If he can string together a few good weeks in a row, it'll help."

"I just hate that he feels like he has to hide away, like he needs to be ashamed of anything." Gripping the edge of the big trough sink, I stammered, "I regret all the times I turned him away. Even though he was using. I thought I was doing the right thing, but..." I hung my head.

Deck exhaled and rose to his feet, coming to stand behind me. "Don't beat yourself up. You were doing the best you could. And like I said, Johnny will get there."

I looked up and met Deck's magnetic gaze in the mirror. "I think part of me wants to expedite the process because I spent so long sectioning Johnny off from the rest of my life," I admitted. "It all seems so stupid in retrospect. Now that I've stepped away from JBC, I see how meaningless it was to spend that much effort worrying about appearances. I want Johnny to know I'm not ashamed of him. Unfortunately, I haven't given him much evidence of that."

Deck dipped his chin thoughtfully before asking, "Cori, do you mind if I make an observation that's kind of personal?"

"Please."

"I know we've only been back in each other's lives a few weeks, and it wasn't exactly a smooth reunion at first—"

I pffted.

He shrugged contritely, still talking over my shoulder. "I'll own that. But I think we can agree that there was a time when we understood each other extremely well. For a long stretch just before I got locked up, you probably knew me better than anyone." My whole body froze, but Deck continued as though he hadn't just said the thing I'd been waiting for him to say out loud since I was sixteen. "I'm still learning about the Cori who went to college and founded a company that made her a millionaire. The Cori who lives in a sweet little townhouse in Seattle, who wears expensive clothes, and rarely curses."

"That's who you think I am? Some rich lady living it up in the city?"

He laughed gruffly. "Absolutely not. I *know* that isn't who you are. That's what I'm saying." In the mirror, I watched as he hesitantly raised an arm, guiding me to turn around and face him. "I'm in awe of the person you are now, the one I'm still getting to know." He rested his hand on my biceps. "But fundamentals don't change, and I know the Cori from this neighborhood pretty damn well. She's the reason I know what the word *expedite* means. She was there for all my best days growing up. It was her voice I heard when I was in prison, telling me I should get my GED and then my bachelor's degree…"

He stopped short, looking abashed.

"Deck…" I murmured. "You've never said that before. How much we understood each other, I mean."

He removed his hand and ran it through his curls, rocking back on his heels. "C'mon, Cori… You know that we… You know."

Baby.

Heart emoji.

I didn't press. Instead, I asked, "You thought about me in prison? After you ignored my letters and refused to see me, I figured you were mad, that you…blamed me."

He shook his head aggressively. "Not even for one second," he mumbled. "And of course I thought about you while I was in. All the time."

From his red face, I gathered that the admission cost him. I offered a lifeline. "What does this have to do with me not being ashamed of Johnny?"

"Oh, right." He folded his arms. "I'm saying that all those versions of Cori are you. Streetwise or sophisticated. Doing what you had to do to protect yourself. Johnny knows that. You were defending the life you'd made. Because it must have been hard for it to feel safe. And permanent. Johnny was a reminder of how fragile it all was."

I leaned my hips against the sink. "Those years after college, when we were getting JBC established, it felt like I'd built my life on sand. Even with all my hard work, I woke up every morning with a low-key fear that someone would come along and expose me, point out that I didn't belong in front of venture capitalists and that being a leader in the industry was for people who didn't grow up in trailer parks. And you're right—I'm not proud of it, but whenever

Johnny came around, it felt like a warning that everything could dissolve in an instant."

"Like I said, you were just scared. Not being a bad sister."

I chuckled mirthlessly. "You know what the most ridiculous part is?"

"What?"

"These past few years, when my nice tidy life started feeling secure, when I finally started to trust it, that was when I realized I didn't even really want it. Once the stress and fog of *Do I belong here* and *Do I deserve this* lifted, I could see clearly. I had always assumed happiness would follow stability. But it just... didn't. After I figured that out, I tried to make it work, but eventually, I admitted to myself that I didn't want the life I'd fought so hard to create and hold on to. That's why I was ready to sell JBC when the offer came."

"So if you don't want your old business and that life, what do you want?"

"I don't know. Something more in the middle, I think. Hopefully, I'll know it when I see it."

"Well, it's good you're helping Rosa while you figure it out."

I shoved away thoughts of the dismal month-end numbers for the Center I'd combed through the day before. "What about you, Artie Decker? What kind of life do you want?"

Two small lines appeared on his forehead as his brow furrowed thoughtfully.

"I don't know about the future yet," he replied slowly, drawing out each word. "The only thing I'm sure of is that I don't want to live with any more regrets." His intensity consumed all the energy in the small space. "I need to be careful. I've messed up enough for two lifetimes, and I don't want to make new mistakes."

He took a step closer, and I held my breath. From this distance, I could make out the onyx rings outlining his dark brown irises. Leaning in, he stretched an arm out, and I watched in slow motion as he grabbed a roll of blue painter's tape from the sink behind me.

"Better get back to work," he said huskily.

I nodded. Once safely in the hallway, I released the air from my lungs.

ROSA WAS AT HOME CARING FOR LUPE. They'd decided to stop all invasive treatments for Lupe's cancer and were working with insurance to come up with a plan for palliative care and, eventually, hospice. It was heartbreaking, yet comforting, to know that Rosa and Lupe could share a long, loving goodbye. Rosa told me they'd been spending time looking at photos, watching movies they both loved, and eating their favorite foods. I was sure there was a lot of pain and sadness mixed into their days, but it was very much in line with Rosa's character that she didn't dwell on it.

Rosa deserved to be at home as much as she wanted to be, and I was determined to cover her operational duties at the Center to make that happen. Longtime employees like Chuck were willing to step up as well. I'd already promised Rosa that she had me for as long as she needed me. When she'd wrapped her arms around me and said, *"Gracias a Dios por ti,"* I felt prouder than the day I'd secured fifteen million in funding for JBC.

While Deck worked on the bathroom repairs, I met with Ana, the fundraiser, and Quincy, the accountant. We'd scheduled the meeting for two hours before the kids arrived, so Marisol joined us.

Quincy and Ana both worked three days per week, overlapping only on Thursdays, though Quincy usually worked remotely. He did freelance accounting for nonprofits to supplement his retirement income after a long career as the CFO of a local restaurant chain. His shiny bald head gleamed like a friendly beacon, and he had the best laugh, the kind of *heh-heh-heh* deep from his belly that made everyone around him join in, even if nothing was funny.

Today was the first time I'd met him in person, and I was immediately charmed. Not to mention reassured by his uncanny ability to drill down on numbers, and his honesty in assessing the Center's difficult financial situation. I already admired Ana's capabilities as a fundraiser, and, of course, Marisol's expertise in running programs that donors wanted to support. Even with a small leadership team, I sensed the potential for success.

"I'm so glad to be in the building," Quincy said, wandering around the atrium and offering compliments for every piece of artwork on the walls. "Rosa lets me work from home since I'm an old man and it's a hell of a commute from my neck of the woods, but I do love being here. I'm happy to come in more often if you think it would help."

"That's a generous offer," I said, considering it. "Why don't we keep having you come in on Thursdays, so at least there's one day where we all work together physically in the same space. It may help us move quicker."

I appreciated Quincy's willingness to be flexible. He already did a lot for the Center, charging well below the prevailing wage for his accounting work. I also suspected he did more than he billed for. But I wasn't going to look a gift horse in the mouth. During his corporate career, he'd been on the board of directors for the Center because he genuinely loved Rosa and believed in the mission.

As I became familiar with the Center's finances, I met dozens of donors and board members who offered to step up and contribute more to keep the place running. We just didn't have enough of those people to solve the problem of long-term sustainability. If I was going to do more than merely provide Rosa with a stopgap for the next few years, we needed to have the funds to establish a meaningful endowment, allowing the Center to operate off its interest, and also mount a capital campaign, which would serve the dual purpose of getting new funders engaged while providing the means to deal with the maintenance backlog and ongoing repairs.

Ana often reminded me that it was significantly easier to get donors to fund new building wings and fancy program initiatives than to provide general funding to keep the lights on and pay the staff. We needed a balance.

"I can also come in more often, if it would help," Ana said. "Happy to do it."

"I may take you up on that, especially closer to the Gala for Kids," I replied, thinking of the event scheduled for early December, only two months away. "We have it budgeted to do half a million, but I think we need at least eight hundred thousand to make up for the fundraising that didn't happen over the summer."

"Sure, just a cool eight hundred, when the most we've ever done is six," Ana chuffed. "You don't ask for much."

Despite her good-natured chuckle, I knew she understood my shoot-for-the-stars attitude. She was ten years older than me and had also attended the Center as a child. She took the part-time job as a fundraiser after going through a divorce four years ago. Her two kids came to the Center even though she could afford to enroll them in a place much closer to their home. When I'd asked her why she picked them up and brought them every day, she'd looked at me like I was nuts.

"Cori, I don't care how fancy the *learning centers*"—she used air quotes—"are by my house. If you had kids, wouldn't you want them to have Rosa and the Center in their lives?"

My respect for her, already high, had cemented.

"I know eight hundred is a stretch," I conceded. "But we have to try. If the event fails, we're looking at immediate cuts to athletic programs, the arts, and music, as well as significant increases in camp fees. I came here to help the Center. I don't want to have to gut it."

Quincy examined one of the bulletin boards outside an art room. He pointed at a smaller canvas pinned in the corner. "Whichever kid did this one, they've got genuine talent."

Marisol smiled. "That's one of Reign's. We rarely get them off the couch, but when we do, it's usually to the art room."

Ana looked up. "Maybe we can ask them to do something for the gala. It might be nice to have the invitations and posters featuring kid art."

"Love that idea," I said.

"Speaking of artwork—" Quincy adopted the expression I'd come to recognize as the one he wore before delivering bad news. "I think we need to look at the website. Online donations are down over sixty percent compared to last year, and while technology is certainly not my forte, I'm wondering if it isn't because our online presence hasn't been updated in a while."

Dejected, I sighed. I hadn't realized the year-over-year numbers were that bad, but the Center's desperate need for a refresh of its website and social media pages was something I'd identified on my first day. I'd hoped the updates could wait until we took care of more immediate fires, but based on Quincy's numbers, they were part of the inferno.

"I have some former work acquaintances who might do that type of work for a reasonable rate, or possibly even free. Sorry I haven't gotten to it yet," I said.

"Cori, it's okay," Ana reassured me, taking a sip of her tea. "We know you're still getting acclimated. You've done a lot in a short amount of time."

"If you know anyone with that expertise, it might be nice if they could get the kids here involved," Marisol added. "Instead of having someone just design a website or get us set up on Instagram or whatever, we could have a few older teens learn those skills. There's some of that in school, but it's hit or miss on how good the instruction is, let alone whether they have the opportunity to apply what they've learned."

"That's a fantastic idea," I said, wheels turning.

Two months ago, my life had been completely compartmentalized. Now, not only was I reintegrating myself into my old neighborhood, but I was also contemplating inviting coworkers from JBC into that world. I could easily envision Jason or Brad writing a check at the gala, but it was murkier to imagine them teaching coding and graphic design to fifteen-year-olds who swore like sailors and had souls older than Methuselah.

But who knew? Rosa always said to have a growth mindset about kids. Maybe I should extend the same courtesy to adults. It wasn't my former coworkers' fault that they'd never had to go back-to-school shopping in a church's charity bin or put water in a shampoo bottle to make it last longer.

"The kids will be here soon," I announced, clapping my hands together. "Let's change the subject to something more fun and talk about how awesome the teen dance will be tomorrow night."

CHAPTER TWENTY-THREE
Deck

"Y ou aim the gun at the juncture of the baseboard and the tile and pull the trigger here," I explained. "Once you have it in a nice, even line, you run this tool over it to smooth it down."

"Alright, can I try?" Reign's eagerness as they reached for the caulking gun amused me. They still mostly communicated with sullen stares and noncommittal noises, but it flowed a little easier since I'd gotten permission for them to help me with projects.

"Yes, but how about you practice on these spare boards first? Then once you find your rhythm, it'll be a lot easier to crawl down and do it on the actual floor tile."

Reign nodded and grabbed the boards.

I stood and stretched. I'd been working on the ground all day. Even though I took breaks and wore knee pads, this type of labor was exhausting.

After assessing the extent of the damage to the bathroom, I'd volunteered to do more than simply fix the toilets and surrounding areas. It wouldn't be a full remodel, but close to it. Juan and I had leftover materials from another commercial job, and the company was happy to donate those items to the Center. I planned to replace all the toilets and stall dividers, along with the tile on the floors and walls. I'd also gotten updated sinks to replace the rusty trough-style one, which looked like something out of a horror movie.

I ran my ideas by Cori yesterday afternoon, and she seemed grateful, not just for my offer but also because the practical discussion put us back on neutral ground. Something we needed after our conversation that morning in front of the same ancient sink.

When she'd asked me what kind of life I wanted.

When she made me realize I still wanted the same thing I had at eighteen.

Except how could I ever have it? After everything.

I wiped an elbow across my brow, keeping an eye on Reign. We needed to wrap up soon so I could help Cori with the dance setup in the gym.

After the first day we met, Reign asked to help me. I wasn't cleared to interact with kids unless there were other staff members or volunteers around, so Marisol came up with a workaround. She made sure there was always a volunteer in the room with Reign and me. Generally, she grabbed the least-invested person she could find—there were plenty of volunteers at the Center who weren't there for any sort of altruistic motives, but rather to earn credit hours for class—with the instruction to stand around and serve as an extra body while I taught Reign how to do things.

So while Reign practiced with the caulking gun, Sandra, the volunteer, played on her phone and ignored both of us.

"I told my dad I was helping the contractor at the Center," Reign told me.

"Oh, yeah?"

"Mm-hmm." They kept their eyes firmly on the boards in front of them. "He's annoyed I don't play sports, and he hates my art, so I figured maybe I'd tell him about this, and he'd like it."

My stomach dropped. I didn't feel equipped for this conversation, fearing its direction.

"What did he say?" I asked mildly.

"He slapped me on the shoulder and said, 'Great idea, Ricardo. Maybe we'll make a man out of you yet.'"

I winced. And I was seventeen again, watching Eliazar's parents reject him.

"I'm sorry, Reign. It sucks that he said that, that he can't see who you are."

They put the caulking gun down, sitting back against the newly mounted stall divider. "I almost didn't come today. When my dad said that, I thought maybe I shouldn't help you anymore. Because, you know, fuck that guy and making him happy. Like maybe I should take a ballet class instead. Or do makeup tutorials online. Even if I have no fucking interest in ballet."

I let the f-bombs slide. "And the makeup?"

Reign shrugged. "Not my thing."

I slid down onto the floor across from them. "For what it's worth, I'm glad you came. For you, not your dad. And you know I'm a construction worker, not a trained professional for working with youth. Marisol or Rosa could probably say things better." I glanced at Sandra again, confirming her continuing obliviousness. "But if you don't mind hearing this from someone whose primary life skill is wielding a drill, I hope you know that the way your dad is acting is a *him* problem, not a *you* problem." I whooshed the air from my lungs. "I could lie and say he'll come around, but he probably won't. The upside is, you don't need to let him get to you either. You can just…not care. You don't have to make him see that he's wrong for you to know that he is."

It was probably shitty advice. To tell a kid they would always fight with their pops. Then again, Reign had been sitting on the couch for months, barely talking to anyone. If they were finally opening up to me, of all people, I sure as hell was going to honor it by being truthful.

Reign nodded. "I hear what you're saying. It's just…a shitty situation."

"True. But it's not your job to fix him, Reign. And just so we're very, very clear. Your dad is wrong. Full stop."

"Thanks." It was barely audible, but I'd take it.

"Out of curiosity, what made you decide to come today? Not that you wouldn't have killed it at ballet."

They smirked. "I really wanted to use this caulking gun."

REIGN DEPARTED THE CENTER ALMOST immediately after we blocked off the bathroom for the night. I asked why they weren't staying for the dance, and they laughed like it was the funniest joke they'd ever heard.

Afterward, I told Cori and Marisol about my talk with Reign. I wanted to be transparent in case I'd done something wrong.

"It's not exactly protocol, but you didn't do anything truly *egregious*," Cori said, and we shared a fond look at her use of another SAT word.

Marisol practically bounced. "It's progress. I mean, it sucks that their dad is a dick and still calls them by their dead name, but the fact that Reign confided in you is great. Sometimes, they talk to Rosa, but not about this."

"Okay, good. And for the record, Reign is a natural at construction and has been genuinely helpful."

Shouting came from the gym, reaching us all the way in the atrium.

"I'm going to see what's up," Marisol said. "It's been crazy today with all the kids packed into one side."

That morning, Chuck and I had heaved a massive, accordion-style divider into the center of the gym. One half was still available for basketball, while the other was off-limits because of the dance setup. I'd attached four spotlights to the rafters over the stage Cori rented for the DJ, along with string lights across the center of the space. The DJ had already arrived and was hooking up her PA to the gym's central system. I still had to hang the giant disco ball and set up tables for food.

Cori eyed me carefully. "That conversation with Reign... I'm guessing it made you think of Eliazar."

My lips tightened before I said, "Eliazar always felt bad. Not for being gay, but for letting down his parents. There was no way to square that circle." I pushed a fist against the counter, remembering. "Having his mom and pops reject him broke something inside him. He used drugs and sex to numb out. Having us—his brothers—wasn't enough."

Cori covered my fist with her hand, pulling my arm down. "You were enough, Deck. Eliazar just got caught up." She held my gaze. "And it's not going to be that way for Reign."

The unmistakable slapping sound of hits landing on bodies cut through the air.

"I'd better find out what's happening," Cori said.

Following her hurried steps to the open half of the gym, we found Chuck and Marisol attempting to break up a fistfight.

Two older boys were throwing punches while the other kids formed a loose circle around them. Wide-eyed volunteers kept the onlookers away from the fighters.

After one boy landed a vicious kidney shot, his opponent's grunt of pain echoed off the concrete walls.

"Jayden! Tycho!" Chuck yelled. "Knock it off!" Even though Chuck was extremely fit for a man in his late fifties, he struggled to insert himself between the two young men. They attacked one another like rabid dogs, hurling their fists with no skill or finesse. Street brawling, my brother Emilio would call it.

One of the teens turned his face toward me. Jayden. I'd learned his name over the past few weeks because he attracted a lot of attention. The kid was a hothead, regularly breaking the rules and getting sent home. For a moment, we locked gazes, and it was just enough time for the other kid, Tycho, to launch his knuckles into Jayden's jaw.

Jayden's head whipped to the left, taking the hard hit, and his body followed the motion as he stumbled backward to stay on his feet. He spat blood onto the gym floor. "That all you got, dickface?" he taunted.

Before Tycho could fly back at him, Chuck took advantage of the break to step between the two, grabbing Jayden from behind and tightening his arms at his sides. "That's enough! Cool down. Now!"

Marisol attempted to apply the same hold to Tycho, but took a slap to the cheek when he resisted. Her hand flew to her face where he'd struck her.

The sight of Marisol touching her jaw—on the side where the burn scars were—momentarily stunned the room.

Everything in me wanted to beat the crap out of the little shit, but I held myself in check, conscious of the fact I'd just gotten off parole.

Tycho was instantly contrite. "Oh shit, Miss Mari. I'm so sorry. I didn't mean to hit you. It was an accident, I swear. I would never—"

Marisol held up her hand. "It's okay, Tycho. It was just a tap. I know you wouldn't hit me on purpose." She exhaled. "But I wish you would have shown Jayden the same respect. I'm getting so tired of telling you boys not to solve things with your fists. You shouldn't be doing it out on the streets, and you definitely shouldn't be bringing it into the Center."

The kids who had been holding their phones lowered them quietly. I'd seen my sister in action since I'd started working through my repair list, and this was another example of her top-notch leadership. I was so proud of the way she kept her cool. And especially the way she commanded everyone's respect.

Marisol glared at Jayden. "Do I even want to know what the fight was about?"

"Nah. Just some shit from school."

"Shit from school!" Tycho snarled. "Is that what you call it when you fuck my girl!?"

A slow smile spread across Jayden's face. "Is she really your girl if she begged to suck my dick?"

"Motherfucker!"

Jayden's gaze narrowed. "You get one of those, asshole," he said to Tycho, voice deadly serious. "I'll let it pass since, yeah, I fucked your girl. But unless you wanna get jumped tomorrow, I'd fucking let this go, bruh."

Chuck and Marisol exchanged glances as though silently communicating about how long to let the conversation play out. Since the teens seemed to be calming down, they didn't intervene.

"Fine!" Tycho sneered, a flash of fear crossing his features.

"Alright, both of you yahoos need to get out of my gym," Chuck said.

I didn't realize Cori had slipped away until she reappeared at my side carrying an ice pack, holding it out to Marisol.

"Chuck is right," Marisol said levelly, putting the cold gel against her cheek. "And you're both suspended until next week. Come back on Monday. With much better attitudes."

"Yes, Miss Mari," Tycho said. He sidestepped around Jayden to grab his backpack from against the wall, mumbling, "Sorry again," to my sister as he passed us.

Jayden sat down, wiping his wrist against his bleeding mouth until Chuck came up to him with another ice pack. "Take this and get out of here, Muhammad Ali. See you Monday. And just come for basketball, okay, not MMA."

Jayden chuckled, accepting Chuck's hand to lift himself off the floor. "I'll try, man. But you know how it is."

Chuck neither agreed nor disagreed. He blew his whistle and did his best to wrangle the other kids back into some semblance of a game, reminding them to keep their noses down unless they also wanted to get suspended and miss the dance.

On his way out, Jayden paused by Marisol and said, "I didn't know Shayna was his girlfriend. She never said. I wouldn't have gotten with her if I'd known 'cuz that's fucked up."

Marisol nodded. "Just leave him alone now, alright? It's over."

"Dang," I said, once Jayden was outside. "That was exciting."

Cori watched until he reached the sidewalk. "He really is a good kid. Deep down. I wish we could figure out a way to channel all that energy into something positive."

"We'll keep trying," Marisol said.

"What's his deal, anyway?" I asked. "I don't want to judge or anything, but he doesn't seem like a kid who'd come to the Center. Especially not at his age."

"He comes because his mom wants him to," Marisol explained. "His brother, Greg, got locked up a few years ago, and now their mom is terrified Jayden will end up the same way. He comes here to make her happy, but you can see it in his eyes. He wants something more. Greg was a petty dealer, maybe worse. Before he went away, he had money and a sweet car. I know that's in Jayden's head."

"Too bad the going to prison part isn't in his head," I quipped.

"From your lips, brother," Marisol said. "Greg's old crew wouldn't mind adding Jayden in, if you know what I mean. But he doesn't want to break his mother's heart. Maybe coming here helps. I hope."

"It helps," Cori said, slinging an arm around Marisol's shoulders. "Every day he's here and not out there helps."

Optimistic words. But I saw the look in Jayden's eyes after he threw that punch. I'd seen it before. In the mirror. Reminding me it only took one bad decision to ruin everything.

CHAPTER TWENTY-FOUR
Cori

By the time eight o'clock rolled around and the DJ was pumping Tyler the Creator, most of the kids had stopped talking about the fight between Tycho and Jayden.

Deck had rigged the disco ball so that the gym took on a starlit quality, a real accomplishment considering how old and dingy the walls were. He'd stayed for the dance, telling me he wanted to see his hard work in action.

"Nothing better to do on a Friday night?" I teased.

He scoffed playfully. "Hardly."

I realized that with our focus on helping Johnny and the Center, we hadn't caught up much on the more mundane details of Deck's life. It was a metaphor for our relationship that I knew about his soul-crushing inertia due to blaming himself for the past, but not what his favorite restaurant was or whether he went hiking on the weekends. How had he come to start a construction business? Did he enjoy living in Mountlake Terrace?

He lived alone, but did he...date?

The thought of Deck having a relationship sat in my stomach like a brick. But I didn't know what to do with that feeling. Acknowledging any sort of romantic interest in him would be a huge step, affecting not just us, but my brother, our families, and the Center. And even though my life had changed drastically in the past two months, I hadn't completely abandoned the caution that kept me sane for a dozen years. But regardless of where we were headed, my pull to him was as intense as ever. I wanted to know him more.

Stationed near the food tables, he watched the kids on the dance floor with his arms crossed.

I came up beside him and grabbed a cookie. "What would you be doing tonight if you weren't here looking like a bouncer?"

He chuckled, dropping his arms to hook his thumbs into his belt loops. "Honestly? I'd probably be home watching TV. I'm usually cashed on Fridays after the stuff Juan and I do all week." Glancing at me, he added pointedly, "I almost never go out. Sometimes we go to this bar, Tubby's, to watch a game or whatever, and I visit my family, but that's about it."

I nodded in answer.

"What would you do?" he asked. "If you weren't here, I mean."

I kept my gaze on the kids as I replied, "Same as you. TV probably. Or reading. Scrolling on my phone. On Sundays, I usually have brunch with my best friends, but that's about the extent of my social life. I used to work a lot on weekends." I turned to him. "But now that everything's changing for me, I'm thinking about trying new things."

"That so?"

"Yeah. I—"

"Oh my gosh, you guys, I'm so annoyed!" Marisol rushed up beside us. "I keep catching the girls in the bathroom trying to change their outfits. Two of them were practically naked."

I shook my head, snickering. "Guess nothing has changed, huh? I remember girls in high school would put on the outfits their moms approved of to leave the house, but immediately go into the bathroom before homeroom to sex things up. Switch out leggings for short shorts or take off a sweatshirt to show off a tight tank top. Not to mention all the makeup and perfumy body lotions."

"Don't belittle my pain, Cori," Marisol groaned. "Poor Chuck is monitoring the hallways and dark corners for things that would definitely not be mom-approved."

"I know it's tough to supervise, but on the bright side, the kids seem to be having a good time," I said.

"They really are," Marisol agreed. "This is the best turnout we've had for a late night in years. I have to admit I was nervous when you suggested a dance. I thought the kids might think it was corny or want to hang out on the edge of the gym all night."

Her words warmed me. The kids might be enjoying themselves, but there was no way they were happier than I was, watching them laugh and goof around with their friends.

Deck turned to grab a taco from the table. "What I'm loving are these tacos. I thought you were just gonna grab some cheap pizzas, but these are amazing."

"That was the original plan," I said. "Then I remembered Rosa telling me about this truck parked near the elementary school that makes tacos almost as good as hers, and I figured it would be cool to support a local business with a huge catering order." Not to mention the satisfaction of finally having a real taco at an event. Even if it was only a teen dance. I grinned, imagining the Center kids eating cauliflower tortillas and steak tartare.

"What's that smile on your face?" Deck asked.

"Nothing. Just happy to be here."

The three of us resumed watching the kids. It seemed like no matter what music played or at what tempo—Olivia Rodrigo or Billie Eilish or J. Cole—they saw it as an opportunity to grind on one another.

"It's amazing what passes for dancing nowadays," Deck observed.

"Sorry, Grandpa, but I think it was the same when we were kids," I countered. Though I'd attended exactly one dance in high school, so I couldn't say for sure.

"Nah. There were at least a few times when we turned around and faced each other or danced in a group." He frowned at the couple nearest us, the girl moving her butt against the boy's zipper. Not even in time with the music.

"I do feel slightly cheated," I joked. "Early 2000s teen romcoms and TikTok have led me to expect more synchronized dancing."

"Should I get them to tone it down a smidge? Tell them to make room for Jesus?" Marisol smirked.

I chuffed.

"Seriously, you couldn't fit a piece of paper between those two," Deck grumbled.

"I never pegged you for such an old man, big brother."

"C'mon," Deck protested. "I'm not a prude or anything. At least I didn't think so before I started watching these guys. *¿Es indecente, verdad?*"

Her brother's outrage clearly amused Marisol. "Alright, then." She cocked her hip. "If you're so offended, why don't you show these kids how it's done?"

Deck pffted. "You want me to dance?"

"Uh, no. No one wants to see that. I want you *and Cori* to dance. Together." She clapped her hands in front of her. "And I know just the song."

"Hey—" Before I could object to getting pulled into their argument, Marisol scurried away to the DJ.

"Sneaky little wannabe matchmaker," Deck muttered.

Marisol's complete lack of subtlety made me smile. Suddenly, she was seven years old again, trying to get Deck and me to hold hands on the couch while I babysat.

"We don't have to do what she says," I assured him. "I certainly don't know how to dance any better than these kids."

"You don't know how to do better than rub your ass on someone's privates?"

I hiccuped a laugh. "Dancing's never been my thing. I went to one formal in ninth grade, and I've done the YMCA at weddings, but that's about all."

The song ended. A confused murmur rippled among the teens as the first notes of the Beatles' "Something" came through the PA.

Peering over at Deck, I prepared to share a smile over his sister's complete lack of chill, only to find him staring at me with a serious look on his face.

To my shock, he held out a hand.

"Marisol might have a point. C'mon, *wife*. Let's show them how it's done."

I paused, looking down before giving him the slightest of nods. My hand felt as though it belonged to somebody else as I slid my fingers into Deck's warm palm and allowed him to lead me to the center of the gym.

Most of the kids retreated to the tables and bleachers, although a few brave couples remained. Thankfully, no one tried to grind to George Harrison.

Deck pulled me toward him, bracing my hips with about eight inches between us. I looped my arms awkwardly around his neck as we began swaying side to side.

Into his ear, I whispered, "You surprised me. I figured you'd shut Mari down."

"Don't think too hard on it. I...wanted to dance with you."

Inching closer, I almost stepped on his boot. "I'm glad."

Glad was an understatement. It felt like floating. The soft touch of his fingertips invaded my senses, the pure *rightness* of being in Deck's arms. How many times had I fantasized about this? How many times as a teenager had I wished Deck would ask me to homecoming or prom? It was a dozen years later. Yet somehow, it felt exactly the way I'd imagined.

It felt perfect.

Without deliberation, I closed the last of the distance between us and leaned my cheek on his chest, looking up at him. I felt the insistent thumping of his heart. He tilted his head down and locked our gazes together, the silver light of the disco ball making a halo around his dark hair. His Adam's apple bobbed as he swallowed. Sighing, I closed my eyes.

His grip tightened on my hips, and I heard the undertones of his mumbled, "Fuck it," as he moved his fingers to the center of my back before circling his arms around me, cementing us together.

Deck held me in his embrace as we continued to sway and rock to the music. He maneuvered slightly to rest his chin on my head, and I linked my arms around his neck. I felt the heat of his skin, the outline of the hair beneath his T-shirt, and the hard planes of his thighs.

"Ahem." Marisol walked up next to us, clearing her throat dramatically. "Do I need to remind you to leave room for—"

"Don't even say it." Deck stepped back from me. "Sorry, Cor," he said. "I forgot where we were for a minute there."

I noticed he didn't apologize for holding me close, only for where he'd chosen to do so.

"It's fine, Deck. Me too," I said. "It was a nice dance. Thanks." I saw a few of the kids watching us. Luckily, since Deck and I were still new around the Center, they didn't seem to care too much. If Marisol and Chuck had danced like that, it would have been a different story.

Marisol raised her eyebrows at her brother. "Tell me again about how the kids' dancing was too sexy?" She fanned herself with her hand.

"Knock it off," he chided her. "It was just a dance. And it was way tamer than what the teens were doing."

"Sure."

Fate conspired to keep Deck and me apart for the rest of the night. He got pulled into an extended emergency repair of one of the bleachers while Marisol and I navigated the drama when Shayna, the petite vixen at the center of the fight between Jayden and Tycho, showed up.

I appreciated the distance. It gave me a chance to consider my reaction to being held in Deck's arms. He was the only man who'd ever inspired strong emotions in me, and it was becoming harder to deny that I wanted him. That I didn't want to be careful. Not after all these years.

And it would need to be me to light the fuse. Because Deck had been talking himself out of his feelings for years. He might let his guard down and put an arm around me on the couch or ask me to dance—things he could dismiss because of our friendship and our history—but he'd never admit he wanted more unless I did first. For all Deck's talk about being a live wire, he'd always been incredibly disciplined with his words, at least when it came to me. He'd only slipped once.

Baby.

Heart emoji.

CHAPTER TWENTY-FIVE
Cori

Two days after the dance, I was still going back and forth in my mind about talking to Deck, trying to game-plan my approach.

Oh, hey, Deck, I know you went to jail for nearly beating to death the guy who almost raped me, and my drug addict brother with newly-diagnosed HIV is a big factor in both our lives, and you feel guilty about everything from your sister's burns to Eliazar dying, and I'm traumatized from my mom being a sex worker and wondering all the time if my brother and I were going to get taken away, and I turned my back on my entire childhood and created a double life for myself in the corporate world, and I need to save the one place I loved growing up from financial ruin, and a month ago, we were barely speaking while prowling around a nasty drug house stepping over vomit looking for Johnny, and you still probably feel you're bad for me, BUT I think we should start holding hands and going out to dinner and watching baseball games and stuff because I might be a little in love with you, and probably have been for basically my whole life, and, oh yeah, I think you love me too.

Even picturing the conversation made me nauseous.

It was a terrible time to upset our status quo. But for the first time in my life, I didn't care. I wanted to do the messy, fucked-up thing. But not necessarily right this minute.

I felt like I could go slow acclimating myself to the idea first. It was enough for now to enjoy my rediscovered friendship with Deck and not rush into the next step.

Maybe I'd have a better answer when Deck came over later. I'd invited him to Sunday brunch with my friends, hoping it would make my brother feel more comfortable to have him there as a buffer.

A few minutes before Britta and Marcus were set to arrive, Johnny was still fumbling with the buttons of his polo shirt.

"You don't have to wear that," I said. "We aren't formal or anything."

"I wanna make a good impression on your fancy friends."

He was nervous. Since leaving rehab a week ago, he'd been holed up in my house. He'd turned my guest bedroom into a hurricane of clothes, candy wrappers, and soda cans, plus his meds were in the hall bathroom cabinet, but other than that, it was like living with a ghost. I knew I needed to approach the subject of trying a different rehab, but Johnny barely seemed able to navigate the menu on my TV, let alone discuss options for his continued recovery.

At least he hadn't relapsed, and it had been over a month since Deck and I pulled him out of the hell house. That was something.

Since I couldn't coax Johnny outside, I'd decided to bring people who weren't Deck and me to him. Britta and Marcus were a soft landing. I knew they'd be kind, and I wanted Johnny to see that he fit with the other pieces of my life.

"My friends aren't fancy," I insisted, pulling his hands from his collar. "They're like me."

Johnny's forehead stretched. "Sorry, Sis. You fancy."

"I am not!"

"Let's examine the evidence, shall we?" He counted off on his fingers. "When we order takeout, you put it on plates instead of eating out of the boxes. You have spare toothbrushes for guests. Your fridge has one of those thingies to get ice and water. And you have a switch on the wall to make the shades go down over the windows."

"Only the high ones I can't reach!" I flicked him on the arm, pleased to feel a little meat under my fingers. "You have a low bar for what's fancy."

"What can I say? I grew up in a trailer park." He grinned. I'd missed that smile.

"Well, you'll love Britta and Marcus. Fancy or not. And they'll love you."

"And they know about...everything?"

"They're my best friends, Johnny," I said gently. "I already told you they know. And they're not judging you. Just be yourself. That's all you need to do."

He inhaled warily. "'Kay."

Britta and Marcus showed up carrying a casserole dish and a reusable grocery bag with a bottle poking out of the top.

I intercepted them in the doorway and motioned to the bag. "We should probably skip the mimosas today."

Britta winked. "It's sparkling cider."

I shook my head. "Sorry."

"No worries. I know this is weird. We're just excited to finally meet your brother."

"I already met him once," Marcus said. "When Cori and I were engaged. Although he might not remember."

"I suppose that means I was high or passed out." Johnny entered the main room with a self-deprecating chuckle.

Marcus's cheeks paled. "Apologies, man. I didn't mean to imply anything." He held out his arm, and Johnny stared at it a fraction of a second before shaking his hand.

"No offense taken. I know it wasn't a shot."

"Definitely not," Marcus stated firmly before pulling his hand back. "It's very nice to see you again, Johnny. This is my wife, Britta."

Britta pushed the casserole dish into Johnny's chest. His arms raised instinctively to cradle it. "Lovely to meet you," she said. "Can you help me take this stuff into the kitchen since my husband and best friend here apparently weren't going to offer?"

"Uh...of course."

He walked into the kitchen and deposited the dish on the countertop.

Britta followed, asking him, "Do you know where the plates and a spatula are so I can work on this quiche? I'm not certain where your sister hides those things."

"Sure."

After hundreds of brunches, Britta knew perfectly well where everything in my kitchen was. She chatted amiably with Johnny as she kept finding more tasks for him. *Would you please unwrap the scones? Don't you just love orange chocolate? Or are you more of a blueberry man? Let's get the sausages in the skillet now. I got the links. Do you prefer those or the patties?* I sent up a prayer of thanks that Marcus had the good sense to break up with me and bring this amazing woman into our lives. Within five minutes, Britta and Johnny were engrossed in a detailed discussion about a true crime documentary they'd both watched recently, shooing me and

Marcus into the living room so they could debate the merits of underwater evidence collection.

"Johnny seems alright," Marcus said once we were out of earshot. A statement and a question.

"He is," I agreed. "But unless we can get him into some kind of rehab program, this all feels like a ticking clock, just biding time until his next relapse." I raised a shoulder at Marcus's answering frown. "It would be nice to feel differently, but I've been down this road too many times not to be pessimistic."

"But this is the longest he's been clean in a while, right?"

"He had a few months sober after our friend Eliazar died. But there's also more at stake now, with his heart and the HIV." We heard the rumbling sound of a truck pulling into the driveway. "That would be Deck," I said.

"This is the guy who was Johnny's friend when you all were kids? The one who's been helping you at the Center?"

"Mm-hmm," I replied absently.

Marcus's gaze sharpened. I hurriedly opened the door.

This was the first time I'd seen Deck in anything other than the worn jeans and gray T-shirts he wore at the Center. His ribbed navy sweater fit his broad chest and lean torso like a glove, gold chains peeking out from the neckline. His dark jeans, a brown belt, and matching brown lace-up boots looked like they'd come straight off a store mannequin, and his haircut was fresh, glossy black curls falling roguishly across his forehead.

A subtle smile played across Marcus's lips as he looked from Deck to me. I'd been drawn to Marcus in college because he exuded such a safe balance between being attractive and being approachable. He possessed a readable face that put people instantly at ease. The stark contrast between his openness and Deck's enigmatic expression struck me.

"Thank you for inviting me," Deck said formally. Holding up a bag, he added, "I brought roasted potatoes."

"Mamá Decker's recipe? With the peppers?" I asked hopefully.

He relaxed, grinning. "Yeah."

After introducing Deck to Britta, the five of us sat down to eat. Surprisingly, Johnny carried the brunt of the conversation, eager to continue engaging with Britta about their similar taste in movies and TV.

"Deck and Cori only want to watch dumb comedies," he complained. "Like, ever since we were kids, I'd vote for Tarantino or some cool horror movie, and these two would be like, 'Nah. Let's watch *Forgetting Sarah Marshall* for the five millionth time.'"

I tsked. "You've never had any taste, Brother."

"No, I'm with you, Johnny," Marcus said. "When Cori and I were engaged, I'd suggest dramas or action movies, but she'd only ever agree to go see comedies."

Deck's fork clanked loudly as he dropped it on his plate. Four pairs of eyes turned to him.

"Sorry," he stammered.

Britta observed him keenly before smiling. "Deck, has Cori not filled you in on our friend group's sordid history?" she asked.

"Oh, stop." I made a face at her.

She ignored me, turning to Deck. "Once upon a time, Marcus and Cori were a couple. And they got engaged. But then they broke up—"

"Marcus dumped me," I interjected.

"Sort of," Marcus corrected.

Britta grimaced, shutting us both up. "Anyhoo," she continued, "they broke up but stayed good friends. Because that's all they ever should have been. Then Marcus met me, and we got married. Cori stood up for us at our wedding and gave a very bland and boring toast at the reception. Now we're all friends. Except Cori's better friends with me than her ex-fiancé." She gave Marcus a triumphant smile.

"Well, that's mostly true," I said. "Except it was a fantastic toast."

"You quoted Lana Del Rey," Britta argued.

"Like I said, fantastic toast."

Deck chortled with the rest of us, but seemed unsure.

"So Deck," Britta began, giving me a shit-eating grin, "Cori told us you and Johnny were close growing up, but it sounds like maybe you were all friends?"

My neck heated.

Deck shifted in his seat. "I guess it would be fair to say that. Cori used to come over to my house and babysit my sister. Plus, Johnny let Cori tag along with us a lot when we went places."

Britta hummed, exchanging a glance with Marcus before letting the subject drop. She and Johnny carried the conversation for the rest of the meal, mostly discussing the merits of *Squid Game*.

Deck exited quickly after eating, apologizing awkwardly on his way out the door, citing prior plans with his parents. After he left, Johnny admitted to running on fumes, still adjusting to his withdrawal and his new medications.

Britta pulled him into a tight hug before he went to lie down. "It was a pleasure meeting you. I hope we can do it again soon."

"Yeah." He scratched at his scalp. "Same. I mean that."

Marcus snuck out on the deck to take a phone call while Britta helped me wash dishes. I thanked her for putting my brother at ease.

"Don't worry about it," she said. "Johnny's a sweetheart. I totally see what you meant when you described him as charming. Let me know if there's anything I can do for either of you to help with the situation."

"You're already doing it. Treating him the way you did."

"Well, that's too easy." She put down the sponge and leaned against the sink, checking to make sure Marcus couldn't hear before turning to me with a leer. "And not to change the subject... But how about you tell me what's up between you and that sex-on-a-stick man who ate brunch with us?"

My jaw dropped.

"Oh, come off it, Cor." Britta laughed. "I know you. And ohmygod why the heck didn't you mention how hot he is? That tight body and all that yummy black hair. Don't get me wrong, Marcus is a total dime, but Deck is like that mysterious broody type who makes you want to...decipher him."

I huffed. "I'm glad you liked him. But there is no *deciphering* going on. How about we return to our discussion on the great solar panel installation saga of our lifetime?"

"Nuh-uh. This is so much more interesting—"

"Are we talking about how Deck wants to throw Cori down on the bed and do dirty, dirty things to her?" Marcus asked, coming in from outside.

"What!?" I squawked.

Britta gave me a *see, I told you so* look, crossing her arms gleefully.

"Oh, he definitely does." Marcus waggled his eyebrows. "The air was full of horny pheromones, and he eye-fucked you the whole time."

"Horny pheromones? What the hell?"

Marcus held up his hands. "Whatever."

I knew they thought they were being playful, funny even, but they didn't understand my history with Deck. It wasn't something I could be flippant about. Or sanguine. That would never be our story.

"Guys, I know you mean well. And I'm not trying to be coy…" Sitting down on the couch, I squeezed my eyes shut for a second before opening them again.

Britta and Marcus sobered.

"What's going on, Cori?" Britta asked.

I exhaled the air from my lungs. "So…long story short…When we were teenagers, Deck and I had more-than-friendly feelings for each other. Ones we never acted on. Now that we're back in each other's orbit, that pull is still there. But there are reasons we don't acknowledge—" My voice faltered. "It's complicated."

Britta seated herself next to me, placing a hand on my knee. "We're missing something here, obviously. It's more than what's going on with your brother?"

I nodded, releasing another deep, slow breath. After twelve years, I was finally ready to share with them.

"It has to do with the last night I saw Deck when we were kids."

Speaking rapidly, I spared nothing. I told them about Deck and me, how our relationship evolved from friendship into lingering glances and stolen touches, always with our feelings unstated.

Detailing how Deck, Johnny, and their friends fell in with criminals, and how that situation spiraled, I then recounted Chi-chi's assault in painstaking detail, down to my bloody foot. I finished with my recollection of Deck nearly killing Chi-chi with his bare fists, and the look on his face when they shoved him into the back of a police car.

"I sent him a few letters after he got locked up," I added. "When he didn't reply, I figured he was done with me. After my mom died, it just made sense to…leave it all behind. Leave him behind. I became a new Cori, a successful Cori. To use Marcus's term—*Robot Cori*. Being back in Everett now, spending time with Johnny, and having Deck in my life have given me back little pieces of my soul.

Showed me what's been missing. I feel whole again, a whole person who can own her truth, who can finally tell you about the night Chi-chi held me down on my bed and almost raped me."

A tear fell down Britta's cheek. Her fingers on my knee clutched tightly.

"I don't know what to say," Marcus breathed out, shaking his head slowly. "All this time, I didn't know."

"I didn't want you to know," I said. "Keeping the most horrible details to myself gave me a sense of control over the narrative. I'm telling you now because I'm letting go of that. Finally."

Britta wrapped me in her arms. "I'm so sorry that happened to you," she said.

Pulling back, I gave her a firm glance. "I'm okay. I've done some therapy, and like I said, every day it gets easier." She waited as I gathered myself and continued, "But maybe don't make jokes about me and Deck, how he looks at me or whatever. I'm not ready to be normal with it yet. To treat it like some random attraction. Let alone open it up to commentary. It's heavier than all that. And I'm still figuring out how to deal with that *weight* between us."

Britta was instantly contrite. "Of course we won't make light of it anymore! We never meant to make you feel uncomfortable."

"It's okay," I assured her. "Under all usual circumstances, I *like* that you joke around with me. It feels like something regular people do. I don't want anyone's pity. Or to be treated differently."

Britta pointed at her nose, exaggeratedly rotating her finger in a circle. "This is not my *I pity you* face. This is my *I'm so glad you told me, and I'm so proud to be your friend, and I love you* face."

I laughed. "I love you too."

Slumped in a side chair, Marcus grunted as though to agree, but he still looked wide-eyed. It was understandable, considering he'd known me for over ten years and most of this was new information.

Britta peered at him before facing me again. "Can I ask one thing? You don't have to answer if you don't want to."

I eyed her. "Okay."

"Why didn't you and Deck get together back then? Before all the stuff with that Chi-chi character? You said you never told him how you felt, but you also said he probably felt the same way. I know you were young, but..."

I looked up at the ceiling. "It's not my place to give up his secrets, but Deck has his own demons. They gave him a reason to run from me. Going to prison convinced him he was right all along to stay away."

"That's why he didn't answer your letters," Marcus spoke up. "To give you a clean break from his 'demons.'"

"I don't know if that's incredibly sad or incredibly romantic," Britta said. "For what it's worth, he looked at you today like he really, really liked you. And if you're working through the stuff from your past, maybe he is too."

"Maybe."

"Hopefully, this is okay to ask..." Marcus said slowly. "But whatever happened to Chi-chi? Are you safe?"

I hmphed. "Interesting footnote. Turns out, the cops had eyes on the big man Chi-chi ran scores for and had plenty on him already. That's how they picked up Cruz. In exchange for a reduced sentence, Chi-chi rolled on his boss and got a nasty prison-yard death for his trouble. Shanked right in the back. Bash got the same two months later."

"Jesus," Marcus breathed out.

I shrugged. "Meh. That's what you get when you snitch like a little bitch." I couldn't drum up much compassion for the man who'd assaulted me.

Marcus did a double take. "Damn, Cori. At no point in our re-lationship have I ever thought I'd hear you utter the phrase 'snitch like a little bitch.'" He cracked a smile.

"Shut up." I laughed.

Britta cackled. "Oh my god. Say it again. Except give me a sec to grab my phone. I want to record it for Instagram."

"Fuck off." I threw a pillow at her.

I knew they weren't making fun of me. They were letting me know that, whoever I was and whoever I'd been, it was all okay with them.

By the time they went home, our conversation had turned to the more benign topics of Marcus's squabbling interns and Britta's next work trip. But the glow of unburdening myself lingered, of finally being in the right headspace to relay all the gory details of my past.

I wondered about Deck. Being in his arms was one thing, but being in his head was another. I didn't understand the full extent of his demons, but I couldn't stop myself from imagining what might be on the other side of him conquering them.

CHAPTER TWENTY-SIX
Deck

M onday morning, I arrived at the Center early to work on the bathroom tile. Reign would be in to help later, and I needed to make good progress for the project to remain on track, since it took longer when I spent time instructing them on how to do things.

I was also hoping to run into Cori so I could apologize. I'd been sort of rude yesterday, especially after learning she and her friend Marcus had once been a couple. Been engaged.

It shouldn't have taken me by surprise. Obviously, Cori had lived her life while I'd been locked up. Not to mention the past few years. I knew from Johnny that she didn't date much. Had Marcus been her only serious relationship? And was that the kind of man she was into? A perfectly nice and boring white-collar guy with awesome manners who probably had a closet full of, like, sport coats. He seemed like the type of person who kept in touch with his fraternity brothers and had a favorite author. Meanwhile, I'd had to buy a new outfit to avoid embarrassing myself at brunch, and the only reading I did these days was my daily doomscroll through social media.

I thought we'd been getting somewhere on the dance floor. The euphoria of holding her in my arms had flooded my senses. But I'd let myself have it. And made no apologies for wanting it.

Then I met Marcus, and the familiar insecurities came rushing back.

When I reached the office, Cori was on a Zoom call with Quincy, the accountant. I lingered outside, trying not to eavesdrop. Then I heard my name. Quincy's voice was muffled, but I caught snippets of Cori's end of the conversation.

"Deck is saving us a ton doing all this repair work for free... I know. I saw the maintenance line item, we will need to fix that... Yeah, the foundation is pulling back on all their grants, so we only have this year... We pushed him on fulfilling his get-or-give commitment, and he quit the board instead... No. Ana feels good about it. Goal is still the same."

Hearing the click signaling the end of the call, I rapped on the doorframe. Cori sat at the desk—in a new chair—with her head in her hands.

When she looked up, I confessed sheepishly, "Sorry, I might have overheard some of that conversation."

She waved her hand. "Don't worry about it. You're part of the team now, right? None of this is sensitive or confidential. I can tell you straight out that the Center's finances are still totally fucked. We need an influx of money. There's no way to get out of this with cuts or efficiencies. We need the gala to make eight hundred thousand. Minimum. That'll buy us another year to figure out a long-term plan to remain sustainable."

"And if the gala doesn't make that much?"

Cori's expression tightened. "We'll look like a sinking ship. Funders will pull out. It'll snowball. Donors don't like throwing money at lost causes. That's why some of our board members have already bailed. They thought the numbers were too daunting."

"But Ana is optimistic?" I asked hopefully.

"Honestly, it's fifty-fifty. We had some promising leads that didn't pan out. The good news is, we already have five hundred in pre-funding secured—those are donors who have committed to raising the paddle for certain amounts that night—so finding the other three hundred is possible since we still have two months."

"Finding" three hundred thousand dollars sounded overwhelming, but I supposed that was why I was ripping up tile while she pored over spreadsheets. "The Center is lucky to have you," I told her.

Cori came around to the other side of the desk, crossing her arms and ankles as she leaned against it. "No, Deck, like I said to Quincy, the Center is lucky to have *you*. You're taking on so much work that would otherwise get pushed aside. It's no less important than what any of the rest of us do." She unfolded her arms. "Actually, check that. Marisol and the program staff have the most important jobs, but the rest of us are necessary too. Including you."

"Thank you."

"Out of curiosity, how did you come to be involved in construction? I realize I don't know much about your life since you got out. Or even before then."

I scraped a hand through my hair. "Well, I guess it started in prison. I took classes to earn my GED and then my bachelor's degree. One instructor suggested that people with my learning style tend to thrive in jobs that involve hands-on work. I got lucky there was a program that allowed me to learn a trade on the inside, and once I started, everything just fell into place. There were opportunities for day-release work programs, so I got the experience I needed. I met Juan there too. He made parole three years before me, and when I was released, he was waiting for me with J&D basically ready to go."

"Wow. That's amazing. He sounds like a great friend."

"He is. At first, I didn't want to accept the help—"

Cori snorted. "Sorry. Sorry." She held up her hands.

I grinned. "But Juan pointed out how stupid and stubborn I was being. We worked out an arrangement where I could buy into the business over time, but he's never treated me like anything less than an equal partner."

"That's awesome, Deck. Truly. I hope I can meet him someday."

As soon as she said it, I recognized how much I wanted that. To have her meet Juan the way I'd met her friends.

I sighed. "Hey Cori, I'm...uh, sorry... For yesterday."

Her brow furrowed. "Huh? What happened yesterday?"

"I know I was pretty quiet during brunch. Then I left so quickly. I don't think I made a very good impression on your friends."

Her face relaxed. "It's all good, Deck." She hopped onto her feet, closing most of the distance between us. "Trust me, they liked you. But as long as you're bringing it up, is there a reason you were so quiet?"

I felt her breath on the bottom of my chin. Her blue eyes stared up at me. Challenging.

"I...I...don't know," I stammered. "Guess I was just... surprised."

"Surprised?" She angled her head sideways.

I swallowed nervously. Why had I brought this up? ¡*Estupido*! Of course she was going to ask me to clarify. "Don't know," I mumbled. "I don't know why. I just thought I owed you an apology for clamming up."

"Hmm," she replied inscrutably.

"Cori!" Marisol came bursting into the office. "You need to pick up line two. Mr. Samuels is on the phone, and he wants some answers about the allocation of funds."

"That sounds urgent," I said, stepping back. Even I knew Evan Samuels was one of the Center's largest donors. I backed away, grateful for the reprieve. "I'll leave you to it, then."

Cori sighed. Before picking up the phone, she said, "Deck, I'd appreciate it if we could have lunch today. I'd like to finish this conversation." Under her breath, she murmured, "Finally."

The look on her face showed she wouldn't take no for an answer. "Sure thing, Cori." I stumbled into the hallway.

Terror gripped me. Followed by the freedom of surrendering to the inevitable. I had a few hours to prepare for a conversation we'd needed to finish for twelve years.

The rest of the morning, I deliberated about what to say to her. I kept coming back to the same crazy thought to put it all out there, tell her I'd gotten weird about Marcus because I was jealous he'd gotten to be with her in a way I'd always wanted to be.

It seemed useless to attempt a half-truth or an outright lie. For as long as I'd known Cori Raney, she'd never fallen for anyone's lines. That quiet competence was one of my favorite things about her.

Over the past few weeks, I'd watched her placate nervous donors and board members, help Ana coordinate sponsors for the gala, and work with Marisol to manage programs so Rosa could be with Lupe. This was all besides the times I'd caught her having fun on the job—reading to the kindergartners, making dreamcatchers with the upper elementary group, or working the scoreboard for Chuck during an ad hoc soccer tournament.

Cori 2.0 certainly seemed a lot like Cori 1.0, but I got the feeling this grown-up version wouldn't put up with my mixed signals the way sixteen-year-old Cori had.

This Cori wasn't going to pretend I hadn't held her close on the dance floor. She knew why I'd been shocked into silence after finding out she'd been engaged. She'd stood in front of me just now, practically demanding I admit it.

So I would. That was my plan. After everything we'd been through, I wasn't going to wait around while she found another Marcus to get engaged to. I was going to tell Cori I wanted something more than friendship.

She knew my flaws, my pain, and my regret. If she wanted me anyway, then I would be grateful, not scared.

Expressing my feelings felt a bit like standing on the edge of a cliff, trying to capture gravity. But she deserved to have the information and decide what happened next. And if she wanted to put the genie back in the bottle and tell me it wasn't a good idea to change things, that we were better off as friends, then so be it.

But I hoped she'd say something else.

Chapter Twenty-Seven
Deck

A Mediterranean food truck was parked half a mile from the Center. Cori and I took advantage of the mild weather to walk there. Since it was midday on a Monday, we mostly had the sidewalk to ourselves. I'd prepared myself to say my piece, but she spoke first.

"Thanks for having lunch with me, Deck. I know we have some stuff to talk about, but to be honest, I just had a hell of a morning making some extremely obnoxious phone calls, and I need to get some food in me before we discuss anything heavy."

I smiled. What were twenty more minutes after more than a decade? "Do you want to talk about the phone calls? Maybe it'll help to vent a little?"

She hiked her purse up on her shoulder aggressively. "Just talking to some of our longer-term donors. Everyone wants answers I don't have. I can't guarantee success in the future if we don't have the money pledged. So it's kind of a chicken and egg thing, you know?"

"That sounds annoying. Sorry."

"It's okay. Part of the gig. I'm hoping all these folks will be at the gala. Once they see the programs in action and are reminded of the mission, I'm betting they'll be all in. But our best hope for long-term sustainability lies in attracting new donors. I have a number of contacts from JBC who will be attending the event. I'm just not sure that'll be enough." She exhaled. "I don't know. This is exactly what I signed up for when I said I'd help Rosa. I think I just forgot that some days feel this way, no matter the job."

"Your old job was like this?"

"In the sense that I often got so frustrated I wanted to throw things," she said wryly.

I had trouble picturing Cori as anything other than cool and composed. "It sounds like you don't miss it?"

Her pace slowed. "No. It was good for a while, and I learned a lot, so I don't regret my time there, but I'm done with the corporate world. That's one of the few things I'm sure of."

A whisper of laughter escaped me.

"What?" she asked with a smile.

"This is going to sound nuts, but that's kind of how I feel about prison. Before I went in, I was really spiraling. I mean, I almost killed someone with my bare hands. Being inside grounded me. I got an education and found my place. I regret a lot of the things that led to me being thrown in a cell, but the experience itself changed my life. It would be a stretch to say it was good for me, but I came out better." I chuckled again. "Also, like you, I'm definitely done with it. No way am I going back."

Cori's brows drew together. "Of course not."

I appreciated how confused she seemed by the mere suggestion.

We reached the truck and both of us ordered falafel sandwiches. They were messy to eat while walking, so we sacrificed more than a few bits of cucumber and dollops of tzatziki sauce to the pavement gods.

Three blocks from the Center, we came to the little corner market that had been part of the neighborhood for as long as I could remember.

"Can we stop at the store?" Cori asked. "That pita was great, but it's not going to hold me until dinner. I want to grab a bag of pretzels. Then maybe we can have our talk?"

"Sure. Is it alright if I buy Reign a candy bar? They're coming to help me this afternoon, and I know they like Twix. But I don't want to get in trouble for showing favoritism or anything."

"It's okay, Deck. That's nice. As long as you don't give it to them in front of all the other kids, I think it's fine."

We walked through the glass door to the familiar *ding* announcing our entrance, and I upnodded Amos behind the counter. Amos had been a few years ahead of me in school, and we were in prison together for a while when he served time for robbery. When I first got out and lived with my parents, I'd run into him at the market, so I knew he'd been working here for a few years. His name tag said *Assistant Manager.*

The ancient building was long and narrow. The market consisted of only two aisles with chest-high shelving in between. Fountain soda machines, a slushy dispenser, two freezers full of ice cream novelties, and cold cases housing single-serve drinks lined one wall. I recalled the way my friends and I used to give that slushy machine a workout. I grabbed Gatorades for myself and Reign, along with the Twix. Cori stood in front of the pretzels like she was studying the *Mona Lisa*.

"Why can't I ever decide between the jalapeño and mustard flavors?" she whined.

"That means you need bo—"

"EVERYBODY DOWN ON YOUR FUCKING KNEES!"

With instincts honed since birth, I swung my arm around Cori and pulled us both to the sticky linoleum floor, covering her body with my own.

Turning her head to mine, I put my pointer finger over my lips in the universal *be quiet* gesture. She nodded.

"EMPTY THE FUCKING REGISTER! NOW! AND THE SAFE IN THE BACK!"

Cori and I were on the opposite side of the market from the front counter. From our vantage point on the floor, I saw the back of a man dressed in black sweats, with a black beanie and neck gaiter covering his hair and the lower half of his face. In his hand, he waved a coal-black pistol. A nine-millimeter double stack Glock, if I wasn't mistaken.

"HURRY, MOTHERFUCKER. HURRY!"

Amos didn't appear to move any faster as he pressed buttons on the register, and the drawer snapped open. The old-fashioned radio he had next to the cigarette case droned with sports news.

Next to me, Cori raised her head. Her eyes went wide as plates. Too quietly for Amos and the gunman to hear, she whispered, "Deck, that's Jayden."

"What?"

"It's Jayden. You know, the kid from the Center. The fight last week."

It took me a beat, then I remembered. His eyes. "How do you know?"

"I recognize his backpack, plus I just know. It's him."

I hadn't even noticed the backpack. I recalled everything Marisol told me about Jayden, about him being drawn to his brother's old crew. Stupid kid. He was no pro, and those guys weren't doing him any favors with this job. Sending him in with a recognizable backpack to rob a store in his own neighborhood in broad daylight in a market covered with cameras. I shook my head. This was it for Jayden. The choice that was going to change everything.

Cori shook my wrist.

"Deck, we need to do something."

"Huh?"

She hitched her head toward the counter. "You know, stop him. He's going to get picked up, and this will ruin the rest of his life. His poor mom will have two sons on the inside."

I blanched. "What do you want me to do? That's a serious piece he's packing."

Her eyes teared up.

The *ding* sounded again. Amos's and Jayden's faces whipped to the door. Jayden's gun hand twitched, and he lifted his arm to aim at the person who'd come in at the exact wrong moment. The customer, a middle-aged businessman-type, froze.

His hands slowly rose. "Please," he squeaked.

Jayden's gaze narrowed sinisterly above the gaiter. His index finger brushed over the trigger. With a click, his thumb clamped down on the safety, disengaging it.

The customer squeezed his eyes shut.

Seconds ticked by, but Jayden didn't pull the trigger. He merely stood there, aiming at the terrified man as his arm shook. Monotone voices continued blaring from the staticky radio.

The customer sensed Jayden's hesitation and opened his eyes. In a flash, the man bolted out the door. He jumped into his car and drove off on screeching tires.

Seconds later, another car peeled out of the parking lot.

"*Hombre*, I think your getaway driver just hung you out to dry," Amos said to Jayden. "And that *gringo* you let escape is probably calling the cops right now."

Jayden's eyes went wild. He swung his gun arm, pointing it at Amos. I heard the harshness of his breathing through the thick fabric and could practically smell the sweat soaking his skin.

Amos held up his hands. "Whoa. You don't wanna do that."

"JUST EMPTY THE FUCKING REGISTER!"

The hollowness of Jayden's voice got to me. Like I was watching myself thirteen years ago, doing jobs for Chi-chi because I didn't know a way out of it.

I decided that Jayden's not pulling the trigger was the actual choice that mattered on this day. His moment of conscience would be the thing that defined him, not his decision to rob a store.

Standing, I walked slowly toward him with my hands raised. "Hey, man." I spoke deliberately.

Jayden snapped his head to me, gun arm outstretched. "Get the fuck down!"

I crouched but stayed on my feet. "I'm only trying to help you. It's not too late to get out of this."

"I am getting out of this. I'm taking the cash and leaving." Jayden turned back to Amos, thrusting the backpack into his hands. "Put the money in that!"

Amos gave me a nod before shoving the bills from the register into the backpack.

"It doesn't look like much cash," I said casually, moving closer to the front. "Most people use cards these days."

Amos finished loading up the backpack and slid it across the counter. Jayden picked it up, apparently no longer interested in the safe, and hunched it over his shoulder.

In the distance, police sirens blared.

"Give it back," I said. "You're never getting out of here with it. They'll be looking for a young male dressed all in black. Armed robbery is years, Jayden. Years."

He flinched. "You know me."

Shit. I'd let the name slip. Well, no help for it.

"Jayden!" Cori stood and walked toward us. She held her arms up, but Jayden didn't bother to raise the gun at her. Instead, he flicked his thumb to re-engage the safety. "You need to give the money back right now," she implored him. "Let Deck help you."

Cori looked at me beseechingly. Based on the sound of the sirens, cops would be here in less than a minute. As a single tear slipped from Jayden's left eye, I sprang into action.

I tossed the backpack to Amos and pulled the gun from Jayden's quivering hand, giving that to Amos as well. Amos quickly shoved the cash back into the drawer and went into the office to stash the Glock. Cori pulled off Jayden's beanie and gaiter and stuffed them in her purse, fluffing up his hair with her fingers.

That was when I saw the woman.

She must have been lying down in the other aisle.

Cori muttered, "Shit," under her breath as she took in the same impeccable makeup and complicated updo I saw. The woman was obviously young, in her mid-twenties at most, but she was dressed like someone's wealthy grandma, wearing a pale purple suit dress and pearls, along with shiny heels and a matching purse. Standing, she brushed off the front of her thighs.

"Please!" Cori pleaded as the sirens grew closer. "He's a good kid. I promise. He deserves a chance."

A police cruiser pulled into the parking lot. I'd been hoping Emilio might be called to the scene, but no such luck. The two officers inside the vehicle initially seemed to be assessing the situation through the windshield. Amos and I started fake laughing like we'd just shared the most hilarious joke, and I slung my arm around a still-wooden Jayden.

Ding. The bored-looking officers came through the door.

"We heard there was a situation?" one officer said, more a question than a statement.

"Someone reported a robbery in progress," the other officer spoke directly.

Amos's forehead creased in an Oscar-worthy performance of *confused corner store cashier*. "Must have been someplace else. I've been on shift since eight this morning, and it's been quiet all day."

The first officer seemed ready to shrug and call it a day, but the second officer peered around suspiciously. His eyes landed on Jayden, who did not look up. "You okay, son?"

"Good," Jayden mumbled.

"He's fine," I said, still squeezing his shoulders. "This is my little cousin. He's pissed I caught him cutting. I was about to take him back to school, but we stopped off for a hot dog since he missed lunch period."

Amos plucked a hot dog off the roller, putting it in a bun and handing it to me.

The officer continued looking around. "What about you?" he asked Cori. "Seen anything suspicious?"

"Nope. Just came in for some pretzels on my lunch break. I'm helping at the Center while Rosa takes care of some personal business."

This sparked the interest of the first officer. "How's Rosa doing these days?"

"She's good," Cori replied brightly.

"Well, tell her Officer Ripley says hello," he said.

"Will do."

"What about you, miss?" the second officer called to the young woman in the back. "Did you see anything happening in the store, or nearby maybe?"

The woman darted nervous eyes between Cori, Jayden, and the officers. "Oh...um...no, sir, officer, sir. I didn't see anything. I just was minding my own business buying a Diet Coke."

Damn. I wished the lady was a better actress, but at least she wasn't giving Jayden up.

The second officer turned to Amos. "You got cameras?"

"C'mon, Dawson. Leave Amos alone," Officer Ripley said. "Nothing happened here. I'm not trying to do extra paperwork because some guy got scared and confused a kid in a hoodie with an actual criminal."

The second officer nodded. "Yeah. Okay."

They shuffled out the door. Officer Ripley leaned back and mouthed, "*Clean it up,*" to Amos.

After the police car drove off, Amos flipped the sign on the door to CLOSED.

"Thanks, *bróder*," I said to him, grateful that even though we hadn't had anything close to a heartfelt conversation since I'd gotten out, our neighborhood bonds still kicked in when it mattered. "Can you take care of the gun?"

Jayden spoke up. "I need to give that gun back."

Amos breathed out roughly. "I'll give it back for you, kid. This is your lucky day. Your brother was my boy, and his crew owes me. Imma give the gun back and tell them to leave you the fuck alone. Your mom has been through enough. Why the fuck you tryna break her heart, acting like a little punk?" He crossed his arms over his broad chest, shaking his head once.

"I know, okay! I know!" Jayden exploded. "But when Alejandro asked, I couldn't say no."

Amos and I exchanged glances. Alejandro wasn't someone to be messed with. But I trusted that Amos meant what he said, that he could get Jayden out of whatever he was into. I didn't need to know the details.

"Listen." I put a hand on Jayden's shoulder. "No one knows better than me and Amos how hard it is to say no. But you're gonna fucking have to. From now on. We all just put our lives and reputations on the line for you... Me, Amos, Cori...and this nice lady in the purple dress—"

"Mia," the woman offered.

"And Mia. We all covered for your dumb ass. And we didn't do it so you could keep making the same stupid choices."

Cori stepped in front of Jayden, forcing him to meet her eyes. "Amos was right when he said you got lucky. Someone was definitely looking out for you. And now it's time for you to step up."

Jayden squinted at her. "Don't get me wrong, Miss Cori, I like you. It's dope you've been helping out at the Center and all. But with respect, what the fuck does a rich lady like you know about what I need?"

Amos reached across the counter and tapped Jayden on the back of the head. "Shut your mouth, *pendejo*. You don't talk to her like that."

Cori gave Amos a little wink—*a wink!*—before speaking firmly to Jayden.

"I know more than you think, Jayden. I know that if you squeeze the handle on the red slushy machine just right, some of the blue slushy gets mixed in. I know Amos puts these little squares of aluminum foil out on the counter so the addicts don't steal the full rolls. And I know things around here have changed a lot, because ten years ago, the cops wouldn't have shown up nearly as quick. I grew up in this neighborhood, too, in that shitty trailer park three blocks from the high school." Jayden startled slightly, but Cori wasn't done. "The main thing I know is that no good can come from you being charged with robbery today. No good for you, anyway. But you need to look at this turn of events, this intervention, as a kind of miracle. Because ninety-nine times out of a hundred, you'd be on your way to jail right now, getting ready to spend your twenties behind bars. But instead, all of us are going out on a limb for you."

Jayden tried to look down, but she didn't allow it. Arching a brow, she said, "Tell me you understand."

His eyes were thunderous, but he nodded.

"Here's what's going to happen," I said. "You're going to say thank you to Amos for dealing with Greg's crew for you. And then you never speak to them again. Especially Alejandro. What's more, you aren't going to tell anybody about this, ever. I doubt the assholes who peeled out of the parking lot will say anything. You're going to take this gift for what it is. And that means respecting the code of silence."

"I'm definitely not going to say anything," Mia interjected awkwardly. Amos smiled.

"Thanks," I said to her.

"Are you going to tell my mom?" Jayden asked, the first hint of remorse in his tone.

I wordlessly communicated with Cori over Jayden's shoulder. "No," I replied. "She's been hurt enough. But make no mistake. We are buying something from you with that agreement."

"What do you mean?"

"He means you're not getting off free and clear," Cori said. "This was way too big of a misstep to shrug it off. We just helped you out of a felony."

"So what happens?"

"You're going to come to the Center," Cori declared. "Every day. Where I can keep an eye on you. No fighting. No mouthing off. No leaving to hang out with Greg's old crew."

"And when I'm around, you're going to help me with the building repairs," I added. "It'll do you some good to work with your hands."

Jayden made a face but didn't protest.

"This is day one, homie," Amos said. "Deadass. There won't be another chance."

Looking at Amos with fresh eyes, I took in all three hundred pounds of him, tatted up from his hands to his neck to most of his shaved head. I wondered how he appeared to Jayden. I saw only my old acquaintance—after this day, my true friend—but I guessed Jayden saw someone harder, someone whose word should be respected.

Nothing like two ex-cons to convince the young folks to just say no to a life of crime.

"You understand?" Cori asked Jayden.

"Yeah," he responded grudgingly, but some of the tension left his shoulders.

"The Center's closed on weekends, right?" Amos asked.

"Unfortunately. There's no budget for regular programs, just sports leagues," Cori answered.

"*Perfecto*. Then, since Jayden won't be there, he can come here. I could use a part-timer to help clean up and stock shelves, maybe even learn to work the register."

"For real?" Jayden perked up.

"Yeah, kid. I gotta do my part for the neighborhood, too. I see my homeboy Deck out here hammering and sawing for the Center, plus Cori back in the hood making things right. You're a little shit, but you can be my good deed."

I laughed, and it felt okay. Even Jayden cracked a smile.

"Pardon me." Mia inched closer. "The last thing I want to do is intrude, but if I may—" She looked directly at Jayden. "I want to say that I'm going to keep my promise. No one will hear about this from me." She squared her shoulders. "Obviously, I don't know why you felt the need to pick up a gun and rob a store, but I do know how lucky you are to have people willing to step up for you like this, people who see your potential, who think you can be better tomorrow than you are today. And I have a gut feeling their faith in you is justified."

None of us knew what to make of the demure young woman dressed like a congressman's wife. But for whatever reason, it seemed to be her words that finally got through to Jayden.

"Thanks," he said. "I know I got lucky."

"That's good to hear," Mia said, tapping his shoulder briefly. She held up a Diet Coke and put five dollars down on the counter in front of Amos. The *ding* echoed as she walked out the door. Cori ran after her, I assumed to thank her again.

"None of what comes next will be easy," I said to Jayden. "It's why I want you to help me at the Center. Working with your hands is good for fixing things up here." I pointed to my head.

"Definitely not easy," Amos agreed. "But it'll be better than prison." He handed Jayden his empty backpack. "See you Saturday at noon for your first shift. Now get the fuck out of my store."

CHAPTER TWENTY-EIGHT
Cori

By unspoken agreement, Deck and I put our conversation on ice. After the incident at the market, we drove Jayden to school in one of the Center's vans. Shockingly, he told us he'd made it to his first four periods that morning, so evidently his plan had been to commit a casual felony during his lunch period. We extracted a promise from him to come to the Center that afternoon, and maybe it was naive, but I had no doubt he'd keep his word.

When Deck and I were alone again in the van, he asked what I'd said to Mia.

"Nothing much," I replied. "I thanked her again, and she said she was glad it was her and not someone else who might have done something different. She said that she was only in the store because she'd had lunch near the waterfront earlier and got turned around since she doesn't know the area."

"Explains the church clothes."

"I gave her my card and told her to reach out anytime, in case she wanted to check on Jayden."

Deck hummed thoughtfully. "It's nice to be reminded there are good people in the world."

I nodded. "I only hope Jayden saw. Not just Mia but also you, me, Amos, and even that one cop who clearly knew something was up."

"It's tough to get a kid like that, with such a big chip on his shoulder, to see he has people. Being part of his brother's old crew is tempting because no one's asking him to make a hard choice."

"Wild how robbing a store is somehow the easy choice."

"Neighborhood logic." Deck lifted his shoulders as we pulled into the Center's parking lot.

When Jayden arrived a few hours later, he'd switched out his hoodie for a plain white T-shirt. He checked in with Marisol, just as he did on any other day, as I stood next to her at the front counter.

"Remember, no more fights with Tycho." She gave him a warning stare.

"We're cool. Imma keep my head down," he said, eyeing me.

"Glad to hear it," Marisol replied.

"Jayden, I was wondering if you'd like to help Deck," I said. "He's working in the bathroom."

The teen stuffed his fists in his pockets. "Uh, yeah. Sure."

If his quick agreement surprised Marisol, she didn't show it. "That's a great idea, Cori."

"It was Deck's idea, actually."

I walked with Jayden across the atrium to the bathroom, lifting the caution tape. Inside, Deck and Reign kneeled on the floor. Sandra, the volunteer, sat in a chair engrossed in her phone. Since the bathroom project had evolved from a repair to a full makeover, it looked nicer every time I came in. There were still holes in the ground where toilets should be, but the freshly installed sinks gleamed.

Deck saw me noticing them.

"Those are leftovers from an apartment project we worked on in Bellevue," he said. "I know they're modern, but they're commercial-grade and should hold up fine."

"They're gorgeous," I said. "A real upgrade. I just hope they don't put the rest of the place to shame."

Deck smiled with the cocky confidence I'd seen way too little of this past month. "Don't worry. I have a few other tricks up my sleeve. When I'm done, this bathroom will shine like it's brand new. In fact, I spoke to Juan this morning, and I can do the other downstairs bathroom to match, if you want. The project owners are fine with donating their excess materials."

"That's incredibly generous, Deck. Of course I won't say no."

He stood and waved an awkward hello to Jayden. Reign paused in their work, watching from the floor with flattened lips.

"Hey, Jayden." Deck tipped his head downward. "Do you know Reign?"

"Yeah, I've seen them around." Jayden glanced at the other teen. "'Sup."

Reign looked suspicious but nodded at Jayden before turning back to the tile, making a point of slipping in earbuds first.

"Reign helps me with projects, too," Deck told Jayden. "That won't be a problem, will it?"

"Huh?" Jayden's attention was stuck on Reign's movements. He seemed genuinely curious about what the other teen was doing. "I got no beef with Reign. I know some people are assholes about the non-bi—... the non-bini—...the not a boy or a girl thing, but far as I know, they never did shit to me or mine, so we're cool."

"Nonbinary," I said, stepping forward and checking again to make sure Reign's earbuds were in. "That's good to hear. Maybe it helps that you're a few years older. I hope Reign will have more friends when kids are mature enough to understand. Also, watch your language."

"Sorry." Jayden made a face. "But so you know, Reign would have plenty of friends if they'd just chill the eff out. They act like a pit bull guarding a fence—getting all mad before you even know if someone's just walking by or tryna be nice."

My heart hurt for Reign. Rejecting people before they could reject you was an isolating defensive strategy. Like me hiding my truth to avoid others' reactions to it. Or Deck denying access to his life in the name of protecting me. So much coping. So much surviving. It sucked. I just wanted to open myself up to happiness. And I wanted that for Reign too. And Jayden.

"Jayden, there's an extra pair of knee pads." Deck pointed at a box under the sink. "How about you grab them, and then you can help us grout this tile?"

Jayden looked excited as he slipped on the pads. Giving Deck a salute, I slipped from the bathroom. My phone buzzed as I headed toward the office.

GRAHAM EVANS: Hi. Not trying to pester you but still hoping you're up for coffee? Just thought I'd try once more. Don't worry, I'm not a crazy stalker. If you don't reply to this one, it'll be my last. ***smiley face emoji***

Shoot. I'd gotten so bogged down with everything, I'd never set up that coffee with Graham. Probably a good thing since Deck and I needed to hash out our stuff, and I didn't want to get distracted by anyone else until that happened.

But Graham was a good guy. And if he was okay being just friends, I was too. And maybe he would give me some advice about the Center. He knew a lot of people who could help with our website and social media problems. Was it slightly savage to ask him for favors when I knew he was hoping for more than friendship? Possibly. But he was a big boy, and he could turn me down if he wanted to. No harm done. Stabilizing the Center required a certain ruthlessness. And time was ticking. I needed to cast the net far and wide, giving as many people as possible the chance to invest in these kids' lives.

ME: Sorry for not getting back to you sooner. My new project has taken up a ton of time. I promise it wasn't intentional. Also, to make sure we are on the same page, this is a coffee between friends. Not a date.

GRAHAM EVANS: You've made that clear. Can't say I'm not disappointed, but I'll take friends. I'd love to hear about this project.

ME: I was hoping you'd say that. Any chance you're free now?

I ORDERED FOR BOTH OF US THROUGH the Starbucks app, and Graham picked up our coffees on his way to the Center.

When he arrived, I handed him a visitor's badge and gave him a tour. The Center showed very well that afternoon. In the large art room, kids finished clay pots using the new kiln donated by a local pottery studio. Chuck ran a kickball tournament for the middle schoolers on one side of the gym while the kindergartners giggled through a limbo contest on the other. A dozen older teens completed homework in the computer lab while others hung out in the atrium playing *Mario Kart*. The Center had multiple gaming subscriptions and physical cartridges for the older consoles, but nine times out of ten, the kids wanted *Mario Kart*.

Passing behind the beat-up couches in front of the TV, Graham lingered. When the next game started, he glanced at me for permission before asking to play. At first, the kids thought it was hilarious, considering Graham had on a three-piece suit and shiny shoes. They rolled their eyes when he asked to play Yoshi. Then he kicked all their butts, and his resulting glee made me laugh. Whatever happened, I hoped Graham and I would stay friends.

"I don't think I've ever sweat so hard playing video games," he said after we retreated to the office. He dropped into the seat across from the desk, fanning himself with his hand as he removed his suit coat. "Those kids are almost as merciless as my nephews."

"I'm glad you enjoyed yourself."

During our tour, I'd given him the rundown on what I'd been up to at the Center. He was no dummy, so I knew he was waiting for me to ask him to get involved. As he peered at me from above his coffee cup, I detected the hint of a smile. He was having a fine time making me work for it.

"I did enjoy myself, Cori. Thank you for inviting me. I had no idea this place existed." This time, his grin broke through, and he finally asked, "Alright, how can I help?"

"Well—" I smiled back at him. "I'll tell you since you asked, but only because you were so pleasant wiping the floor with those high schoolers." I sipped the last dregs of my latte. "First, I want to say again how sorry I am for not texting you when I said I would. I promise I'm not usually so flaky."

He relaxed in his chair. "No harm. I appreciate your honesty."

I cleared my throat. "In the spirit of honesty... When you initially texted me, I might have been more open to the possibility that this could have been a real date, but now I'm sort of in a *situationship*, so my friendship and undying gratitude for any help you're able to offer the Center is all I can offer."

Graham nodded once. "I figured. Can't say I'm not sorry, but I can take a no." He shifted in his chair. "Anyway, let's steer the conversation away from that awkwardness into how you're going to convince me to help this place. Because these kids clearly need help with their gaming skills."

I barked a laugh. "I think what you meant to ask is how I plan to give you the opportunity to make a significant positive impact on the lives of kids who truly deserve it."

He leaned back. "I almost forgot how good you are in the boardroom."

"Thank you. Now, I have a few ideas about how you and Trem-Mark can help..."

Half an hour later, Graham and I shook hands across the desk. He'd been generous. He didn't have the authority to promise a significant financial gift from TremMark without consulting the other executives, but he felt confident that they could make a six-figure commitment spread out over five years through their corporate giving program. Youth service was one of the company's core philanthropic missions. The Center would probably have to rebrand the science room with the TremMark logo and have a ceremony with a giant check, but that was par for the course. Graham also agreed to host a table at the gala and ask some deep-pocketed friends to join him for the event.

"I'm going to ask Jason and Brad to host tables as well," I said. "You're the first person from JBC or TremMark I've spoken with about this."

"I'm honored."

"Well, I appreciate the soft landing. The JBC folks don't know I grew up here, or how invested I am in this place. I'm excited to show it off." Hearing the words leave my mouth felt liberating. I'd spent so long thinking I had something to hide.

"You deserve to be excited. And proud." Graham shrugged his coat on.

"Let me walk you to your car."

Graham waved to the *Mario Kart* group as we passed through the atrium. In the parking lot, he stopped in front of a sleek white Range Rover.

"I'm so glad you came by today. Thanks again." I smiled and gave him a stiff hug.

"Me too," he said, leaning close to my ear. "I hope we do it again soon. And I'll set up the meeting with the giving team."

We pulled apart, and he grasped my shoulders, running his palms down my arms to squeeze my hands before getting into his car and driving away.

I turned toward the Center.

Deck stood at the entrance. Based on his expression, he'd seen it all—the smiles, the hug, and Graham running his hands down my arms.

Expression tightening, he went back into the building.

Dammit.

I released a groan into the deserted parking lot, raising my eyes heavenward. Sometimes Deck made me crazy because I wanted him so much. Other times, he made me crazy by being a big, insecure self-saboteur.

I shook my head.

It wasn't going to go down like that. Not this time.

This time, we were putting those demons to rest.

Chapter Twenty-Nine
Deck

I'd barely answered the knock on my front door before Cori barreled through. I couldn't believe she'd shown up at my house.

"Cool trick avoiding me the rest of the afternoon at the Center, Deck. But we need to talk."

The TV in the living room blared with some movie I'd put on when I got home. I'd thought about calling Juan to see if he wanted to meet up at Tubby's but decided I'd be shit company. Better to wallow in my own misery than inflict it on my best friend.

What I hadn't expected was for Cori to show up unannounced, no warning text or anything.

"Is everything okay?" I asked. "Johnny?"

She stopped short in the entryway, removing her shoes and throwing the delicate flats into the box with my dirty boots. Bastardo immediately jumped in and curled into a ball on top of them. "Johnny's fine, I'm sure. Probably chilling on my couch the way he has been for weeks. I wouldn't know since I came straight from the Center. I would have come sooner if I hadn't agreed to an evening

Zoom call with one of the board members. And you know full well why I'm here."

Flouncing into my living room, she turned around with her hands on her hips. She seemed mad but also...energized.

"Actually, I'm not sure why."

"No, Deck. Nuh-uh. We're not playing the game that way anymore. I'm here because you got all weird when you saw me with *my friend* Graham."

I sighed. "You can do whatever you want, Cori."

"Pfft. Come off it." She paced back and forth in front of my makeshift coffee table before releasing a sound that was half laughter and half annoyance. "Stop being infuriating. You know it bothered you to see me with him. Just like it bothered you to find out about Marcus." She lifted her forehead as though daring me to disagree. "Even if it's not rational. You don't believe for one minute that my visit with Graham was anything more than exactly what it was—two friends sharing a conversation. It just suits your purposes to pretend it could be more. Something that entitles you to be all...all..." She flicked her fingers back and forth. "Huffy."

I scoffed. "That doesn't even make sense."

She stopped pacing and stepped nearer to me. "Not everything makes sense, Deck. Especially the scary stuff."

I crossed my arms. "Am I scared in this scenario?"

"Terrified," she stated boldly, inching closer. "And we both know why."

"Is that so?" I aimed for detachment, but the words left my throat sounding hopeful.

Her hands snaked out to pull at my wrists tucked into my armpits. Her breathing remained deep and even as she locked our eyes together. "You need to say it out loud, Deck. I can't make that leap for you, can't force you to get over yourself."

I tried to step back, but she held my hands in a vise grip, mouthing, *"Not this time,"* as she kept her gaze on me.

"You already know, Cori." I closed my eyes before opening them again in slow motion. "You know I'm not like…those other men." I bit down hard on my bottom lip. "It's unfair to let myself want things when that's what you're used to. You're sophisticated and smart and strong. You deserve everything a man like Graham can give you."

She scowled. "Unfair to who? That's what you don't seem to understand. Graham is a great guy. And he is very educated and knows lots of interesting people. But there are important things he doesn't know."

I froze as her hands traveled up my forearms to my elbows.

"He doesn't know the correct ratio to mix hot sauce packets from Taco Bell into pasta when that's all you can afford for dinner. He doesn't know how to avoid bill collectors and process servers and cops. He doesn't know what it's like to master your mom's signature so you can sign all the permission slips for school. He's never had to search for laundry quarters in the couch cushions, or put on a face for teachers or coaches or social workers. And Deck—"

Her thumbs scratched circles into the sensitive skin of my inner elbows, making my arms tingle.

"Yeah?"

"Graham would have turned Jayden in to the police today. Not because he's a bad guy, but because of all the things he doesn't know." She ran her hands back down to link our fingers together, so our wrists and torsos touched. "He doesn't know *me*, Deck. He can't. And as far as what he can give me…"

I swallowed, captured wholly by the most beautiful eyes I'd ever seen, the ones that had haunted me since I was a teenager.

"He doesn't make my heart race. He's never made me crazy. Guys like him and Marcus, they're nice. But I want more than that."

"You make me crazy too," I rasped out. "And you deserve everything. The entire world."

She pressed herself flush against me. "And what do you deserve?"

My body was as rigid as a statue but also a fucking inferno. Her question hung in the air, loaded and tense. I felt every inch of her soft curves, saw the tic in her neck as her pulse beat a rapid rhythm. The words stuck in my throat like glue. I had to force them up past the threat of pain, force them up through years of guilt and self-recrimination.

At last, raggedly, they broke through.

"You, Cori." The rough rise and fall of my lungs turned the words into stormy syllables. "I deserve a chance to show you how much I want you. How much I always have. More than anything."

"Yes." Her forehead pressed into my neck. "Because I feel like I'm awake for the first time in twelve years, and I didn't even know I'd been asleep." She ran her nose across my chest, murmuring, "And I want it. To be so known by someone that it makes me more alive, puts me at the mercy of my battered, beating heart." She placed a soft kiss on my T-shirt. "Only you've ever made me feel that way, Deck. Like I wanted someone so much I wasn't totally in control of it. Only you."

"Only you," I whispered.

She tilted her head back to gaze at me. "After everything, we deserve to try."

Moving one hand to my front, she pulled up my shirt to place the bare skin of her palm on my belly, crawling it slowly up my torso.

And then my mouth was on hers, pulling her into me with the raw hunger of a man long denied. My first taste of Cori was not the delicate exploration it might have been when we were teenagers. This kiss was a brutal demand, communicating years of pent-up desire. My hands on her hips kept her firmly anchored as my lips sought purchase, my tongue darting out to wet the seam of her lips, seeking entrance. She opened for me with a low groan.

One of her hands held fast to my shoulders, but the other beneath my shirt continued its exploration, fingertips raking through my chest hair, pulling on my chains and tweaking my nipples.

I came up for air, looking at her with a question in my eyes.

She understood immediately and nodded. "Yes. I want everything, Deck. Everything. We've spent too long denying ourselves."

"You're sure?" I asked, feeling the swell of disbelief and wonder in my gut.

"Absolutely."

I replied with something close to a growl, then kissed her again. After a moment, she pulled back, panting. "Please tell me you have an actual bed and not, like, an air mattress on top of U-Haul boxes."

I bent down and picked her up as she circled my waist with her legs. "Let's go find out."

My bed—including not only a cushy mattress but also a box spring on top of a maple frame—was made neatly and efficiently, with a sage green comforter and two pillows. The bed-making habit had stuck after prison. When I'd first gotten out and stayed with my parents, I'd tried to revert to my teenage mode of being a slob, as though to solidify my return to civilian life. But after a while, I'd missed the ritual.

I flipped the switch, turning on the small lamp by my night-stand. Seeing the light streak across my pillows reminded me of something I needed to tell Cori before we got too far.

Reluctantly, I put her down in front of me, stepping back.

"Is something wrong?"

"No." I said shakily, placing the heel of my hand against the tent in my pants. "I need...before we... I have to tell you..."

She smiled softly. "What is it?"

A long, slow exhale left my lungs. "Well, it's just... You're the first person I've ever had in this bedroom."

She looked confused for a moment before breaking into a smile. "Are you trying to tell me you haven't brought a girl here before? I sort of gathered there hasn't been anyone serious since you got out."

I shook my head, looking down. Logically, I knew I didn't need to be embarrassed, but for some reason, it was hard to say. "Definitely no one serious. But also, not really anyone *not serious* either."

She paused before reaching for my hand again, grasping it reassuringly. "I think I understand."

Meeting her gaze directly, I said, "I had a few one-nighters when I got out, but nothing since I bought the house. And even before, in high school, there were only three."

"So you put the brakes on just now to tell me you haven't had a lot of experience?"

I nodded. "I feel like I need to warn you because I'm afraid I'll be...that I won't meet your expectations."

She sat down on the bed, patting the space next to her until I sat, too. "Listen, Deck, so we're clear, I haven't exactly been racking up my body count since we were teenagers. You don't need the number, but let's just say it's nothing that would bring me to an expert level. Maybe advanced beginner if the scale is generous." She scooted closer and turned toward me. "Nothing that happened in the past, for either of us, matters now."

I ran a hand over her thigh. "You're sure? Because I still plan on blowing your mind. You might just need to give me some time to figure things out."

"Let me tell you something…" She swung a leg over my lap, straddling me on the edge of the bed. Her fingers twined behind my neck, and she rocked her hips seductively before tugging my tee off and tossing it on the floor. "I've never wanted anyone the way I want you." She ran her hands through my chest hair. "Touching you like this, being with you in literally any way, is something I've only dreamed of. That kiss we just shared in your living room—that was the best kiss of my life. And it's not even close. You don't need to worry about blowing my mind because my mind is already blown. I'm already melting right into you, wanting you to touch me and make my body lose control the way you've been making my heart and mind do for so long."

"*Fuck*," I mouthed as she pulled her sweater over her head, exposing a lacy black bra.

"I want you, Deck." She leaned forward and touched her lips to my collarbone, speaking directly into my overheated skin. "Put your hands everywhere. I want you to touch me and explore me and learn me. I don't care what you've done, or what I've done. Where we've been. None of it matters because this is the only thing that does." She peppered feathery kisses up my neck and along my jaw. At my ear, she whispered, "We're finally together. And I've never wanted to be anywhere more than I want to be in this bed right now."

I let out a hushed groan. "*Mi preciosa. Te adoro.*"

"I'm yours, Artie Decker." She ground her center against my cock, the edges of her bra teasing my nipples. Unseating herself from my lap, she stood back and took off her socks, then the rest of her clothes—efficiently, with her eyes glued to me the whole time. I sat back and watched as each piece of clothing came off, rubbing my erection through my pants.

When she stood fully naked in front of me, hands loose at her sides and red hair cascading down her back, I took a moment to enjoy the view. "You're perfect, *mami*."

"Show me."

I swayed forward and pulled her closer, kissing her belly as I trailed my way up, licking a path along her skin as I rose slowly to my feet. Her hands undid my belt. I continued the journey of my kisses over her face, paying special attention to the tiny moles on the apple of her cheek that had played a part in so many of my Cori fantasies.

My pants fell to my knees, and I stepped out of them while holding her jaw in my hands, returning my lips to her mouth for another taste. Our tongues danced as her hand dipped into my boxer briefs, stroking the underside of my cock with a firm palm, pushing my erection against my stomach and swiping her thumb along the slit to gather the precum there.

The back of my knees pressed against the edge of the mattress as we pulled apart. I put my fingers under the elastic of my waistband, and she watched intently as I removed my boxers in one quick movement, followed by my socks. For a few moments, we stood there naked, next to the bed, staring at each other.

Eventually, one of her hands settled on my chest while the other returned to stroking the steel pole between my legs. I closed my eyes as her fingers worked their magic.

Not only had I not been with anyone for almost two years but I also wasn't a prolific masturbator. In prison, I'd rejected the numerous offers to have my dick sucked and thankfully hadn't attracted the kind of unwanted attention I'd seen depicted in movies and TV. The lack of privacy had dimmed my sexual appetite because I could never stomach jacking myself with a cellmate around, and certainly not in the showers, where it might have been viewed as an invitation. As a result, beating off had been infrequent and quick when it did happen. And as with the bed-making, I'd carried that habit with me after my release.

Which was why having Cori's hands on me felt like more of a revelation than it might have for a different sort of thirty-one-year-old. Every soft touch was a precious gift, every second bliss, every moment worth memorizing for all eternity.

"Cori, you feel so good... I... Thank you."

She leaned forward and kissed me again before sliding her nose along my cheek to my ear. "You're welcome." Inhaling deeply, she murmured, "Your cock feels so thick and hot in my hand. I love touching you. I can't wait to feel this inside me."

Her words excited me almost as much as the thumb that began circling the sensitive spot beneath the head of my dick. The sensations were so much, I could barely stand it.

"I'm so turned on right now," I said. "I need to sit down before my knees give out."

"That's what a girl likes to hear." I slumped onto the mattress. "Hold that thought," she said, turning around and exiting the room, giving me a fantastic view of her perfect peachy ass. A moment later, she came back waving a condom. "From my purse," she said, tossing it onto the mattress near the pillows.

"Such a Girl Scout." I scooted back until I lay all the way across the bed, with my head on the pillow next to the foil packet.

She put one knee on the bed and crawled slowly up my body until she was stretched out on top of me. Folding her arms across my pecs, she rested her chin on top of her fists, looking down at me and grinning. I ran my hands up and down her back and over her ass, squeezing the round cheeks firmly. She lined her center over my cock and began sliding back and forth over it. She wasn't moving fast enough to get me off, only enough to tease me. Keeping me horny while promising things to come.

The mattress jostled unexpectedly, and I peeked down by our feet to see Bastardo had jumped onto the bed.

Cori glanced down too, a titter of laughter escaping her.

"No way, *gato demonio*," I said, shooing him with my hand. Bastardo glared at me and proceeded to groom his chest, licking aggressively.

Cori lifted one foot slightly, urging the cat off the mattress. When her prod became more of a gentle shove, Bastardo got the message and hopped off, giving us a murderous glare on his way out the door.

"I hope he still likes me after that," Cori said, burying her face in my chest. "But even if he doesn't, it was worth it."

"He'll get over it." My voice sounded wrecked to my own ears. I gripped her hips, encouraging her to resume rocking over my erection.

Cori closed her eyes and hummed, then lifted herself up. She leaned back on my thighs, spreading herself over them. I looked down in awe at the place that was warm and wet and open, waiting for me to fill.

"Fuck, you're so beautiful," I murmured.

She gazed down at me with the intensity that was so much a part of her, her eyes full of secrets and knowledge. I'd never been able to hide from those eyes. And I didn't want to now.

"Hand me the condom," Cori commanded roughly.

I startled. "You're ready for... Now?"

"Now. I need to feel you."

"But I...wanted to taste you." *And I don't want this to be over too soon.* "I want to make you feel good."

She scoffed playfully. "I'm betting that thick piece you've got keyed up between your legs is gonna make me feel pretty good. And as far as tasting me goes, I want to do the same for you. And we will. There will be time for all the things. But right now, I need to get you in me."

I handed her the condom, mesmerized as always by her competence. Letting her take the lead felt right. I'd denied her for so long, lied to myself. She deserved to set the pace.

But she also needed to hurry. Because I would not last long.

She rolled the condom on before sliding down on top of me, taking me into an enveloping heat that had me closing my eyes and questioning honestly if a person could die of pleasure.

"This is..." I grunted, the guttural sound vibrating off the walls. "It's so—"

"Amazing," Cori whispered as she seated herself fully, her wetness spread out and mixing with my dark curls. Our bodies connected in the most intimate way possible. She tilted forward and toyed with the chains lying on my chest. "I'm actually pretty close already, Deck," she said, inspiring a small shiver of satisfaction. With her other hand, she reached for one of mine. Grabbing my pointer finger, she brought it to the place where we were joined. "Rub my clit. Fast."

I did my best to follow orders. Thanks to the internet, I had a general understanding of the female anatomy, even without extensive firsthand experience. As I furiously worked the little nub, Cori squeezed herself around my cock and writhed on top of me. Darts of ecstasy crossed her features, and getting her off became the most important goal of my life.

Before I knew what was happening, she came with a cry. The trembling cascaded down her body to her thighs. Her inner muscles massaged my cock.

As she gasped softly through the aftershocks, I grabbed her hips and flipped her over, my shaft slipping out. Cori reached for me as she settled into the pillows. I inserted my cock inside her again, holding myself up on my arms.

I gazed at her eyes, her mouth, and the place where my gold chains fell loosely on the perfect pink tips of her breasts. "You're gorgeous, *mami*," I whispered. "This is the best night of my life."

She looked at me with a penetrating stare, acknowledging my words with a smile I'd never seen before. A smile between lovers.

We kept our eyes glued together as I thrust myself into her. It didn't take long. Ten quick strokes and I shuddered fiercely, releasing into the condom. Cori widened her eyes beneath me as I experienced the best orgasm of my life.

As the pleasure subsided, I fell on top of her with a long, cleansing breath.

This woman. This woman was everything to me.

I would never let her go again.

SEVERAL HOURS LATER, WE LAY CURLED up together. There'd been no question Cori would spend the night. If I had my way, we'd be figuring out how to spend every night together from then on. My place. Her place. It didn't matter.

Bastardo made his way back onto the bed, settling himself next to Cori, who he'd apparently forgiven. I could get used to this. Sleeping next to a magnificent woman, having someone to care about at the end of a long day. Making a family with my temperamental cat.

This could be real. This could be a life. My life.

A rattling phone cut through the early morning darkness like a bullhorn.

"Has to be yours," Cori drawled sleepily. "Mine is still in my purse in the living room."

"It's fine. Whoever it is will call back."

I pulled her into my arms.

The phone shook again.

Silencing it required me to leave the cozy cocoon of the bed, since I'd left it on the dresser. But when I turned it over, something compelled me to answer the unknown number.

"Hello?"

"Hello. Is this Mr. Arturo Decker?" the harried voice asked.

I cleared my throat. "Yes."

"This is Natty Garfin. We've been trying to get ahold of your wife, but she isn't answering her phone."

My wife? My... Oh... Oh fuck.

"She's here with me."

"That's helpful. Well, I'm a nurse at Everett General. We've been trying to get ahold of Ms. Cori Raney—I suppose you two have different last names—but now that I have you on the line, I'm sorry to have to inform you that your brother-in-law is in our intensive care unit."

"Wait. What?" I pulled on my boxers as I held the phone against my ear with my shoulder. "What's happened?"

"Something's wrong?" Cori asked from the bed. I turned to her, and she diagnosed the look on my face immediately. "Johnny," she mumbled.

I nodded softly as she began getting dressed.

"Mr. Johnny Raney is in the ICU," Natty said again, very matter-of-factly. "We can't be sure until all the tests are back, but we believe he's had a cardiac incident. The doctor also suspects an overdose. I'm very sorry to have to tell you this over the phone, but it's important that you and Ms. Raney get to the hospital as soon as possible."

"We're on our way."

"Good. And...you should hurry." The first flicker of emotion entered Natty's voice. "Again, I'm very sorry."

Cori was already dressed. "Where is he?" she asked.

"Everett General." I paused before deciding there was no shielding her from the truth. "And baby, it doesn't sound good."

Chapter Thirty
Cori

I resented how eerily familiar the hospital waiting room felt. Hated that I'd been here less than six weeks ago, sitting in the same vinyl chairs, sipping the same tepid vanilla latte.

Waiting to find out if my brother would die.

And just like before, Deck sat next to me, paced behind me, and fidgeted with the vending machines. Except this time, it felt completely different.

Every few moments, Deck's hand brushed over my shoulder. He'd brought me the latte with a kiss to the cheek and the warm reassurance that, "Johnny's tough." He called Marisol, Rosa, and his parents. After pulling their numbers off my phone, he texted Marcus and Britta as well. When we arrived, he helped me obtain information from the harried nurses and saved me the burden of paperwork by filling out most of it himself.

In speaking with the hospital staff, he referred to me as "my wife."

Everything had changed for Deck in the few hours since we'd spent the night together. And I knew I needed to lean into it, knew that the change was warranted. It hadn't only been one night. It had been twelve years. I'd wanted this since the eighth grade.

But it was tough to swallow. We hadn't had five minutes to settle into a new normal before shit hit the fan. And long-standing coping mechanisms had a way of surfacing in stressful situations. No matter how much I'd done over the past few months to heal, the allure of *Robot Cori* called to me like a siren's song. That woman could make decisions without worrying about anyone else's opinions. She functioned best as an island.

Now I had supportive messages coming in from Britta, Marcus, and Marisol. Suddenly, I was a kid again, and everyone knew my dirty stuff.

All I wanted was to check off a to-do list. Step by step. Be in total control. Whatever it took to fix Johnny. And if I couldn't, I wanted to fail without eyes on me.

I resented feeling exposed almost as much as I did being back in this stupid waiting room.

From the way Deck described it, his phone conversation with the nurse had not been promising. When we arrived, we found out that Johnny had been found under an overpass near I-5 in Everett, in a popular hangout for addicts and the unhoused. When the EMTs arrived, they administered Narcan and revived him. He'd been lethargic but had conversed with the EMTs for a few minutes before surprising them by fainting. The medics took him to the hospital. During the ambulance ride, they had to shock him, and he was breathing on his own by the time they reached the emergency room.

The ER docs hadn't initially been optimistic, but as Johnny's heart continued to beat, they became more so. They transferred him to the ICU for more tests and observation. By the time Deck and I burst through the hospital doors, he was still critical, but stable.

Two hours after we arrived, after I'd downed the last dregs of my latte, a nurse led Deck and me back to a separate ICU waiting room. Dr. Alvarez walked in a moment later, wearing scrubs and an exhausted expression. The eerie, familiar feeling returned.

"Mr. and Mrs. Decker," he said. "I'm sorry we have to meet again under these circumstances."

"Um, she's still Raney, like Johnny," Deck said.

"My apologies," Dr. Alvarez replied, pinching the bridge of his nose. "You'll forgive me for that mistake. I'm usually more careful about those types of things. But it's been a heck of a roller-coaster ride with your brother-in-law today."

"It's okay," I said, looking over at Deck, silently asking if he remembered it was Dr. Alvarez who'd given us the bad news on Johnny last time. Deck nodded subtly, slipping his hand into mine. I tamped down my instinct to pull away. "I appreciate you taking care of Johnny...again," I added wearily.

"Yes," Deck chimed in. "Thank you."

Dr. Alvarez sat down in a chair across from ours. "I'm grateful to be the doctor on call tonight. The last time he was with us, your brother was a very popular patient. He's certainly *fun*, not to mention polite to the staff. We were all hoping for a better outcome. Not such a quick return visit."

I hummed hollowly.

"We know the feeling." Deck squeezed my palm.

"Yes, well..." Dr. Alvarez cleared his throat. "On the positive side, I can see from his lab results that Johnny's been trying to take care of himself. He's put on a bit of weight, and his HIV meds appear to be in order. His viral load is significantly lowered." The doctor glanced at his tablet and then back at us. "Not to be too blunt, but I take it rehab didn't work out?"

Tears welled up behind my eyelids. "No," I ground out, barely audible.

"He checked himself out after about two-and-a-half weeks," Deck said. "He's been staying with Cor—...um, with us, barely leaving the house. We were out tonight, though, so he was on his own." Deck pulled his hand out of mine to fist it in his lap. "Doctor, can you tell us anything more about what happened?"

Dr. Alvarez leaned back. "Johnny went into acute cardiac arrest, likely due to a fentanyl overdose first responders initially reversed with naloxone. Essentially, your brother overdosed and was revived, but that trauma put a lot of strain on his heart, and he fainted. Based on what EMTs saw at the scene, it looks like Johnny smoked a laced joint. Another overdose happened about a half hour after your brother in the same vicinity, so maybe they were sharing, or it's a bad batch on the street." The doctor exhaled loudly. "The police will figure that part out. Johnny doesn't appear to have any other drugs in his system, other than THC, so I suppose if there's a silver lining in all this, it's that. We were able to shock his heart into a normal rhythm, but we won't know for sure if there is any cognitive damage until we can speak with him further. He's still groggy. We ran tests that will determine the severity of the damage to his heart, but we don't have all those results yet, either."

"Can we see him?" I asked.

"He's getting scans done now. You're welcome to wait, and he should be back in his room in about forty minutes."

"Dr. Alvarez?" I asked as the man rose to his feet. "Do you know how long Johnny will be here? Or what comes next?"

He looked back at his tablet. "I'm optimistic that Mr. Raney had a mild cardiac event. We need to monitor it, but I doubt the cardiologist will recommend surgical intervention at this time, although she may recommend some changes to his meds. The tests will tell us more. We'll keep him here a few days for observation, but I'm guessing he'll be ready for discharge before the weekend."

Deck looked as overwhelmed as I felt. "Thank you," he said dully.

While I was grateful Johnny was breathing and apparently had been very lucky, the prospect of him coming home with me was terrifying. Like the clock on the ticking bomb would simply restart again. Why the hell had he been near that overpass?

"Johnny needs to go back to rehab," I declared. "There's got to be someplace." Speaking to the doctor, I asked, "Can you recommend an in-patient facility that can accommodate his needs? Maybe one a little less *polished*."

"Conscious Horizons was a bust," Deck added.

"Ah," Dr. Alvarez mused, tapping his chin. "I'm familiar with Conscious Horizons. I can see how maybe Johnny didn't mesh there."

"Is it possible there's a place that's a bit more...Everett?"

The doctor's lip twitched. "I might have a suggestion. Not quite as posh, but still effective. Are you opposed to him being in Oregon?"

I sighed. "Doctor, at this point, I'd be willing to put Johnny on the moon as long as they could figure out a way to make him better."

Dr. Alvarez nodded. "I'll make a phone call." As he opened the door, he looked back at us. "For what it's worth, we're all rooting for Johnny."

Him saying that was worth a lot, actually. It was a new experience, feeling like I had a community of people who wanted to help my brother. Not only Deck but also Deck's family, Britta and

Marcus, and everyone at the Center. But getting my head around that understanding was going to take a minute.

Once we were alone, Deck hunched over in his chair. "I suppose it could be worse," he suggested weakly.

I frowned, and he shook his head. "Sorry, baby. That was a dumb thing to say."

Baby. We were finally there, and I couldn't even enjoy it. At the moment, I couldn't see it as anything other than weight.

"Deck, you can take off if you want to," I said, not meeting his eyes. "I'm good here for now."

"What?" His face pinched in confusion. "I'm not leaving you."

"It's amazing you're offering to stay, but you really don't need to. I've got this."

Deck stiffened. "I know you've got this. No one who's met you would doubt that. But you don't have to do it on your own."

I turned toward him. "Deck, I appreciate everything you're trying to do, but I really am fine. I know you have other obligations, and I don't want to keep you from them."

"What obligations?"

I sensed his burgeoning frustration. That wasn't my intention. I just wanted to be by myself so I could stress and not have to fall apart in front of him. "I'm just saying I know it's a lot. You're trying to keep up with your work with Juan and J&D while you do the projects for the Center. Plus, there's your house, and, and...Bastardo."

"You think I should leave you here alone to deal with your brother who almost died to take care of the cat?" He drew out his words.

I waved my hand. "The cat, and all the rest of the stuff I said."

Deck scoffed. "Cori, did anyone ever tell you subtlety is not your strong suit?"

"Huh?"

"Bastardo could survive the apocalypse with zero help from me," he stated. "I know what's happening. Except this time we're in opposite land because it's you pushing me away. The only thing I don't understand is why."

I bit my lip, still spinning it over in my mind, trying to figure out why I wasn't leaping into his arms.

"I'm sorry, Deck." I'd waited forever for him to admit he wanted me. And now I was acting like he should go. He didn't understand it, and neither did I. Not fully. "I'm still learning how to do this, how to let you in."

He tugged on his collar. "We can learn together."

Moving to sit in the chair next to him, I laced our fingers, resting them on the faux-wood armrests between us. I looked down at the way our hands fit.

"Being with you last night was one of the best experiences of my life," I said.

He inhaled. "For me too," he murmured.

I turned my head, meeting his gaze. "I love you, Arturo Decker. You know that, right? No matter what I say or do. No matter how jumbled my thoughts are. That never changes. I love you so much it hurts sometimes."

His eyes practically glowed with intensity. "*Te amo*, Cori," Deck said. "I love you too. Always."

My heart leaped. After a dozen years, there it was. Both of us declaring our love. Quietly. After all the history and turmoil, it made sense that the words were hushed, uttered in the sterile white midst of a hospital waiting room. Because our love still had to be tentative and careful, marked as it was by the chaos around us.

I didn't know how to love Deck loudly yet. Couldn't love him in full color. I wasn't ready. After loving him silently for so long, it would take more than a few hours to feel different.

"I love you," I continued. "Except you deserve to know that every instinct in me is screaming to be alone right now. Because that feels like control." I squeezed his palm as my thoughts came together in real time. "You know, you're the only person I've ever allowed to see me struggle like this. I haven't had that for years, being my full messy self in front of anyone."

"Not even Britta and Marcus?"

"No. I only just told them about Chi-chi."

Remorse flashed across his features. "I regret it so much, staying away these past few years. Or even when I was inside, I could have answered your letters." His thumb brushed back and forth over mine. "I can't go back and change it. But I can stop making the same mistake." He lifted our joined hands to kiss my knuckles softly. "I'm not going to push you away anymore, Cori. Never again. I'll give you space if that's what you need, but I'm not going anywhere. Not when you're telling me you love me and the thing holding you back is all the bullshit you're dealing with in the moment. Hard times pass. And when this does, I'll be here waiting for you, ready to explore this next chapter between us."

I rested my head on his shoulder. "Do you know what I did after you went to prison?"

He chuffed. "Finished high school, finished college, and became a badass rock star in the business world."

I smiled. "Besides that?"

He angled his neck to kiss the top of my head. "What are you driving at?"

I untangled our fingers and stood. A small window looked out onto the hospital parking lot. Pressing my shoulder into the wall,

I stared out of it. "After you ignored my letters, I let go of my little girl fantasies. I gave up. Moved on. I wasn't pining, wasn't waiting for you to come back into my life. Because I knew it wasn't going to happen. Because growing up, I'd learned that nothing is fair, and for damned sure nothing is guaranteed. Over the years, there were times when I thought of you. Of course I did. I'd never felt so in tune with anyone, and once that was gone, I missed it. Because even with all the fucked-up shit, my mom, the drugs, Chi-chi, whatever, something still felt innocent about all the times we spent together. The last of that innocence didn't end when Chi-chi pulled out his nasty dick. It ended when you got shoved in the back of that cop car—"

"I saw your eyes that day," Deck interrupted gruffly. "The way you looked at me, I thought you hated me."

Turning from the window, I stared at him. "There was a split second when I thought maybe I did. But what I really hated was that the last bitter hopes of my little girl dreams rode away with you."

His eyes clouded. "I remember riding to the station. There was so much blood on me. I'd never felt so filthy."

"It was a terrible night. A *defining* night." I sat back down next to him and entwined our fingers again. "But what I loved about you when we were kids still stands. You're a good man. You want to take care of people and do the right things. And I can see how much you've grown. How you've overcome some of the worst impulses you had as a teenager."

He swallowed audibly. "I think about it sometimes. That I nearly beat someone to death. I hope and pray I'm not that person anymore."

"I have faith you're not. But it doesn't change the fact that, as far as our history goes, I'm just as affected by the experience of forcing myself to let you go as I am by loving you."

"And I got good at pretending not to love you," he said sagely. "We both have baggage to untangle."

"That's right. We've waited our whole lives to be together. I don't want to fuck up the opportunity by trying to put a label on our relationship while all this other stuff is going on."

He chortled glumly. "It's hard to believe that it hasn't even been twenty-four hours since Jayden tried to rob the store."

"Gawd," I breathed out. "Isn't that the truth?" I brought my knee up to rest my chin on it. "But I meant what I said. I love you. Being with you last night felt like taking back some of that innocence I lost." I stared out the tiny window again.

"Where does that leave us?" he asked.

"I'm not in a place right now where I can think clearly about how to move forward. And I've never been more terrified in my life that I might fail at something. It's hard to trust it when it's so new."

"You don't trust me?"

"No, Deck." I volleyed a finger between us. "It's this I don't trust. Not yet. But I could. If we give it time and take it slow. I could trust it. I want to." Sadness weighed my voice. "I know I'm such an idiot. Getting the thing I've always wanted most and then not knowing what to do with it."

"You're not an idiot," he said firmly. "If you need to step back from us as a couple right now to focus on Johnny, or just to get your head on straight, I can respect that. One thing I owe you, maybe more than anything, is time."

"Thank you."

I thought about how I'd asked Marcus to settle for less than he deserved. No way could I do that to Deck. "I want to get this right, Deck. You deserve to be loved the right way."

"*Mi amor*"—He grabbed my chin—"I loved you every day I was locked up and every day since I've been out. You've always loved me the right way. You've always loved me better than anyone else."

The sincerity shone in his eyes. I saw the boy in him, even as the man he was always meant to be said the perfect thing.

"I don't know what will happen next, Deck. Not with Johnny, or the Center. Or with us. But you're right. Bastardo can figure it out on his own for a day. I'm grateful to have you by my side."

"I'm here."

CHAPTER THIRTY-ONE
Cori

When the nurse came in to let us know Johnny was awake and talking, Deck and I still had no concrete resolution. All I knew was that we loved each other, and I wanted to be with him, but the idea of it also completely overwhelmed me. I envied sixteen-year-old me, who loved Deck with her whole heart and had no reservations. Twenty-nine-year-old me was too afraid of showing my belly or doing things wrong.

The nurse offered to walk us to Johnny's room, but then her tablet beeped.

"Shoot," she said, swiping at it. "I need to head in the opposite direction. Do you think you can find your brother's room on your own? It's at the end of the hall and around the corner."

"No problem," I replied.

I held Deck's arm as we made our way. Outside, the early morning light was dim, but inside, with the bright fluorescents, time had no meaning. I whispered in Deck's ear, "I don't want to tell my brother, or anyone, that we're together yet. That feels like extra pressure we don't need."

"I think everyone we know will be happy for us. But if that's what you want, that's what I'll do." He leaned over and kissed me on the head. "I'm just happy to hear you say we're together, *mi preciosa*."

I laughed. "We're together, but I have no idea what that means, and I don't want anyone to know. Also, I reserve the right to wake up tomorrow morning and say something different and overthink and have new hang-ups."

He grinned back. "Fair enough. Now let's go take care of our brother."

We rounded the corner and heard the heavy sound of boots hitting the linoleum. Another man headed our way from the end of the corridor. He wasn't wearing medical scrubs, so I assumed he was a visitor like us.

The man came closer, and Deck's arm grew stiff in my grasp. I peered sideways, startled to see a fierce, thousand-yard stare on Deck's face. A moment ago, he'd been smiling. Now, he was clenching his jaw, nostrils flared. He looked hard. Unyielding.

As the man passed, I saw that he was young, perhaps in his mid-twenties, dressed in a white T-shirt and baggy jeans, with a black baseball cap. He narrowed his gaze on Deck, and Deck met his eyes directly, keeping his posture stiff. The man's features eased slightly before he gave Deck the barest of upnods. "'Sup," he said gruffly, walking on without an answer.

Once the man turned down the corner and was out of earshot, Deck relaxed. The intensity in the air took a few more beats to dissolve.

"Who was that?" I asked in a hushed voice.

"Alejandro."

"The guy who gave Jayden the gun?"

Deck dipped his chin. "That's the one."

"He knows you?"

"Probably just from around the neighborhood. I only know his face because Emilio pointed him out once. Benefit of having a cop brother, I guess, but I've heard his name plenty."

We were almost at the door to Johnny's room. I stopped Deck, pulling him to the side of the hallway. "Why did he look at you like that?" I asked. "Like he had a problem with you or something?"

Deck rubbed the back of his neck. "*No sé.* Doesn't matter how many businesses I start or years I stay away from the game. I'm always gonna be the guy who went to prison for almost killing Chi-chi. It gives me cred but also invites *interest.*" Deck moved to pull me into his arms. "It's fine, Cori. You've been away from all this for a while, but you remember how it works. He's just a dog trying to make sure I don't want to piss on his tree."

The prison stint would follow Deck for the rest of his life. I admired how he didn't feel the need to *fix* his narrative or hide it like I had.

"Well, I liked that scary-looking mafia boss face you made at him," I teased. "Very sexy."

He choked on a laugh. "Let's go see Johnny."

We walked into my brother's room, and I felt optimistic. Somehow, Deck's exchange with Alejandro had grounded me. We could all do hard things, including Johnny. I probably had no business feeling that way, considering the beeping machines hooked up to my brother. Not to mention how ragged and pale he appeared. But even with looking wrecked and all the wires amidst the antiseptic-smelling hospital air, Johnny reminded us immediately that he was still himself.

"If it isn't the happy couple," he whispered, mischief lacing his words. "I'm assuming you're here to discuss the blissful joys of married life."

"Cut the shit," Deck said, fighting a smile and taking a seat on a rolling chair next to Johnny's head. "You really scared us."

"What Deck said," I agreed, sitting on the edge of the bed. I wanted to say more, but the events of the day must have caught up to me because words got stuck in my throat as I struggled to keep myself from crying.

Johnny noticed my watery eyes and frowned. "I'm sorry, Cor. I didn't mean for this to happen."

"We almost lost you, brother," Deck said. Like me, he seemed too overwhelmed with relief to be angry. "What the hell were you thinking?"

Johnny exhaled. He fidgeted with his blankets a little, drumming his fingers on his thigh before answering. "You know I've been trying to stay good. Being at Cori's place has been helping, I think. But my boy Rocco has been asking to meet up ever since I got out of rehab—"

"Since you walked out," I corrected.

"Whatever," Johnny said with minimal bite. "Anyway, Cori texted she was gonna be pretty late at work. And I dunno, I thought maybe it would be okay. That I could at least try to see. Rocco's a good guy. He was there for me after...after Eliazar died. And even tonight, when someone offered me the pipe, he got in the way, saying I was clean. He was trying to respect it, ya know?"

"So how did you end up in the hospital?" Deck persisted.

"I'm not sure. Someone offered me a hit off a joint. And I thought that would be okay. It's legal, right? What's crazy is I wasn't even feeling tempted by the hard stuff. But I've been so tense lately. Figured one toke couldn't hurt. Next thing I knew, the EMTs were over me, asking questions. Then I woke up here. They told me I had fentanyl in my system, so it must have been in the weed."

He was a good liar. I wouldn't put it past him to lie about this, but his story rang true. Deck and I exchanged a glance that told me he believed Johnny as well. I decided not to argue right now about his marijuana-doesn't-count logic, but I took some comfort in knowing he hadn't gone out in search of hard drugs.

"You realize you're going back to rehab," I told Johnny. "It's not even up for debate."

He looked toward the window. "Yeah, I know."

Deck's phone buzzed. He pulled it out and glanced at it. I saw a long text but couldn't make out who the sender was.

"It's nothing," Deck said, slipping the device into his pocket. "Work stuff."

I turned back to Johnny. "Dr. Alvarez said he can recommend a facility he thinks you'll like better. Once you're cleared to leave the hospital, I'm taking you."

Johnny blew out a breath. "I'm not going to fight you, Cor. Not anymore. These past few weeks being at your place have been great. It's like I forgot what life can even be. Clean showers and watching Seahawks games and seeing you every day. Fucking *brunch with the besties*. I don't know why I couldn't say no when Rocco texted. I guess I just wish I could have both."

"You can't have the part with the drugs, or the people who do them," I said definitively. Just like Deck and me, Johnny was going to have to figure out a better way to marry his past and his present.

"I know. I know." Johnny nodded resignedly.

The nurse from the waiting room popped her head in. "I'm glad you guys had time to talk, but since we're outside of regular visiting hours, I'd suggest you go home for now. Mr. Raney can rest, and you can come back later."

"Johnny," he corrected the nurse with a wink. The corners of her mouth turned up.

"Of course," I said. "I appreciate you making the exception."

I leaned over to kiss Johnny's forehead. "See you later, Big Bro."

Deck clasped palms with him. "We'll be back soon."

Johnny was practically back to sleep by the time we closed his door. I leaned against Deck as we walked to the parking lot.

"Johnny definitely seems like himself, so hopefully we got lucky again and there's no cognitive damage," I said. "I'm so angry that this happened, but also relieved, and probably at least a little manic from lack of sleep." As if proving my point, a demented laugh escaped me. "Part of me wants to sit with my brother, but I'm glad the nurse ordered us away because I really need to go to sleep and put a period on this day, or two days, whatever you want to call it—"

"Cori." Deck stopped me as we exited the building, bracing ourselves in the chilly air. "I need to tell you something." He wrapped his arm around my shoulders. "As much as I wish this could wait, we're going to have to give Johnny some bad news before one of his bonehead friends does."

"What bad news?"

"That text I got earlier wasn't work. It was from Emilio. He's on duty tonight. He was waiting until the family got notified to tell me, but that guy Johnny mentioned, Rocco..."

"His friend? Yeah. I've heard his name from Johnny before."

"Well, Emilio knows they're bros. They've been picked up together before, apparently." Deck inhaled. "He wanted to let me know Rocco's dead. Overdosed earlier tonight. He told me so we could give Johnny the heads-up. Figured the news should come from one of us."

"Shit," I breathed out. I was sad for Rocco and his family, but mostly, I worried about how this would affect my brother. Over the years, Rocco was the only acquaintance of Johnny's whose name I'd ever learned. My brother would take it hard. But I couldn't help being grateful it wasn't Johnny who'd stopped breathing for good tonight. "We'll tell him together this afternoon."

Deck nodded, then asked, "Where am I going, Cori?"

"Huh?"

"We took your car here. Are you dropping me off, or..."

I waited for my lizard brain to insist I push him away.

It didn't.

I knew it still might in the morning, that I hadn't magically figured out how to share my burdens in the past hour, but for now, I was taking the W.

"We already slept in your bed," I said levelly, reaching for his hand. "After all the stuff with Johnny tonight, I really need to see what you look like in mine."

He stepped closer and cupped my cheek. "*Sí. Te amo.*"

I shivered as the intensity he'd had in his eyes when he stared down Alejandro returned. Except this time, the force behind it carried no menace. Only a promise.

DECK AND I WENT BACK TO MY HOUSE and, contrary to the sexy implications of his words outside the hospital, fell asleep almost immediately. I woke up first and gave myself a few minutes to marvel at the sight of him lying in my bed. He'd stripped down to gray boxer briefs and slept on his stomach, clutching a pillow. His smooth skin rippled with muscle, and his inky-black hair spilled out over my sheets. He looked soft like this, sweet even, and I smiled recalling his fumbling admission of his lack of experience last night. Sixteen-year-old me squealed internally. *He's here*, she said. *We made it. He's so beautiful! We love each other.* And then, inevitably, *fuck you, Chi-chi.*

Deck had been to my house enough times over the past few weeks while visiting Johnny to feel comfortable in the downstairs spaces, but he'd never been in my bedroom. Yet he'd had no hesitation when we'd climbed the stairs earlier, almost like he knew how much I relied on his certainty. I'd fallen asleep on his chest and woken up with his arm draped across my torso. Now, his jeans and T-shirt hung over the chair by my window, and his presence in my bed didn't feel new at all.

Around noon, I woke him up and told him I was headed back to the hospital. We agreed he'd go by J&D to check in with Juan and then meet me in Johnny's room. I'd wait for Deck before telling my brother about Rocco.

When I got to the hospital, I was surprised to find Marisol coming out of Johnny's room.

"You came to visit my brother?" I asked.

"Deck texted us last night. *Mamá* made the brownies Johnny likes and asked me to bring them since she had to get to work."

"The brownies with the spicy chocolate?"

"You remembered."

"Of course. Johnny told her once when he was twelve how much he liked them, and she sent me home with them all the time after that."

"Mamá cares about him." Marisol shoved her hands into the back pockets of her vintage-looking corduroys. "We all do."

Studying her face, I saw genuine concern in her eyes. Marisol had known my brother her entire life. She'd been young when Johnny had come around every day, but that didn't mean she cared any less. And over the past twelve years, the Deckers had done what they could for him, operating on the same tough-love principles I had while still trying to make sure he knew they loved him.

"Thank you," I said. "Hopefully, your mom won't mind that at least one of those brownies will be mine."

Marisol tittered lightly. "I'm sure she was counting on it. If Johnny eats the whole pan, he'll have to add diabetes to his list of problems."

I laughed. "You've got jokes. Even now. No wonder you and my brother get along."

"Cori, whatever you need, you know you have us. All the people who love you and Johnny, especially my family."

"Thank you, Mari. Johnny and I are very lucky to be honorary Deckers."

"About that..." She grinned slyly. "I heard a rumor that it's not so honorary."

I tensed. Deck and I had agreed not to tell people about us. He wouldn't have told his sister?

"What do you mean?"

"When I asked the nurse if I could bring the brownies, and gave her my name, she said something about how one brownie wouldn't hurt, and it was fine for me to visit, because I was family, you know, since Johnny's *brother-in-law's* last name was also Decker." She folded her arms and raised an eyebrow, trying not to crack up.

"Long story," I mumbled. "Don't ask."

"I'd like to hear it sometime," she said. "But you're saved for now because I need to get back to the Center. Gotta unleash some positive adult mentorship and guidance on the kiddos blah, blah, blah."

My lips twitched. "Thanks for holding down the fort," I said. "Can you do me a favor and text if Jayden doesn't show up today?"

She gave me a quizzical look before nodding, but didn't ask for more details.

"Appreciate it."

Marisol rocked back on her heels, assessing me thoughtfully before offering, "Cori, just so you know, no one would be happier than me if Decker were your last name. As much as I love the twins, you've always been more of a sister to me than they have. If you and Artie ever pull your heads out of your asses, I'll be the first one cheering on the sidelines."

She turned and walked away before I could reply. But her effusiveness firmed my conviction that Marisol's brand of cheerleading, or anyone's, was more than we needed to contend with right now. I was going to protect the bubble Deck and I created last night for a little while longer. Marisol wasn't wrong. Everyone we knew would likely be excited to learn Deck and I were together. That didn't change the fact that each new level of making it "real" felt like a problem to be solved. We could check Johnny into rehab, get past the stress of the gala, and then accept the well-wishes. For now, it was enough to have Deck by my side and in my bed while I focused on trusting this relationship and he worked to feel like he deserved it.

I entered Johnny's room and found him staring hard at a plate of brownies well out of reach.

He glared at the plate, then at me. "Did you know Deck's little sister is a sadist? She brought over some of Mamá Decker's brownies and then only let me have one."

I chuckled, sitting on the stool. "You're lucky the nurses let her give you that much. Good thing you're such a charmer."

"Can't help it." He shrugged. After a moment, he added, "She's really something. Marisol, I mean. Doesn't put up with anyone's shit."

"No, she doesn't," I agreed, smiling. "That's why she's so good at the Center. A little mini Rosa."

"Yeah." He lolled his head toward me. "Why don't you fill me in on what's happening there. You haven't given me an update on those kids who got into a fight before the dance you told me about. That was entertaining."

I almost burst out laughing, or crying, thinking about everything I could tell my brother about Jayden. I wouldn't, of course. Instead, I said they were fine and started babbling nonsense about the gala, attempting to stall until Deck showed up and we could tell Johnny about Rocco.

The sound of boots hitting the floor echoed in the corridor, and we turned our heads in time to see Alejandro pass by Johnny's room.

Johnny registered the tension in my shoulders. "You know Alejandro?" he asked.

"Only by reputation."

"Damn," he said, impressed. "You really have returned to the neighborhood."

"Shut up." I flicked his arm.

Johnny murmured low, "One of his boys is in a room down the hall. I heard the nurses gossiping. Apparently, he got hit by a car."

"Hmm," I said, and we didn't speak more about it. Not our business.

Ten minutes later, Deck walked in. Without too much buildup, we told Johnny about Rocco. The light dimmed in my brother's eyes after that. He asked a few questions, but since we didn't have many answers, we mostly just let him process. I wondered if it had been like this when Eliazar died. At least now Deck wasn't in prison, and I was more present in Johnny's life. He wasn't alone.

Unsurprisingly, Johnny asked to be by himself for a while. This worked out since Deck and I wanted to stop by the Center to check on things. Marisol texted that Jayden had shown up, and also that both he and Reign were wondering if Deck would make it in.

Before we left, I slipped my brother another brownie and squeezed him as tightly as I could around the wires. I saw his eyes as I pulled back. He was waiting for us to leave so he could break down. It broke my heart, but it was also a bittersweet reminder that Johnny and I were a lot alike.

Once safely out of Johnny's sight, I slipped my hand into Deck's. It felt like our love had grown in only a few short hours. Even though most of them had been spent apart. "Let's go check on the Center and then go back to your place," I said. "Pizza and an Adam Sandler movie?"

"*Perfecto.*"

"And we should stop at the pet store on the way. I owe Bastardo a few treats."

CHAPTER THIRTY-TWO
Deck

When Cori and I arrived at the Center, her expression and posture changed immediately into the mode I'd come to think of as *Boss Cori*. Walking through the doors was like crossing into a portal, where she had tunnel vision about stabilizing the Center's finances and ensuring the gala's success.

In the car, she'd told me about her friend Graham and the commitment to donate he'd made on behalf of his company. She planned to call other former colleagues to invite them to the gala, and if they couldn't come, she'd ask them directly for donations. Her exact words were, "My goal is to make them understand that 'no' is not an acceptable answer."

Boss Cori was so hot.

After checking in with Marisol, Cori went straight to the office, and I headed to the first bathroom, which was nearly complete. It only needed paint and grout on the tile. I found Jayden there but not Reign. Sandra, the volunteer, scrolled on her phone in the corner, especially oblivious today with her earbuds in.

"Where's Reign?" I asked Jayden.

"They're with one of the staff, doing some art for the big event thing coming up."

"The Gala for Kids. Good for them. How is the grouting coming along?"

Jayden kneeled on the pads set up under the sinks. Wiping his hands on his thighs, he complained, "I don't think this work is for me, man. When Reign does it, it comes out smooth. With me, it's like I'm drunk or blind or something."

Examining the tile in front of Jayden, I saw that the grout appeared obviously uneven. That's why I'd had him start behind the sinks, where no one would notice the imperfections.

"Don't worry," I assured him. "You'll get it."

"I can see from your face that it sucks," Jayden snarled, rising to his feet. "I don't fucking need this." He moved to shove past me.

"Stop!"

I sighed. After everything Cori and I had been through, I'd hoped things with Jayden would go down a little easier. But that was asking too much of the universe. At the first hint this might be difficult, of course Jayden forgot everything we'd discussed the day before.

"We had an agreement. Don't even think about leaving," I said. "We put ourselves on the line for you yesterday, and you need to honor your word."

Jayden cursed under his breath. "I know. But—"

"No *buts*. I can teach you to grout and paint and all the other stuff. But we both know you're the one who needs to deal with the shit in your head. You've been given a gift. And not just by me, Cori, and Amos. That random lady yesterday could have easily talked to the cops and had your ass thrown in jail."

Jayden shrugged. "Whatever."

"No, not whatever." I mimed his shrug. "You tried to rob a business. With a gun. That wouldn't have been some bullshit juvie stint or community service, kid." The gun part, especially. I might have done less time if I hadn't had the bat. According to the justice system, it counted as a "deadly" weapon.

"I'm not a fuckin' kid." Jayden straightened his shoulders.

I raised my eyebrows. "Yeah, you are," I drawled. "Because only a kid would think it wasn't a big deal to do something that could get you locked up. Only a kid would think prison wasn't something to be avoided at all costs."

Jayden studied me. I met his eyes directly, staring until he looked away. Finally, he asked, "You were in, weren't you? Miss Mari never said, but—"

"Not that it's any of your business, but yeah. Did almost ten years."

"You're the one who got Chi-chi, right? I heard about that."

I mentally rolled my eyes. At what point would my turning Chi-chi's face into hamburger not be a neighborhood legend?

"I'm not gonna give you details. It's enough to say I made a bad fucking choice, on top of a series of bad choices, and that was it. Once you start down that road, there's a good chance one of your bad choices will be the last one you make. Unless you get off that ride."

"Easy for you to say."

"What part of nearly ten years in prison do you think was easy?" I growled. "Yeah, I turned it around in there, made the most of my time. I guess in that sense, I was luckier than some. But 'easy' isn't a word I would use. So maybe shut your mouth about shit you don't understand, alright?"

Perhaps in response to the icy stare on my face or the knowledge of what I'd done, Jayden relented a fraction.

"It's not that I want to get locked up," the teen muttered. "It would kill my ma. My brother, Greg, is inside, and it's making him...into something else. Even if he does come home, it won't be him, you know?"

"Hundred percent." Jayden was a cocky little shit—Amos was right about that—but a perceptive one.

"I just don't..." Jayden faltered. "I don't know what else to do."

"What? You mean like, with your life?" I eyed him.

Jayden nodded. "I always saw myself just doing whatever my brother did. He seemed happy."

"That's crazy, Jayden," I said honestly. "You have options. I know this is a tougher neighborhood, but plenty of kids here go on to do great things and have successful careers. I get that it's harder, that there are more opportunities to make bad choices maybe, but there are also ways to make the right ones. And as far as not knowing what you want to do with your life, that's okay. Since you're only sixteen."

"I don't feel sixteen," Jayden admitted quietly. After a lengthy pause he asked, "Do you regret it? What you did to Chi-chi?"

Instead of answering directly, I responded with, "Can I tell you a story?"

He shrugged, and I interpreted that as agreement.

I propped my back against the cold porcelain of the new sinks and ran a hand over my face before speaking rapidly. "When I was eleven and my little sister was two, my parents went out one night and left me in charge of her. While I was upstairs getting her bath going, I heard shouting from the kitchen. Somehow, she'd managed to light one of the burners on the stove and set her clothes on fire." I paused, gathering myself. Most people in my life knew this story, so it had been a while since I'd had to tell it. "I jumped on top of her and rolled around, smacking her with a dish towel until

I put out the fire. I called 911, but she was screaming. Screaming in a way I'll never unhear it. The paramedics got there quickly, but there were burns on twenty-five percent of her body. She had medical issues and surgeries until she was in fifth grade."

Jayden digested the information stoically. "That's what happened to Miss Marisol? Her scars?"

I nodded grimly. "That was my first bad choice."

He shook his head sagely. "Nah, man. That was an accident. No one would blame you for that."

"I see that now," I said, "but only now. And that's the bad choice I'm talking about, not believing everyone who told me it wasn't my fault. My parents. My siblings. Even Marisol, once she was older. Instead, I beat myself up about it. For years. I used it to define myself as a fuckup."

Jayden rested his shoulder against a stall door across from me. "Everyone likes Miss Mari," he said thoughtfully. "What happened to her sucks. But what does that have to do with Chi-chi?"

"Two reasons. The first is to tell you it's not the thing that got me locked up that I'd change if I could go back. It's the choice to take all the blame for Marisol's accident, because that one choice poisoned every choice that came after it. My hunch is you've already made a lot of poor decisions, especially lately. But you've been given an opportunity here to change things. The other reason is that I should have listened to the people who loved me. I should have listened when I asked for forgiveness, and they said there was nothing to forgive. I'm holding my situation up to you like a mirror because I want you to see. You say you don't know what to do. I'm reminding you that you have people to ask. People who love you. People who will help you. Your mom. Everyone at the Center. And now me, okay? Even if you don't have it all figured out, you know who has your best interests at heart. And it's not your brother's old crew. Or Alejandro. Or anyone else who doesn't care if you get locked up, understand?"

Jayden fell into a crouch like a blunt object had struck him. "Yeah."

"Being here is a good start. But stop pretending to have a hissy fit because the grout looks bad. You know that's not the problem."

Jayden eyeballed the tile. "Reign is good at it. I'm going to ask them to help me."

"Reign is a natural," I agreed. "I'm sure they'd be happy to know you think so too."

He stood back up and faced me. "It's almost five. Can I take off? I promised Amos I'd go by the store to fill out paperwork."

"Uh-huh. But think about what I said."

Jayden made a noncommittal sound that I supposed was better than open hostility. When he turned to leave, we saw Cori leaning outside the doorway.

Jayden brushed past her with a mumbled, "Hey, Miss Cori."

"Nice to see you too, Jayden," she called after him. She tapped Sandra on the shoulder to get her attention. "You can head out into the gym with Chuck to finish your shift," Cori told her. "Deck won't be working with the kids any more today."

Sandra appeared startled to find herself in the same reality as us, but after looking up from her phone for a few seconds, she seemed to reorient to her surroundings and plodded off toward the atrium.

"How much of that did you hear?" I asked Cori.

"Your conversation with Jayden? Enough to make me remember how stubborn you were about letting me help you with your schoolwork." She smiled.

After checking to make sure we were alone in the bathroom, I circled my arms around her waist and pulled her to me.

"You're right, baby." I spoke languidly into her ear. "I was extremely *recalcitrant* back then." I kissed the hollow of her neck, causing her to shiver. "Definitely *obstinate*." I pressed my mouth to her exposed collarbone. "And of course very, very *intractable*." She pushed me away as I nipped the underside of her jaw.

"You make me forget myself," she admonished breathily.

"Wait till we get home," I promised, picking up the tools Jayden had strewn about the work area.

She sighed, shoulders sagging. "Actually, when we get home, I might have to jump back on my emails for a while."

I registered the worry in her tone. "What's wrong? Is it Johnny?"

"No." She shoved her hair behind her ears. "Ana and I got some bad news. One of the donors who made a six-figure pledge for the gala months ago backed out. Something about wanting to support larger-scale initiatives. Which is bullshit, but whatever. The bottom line is we have to find that money somewhere else, and time is ticking. We'd been making a dent in the three hundred thousand we needed, but now we're back at square one. Worse than that even, now we need to raise three hundred and thirty thousand. And with less than seven weeks left."

"What about your friend Graham? Doesn't that help? And your old business partners?"

"Graham can give personally, but the corporate gift needs to go through red tape at TremMark. That will take a minimum of a few months. Jason and Brad both agreed to attend the gala, and I'm sure they'll be generous, but neither of them is in a position to cover a gap that large. I have more people to call, so it's not like I'm giving up. The job just got a lot harder, though. I'd really wanted to go into the event knowing for sure that we'd secured all the money, but I think we're going to be doing a little bit of finger crossing and a lot of praying that night."

"I'm sorry, Cori. I wish there was more I could do."

"The stuff you're doing with the repairs is massive. I know how hard you've been working to be here when you can and still keep up with J&D. And I feel guilty myself. Part of me thinks I should just float the Center this money, but I really can't, not right now when I'm going to be paying out of pocket for Johnny's treatment. Not to mention his meds. Plus, I'm not working, and I don't know when I will be. I made a lot of money selling to TremMark, but it's not infinite. I can't just burn through it all. My brain doesn't work that way."

I pulled her close and tucked her head under my chin, taking satisfaction in the relieved breath she released. "You don't have to save the world all by yourself, baby. You've got me now."

She peered up, pouting her lips a little. "I don't suppose you have a spare four hundred thousand in that toolbox."

"Nope." I chuckled. "I might have a stick of gum and a few quarters, though." Carding my fingers through her hair, I spread the red-gold strands over her shoulder. She was so *ethereal*. "How about you let me take you home and rub your feet while we eat that pizza and watch *The Wedding Singer?* It's a classic, right?"

"It's an ancient relic, but yes, I love it."

"I remember. We'll watch, and then you'll let me take you to bed, okay? We won't worry about Johnny or the gala or anything. We're taking a few hours off from all that to just be Deck and Cori."

She tipped her head down to rest her forehead against my chest. "Maybe we can go extra stealthy and be Arturo and Corona, just for tonight," she mumbled.

A laugh escaped my throat. "I forgot you were named after your dad's favorite beer."

"Yep. People still always assume it's Corinne or something, and I never correct them. Just like Johnny's named after Dad's favorite liquor. Our names are basically the one thing we got from that guy before he dipped. Only an elite group of people know that."

"I feel lucky."

"You should," she teased, chuckling in the muted way that brought me back to playful conversations at *Mamá's* kitchen table, when I'd barely let myself dream about touching her.

"No, Cori." I tipped her chin up with my finger so she could see the seriousness of my expression. "I feel very lucky. *Te amo.*"

I kissed her softly.

———

ON SATURDAY, CORI MET BRITTA AND MARCUS at the hospital to visit Johnny. They'd moved him from the ICU to a different wing, and he'd be leaving soon for the rehab Dr. Alvarez suggested. I offered to tag along, but Cori told me to take the night off. I'd been spending a lot of time at the hospital because she'd been on Zoom calls with Ana and Quincy basically nonstop ever since that donor had pulled out of the gala.

After she left, I texted Juan to see if he wanted to meet up at Tubby's for wings, and he said he'd see me at six.

On the way, I stopped off at the corner market to check in with Amos about Jayden.

"How'd his first day go?"

"Pretty good," Amos said. "He was quiet. I think he thought some of Greg's old crew might turn up."

"Shit. I didn't even think about that."

"*No te preocupes, hermano,*" Amos reassured me. "When I took the gun back, I made sure they knew Jayden was out and needed to stay out. And also that it was a good idea for them to stay away from the store for a stretch."

"How'd you manage that?"

Amos's demeanor changed in an instant. He gave me a hard stare.

I raised my palms. "Sorry, sorry. I don't need the details." *Dios*, I'd gotten stupid.

He nodded firmly before saying, "Kid's a hard worker. I had him stocking shelves, and he surprised me by not fucking around with it. Just put his head down and got it done."

"That's good to hear. Let me or Cori know if anything changes, and I'll tell you if he gets into any trouble at the Center."

Amos huffed a laugh as he began counting out his register. "Yeah. He has beef with some kid named Tycho."

"Normal teenage bullshit," I said. "Getting him to where that's his biggest issue would be a win."

After nodding in reply, Amos asked, "Did you hear anything from the lady who was here that day? Mia? No chance she'll change her mind about keeping quiet?"

"Cori mentioned Mia texted yesterday to check in on Jayden. I think we got lucky with that one."

"*Eso está loco*." Amos slammed the register door shut and put the cash in an envelope. "Tell Cori to let Mia know anytime she wants to come in, her Diet Coke is on the house."

───────

I GOT TO TUBBY'S JUST AFTER SIX. Juan hadn't arrived, so I sat at the bar to wait.

There were three stools available. I lowered myself onto the middle one and raised two fingers at the bartender.

"Hey man, can I please get two Cokes and a basket of wings? Level four."

As the bartender typed into his tablet, I felt the man seated next to the empty stool on my right go rigid. After a beat, he asked, "Meeting someone or just extra thirsty?" in the raspy, rattling voice of a heavy smoker.

A jolt went through me. My eyes traveled from the bar top, where the man's fingers gripped a water glass, up the length of his dark arms, covered in faded tattoos, to the short sleeve of his blinding white T-shirt, until I found myself staring into eyes I hadn't seen since I was eighteen.

"Cruz!" Without thinking, I launched off my stool and embraced him fiercely.

He stiffened but didn't push me off. Just sort of sat there until I was done.

"I see prison somehow turned you into a bigger puppy." His jaw ticked when I pulled away.

I slapped him on the arm. "Shut the fuck up, brother. I can't believe you're here. So you're out? Why didn't you say anything?" Cruz hadn't responded to any of my attempts to reach him in prison since I'd gotten out.

The jaw tic never materialized into a smile. His face went blank. Then hard. "I got out last week. I was gonna call, kinda working my way to it, but now..." He gestured at the barstools.

My phone buzzed. A text from Juan canceling on me in favor of a Tinder match.

I chuckled, pushing a soda to Cruz. "This one's yours now," I said. "I can't believe you're here."

He accepted the drink, taking a long sip from the glass rather than the straw.

The years had been both kind and unkind to Cruz. His body was heavily built and muscular. It didn't surprise me that he'd been one of those inmates who spent a lot of time working out. His hair was in a close buzz cut that suited him more than the slicked-back look we'd both had as teens. There were a lot of shitty prison tattoos on his arms and a few on his neck. A decent artist could make them into something, probably. His teeth seemed okay—I'd noticed a lot of guys really let that go on the inside—but his skin was gray-tinged. The faint smell of cigarettes clung to him, and he looked tired behind the eyes.

I had a million questions, especially about how he was here when he was supposed to serve twenty years minimum, but I could tell he wasn't up for answering. Some things never changed. For now, it was enough that I was sitting with one of my best friends, and I still felt the undeniable bond between us.

Unsurprisingly, I did most of the talking. I told him about Juan and J&D, and a little about what I was doing at the Center. Our conversation turned to Johnny, and I filled him in on the heart disease and HIV and the plan for a new rehab. Cruz seemed completely unfazed by the fact that Cori had the financial capacity to take care of her brother.

"I always knew Johnny's little sister would do great things," he said. "I'm glad what that motherfucker Chi-chi did that night didn't knock her off her game."

"Nah. She's tough," I said, trying not to grin.

Cruz hmphed in answer. "Alright, so Johnny's going to rehab," he said. "Where's Eliazar? What's going on with him these days?"

Oh.

Shit.

CHAPTER THIRTY-THREE
Cori

Johnny and I pulled into Green Pines Treatment Facility on Tuesday morning. He'd been quiet during the long drive, still tired from his hospital stay, and still grieving for Rocco.

The one bright spot for my brother over the past few days was when Deck took Cruz to visit him in the hospital.

The visit was probably also good for Cruz. It had blown my mind on Saturday night when I arrived at Deck's and he told me he'd run into Cruz at Tubby's. And that he'd had to break the news to him about Eliazar. I hoped spending time together before Johnny went into rehab had been cathartic for all three of them.

My brother would stay at the treatment facility for ninety days. I'd be able to visit him after the first thirty, but mostly he'd be on his own since it was four-and-a-half hours away.

I started exiting the car, but stopped when Johnny remained seated. "Do you remember when we were kids and we used to trade off cooking dinner?" he asked abruptly.

It took me a second to process the out-of-left-field question before I guffawed. "Sure. On my days, I'd cook, and you'd sit at the kitchen counter, critiquing me and being annoying. On your days, we ate cereal." I pushed my crown against the headrest. "Why?"

"I've just been thinking about that stuff a lot these past few days. Maybe because Cruz came back, but it reminded me of how you and I used to be. Like, Deck, Cruz, and Eliazar were my boys, but you were my *family*."

A golf ball grew in my throat. "I remember. I feel terrible that you lost that sense of family when I left. I guess I...didn't think about it. Not until it felt too late to change it."

"You didn't do anything wrong, Sis. That stuff with Chi-chi..." His voice grew hoarse, and he stared straight ahead through the windshield. "I live with that too. Hiding out while...everything happened."

I put my hand over Johnny's on the console. "I promise that I never blamed you for any of it. Never. And I'm always on your side. You're my big brother, and I'm grateful to have this chance to be close again."

He eyed me directly. "I understand why you had to leave after Mom died. And I can see why you came back now. You weren't ready before, but things are different."

I nodded.

He gazed out at the grounds of the rehab. The drab brown wood plank buildings looked like an old-timey summer camp from a slasher film, but the setting was peaceful and beautiful. "I think I'm good this time," Johnny said. "To get clean."

"I hope so, J. But no matter what, I'm here for you."

We got out of the car and Johnny slung his duffel over his shoulder. "I'll go in on my own," he said. "They're expecting me."

I wasn't thrilled with that, but figured I could hug him in the parking lot as well as the lobby. "Alright."

"Make sure that husband of yours takes care of you. I feel better knowing you have each other."

"Deck and I—"

"If you're about to tell me you two aren't together, you can save your breath." He rolled his eyes. "One of the reasons I let him be stupid and not tell you he was out right away was because I knew he needed to be ready, too. I never doubted he'd figure it out eventually. Deck's been waiting his whole life to love you, Cori. Even if he didn't admit it. No need to deny he finally wised the fuck up."

I smiled. "I won't."

"Good." He headed toward the entrance. "See you in ninety days."

I wanted to scream at him to work hard, be good, take his meds, pay attention, eat his vegetables, do what the doctors told him, and a million other things. Instead, I said, "I'll be here."

———

When I arrived at the Center later that day, Rosa was in the office.

"Rosa!" I exclaimed, running to the side of the desk to give her a hug. "Is everything okay? What are you doing here?"

"*Lo siento, nena.*"

"You don't need to be sorry. It's good to see you, especially today."

"I knew you were taking *tu hermano* to Oregon." She looked at me fondly. "*Tendría que haber sabido que eras demasiado responsable como para tomarte un día libre.*"

My lips tugged up into a smile. "Even I'm not that responsible. I know they can handle things without me. But traffic wasn't too bad. Since I got back into town early, I figured I'd get a few hours of work in." I hugged her harder. "But dropping off Johnny was tough, so I'm happy to see you. And Marisol and the kids, for that matter."

"*Me alegra haber podido ayudar en algo.*"

"My Spanish isn't great, Rosa, but I know you didn't just imply that you're not an immense help to me at all times. Do I need to tell you again how much I appreciate being able to do this for you and the Center?"

Rosa chuckled. "Your Spanish is better than alright," she said, grabbing my chin gently with her hand. "I really missed you, *mija*."

"Me too." I moved to the chair set on the opposite side of the desk. "How's Lupe?"

Rosa fingered the faux pearl necklace that lay across her collarbone. "According to the doctors, she's doing much better than they expected. She may be with us for more than a year."

"That's amazing news. I'm so glad."

"Having you here has helped more than I can say, *nena*."

"And you know I'll stay for as long as you need me," I assured her.

I didn't allow myself to spend too much time thinking about the dent full-time near-volunteerism was making in my bank account. For the first time in my adult life, I didn't care. All the money I'd made since graduating from college had never bought me anything as significant as the look on Rosa's face as she told me how grateful she was.

We spent the next half hour going over the books. I gave her the sunniest version of the truth, something Ana, Quincy, and I had agreed on. I mentioned we were still looking for donors for the gala, but followed it up with the not-untrue statement that I still had former colleagues to call.

But she must have seen something in my expression.

"What's wrong, *mija*?"

"It's nothing," I rose hurriedly without meeting her eyes. "I'm going to see if Marisol needs help."

"*¡Un segundito!*" Rosa spoke firmly, then softened it with, "*Por favor.*"

I sighed, halting in the doorway. As much as I knew it was for the best not to cause her to worry unnecessarily about specifics, it was difficult to hide my burdens.

"Truly, Rosa. I am hopeful," I said, sitting back down to face her. "But these past few months have reminded me how much is at stake. If I hadn't been a Center kid, I don't know what would have happened. The story you tell every child who walks in the doors—no matter how fucked up they are or what situation they're in—is that they have the chance to do great things. I remember being eleven, coming in for the first time, feeling that. My mom used to tell me I was special, but I never really believed it until I came here. And nothing's changed. What would kids like Reign do without it?"

Instead of replying directly, she folded her hands on the desk. "I always knew you'd come back," she said. "And not to the trailer park, or even the Deckers' house. You see the Center as home, a place to land."

I bit my lip, whispering the question that haunted me, "But what happens if I can't save it? What if I wake up the morning after the gala and realize things are too far gone, that the hole is too deep?"

Rosa appeared to consider my question. "I'm going to speak *en inglés*, to make sure you understand," she said. "As I'm sure you know, nonprofits close every day. If that's what happens to the Center, then that's what happens. We're going to do everything we can to save it: you, me, the staff, the board, and everyone who loves it. And even then, it still might not work. And I understand your distress. I'm the one who took my eye off the ball when Lupe got sick—"

"No one would blame you for—"

Rosa held up her hand. "Let me finish. If we can't raise the money, there will be plenty of guilt and sadness to go around. But if the Center closes, that doesn't take away from the decades of good it's done and how many lives have been changed for the better. If you wake up the morning after the gala and have to tell me it's all done, then so be it. You'll know you did your very best, and it was just time. It'll be okay, and something new will come along for kids like Reign."

"I don't know if I can live with that," I murmured. "Failing with that much on the line."

Rosa stretched her arms across the desk and enveloped my hands in hers. "Of course you can. If you weren't prepared to do that, you wouldn't have come home."

CHAPTER THIRTY-FOUR
Deck

"**M**iss Mari said Miss Cori took her brother to rehab this morning, that he OD'd last week."

I startled at Jayden's bluntness as I watched him spreading mastic on the rubber baseboards. "There's no way my sister told you that."

He smirked. "Nah. She didn't. I came to the Center during lunch to see if Miss Mari could help with those papers Amos needs me to fill out. I overheard her on a phone call outside the office."

"You eavesdropped?" I glared at him.

"I just didn't leave, man." Jayden shrugged. "She was the one who left the door open."

I couldn't argue with his logic. Marisol was probably updating my parents.

I wasn't a Hope Center staff member, so I supposed I could plead ignorance about the rules regarding discussing personal stuff with the kids. I was still trying to get Jayden to trust me. Glancing at Sandra, I confirmed she was deep in her scrolling, earbuds in place. Still, I lowered my voice. "Miss Cori's brother—Johnny—is going to be okay. He went straight to rehab from the hospital."

Jayden tsked. "Well, good luck to that guy. I ain't seen rehab work for nobody."

I tried hard not to share his pessimism, focusing on reasons to be hopeful. The program Dr. Alvarez recommended had a much higher-than-average success rate. Also, Johnny had been a different person since he'd reconnected with Cori. He was still upset about his friend Rocco, but seeing Cruz yesterday seemed to cheer him up.

Cruz barely spoke for the two hours we spent in Johnny's room—nothing new there—yet it still felt right. My chosen brothers. Together again. Eliazar's death remained a fresh wound, but being able to grieve him in the same space, even without mentioning his name, I knew that meant something to each of us.

"Johnny's a fighter. Don't count him out," I said to Jayden.

"Well, Miss Cori's been good to me, so I hope that's true," Jayden replied without a hint of sarcasm.

Dios, I was glad we'd all put our necks out for this kid.

"Me too."

Reign came in from the hallway, apparently having heard our exchange. "How come you didn't go with Miss Cori to drop off her brother?" they asked me.

"Not that it's any of your business, but I had to work at my actual paying-money job. My friend Juan has been really cool about me helping out here, but our crew needed me this morning. Besides, why would you think I'd go with Miss Cori to take her brother anywhere?"

Reign rolled their eyes before sharing a knowing look with Jayden. "C'mon, Deck. Everyone can see you and Miss Cori are together."

I struggled not to smile. *"C'mon, Reign,"* I mimicked. "I'm not gonna talk about my personal life."

The appearance of a lovely but tired-looking woman carrying a disposable silver casserole dish interrupted us. It smelled so good my mouth instantly started watering.

She placed the dish on a worktable and glanced at me. "Marisol said I could come back here. I'm Jayden's mother, Gloria."

"Deck." I stretched out my hand.

"Ma?" Jayden said, clenching the woman in a hug. "Is everything okay?"

"Everything is fine, sweetheart," she said. "I just wanted to see all this for myself."

Because Cori, Amos, and I had closed the circle of people who knew what Jayden had done at the market, no one had spoken to his mother. I had no idea what he'd said to her about helping me or getting a weekend job. He'd been coming to the Center most of his life, so it wasn't unusual for him to be here, but as he showed off the baseboards he and Reign were working on and self-effacingly pointed out the rough part of the grout he'd finished, it became evident he'd spoken to his mom in depth, at least about his work with me. That made me happy, knowing he cared enough to share it. Seeing the love between mother and son also reaffirmed my belief that we'd done the right thing covering for him, giving him a chance.

Marisol popped her head in and asked Jayden and Reign to help her unload boxes in the kitchen. Sandra followed them out.

"I asked Marisol to give me ten minutes before she came in, so it didn't look too obvious," Gloria explained. "I was hoping to speak with you for a moment."

"Oh," I said hesitantly. "Everything okay with Jayden?"

"More than." She smiled. "This past week he's been as settled as he's been in a while. And he got that job working for Amos. I don't know how much you know about Jayden's brother, Greg...?"

"Enough."

"I'd imagine. Then you've probably also heard that these past few months have been tough on Jayden. Greg's old crew has been working jobs for Alejandro. You know him?" At my nod, she continued, "I don't want Jayden anywhere near that, but it felt like I was losing that battle. Jayden and I have always been close, but he's been talking back, fighting, and getting into trouble at school. Not wanting to come to the Center. He's a good boy, I promise, but sometimes he makes stupid choices."

"I know he's a good kid."

"And I'm so appreciative of that. After he told me about asking Amos for a job at the market"—*so that cleared up whether Jayden had come clean to his mom*—"of course I was skeptical. But he said he'd been working on projects with you at the Center, and it made him think about things differently. Now, suddenly, he's home more again, and talking to me, and I'm just very grateful for whatever you did. I came to thank you for believing in my boy."

I had no clue how to respond, so I blurted the first thing that popped into my mind.

"Can I give you a hug?"

"Of course!" Her grin widened, and she walked into my arms. Her loose, silver-streaked bun barely reached my chin, but her arms were strong as she gripped me.

After a moment, I pulled back. "I do, you know. Believe in Jayden."

"That's because you, of all people, understand that even the best kids, with the biggest hearts, make shit decisions sometimes."

Her head bobbed, and she patted me on the cheek like a puppy.

I exhaled sharply. "You know who I am... What I did."

Gloria didn't answer. Stepping away and turning toward the mirror, she brushed away a stray hair that had fallen across her cheek. "Chi-chi gave Greg his first joint," she stated flatly. "He was eleven."

Her words echoed off the gleaming new tile, the heaviness in her voice palpable at the mention of her oldest son.

I crooked my elbows before twining my fingers behind my neck. "Amos and I will keep an eye on Jayden," I said.

Gloria nodded, gesturing to the casserole dish. "It's lasagna. My specialty."

I barely had a moment to say thank you before she tapped my cheek again and walked out.

Afterward, I registered the wild thumping of my heart. *Dios.* I loved construction, but the confirmation I'd done something meaningful for Jayden felt like the sweetest high. No wonder Marisol loved her job.

No wonder Cori couldn't sleep at night, worrying about the Center's finances.

———

THE MONTH AND A HALF BEFORE the gala passed quickly. I worked nonstop trying to help Juan at J&D and finish my projects at the Center before the big night. When I could, I got together with Cruz. I worried about him. He was living alone in his dad's old house and had started at a warehouse job working the night shift. He'd meet up with me but never said much. I consoled myself that it was a start.

Cori threw herself into event preparations with a vengeance. She told me she, Ana, and Quincy were doing everything they could to get more people to the event. Much of the gala's success hinged on having a full house. The hope was that the small-dollar donations would add up and put them over the top. I saw the stress on her face and did my best to ease it, letting her vent about sponsors who were late with their contributions or the stage rental that was costing an arm and a leg.

Because of everything going on, the air between us always felt anticipatory and thick with urgency. But we'd turned a corner because now we were each other's safe place. We still weren't public with our relationship, but I was fairly certain everyone around us had figured it out.

At the end of November, Marisol invited Cori to Thanksgiving at our parents' house, which saved me from having to figure out a way to get her there without giving away the game. Except that cover did nothing to disguise the way I looked at Cori across the table, or how I kept inadvertently caressing her lower back.

But Cori had been dead-on about one thing. Not declaring our relationship gave our loved ones the message that it wasn't something we wanted to discuss right now. Not openly. My family knew I'd been avoiding Cori since I'd gotten out, but didn't press for explanations as to why I'd finally come to my senses.

I didn't mind working with whatever timeline Cori needed. As long as I got to hold her in my arms every night, I could be patient. And, whether at her place or mine, we made those nights a priority.

We had so much external crap to stress about, but in the bedroom, it was as though we'd created the most impenetrable bubble around us. Inside that cocoon, we built layers of intimate knowledge that would fortify us when we inevitably took those walls down and invited the rest of the world to know us as a couple. We also discovered that, even after decades, we still had things to learn about one another.

She asked about them in the hush of the dark. The minor burn I'd gotten on my torso the day of the fire, when I'd used my body to cover Marisol's. The overly round knuckle from a broken finger that hadn't healed right after an altercation in prison. And the small silver scar on my arm, from the glass on the ground when I fought Chi-chi—a scar that matched the one on Cori's foot.

Being with Cori was like coming home in a way I hadn't been prepared for. Both the end and the beginning of a path. There were twelve-and-a-half missing years in the middle, but I couldn't regret them entirely. They'd prepared me to accept that this was not only exactly where I wanted to be but also where I was meant to be. Where I deserved to be.

Now that the gala had arrived, I only hoped it would go well, and then we could move on to our next chapter.

CHAPTER THIRTY-FIVE
Cori

Deck and I got ready for the gala at his house. I'd helped him unpack all his U-Haul boxes and replace them with actual furniture over the past month, including the small vanity I was sitting at in the corner of the bedroom. Staring at my reflection in the small makeup mirror, I thought I'd done a passable job with my contouring, but no amount of concealer would disguise the worry lines in my face.

Despite Ana, Quincy, and me calling at least two hundred former donors, we hadn't pre-secured all the funding for tonight. I had a lot of folks from JBC and TremMark attending, and I hoped they would be generous, but by my calculations, we were still two hundred thousand shy of the commitments we needed. And that included Jason's, Brad's, and Graham's confirmations that they'd be raising the paddle for twenty-five thousand each.

We had close to two hundred folks coming tonight whose donation amounts I didn't know ahead of time. I hoped they'd push us past our target. But that was a long shot. I'd received a crash course in nonprofit events from Ana over the past few months and learned that a handful of generous patrons primarily achieved fundraising goals, while most attendees gave at a lower level. Historically, the Center's gala averaged gifts of two hundred and fifty dollars, so quadrupling that would be a stretch. Then again, I'd brought a lot of new energy and supporters tonight. Maybe it would be okay?

Deck came out of the bathroom, tugging on his tie.

"Wow," I said, admiring the snug fit of his dark blue suit. He'd insisted on buying one for the event, the first suit he'd ever owned. Last weekend, he'd gone into Seattle with Emilio to buy it.

Over the past few months, Deck had been doing his best to spend as much time with Cruz as possible, but he'd also been hanging out more with Emilio and Marisol. It was gratifying to watch the siblings reconnect, to see Deck allow himself to have a closer relationship with them. I thought of it as him unpacking metaphorical boxes, along with the ones we'd finally gotten rid of in his living room.

After tonight, no matter what happened, our relationship would be "official." It had been necessary to build it in secret. We'd needed that space, but I was done hiding. We weren't going to announce it or anything. But I'd be on Deck's arm, and that would be enough of a signal to everyone we cared about.

"Back atchya," Deck said, taking in my close-fitting metallic purple dress. He came up behind me as I applied mascara. I'd coaxed my hair into loose waves and pulled them back on one side with a sparkly barrette. He pushed the strands over my shoulder and kissed me delicately on my neck. "Baby, you are the most gorgeous thing I've ever seen."

"Thanks, babe," I said, glancing down shyly. There were still moments when I mentally pinched myself that Deck and I were together.

"I'm going to feed Bastardo so he doesn't destroy the house while we're gone... Also, *babe*?" He smiled.

"Just trying it out," I mumbled.

He coaxed me to stand so he could wrap his arms around me from behind. "I like it, *mami*," he said in a voice so low and sexy my knees wobbled. "Another little reminder that I'm yours for real now."

I leaned into him, enjoying *mami* almost as much as *baby*. Although he never made *baby* sound quite so dirty.

My diamond studs glittered as I secured the posts behind my earlobes. "Are we picking Cruz up?" I asked hesitantly.

"He said he'd get there on his own." I knew that was code for *hopefully he's coming,* but I didn't push.

When we arrived at the Center, I made a mental note to give Ana a massive high five. When she'd floated the idea of moving the event from the waterfront hotel where it had been held the previous few years to the Center itself, both Quincy and I were skeptical. But with so many new donors coming, Ana wanted to make sure they got the most authentic Hope Center experience possible.

Transforming the Center into a welcoming and elegant space, hosting the kind of event that made folks want to part with thousands of dollars, was a serious undertaking. But from the moment I walked into the atrium, I saw Ana's vision.

The furniture had been rearranged to accommodate the rolled black velvet carpet that stretched from the front desk to the gym entrance. Along the way, easels with posterboard-sized collages of the kids welcomed guests. Ahead of the entrance to the gym, a selfie spot with the Center's logo and a massive balloon arch invited attendees to stop and take a picture. A professional photographer captured the guests as they arrived, and she would also record the event. The atrium smelled of the appetizers set up in the gym for the pre-program cocktail hour, and the lobby's usual faint aroma of day-old lunch boxes, feet, and Axe body spray was absent.

The gym itself looked completely different. We'd hired an A/V company to set up a stage and bring in high black curtains to conceal three of the walls. Hundreds of examples of kid art covered the fourth wall, including a gorgeous mural Reign designed for the event. Reign had also drawn artwork for the programs that sat at each seat. We'd rented tables, chairs, and shimmery pearl-colored tablecloths. A local florist, a Center alumnus, donated centerpieces. It barely looked like a gym at all. The only thing we couldn't hide were the two non-retractable basketball hoops. But those had been filled with balloons, and there was something folksy and endearing about that. There was also no escaping that the guests' shiny shoes and gowns were scraping against a weathered basketball court. Chuck and I had debated laying down rolled vinyl to protect the wood, but Deck reminded us that gym floor refinishing was the last thing on his project list, so we didn't need to worry about spiky high heels.

The tables were set up as ten-tops or eight-tops. Before dinner began, I walked around and thanked everyone I saw from JBC and TremMark. I had stopped thinking of them as being part of my "old" life. It was just my life, and I was doing this now. If anyone thought that meant I'd taken a step back in my career, I honestly didn't care.

Jason and Brad would still be around, too. Now that they were part of a more traditional corporate company, they had admitted that the culture there felt a little stifling. Over the past few weeks, we'd laid the groundwork for establishing a volunteer program at the Center to teach coding and design to interested kids, while also addressing the Center's online presence issues. The plans were a win-win, providing Jason and Brad with a creative outlet, offering great opportunities for youth, and upgrading the Center's website and social media platforms.

A small silent auction was set up on long tables on one side of the room, but most of the fundraising would be done during a "raise your paddle" appeal, where guests would be asked to commit to a monetary gift. During the dinner portion, a series of speakers and video presentations were scheduled to entice the audience to give.

I made it a point to find and thank everyone who had already agreed to raise their paddle for more than five figures, including Graham, who sat at a table with a group of his friends. I panicked slightly when he introduced me as "the one who got away," then clocked his wink as he continued, "from TremMark." I chuckled. He really was a good guy.

The emcee came to the mic to announce that dinner would be served soon. The guests began moving to their assigned tables. I hurried to say a quick hello to Britta and Marcus, pleased to see their table full. Most of the people they'd invited were business associates, but Britta introduced one man as Roger, their "solar panel installer extraordinaire."

"That's commitment, coming to a fundraising dinner for a client," I said to him.

"They're more than clients," Roger replied jovially.

"It's true. Roger has been on this project so long, we're basically family," Britta agreed.

"Yes," Marcus added dryly. "He is now the equivalent of that distant cousin you only see for three hours once a year on Christmas, but who still manages to break the Lego castle you spent six months building."

"That is...oddly specific."

"Roger is oddly specific."

I looked over at the man in question, who merely shrugged and grinned at me. "Seems like a great place," he said. "Glad to be here."

My eight-top consisted of me, Deck, Marisol, their parents, Emilio, Juan, and the empty seat we'd reserved for Cruz, who still hadn't arrived.

The first part of the program ran smoothly. Videos highlighted the Center's programs, and two alumni spoke, along with a current parent. I hoped the number of people dabbing at their eyes boded well for the paddle raise.

Because we were serving alcohol, we'd decided not to have kids at the gala. The only exceptions to the rule were Jayden and Reign. The teens sat at the table next to us with a lovely woman Deck introduced me to as Jayden's mother, Gloria, plus Rosa, Ana, Quincy, and several of the Center's board members. At one point, the emcee asked Reign to stand and be recognized for the artwork they'd provided for the event, and then he acknowledged Reign, Jayden, Deck, and J&D Construction for the building repairs.

Deck blushed profusely as he stood and waved at the crowd. I choked up noticing Michael and María staring teary-eyed at their son. Emilio gave him a thumbs-up before turning it into a middle finger salute, which Deck and Marisol laughed at.

Just as Deck sat back down, Cruz snuck in from the back, finding his place at the table and muttering, "Sorry I'm late."

He didn't offer an explanation, and Deck didn't demand one. He clapped Cruz on the back with a simple, "Glad you could make it."

Dragonflies did gymnastics in my stomach when we reached the part of the program where the president of the board of directors would ask everyone to donate. I gritted my teeth as my knees bounced beneath the table, vibrating in anticipation as he made his way to the stage. Deck slipped his clammy hand over mine.

As the board president walked to the podium, a stomping noise behind me caught my attention. Turning in my chair, I noticed a man striding purposely toward our area of the gym. Our tables were on the far side of the room as we'd reserved the prime tables in front of the stage for major donors, so he wasn't drawing too much attention. But by the look on Rosa's and Marisol's faces, I wondered if there was about to be a problem.

The man's eyes settled on Rosa's table.

"Ricardo!" the man whisper-shouted. "I told you not to come tonight!"

Deck leaned into my ear. "Reign's dad?"

"I assume. I've never seen him."

But Rosa clearly recognized the man. There was steel in her eyes as she said, "Don't make a scene, Terrence."

Reign, seated between Quincy and Jayden, seemed to shrink into themselves, staring wide-eyed at their father.

"I don't care," the man snarled. But he lowered his voice and continued, "I told Ricardo not to be here tonight. You and I had an agreement, Rosa. He can come to the Center. It's certainly better than having him sulking around at home, but all this"—he waved in the general direction of his child—"can't be put on display."

Rosa's gaze narrowed. "Reign is being recognized for their artwork and tremendous contribution to the Center. The only thing being put 'on display' is their excellent mural."

"Don't call him that," Terrence hissed.

Reign cowered in their chair, almost like they were trying to disappear. Their behavior was the opposite of the kid I knew, the one full of piss and vinegar, as Deck's dad would say.

Nervous chatter began at the donor table next to ours.

"Should we say something?" Deck asked.

"No," Marisol replied. "Rosa can handle it. Intervening would just draw more attention."

"That the kid you were telling me about?" Cruz asked Deck quietly.

"Yeah."

"Fuck that shit." Cruz shook his head, frowning. "That kid's just tryna live his life. His pops needs to chill." Cruz's gaze lasered on Reign, and I knew he noticed the resemblance to Eliazar.

"Get up, Ricardo. We're going home," Terrance insisted.

Reign remained frozen in their chair. It was Jayden who said to Terrence, "Can't you just go, man? Give Reign tonight. They'll be home later if you need to yell at them or whatever."

Wow. Go, Jayden.

"Who are you?" Terrence demanded.

Jayden schooled his features. "I'm just a kid. But even I know this event ain't about you or your issues. Reign wants to stay, and more important things are happening here."

Standing firm in his ill-fitting suit, Jayden eyed Terrence levelly. Gloria looked like she might explode with pride. Deck too.

Terrence glared at Reign but also seemed conscious that he was beginning to draw attention. "We'll talk about this later," he spat. "Don't think we won't."

Rosa's eyes narrowed. "I'll make sure Reign is looked after."

"Ricardo! It's fucking Ricardo!" Terrence snapped under his breath before turning to leave.

Jayden looked at the handful of folks from nearby tables who'd been close enough to hear the exchange. "It's definitely Reign, not Ricardo," he told them.

I watched Jayden put his hand on Reign's shoulder, grateful that the two had formed a solid friendship.

The board president had finished up his remarks and was about to make the ask. I was thankful his speech had been long enough to give me a few moments to breathe after Terrence's departure, but I worried about its dullness. That it wasn't impactful enough to inspire people to give.

After the official ask, the emcee called for donations at the highest level, one hundred thousand, followed by seventy-five thousand, fifty thousand, and twenty-five thousand. I took out my phone to calculate the total as we went. To my dismay, one of the donors who had verbally committed to seventy-five only raised her paddle for twenty-five. Another had gone down from fifty to twenty-five. *Shit!* Those things always happened, but we really couldn't afford to lose any more. At least Jason, Brad, and Graham had each committed to twenty-five. By the time all the high dollar gifts were accounted for, the total sat at just over four hundred thousand. My phone buzzed.

ANA: We should have been at five after the large gifts. Damn!
ME: There are hundreds of people in this room who haven't raised their paddle yet. We could still get there.
ANA: It's hard to do with nickels and dimes.

Instead of texting back, I met her eyes across our tables and frowned. The tumbling in my stomach intensified.

"Not where you need to be?" Deck asked.

"Getting to eight would be a stretch," I admitted. I leaned close to him. "Thank you so much for being here."

He kissed me lightly on the forehead. When he pulled away, six pairs of eyes stared at us.

Marisol and Emilio smirked. María put a hand to her chest as Michael and Juan gave Deck approving nods. "'Bout fuckin' time," Cruz mumbled.

The emcee moved on to the ten thousand dollar level, and a few takers raised their paddles, including Britta and Marcus. At five thousand, more paddles went up, and even more at one thousand. But in the end, when the last call for two hundred and fifty dollar donations went out, we stood at just over seven hundred thousand.

"I'm going to just fill in the gap," I said to Deck. "I've been fighting it this whole time, but we need to hit this goal."

Deck squeezed my hand. "Cori, you can do that, but I know that's not what you wanted. You've already given so much, not just to the event, but by subsidizing my supplies and all the subcontractors we've used. The *Bank of Cori* can't always be the solution."

"Just for tonight, Deck," I insisted. "So everyone can have this win."

My phone buzzed again.

ANA: It's a bit short of what we were hoping, but it's a lot more than we've ever made at this event before.

She followed it up with a thumbs-up emoji that felt especially flat.

"Cori—" Deck began.

"It's fine, Deck." I gave him a soft look. "Even if I do have to swoop in to make sure this gala is a success. That doesn't mean I forgot that I have people to depend on." I stood and started making my way to the podium to let the emcee know I'd be adding one hundred thousand to the total. It was a lot of money, especially on top of the donation I'd already committed to, but I couldn't see another way.

Deck followed me. "But you're always the swooper. I didn't want you to swoop tonight."

I chortled as he made the word ridiculous. "I'll swoop for you anytime," I whispered.

"No. It's my turn."

Before I knew what was happening, Deck brushed past me and made his way to the front. The emcee, who had been in the process of thanking everyone as he waited for event volunteers to calculate the total for the crowd, looked at me for guidance as my determined-looking boyfriend bumrushed the stage. I shrugged.

Deck tugged on the mic, and the emcee had no choice but to surrender it.

"Hello, everyone. Apologies for interrupting. You may recall that my name is Artie Decker, but everyone calls me Deck. I was the one who had the honor of doing repairs on the Center. Hope y'all enjoyed those bathrooms." He paused, drawing a breath. "Anyway, I want to ensure that everyone in this room understands what a special night this is. Not just for the Center, but also for...for the woman I love." His arm raised in my direction.

Part of me wanted to put my head down as hundreds of pairs of eyes fixed on me. Instead, I found myself gazing directly at Deck as a near-silent, "I love you," fell from my lips.

Deck continued, "And when you love someone, you'd do just about anything for them. Even make an ass of yourself in front of a room full of strangers."

A titter of laughter rippled through the crowd. Cruz snorted loudly.

Deck grinned at him before sobering his features. "There are a lot of great things about this neighborhood. Our little piece of a city that's a mixed bag of rich folks, poor folks, white collar, blue collar, and everything in between. Some of the best people in the world live here. But for myself, and for most of the people I knew as a kid, nothing came easy. Most of the kids who go to the Center would relate.

"One thing about growing up when you don't have a lot is that you expect defeat. Sometimes it feels impossible to find your place. My six siblings, they all seemed to go about life so effortlessly. But not me. I think that's why I was the one who became 'Deck,' even though we all have the same last name. It was my way of asserting myself.

"Lots of young people feel like they can't find a foothold in their own life. So they tell themselves the story of how they won't amount to much. I sure did. Except that's the magic of the Center." His eyes darted over to Rosa's table, where Reign and Jayden sat listening. "The Hope Center is the place for them. Here, kids get a reminder that all youth are amazing and can do great things. Just as they are. You don't have to expect defeat. Unfortunately, my effort to find myself took me down the wrong path, but I'm grateful the Center was here for Cori when she needed it most, and now for kids like Reign and Jayden. Make no mistake, the Center changes lives. Saves them.

"The Center has done a lot for this neighborhood. Now it needs our help. We need to make sure every kid has the opportunity to write their own positive story. Please be generous. Let's not accept defeat."

There was silence in the room for a moment before the emcee took hold of the mic again. "Let's give it up for Mr. Artie Decker!"

The crowd applauded, and the emcee took that as approval to say, "How about we give everyone a chance to raise their paddles again? If you already gave five thousand, maybe you can give another five hundred, or if you gave one thousand, maybe another two-fifty..."

He continued making his pitch. It was unlikely that we could obtain the remaining funds we needed. If Ana had drilled one thing into me, it was that most guests came to an event like the Gala for Kids with a number in mind and very few could be persuaded to adjust it.

But I would forever hold in my heart the memory of Deck trying to move the needle on my behalf.

The emcee began asking for more bids at the five thousand dollar range, and I was surprised to see a few paddles go up. But screw it. Whatever would be would be. I stopped counting as Deck pulled me off to the side of the stage to watch.

"That was unreal," I whispered in his ear. "I can't believe you said all that, but I'm so grateful you did."

Paddles continued to go up at the one thousand dollar level.

"It was all for you, baby. I hope you know that I've found my own story to tell about the Center. It's a love story. A long, twisty love story full of bumps and bruises and near misses for falling off course completely. Being here allowed me to open my heart and tear down my walls so that the love of my life could step over them. Now I know for sure that my place has always been with you."

"Me too," I breathed out, resting my head against his shoulder as he slipped an arm around my waist.

More paddles rose at the five hundred dollar and two hundred fifty dollar levels. When it was finished, my phone rattled again.

ANA: Thank Deck for me, will you? We're still about 20k short, but that's nothing.

She was right. Seven hundred eighty thousand was close enough. Like the win Deck wanted me to have. I breathed a sigh of relief. It felt good knowing he had my back. I could get used to it.

Suddenly, a shaky voice rose from the main entrance to the gym. "I want to donate fifty thousand dollars!"

To my shock, Mia stood in front of the double doors, puffing air as though she'd been running. It took me a moment to recognize her, but she exhibited the same resolute look on her face that she'd had that day at the corner market.

Registering the eyes on her, she cringed but didn't falter, walking demurely toward the emcee. The crowd quieted. Everyone heard as she said, "I'm, uh, sorry I'm late. And I don't have one of those paddle thingies. But I want to donate fifty thousand."

"Well then." The emcee beamed at her. "I'm sure that can be arranged."

My phone went nuts as Ana sent three quick texts in a row filled with nothing but exclamation points. We'd more than hit our goal.

Thanks to Mia.

CHAPTER THIRTY-SIX
Deck

Dios. Mia had saved the day. Apparently, Jayden's misguided attempt at robbery would be the gift that kept on giving.

After the emcee acknowledged Mia's gift to the room, he ended the program by announcing that the Center had exceeded its goal. Guests were then invited to stay for an informal hour of drinks and dancing.

Cori moved immediately to find Mia, while Emilio and Juan made their way to the dance floor. Cruz declared he was going outside for a smoke, promising to walk at least two blocks from the Center. I sat at the table with my parents and sister.

"There have been so many moments I've been proud of you, Arturo, but that may have topped them all," Mamá said.

"Really?" I asked, sounding like the scared eighteen-year-old who knew how often he'd disappointed his parents.

"*Ay, mijo. Tú sabes que siempre estamos orgullosos de ti.* I'm sorry you've ever had to question it." Mamá sighed. "Things went sideways when Chi-chi came into the picture, but we were always proud of who you were in here." She rested her hand lightly on my chest.

I swallowed the lump in my throat.

"I'm glad you and Cori finally found your way to each other," Pop said. "We already love her like a daughter." He feigned a stern expression. "So don't fuck it up."

He teased, but I was stone-cold serious when I replied, "I won't."

More than an hour later, attendees still slowly filtered from the building. The vibes were good, and people lingered to chat or check out the kids' art. I sat at our table and made small talk with Britta, Marcus, and Cruz while Cori and Marisol said goodbye to some VIPs. My parents had gone home already.

Rosa stayed long enough to reassure the board members of her faith in Marisol and Cori before leaving with Quincy, who she'd invited to have a late-night snack with her and Lupe.

"You're sure Lupe is feeling up to it?" Quincy asked.

"*Claro que sí*. She would have been here if she could have. This way we bring the party to her."

"Then it would be my honor," Quincy asserted, following it up with one of his signature *heh-heh-hehs*.

After they left, I caught Juan chatting up Ana. From his body language, I could tell he was interested in more than fundraising tips. That made me smile.

Reign stopped by the table for a quick goodbye before saying they'd see me soon. I hoped that was true. My project list was nearly finished, but I planned to keep teaching construction basics to kids on a volunteer basis.

"Are you going to be okay at home?" I asked.

They nodded. "My dad's an asshole, but he doesn't, like, lay hands on me. He'll yell, but my mom can be okay sometimes. She'll probably make him stop."

I hummed. It wasn't a great answer, but it was honest. "Don't forget to tell your mom how much everyone liked your art tonight. Maybe take home a program so she can see how it was front and center."

Reign nodded noncommittally, but I saw them grab a few extra programs and stuff them into their backpack.

Cori and Marisol made their way back to the table.

I pulled out the chair next to me. Cori glared at it before plopping herself down in my lap.

"I guess now that it's out in the open, you're going full on, huh?" Britta asked jokingly.

Cori laid her head on my shoulder. "No decorum whatsoever. Expect public displays of affection and declarations of love on the daily."

I didn't miss the approving nod Marcus sent Cori's way. Somehow, I knew she had never sat on his lap in public. I looped my arms around her waist.

Cori noticed Mia on the side of the gym and waved at her.

Mia walked over wearing an apologetic smile. "I had to fill out a bunch of forms at the volunteer table. I'm sorry I didn't pre-register. Coming here was sort of a game-day decision."

Cori grinned. "Well, as far as last-minute plans go, it sure worked out great for the Center, so no worries." She gestured to the seat next to Marisol. "Please join us."

Mia lifted the heavy material of her long-sleeved sequined gown, which looked somewhat odd on someone as young as her, and sat. Almost immediately, she began coughing.

"Are you alright?" Marisol asked.

Mia coughed again delicately. "It's okay. I'll get used to it. I think maybe... Probably someone nearby has been smoking."

My eyes shot to Cruz, hunched in a chair two seats away. He'd been quiet for the past half hour since coming back in from outside. While he hadn't been openly hostile, his silent presence wasn't exactly soothing either. I'd thought having him come to the event would be good for him, would show him the positive things going on in the neighborhood. Now I saw how shortsighted that was.

Mia cleared her throat a third time, and Cruz stood abruptly. "My bad," he announced, sounding more surly than remorseful. "I had a cigarette outside an hour ago." Glaring at Mia, he continued, "Habit I picked up in prison."

If he'd meant to shock her, he failed. She observed him placidly before saying, "No, I apologize for being so sensitive to it. I'm sure I'll acclimate in a moment, so there's no need to leave, Mr.... I'm sorry, but I don't know your name."

"Cruz."

"Mr. Cruz."

"Nah. No mister, just Cruz."

Mia nodded once before another cough escaped her. She covered her mouth with a fist. "I'm sure it'll level off in a moment."

Cruz made a derisive sound. "Don't worry about it, princess. I was leaving anyway."

"Hey," I chided him. "No need to be rude."

Cruz sharpened his gaze at me but then turned to Mia with an exaggerated bow. "*Perdón*, madame. I didn't mean to offend the woman who saved the poor kids."

"Cruz!" Cori and Marisol exclaimed.

"What the fuck, man?!" I hissed.

Mia choked another raspy noise from her throat before waving a hand at us. "No, it's okay." Her eyes fell on Cruz. "You're right. I am lucky to be in a position to help the Center. I won't apologize for that. But just so you know, writing a proverbial check is actually a pretty cheap way to contribute, all things considered, since the real work is done by people like Cori and Marisol. I'm only grateful there's a way for me to be involved at all, because lord knows I couldn't put up with what the kids throw at them every day. So I'll keep making donations and leave the *saving kids* part to the staff here."

Cruz's lips flattened. He eyed her carefully before neutralizing his features.

"It's nothing personal, princess. Sorry I made you cough." He looked at me. "I'm going. I don't fucking belong here."

I dipped my chin as he walked away. He'd been incredibly disrespectful, but Mia didn't seem offended. Only thoughtful.

I apologized anyway. "I'm sorry for my friend. He's been through a lot lately."

"Clearly," Mia replied. *Was she smiling?* She peered down at her lap and then her arms. "Thankfully, I'm unscathed."

She was tough, this *chica*. She'd surprised me in the market with Jayden and now again tonight. There was obviously more to her than her kind face and vintage grandma wardrobe.

"Cruz is going through something," Cori agreed, "but that doesn't give him the right to be awful."

"He wasn't awful," Mia countered. "I can see how busting in here and pushing you to your goal in such a *dramatic* way could be construed as vulgar. I'm conscious of that. That's why I'm giving you this gift with no strings attached. Because you know better than me what the Center needs."

"Thank you for that," Cori said. "But I remember the day we met. I don't need any more convincing to know you have these kids' best interests at heart."

"I appreciate you saying that, and if you're open to it, I wouldn't mind hearing more about joining your board of directors."

"That would be amazing. We need some fresh perspectives there."

"Great. Why don't you call me next week?" Mia rose to her feet.

"You're leaving?"

"I left another event to come here. I need to get back."

"Well, I hope no one minds you took a break to pop in and save our butts." Cori laughed.

"It's fine. I doubt they even noticed I was gone."

Cori's smile faltered at the other woman's matter-of-fact delivery, but she recovered. "I'll call you soon."

"Looking forward to it." Mia paused before adding, "I would have gotten used to the cigarette smell. It usually just takes a minute or two, as long as no one is smoking directly in front of me."

"Not your fault. Cruz was out of line," I said.

"Maybe," she replied. "But I hate that he felt like he needed to leave."

"You came in after Deck's speech, so you didn't hear him talk about how sometimes we accept defeat before the battle's over," Cori said. "Cruz is still in the thick of that."

"Aren't we all." Mia tapped her lips. "Sorry I missed it."

THAT NIGHT, I MADE LOVE TO CORI for the first time without the threat of the gala's failure hanging over our heads. Or the need to keep our relationship a secret. We still had to worry about Johnny, Cruz, and the future of the Center, but any uncertainty about who we were to one another had vanished.

In the corner of my bedroom, there was a chair with both my suit and Cori's gown draped over it. Her disgusting natural soda was in my fridge. My spare set of tools lived at her house, and Bastardo had a setup there as well. I'd begun taking him back and forth with me so he wouldn't be alone for days at a time. He hopped up on the bed with us as I held Cori in my arms.

"Thanks for helping me make this house a home," I said.

"You're welcome. Too bad we're about to pack everything up again."

I laughed. We'd decided on the car ride home that we wanted to move in together, and it made the most sense to do so at her house in Seattle. J&D did most of its work in the downtown corridor, and she wanted to keep a little physical distance from the Center—for balance, because she also had a life and friends in Seattle that she loved. She'd still be in the neighborhood almost every day, getting the Center's finances stabilized long term. We'd eventually make a plan for my house, probably using it as a rental, but that didn't need to be decided right away.

"Deck, do you know what my favorite SAT word was back in the day?"

Of course she'd bring that up, even though I'd never mentioned to her that I'd been thinking about those words constantly since she showed up on my doorstep three months ago.

"It's not the infamous dinosaur, the *ignominious*?"

She swatted me. "I can't believe you remember that. No. My favorite was always *ephemeral*."

I thought for a moment. "That's like, something temporary. Fleeting."

"Exactly." She nodded as Bastardo purred loudly next to her hip. "I liked that there was such a lyrical word that seemed to describe my life so well. A good thing would come, then a bad thing would come, like a Ping-Pong game. But I realize now that I focused too much on ephemeral things. I let my mind drift away from what was permanent, because those things were in the background, propping me up and not making themselves known. Rosa and the Center, the way Johnny and I were a team, even my mom sometimes. And you, Deck. Always you. Even when we were apart. What I felt for you never left me. Not in any way that mattered. I went out searching for a foundation I already had."

I kissed her on the nose. "I've loved you for a long time, Cori." Flipping her quickly, I stretched out on top of her, earning a swat from Bastardo. "*Te amaré para siempre.*"

"Forever."

Epilogue

Cori

TWO WEEKS LATER

Deck stood outside the doorway to a room at the end of one of the Center's corridors. When I was a kid, this room had been a multipurpose classroom, but for the past few years, it'd been used for storage. As the last item on his construction list, Deck had transformed it into something entirely different.

We had a grand reveal planned for later that afternoon. All our friends and family, along with the Center's board members, would be on hand for the big unveiling.

But for now, it was only Deck and me. He hadn't allowed me to come in while he'd been working, and he wanted to show me the finished room before everyone else saw it.

He removed the plastic sheeting over the door, and I stepped inside to look around. Colorful murals celebrating the backgrounds and cultures of the Center's youth covered two walls, courtesy of Reign. There were dedicated tables for crafting, with organized cabinets of supplies along a half wall. Kids would have access to everything from crochet hooks to a sewing machine. The library was filled with books suitable for all ages. A large section had been designated as a "chill zone" where program participants could simply hang out away from the noise.

Reign had pointed out that the Center lacked a space for that purpose. Having a calming area would help kids like Reign, whose social battery drained quickly, as well as our neurodivergent youth. The vision for the room was that it would be a place of quiet creativity and introspection, but Marisol had wisely declared that the room would evolve into whatever it needed to be. We wouldn't know what that was until the kids started using it.

I wrapped my arms around Deck, pulling him back to my chest. "He'd really love it," I said.

"You think?"

"Mm-hmm. It's fitting that a room designed to make sure every kid at the Center feels welcome and seen is named after him."

Deck sighed, running his hands along the newly installed plaque he'd made, which read, *The Eliazar Moreno Room at the Hope Center, a space for self-expression.*

"Is Mia going to make it this afternoon?" he asked.

"No. I invited her, but she couldn't come. She sends her best."

Mia had joined the Center's board of directors, but I hadn't seen her in person since the gala. Despite my efforts to be friendly and get to know her better, she was tight-lipped about her situation and how she spent her days. The only things I truly knew about her were that she was an awesome, big-hearted person and somehow had loads of cash.

"That's too bad," Deck said, walking to the other side of the room to open the windows.

I tapped on the plaque. "Love you, Eliazar," I whispered to the wood. "Wherever you are, I hope you know I'm taking care of your brothers."

I felt a pang that Eliazar's other friends were missing this event. Johnny had almost another full month of rehab until he completed his ninety days. Cruz had been MIA since the gala. He was still answering Deck's texts, but Deck's plan to convince him to work at J&D was on ice.

Deck didn't know if Cruz was staying away because he was embarrassed about his behavior, or if the gala had convinced him he didn't belong with us anymore. "It's not true," I mumbled again to Eliazar's plaque. "Deck will always need Cruz, and so will Johnny when he gets back. So don't worry. We're not giving up on him."

"I really think these new windows worked out well," Deck said, his voice echoing in the cavernous room.

"You did a great job. I can't believe how much unused space was here." He had removed two walls of built-in cupboards that had been around when I'd attended the Center, freeing up a surprising amount of square footage.

"I'm surprised at how little effort it took for what looks like a total transformation."

I arched an eyebrow. "You're underselling it. Transformation usually requires a little effort."

He laughed and pulled me into a hug. "But it's so, so worth it."

After confirming for him one last time that the room had turned out fantastic, I gave him a quick peck on the lips and left to meet Quincy and Ana in the office. We'd given ourselves a week to breathe after the gala, but now we were back at it. The Center wouldn't save itself. But at least I felt confident that, whatever the outcome, Deck would hold my hand. No matter how difficult things might get, we'd never take our love for granted.

Ten seconds later, my phone rattled.

Baby.

Heart emoji.

Playlist

"The Way We Get By"
Spoon

"The Line"
Black Rebel Motorcycle Club

"Crown of Thorns"
Mother Love Bone

"Spitting Off the Edge of the World"
The Yeah Yeah Yeahs

"Quick Musical Doodles"
Two Feet

"Perfect"
Ed Sheeran

"Pink + White"
Frank Ocean

"It's Been Awhile"
Staind

"Tidal Wave"
Longwave

"Believe"
The Bravery

"Stuck on You"
Failure

"Autumn Shade"
The Vines

"If I Had a Gun"
Noel Gallagher's High Flying Birds

"Wish You Were Here"
Pink Floyd

"One Day"
The Verve

"Brother Down"
Sam Roberts

Acknowledgements

*O**ur Last Night* is my most personal work to date. I've been writing it between other projects for about three years and the story changed fairly significantly during that time. When I started, I was going through a period in my life where I had lost several family members and friends to substance abuse and mental health disorders. The story began as an exploration of those themes. Then I discovered I don't really have a "literary" fiction book in me. At the end of the day, I like my happy endings, and truly believe good triumphs over all. That optimism guided how Deck and Cori's story evolved. How the "Hope Center" was born.

We all have a past. And we all are at least partly products of how others perceive us. Sometimes letting go of that isn't a huge "rise above it all" moment. Sometimes it happens over time, as we heal. Sometimes the quietest loves are the biggest.

To my author friends, teams and groups— thank you for your inspiration in seeing this one to the finish line. Especially Abby for the final push.

To the Monday stalwarts, Alexander, Alicia, Marc, and Veronica—as always, the early critiques are so helpful in determining the direction and flow of the story.

To the GLA, Aviva, Chun, Erin, Leann, Madison and Woody—thanks for helping to shepherd this from Big Deck Energy to what it became. Love you all!

To Jenny at Editing 4 Indies—I can't thank you enough for your work. You have my deepest gratitude for your incredible edits and attention to detail. I promise that at some point, I will learn the difference between concrete and cement. Also, "upnodding" is a word. It just is. So is dumbfuckery.

To Molly at We Got You Covered Book Design—thank you so much for the beautiful cover. I know it took a while to get there, but I really appreciate you helping to capture the vibe of this book.

Special thank you to Niki for answering my many questions on the medical stuff, and to Veronica for giving my Spanish a once-over and offering great suggestions on how to make these characters' experiences sound more authentic.

To my real-life friends and colleagues, especially Sara, who continue to be my biggest supporters, and who do me the honor of treating this as seriously as I do.

To my readers and friends on Instagram—your incredible support continues to keep the low days at a minimum. It's tough out there and the indie environment keeps changing. I appreciate the evolution and tireless work of this community to stop the gatekeeping and make sure indie authors get their voices heard.

Last but not least, to my main squeeze and my little director. For making me want to come up for air.

About the Author

Rory London is a contemporary romance writer who lives in the delightfully gray Pacific Northwest. Rory would spend a lot more time writing if there weren't so many books to read. When not engaged in something book-related, Rory is likely drinking large quantities of coffee or diet soda, watching football, or using music and podcasts to make it through a gnarly commute.

Rory lives with two other humans who bring laughter, joy, and sarcastic commentary into each day, as well as the world's most lovable dog, and three cats who are secretly plotting their revenge.

Connect with Me:
Website: www.rorylondonauthor.com
Instagram: @rory_london_author
Facebook: Rory London, Author
Goodreads: Rory London
Bookbub: Rory London
Book Playlists: Rory London on Apple Music

Also by Rory London

Standalones
The Outline

––––––––––

Coleman Creek Christmas
Christmas Chemistry
Christmas Comeback
Christmas Crisis
Christmas Crossroads (Fall 2026)